Please return on or before the latest date above.
You can renew online at www.kent.gov.uk/libs
or by phone 08458 247 200

CUSTOMER SERVICE EXCELLENCE

Libraries & Archives

Oisín McGann

CORGI BOOKS

STRANGLED SILENCE
A CORGI BOOK 978 0 552 55862 4

Published in Great Britain by Corgi Books,
an imprint of Random House Children's Books
A Random House Group Company

This edition published 2008

1 3 5 7 9 10 8 6 4 2

Set in Bembo

Corgi Books are published by Random House Children's Books,
61–63 Uxbridge Road, London W5 5SA

www.**kids**at**randomhouse**.co.uk
www.rbooks.co.uk

Addresses for companies within The Random House Group Limited can be found
at: www.randomhouse.co.uk/offices.htm

THE RANDOM HOUSE GROUP Limited Reg. No. 954009

A CIP catalogue record for this book is available from the British Library.

Printed and bound in Great Britain by
Clays Ltd, St Ives plc

For my agent, Sophie,
who tells it like it is

36

Ivor McMorris was on his way to buy some milk when his blind eye started hurting him again. As the first dart of pain lanced through his socket, he instinctively pulled a soft cloth from his pocket to wipe the discharge that sometimes seeped from the corner of his right eye. But that was only a reflex; his eye was fine. It just wanted to hurt him.

It normally happened in bright sunshine. This time it was after nine in the evening and the street was dark. This was an area of council estates and blocks of flats and the streetlamps were poorly maintained. With the fingers of his right hand pressing against his eyelids, Ivor lowered his head and continued towards the convenience store in the small arcade of shops at the end of the street. There was a wind blowing but most of the litter on the street had been pasted to the pavement by the recent rain. A beer can rolled noisily by his feet. Rectangles of orange and yellow glowed out of the wall of terraced houses on either side of him.

The pain always started the same way. The eyeball felt swollen in its socket, even though the doctor had told him it was, in fact, smaller than the left eye. It throbbed, the warm twinges gradually growing in strength, getting sharper and hotter. A particularly vicious one made him grunt in pain.

He had to get the milk and get home before the agony took hold. Ivor had talked to people who suffered from migraines and they said the pain was similar, but he didn't believe it. When his eye wanted to, it could paralyse him. Sometimes he cried like a child.

Ivor didn't like leaving his flat. He knew he would be followed – he was getting used to it now. There were other people on the street, but he could not tell which of them might be there for him. The watchers, wherever they were, seemed content to observe in their unobtrusive way. But there was no way of knowing when that might change. He was afraid that some day they would stop watching and *do* something to him again.

A gang of eight teenagers, none older than sixteen, sat on a low garden wall wasting the evening away as only teenagers could. A stereo buzzed a caustic tune. Kids didn't normally bother

Ivor – he was not one of those adults who had forgotten what it was like. That said, he was only in his twenties and already they seemed like they were from a new era. He ignored them as he walked past. He minded his own business, so they should mind theirs.

But it wasn't that type of street. These kids were looking for entertainment and they were the type who expected others to provide it.

'Hey! Problem with yah eye, man?' a black boy with a skewed baseball cap shouted out.

Ivor kept walking. Another boy, pale and acne-scarred with movements that mimicked an LA gangster, stood up and jogged out onto the road to overtake Ivor. His perfectly white tracksuit and cap said his mother still did his laundry.

'Mah bro' asked you a question, man,' he barked, walking backwards to face Ivor while he talked. ''S rude to ignore 'im like tha', y'know.'

Ivor stopped as he found his path blocked, his hand still pressing against his eye. The darts of heat were getting worse. He just wanted to get some milk and get home. He couldn't make his hot chocolate without milk and he couldn't face an evening without hot chocolate.

'Yes,' he replied. 'I've a problem with my eye. Now, get out of my way.'

There was discharge seeping from the corner

of his eye now. That happened when the socket got irritated. He wiped it away with his little finger.

'I seen you around,' the boy said to him. 'Ain't we seen him around?'

There was a chorus of affirmatives from the others, who were gathering behind Ivor to follow the proceedings. They had indeed seen him around. Ivor wondered if he was supposed to commend them on their powers of observation. He decided against it and went to walk around the boy in front of him. A hand stopped him.

'Stay 'n' talk wiv us, bro',' the boy urged in a voice that spoke to the others as well.

'Excuse me.'

'Nah, man. Ah know yah face now. Yah da hermit. Ain't he da hermit?'

The chorus confirmed it. He was the hermit. They'd seen him around. The pain was white-hot now, and he knew it showed on his face. It seemed to burn like acid along his optic nerve. Soon his whole head would be bursting with it. To hell with the hot chocolate – he had to get home.

'Hey, Lucas, ain't he rich?' the black kid asked his pasty pal.

'Word is that you won da lottery, man,' Lucas persisted. 'Is that true? Is you rich?'

'I have to go . . .' Ivor hissed through gritted teeth.

'No, you don't. You gonna answer mah question, man.'

'I have to— Uurrrgh!' Ivor's voice gurgled into a growl as the pain blinded his other eye. It was unbearable now. It was as if someone had planted a white-hot industrial ball-bearing in his eye socket. He screamed. It made no difference but he screamed again anyway.

Lucas stepped back as Ivor's face clenched up, the older man's breathing coming in harsh gasps. Ivor's skin was glossy with sweat, his brown hair hanging lank over his forehead. His fingers moved with a will of their own, forcing the eyelids of his right eye open. As the fingers dug clumsily into the socket, he jerked his head down once . . . twice. He gave another shriek and his movements became more frenzied.

'Dude's goin' ape, man!' Lucas cackled. 'Someone check his pockets!'

'You check his pockets,' another voice retorted. 'I ain't touchin' the freak!'

Lucas reached round to slip his hand into Ivor's jacket pocket. And that was when Ivor finally succeeded in plucking his eyeball out of its socket. With an agonized roar, he struck out at the young mugger, slamming the eye against the kid's temple.

It hit with a dull crunch and Lucas fell backwards onto the wet ground, stunned. Blood trickled from his temple into his hairline. A shard of glass was embedded in his skin. Ivor looked down at the palm of his hand in dismay; that was the fourth eye he had wrecked. Dr Higgins was going to give him another lecture about that. He tossed the remains of the glass ball away and stared down at Lucas. Parting the scarred, sagging eyelids of his right eye, he gave the kid a good long look at the empty socket.

'Get out of my sight, you little cretin.'

Lucas didn't need any more telling – he didn't even stop to pick up his baseball cap. The rest of the gang were already running. Lucas took off after them.

Ivor sighed and pressed a tissue against the shallow cut in his palm. The army had stopped giving him the more expensive plastic eyes after he'd ruined the second one. Glass eyes were a little cheaper. The pain was already abating – it always did after he got the eye out – but now he felt embarrassed about how he looked. He really needed his hot chocolate. Ever since getting off the painkillers he had avoided alcohol and medication, but he still had to have his little comforts.

Scanning the street, he saw that there was nobody else around now. If there was somebody still watching him, they were doing it from a window or a rooftop somewhere. Let them watch, he was past caring.

Walking the last hundred metres to th... kept one hand over his empty socket while... the milk from the fridge. As he passed the shel... newspapers, he spotted the front page of the *National News*, which had a large, blurred photo of what could be either a flying saucer silhouetted against the night sky, or a dustbin lid thrown into the air. The headline read: WE ARE NOT ALONE. The story was about a 'mysterious shape' seen over a suburb of the city the night before.

'Christ Almighty,' he muttered. 'Can't they find any real news?'

Ivor paid for the milk and then he walked out. He always felt self-conscious about the gaping hollow where his eye should be. Higgins was right; if he was going to keep breaking his eyes, he would have to start carrying spares.

The newsroom clattered with activity as journalists and editors worked to make the deadline for the Friday morning edition. Amina Mir could feel the excitement like static in the air, making the hairs on the back of her neck stand up. Voices called for copy, people argued over headlines and layouts, a woman yelled down the phone at a photographer to email in the shots that were due an *hour* ago and somebody somewhere was cursing at their computer again.

Tomorrow was going to be a big news day and everyone wanted to be finished with this edition so they could harry their contacts in the government, the police and the city council to get a sense of which way things were going to go. Every news-hound in the city wanted to know if there were going to be riots.

Amina loved it all. The *Chronicle* was one of the country's top newspapers and she was getting to see how it all worked. This was where her mother had started years ago. Get a foot in the door doing work experience and if you got lucky, you could make an impression. And Amina was good at making an impression.

She was due to start her second year of university in September – journalism, of course – but her mother had told her that this was how careers were made: getting into a good newsroom and making photocopies or making coffee for the editors. As a favour to her mother, the managing editor, a grizzled old soak named Joel Goldbloom, had even given her some minor human-interest articles to write.

They were the usual tripe that papers used to fill in the side columns: ELVIS MUSIC CHEERS UP DEPRESSED GORILLAS, or HEDGEHOG MAKES IT ACROSS MOTORWAY, or MUGGER FOILED BY CHIHUAHUA. Amina wanted to make the front page before she was twenty-one, but for now she'd settle for writing about human beings . . . and not getting stuck in the horoscopes.

Tomorrow might be her chance at a real break.

She eyed the door to Goldbloom's office. He had her sifting through one of the paper's email inboxes for spam, but he had hinted that he might have another story for her to write. There was going to be a massive protest march tomorrow, calling for an end to the controversial war in Sinnostan. Hundreds of thousands of people were expected on the streets and most of the paper's reporters were going to be occupied in covering various aspects of it.

Amina was sure they'd be able to find her something to do.

'Amina!'

She popped her head round the computer monitor at the sound of Goldbloom's voice.

'Yes, Joel?'

'In my office. Now.'

The editor's office was a large, cluttered space with a beaten-up old desk and a worn leather chair. There were a couple of more modern pieces of furniture in the room but they were littered with paper and treated with thinly disguised contempt by their owner. You had to have spent time in the world before you earned Goldbloom's respect. A wall of glass allowed him to look out on the newsroom and level his evil eye at anyone who appeared as if they might be giving the paper any-thing less than their best. Amina entered and stood in front of his desk like a schoolgirl before the headmaster.

'I have a story for you,' he grunted at her as he flopped back into his chair.

Amina's face lit up with an eager grin. She was an attractive girl; her dark hair and Arabic skin came from her father, but the rest she got from her mother, and she had a gift for smiling in a way that made most people smile back. But not Goldbloom. His red, slightly bloated face showed no sign of reflecting her delight.

'It's a human-interest piece,' he told her.

'Oh,' she said, trying to convey her disappoint-ment without sounding ungrateful. 'I . . . I thought you might need more people out on the streets.'

'The streets are covered,' he retorted. 'And besides, you haven't made nearly enough cups of coffee to earn that kind of credit yet.'

'Right. How much coffee will I have to make, then?'

'Oceans of it,' he said, sifting through some piles of paper. 'And your mother was able to take the photocopier apart and put it back together before she was allowed out on the streets. You can't even change a cartridge yet. Still, you'll be glad to hear there are no animals involved in this one . . . so far as I know. Here, this is it.'

He handed her a piece of notepaper with a name and address on it.

'Young fella – used to write articles for us a few years back,' Goldbloom added, running his hands through his thinning, yellowy-white hair. 'Got on to me recently. He's living on a disability allowance now – was serving in Sinnostan and got wounded in action. But get this: a few months ago he won a couple o' million on the lottery and he's *hardly spent a penny*. Word got out about his win and now he barely sets foot outside his flat. He says there's more to it than just the pests and the begging letters but he wants to talk to someone in person. That's you, sweetheart. He's expecting you tomorrow morning.'

Amina gave her boss another smile. The story wouldn't be quite as dramatic as a riot, but it was a definite step up from hedgehogs. She looked down at the name: Ivor McMorris.

'Thanks, Joel! I really appreciate this.'

'Thank me by turning in a good story. On *time*. Now get your big silly grin out of my office.'

20

Amina stared down the street before her and looked back at the address on the notepaper: 143 Winston Street. This was definitely it. Ivor McMorris lived in flat number five. She blew out her cheeks and continued walking. The Underground station had been grotty enough, but this area was a dump. That didn't put her off. She regarded places like this as hives of social issues such as poverty, drug abuse and domestic violence, buzzing with great stories. She expected to see much worse than this as her career progressed.

The block of flats was a relatively small, damp-looking concrete-cast building on the corner of the street. It wasn't a complete slum – the window panes had obviously been cleaned recently and the bars on the windows were freshly painted in a pale mauve.

Checking her reflection in the stainless steel speaker panel, she straightened her navy suit jacket and flicked back the hair feathered over her forehead. Then she pressed the buzzer for number five.

'Yes?'

'Mr McMorris? I'm Amina Mir, from the *Chronicle*.'

She still got a thrill from saying that.

'Hi. Come on up – second floor.'

The door's lock clicked and she entered, making her way through a utilitarian lobby and up the stairs. McMorris was waiting at the door of his flat. He had only opened it a crack.

'You on your own? Can I see some ID?' he asked.

Amina blinked for a moment, but then fumbled around in her handbag for her wallet. She showed him her citizen's identity card.

'You're just a kid,' he said, the lack of enthusiasm evident in his voice.

'This is . . . I'm at university,' she said haltingly. 'I'm with the paper on—'

'Work experience.' He sniffed. 'Nice to know Goldbloom's taking me seriously.'

He opened the door and reluctantly let her in. McMorris was a few centimetres taller than her, with a square face and curly brown hair. He'd look good enough in a photograph; a little on the thin side, but with wide shoulders that saved him from being skinny. There was a certain rough style in the way he wore his faded jeans and green T-shirt. She always liked to take a few shots of her subjects with her compact camera, just in case she could get one printed.

The skin around McMorris's right eye was marred by a spray of triangular and diamond-shaped scars. Amina made a mental note of them. Hours spent poring over her father's books of battle injuries had taught her to recognize shrapnel wounds when she saw them. That meant that his disability was most likely a missing eye.

He wasn't much older than her – probably in his early twenties – but there was far more experience written on his face. She had seen that look on the face of her father and his mates, one that said they had seen just a little too much.

Behind the door was a basket full of opened envelopes.

'Begging letters, mostly,' he told her. 'People with sick relatives. I get a lot of offers too: "once-in-a-lifetime" chances to invest in start-up businesses. You win the lottery and all of a sudden people start offering you "opportunities" to get rich . . . well, richer.'

The one-bedroomed flat was comfortable, if a little cramped. There were piles of books on shelves and stacked around the edges of the floor. One bookcase was filled with graphic novels, another with films and CDs. The walls were painted in the kind of creamy yellow popular in rented places, but the framed expressionist paintings that hung on them looked like originals – possibly his own.

McMorris's home spoke of a man with a lot of time on his hands.

'Have a seat,' he said. 'You want coffee or tea?'

'Just water if you have it . . . I mean, *mineral water*. If you only have tap water—'

'Don't worry,' he reassured her with a smile, as he opened the fridge in the little kitchenette. 'I don't drink the free stuff any more either. Ever looked up inside a tap? I mean, I'm sure it's safe enough, but . . .'

He had a wide smile with a hint of sadness about it. Amina imagined him to be one of those guys who was more popular with the girls than he realized. She had to remind herself that she was the one in control of this interview.

'Do you mind if I record this?' she asked, taking her recorder from her bag.

He shook his head as he poured two glasses of water from a bottle in the fridge. She sat on the chair that looked towards the television, shunting it round until it faced the couch across the low coffee table. Switching on the recorder, she placed it on the table between them. He handed her a glass and sat down on the couch.

'Now, Mr McMorris—' she began.

'Ivor.'

'Sorry, Ivor. How would you like to do this? Do you want to just tell it your way, or would you like me to get things started with a few questions?'

He took a sip of his water and leaned forward, staring intently at her. Amina was reminded that he was a virtual recluse, and she was probably the only young woman he had seen up close in some time. Her mother had prepared her for times like these. 'Men like talking to pretty young women,' Helena had once said. 'Don't be afraid to use that. Work your advantages. If they want to lose themselves in your eyes or ogle your legs, let them. You know they won't get anywhere with it, and it'll help loosen their tongues.'

It was the main reason Amina wore skirts to interviews.

'Why don't I do the talking?' Ivor said to her.

She nodded and sat up straight, crossing her legs.

'You want to know why I'm afraid to spend the lottery money,' he began. 'But I can't explain that without giving you some background. I wanted to do journalism at university, but the idea of a student loan freaked me out – and besides, I was looking for something more. I thought the army sounded like a good option. Plenty of adventure, sports, travelling, and they had a scheme where they'd put you through university, so I'd get an education without spending the next ten years paying off debts.

'Sinnostan was just heating up. It wasn't a war back then — they were still calling it a "security operation". I didn't think I'd get sent there, but it turned out I had a gift for storytelling and they needed writers. The moment I finished basic training they rushed me through a crash course in journalism and shipped me off to the Media Operations Unit in Kurjong.

'I joined the hearts 'n' minds campaign . . . y'know, putting together news stories to convince the Sinnostanis that we were occupying their country for their own good . . . showing them what great guys we were. Putting a good spin on the whole thing.

'It was exciting stuff, getting to see heavy armour storming up mountain roads, watching fighter-bombers shoot past overhead, riding in choppers and talking to soldiers who were revved up and eager for action.'

Amina found herself nodding. She hated reporters who nodded while they listened. But she had discovered recently that it helped. It showed she was listening — that he had her full attention, without her having to respond to what he was saying. It kept him talking. But she still thought that sitting there nodding all the time looked stupid.

'I wasn't too cynical about it all then,' he went on. 'I had a job to do and I enjoyed doing it. I was getting to cover some thrilling stories. I thought I might even get a book out of it in the end. I didn't spend a lot of time worrying about telling the truth, the whole truth and nothing but the truth – I had officers to keep happy. But on the whole, I suppose I figured we were doing our bit for the cause.

'It seemed like a pretty good gig until my crew went to cover the operations in this tiny village called Tarpan; me, my cameraman and our guide, who acted as translator. Like most of the places in Sinnostan, it's a pretty run-down dump stuck up in a lonely spot in the mountains. Mostly clay-brick buildings, forty-year-old cars made from spare parts, a few rickshaws and a drained bunch of people with those wide-cheeked, wind-burnt, oriental faces who looked like they'd never seen a foreigner before. The winter cold was setting in, and there's a dry wind up there that would cut you to the bone.

'We were sent to the scene of a car bomb in a marketplace in the middle of the village. It was gruesome; the injured had already been rushed to hospital, but there were still a few charred corpses in the burnt-out cars around the site of the explosion. Men with hoses were washing the blood off the road and into the drains. We started filming, even though we knew the insurgents – or the resistance, whatever you want to call the bastards – had a nasty habit of launching follow-up attacks on the people and the soldiers who gathered around these bombsites.'

His hand went up unconsciously to touch his right eye. Amina leaned forward slightly, wanting to urge him on but knowing it was better to let him do it in his own time. Ivor took a sip of his water and leaned back on the couch.

'That's when things got weird,' he said at last. 'This . . . this is what I remember: we were in the middle of filming when the second bomb went off. A suicide bomber on a bloody bicycle, believe it or not. We were caught in the blast and I was thrown against the side of an APC . . . sorry, that's an armoured personnel carrier—'

Amina nodded. 'I speak the language, my father's a major in the Royal Marines.'

'Oh, right,' Ivor said, looking slightly un-comfortable. 'Well . . . anyway, I was knocked out. I didn't come to until I was on a chopper taking us to the hospital. I had a concussion, as well as shrap-nel wounds in my face, arm and leg. And I had a punctured eyeball. They had to keep my head very still for the whole flight. There was a chance they could save the eye, so the medics strapped my head to the stretcher so that I couldn't move my head. They covered both eyes too, to stop me looking around and making the injury worse, so all I could do was lie as still as I could and listen to what was going on. The morphine took care of the pain and it helped with the fear too.

'Everything that followed was what you'd expect: the deafening roar of the chopper's engines, status reports shouted into radios, my hand being squeezed as friendly voices offered reassurances, a dramatic rush to the operating theatre as soon as we landed. And all through it, I couldn't see anything – just blackness with those bursts of light you get when you squeeze your eyes closed. In the clear, painful moments when the drugs started to wear off, I can't tell you how terrified I was that I was going to lose my eye. I could taste and smell blood; I could feel it on my face, along with the fluid from the eye itself. But they told me there was hope. And I believed them . . . God, I wanted to believe them so much.

'But it turned out the surgeons couldn't save the eye after all. That made things simpler for them. Once you take out what's left of it and remove the shrapnel that's lodged in there, recovery is much faster. My other wounds were minor enough, so they just pumped me full of painkillers and antibiotics and a few days later, they shipped me home.'

Ivor paused again, and for a minute he sat there saying nothing at all.

'It must have been absolutely horrible,' Amina said with a sympathetic expression. 'I . . . I've heard stories like this before – from soldiers, I mean. You never really get the same sense of the horror of being wounded from the news. I can't imagine what it must be like.' She hesitated, praying that what she said next wouldn't be too insensitive. 'I hope you don't mind me asking, but—'

'What has this got to do with me not spending my lottery money?' Ivor chuckled. 'After all, that's why you're here, isn't it? Not because I was wounded in Sinnostan.'

'Well, that's not how I was going to put it, but . . . yes.'

He leaned forward again, looking more intense than he had before.

'You see, I said it was weird because that's what I remember, and I could recall it for you in much greater detail than that if I wanted to. It's what I *remember*, but I'm convinced it's not what actually *happened*.'

Amina waited, glancing at the recorder to make

sure it was getting all this. She had a feeling that this story was about to become more than a human–interest article.

'Memory is a fluid thing,' Ivor said slowly. 'It changes over time; we forget names, get things mixed up; confuse times, dates and places. Very few people have perfect recall. But my memory of that time is damn near flawless. I can remember who was in the chopper, how long it took to get to the hospital, how many people were in the operating theatre . . . just about everything. I can remember the times these things happened.'

'It was a fairly traumatic event,' Amina pointed out. 'It's hardly surprising it sticks in your mind.'

'No, it's more than that,' he insisted. 'I was drugged, remember? Morphine sends you into outer space; it should all be a blur. But I can remember what times each stage of the event happened. I went and checked the incident report afterwards and I was accurate to the minute. I can remember it like it was *timetabled*. The recollection of it sits solid in my mind while the rest of my memories flow around it like . . . like . . . it was a rock in a stream. It's just not possible.'

'So . . . what? You think these memories aren't real?'

'Yes . . . no. I think . . .' He hesitated. 'I think I've been made to forget what really happened and had these false memories . . . implanted into my brain.'

'You're saying you've been brainwashed?'

Ivor winced at the term, with all the science fiction it implied, but nodded reluctantly.

Amina gazed out of the living-room window at the blocks of flats beyond, trying to avoid meeting his intense stare. She was becoming less and less certain about his state of mind. Goldbloom would not thank her for writing about the ravings of a shell-shocked war correspondent. Although maybe there was an angle on the man who was too mad to spend his lottery winnings.

'I've mentioned this to other people,' he continued, becoming increasingly animated. 'But nobody paid much attention to me. Post-traumatic stress disorder, they called it. I just needed therapy, they said. I've had bloody therapy! I know what I remember . . . and I know it's just plain wrong!

'The army just ignored me! They ignored me right up to the day that I won the lottery.'

He looked pointedly at her. Amina waited to be enlightened, sitting a little further back, grateful there was a coffee table between them. Ivor seemed ready to burst.

'And then what happened?' she asked, when she realized he was waiting for the question.

'Then they started having me followed,' he breathed.

Amina wondered if this was the time to turn off the recorder and get out, but she didn't want to do anything that would set him off. He could be dangerous as well as delusional. Better to hear him out, let him calm down a bit, make her excuses and leave as inoffensively as possible.

'I was rich, see?' Ivor said, opening his hands towards her. 'There are thousands of hacked-off soldiers with paranoid gripes against the army, but the world doesn't listen to them because they're nobodies. But suddenly I'm a millionaire, and if I want, I can start using all that money to shove a great big thorn up the army's backside. They're not ignoring me now because all of a sudden I'm rich enough to cause them real problems.'

'So why haven't you done it?' Amina asked. 'You haven't done anything with the money. You told Goldbloom you've hardly spent a penny!'

'I've been afraid of what they'll do,' Ivor said in a hushed voice. 'I mean . . . I don't even know what they've done to me *already*. I know they're watching every move I make and I don't know how they're interpreting what I do. I think they might hurt me . . . or . . . or they might mess with my mind again. I didn't want to do anything that might make them . . . angry with me.

'I could go out and buy . . . y'know, the wrong thing, and they read into it and decide I'm a threat to whatever they're doing and the next thing I know I'm being pulled into the back of a van. I can't spend the money because I'm afraid of what they'll do.'

'But if you're scared that they'll come for you if you make trouble . . .' Amina asked slowly, a quizzical expression on her face, 'why did you ring Goldbloom and tell him you wanted to tell your story?'

'Because I'm sick of waiting for it,' he sighed. 'Whatever's going to happen, I just want it to be over.'

15

Ivor watched from the window as Amina walked away down the street. He knew she was sceptical, but she'd still listened to everything he'd had to say. The sense of dread that he'd been feeling for the last week had lifted slightly. It was like confession, he supposed. It was all out in the open now; whatever they wanted to do to him, at least he'd had his say.

But he was already getting that queasy churning in his stomach. Maybe he should call her and tell her he'd changed his mind. She had left him her office number. He could say it was all in his head – he was just confused. He could say he was on medication that was affecting his judgement.

It was too late. What was done was done. Ivor kept his gaze on her as she made her way towards the turn for the Underground station. She was a beautiful girl, and it had been a long time since he'd spent time with any girl, gorgeous or otherwise. What age was she – seventeen? Eighteen? He looked away. Even at twenty-three, he felt like a burned-out old man. His hand went up to his glass eye, touching it tentatively. An ugly, disfigured old man.

He looked back at her tiny figure as it headed for the end of the street. Somebody stepped out of an alley and walked after her. Ivor uttered a curse and reached for the binoculars that hung from a hook behind the curtains. A close look at the man told him nothing. He could just be going the same direction as Amina. There was no way to tell. She disappeared round the corner and the man followed a few seconds later. Ivor released his pent-up breath and turned away from the window. He had said what needed saying. There was nothing to do now but wait and see if there was a price to be paid.

Amina's mind was racing as she strode away from Ivor's block of flats. He was seriously delusional; there was no doubt about that. Her father was a senior officer and she knew the military didn't always do their best to look after their people, but she didn't believe for a second that the top brass deliberately screwed with their troops' heads. Over the years, her father had taken their family with him as he was posted to one military base after another, and she had met a number of soldiers suffering from post-traumatic stress; she knew what it could do.

Men and women returning from conflict zones were often traumatized by what they had seen and done there. She had seen the strongest men, battle-hardened men, reduced to shadows of themselves; constantly trembling, sick and unable to sleep. Paranoia was common, as well as hallucinations, unpredictable aggression and other psychotic behaviour. War could drive you insane.

As she walked, Amina became aware of people walking past her carrying placards; protestors on their way to the march in the city centre. She played with the idea of following them, but knew she had to get back to the newsroom to start work-ing on her story . . . whatever it was going to be. It was easy to dismiss Ivor's theories as lunacy, but Amina found herself feeling sorry for him. In other circumstances, she might have found him quite attractive, what with that worldly look and the sad smile. She wasn't as freaked out by the whole one-eye thing as most girls would have been. Whatever had happened to him, its effects were real enough. Something really had blown his mind.

She stopped short.

Maybe she was looking at this the wrong way. What if his memories really were distorted? Maybe he had seen something, or done something that his mind couldn't deal with, and he had blocked it out. Some atrocity, a war crime – maybe even some barbaric act that his own troops had committed. People who had suffered trauma often suppressed the memories of it. Whatever horror he had experienced, his psyche had put a shield up around it. But he knew something wasn't right, so he had concocted this idea of being brainwashed to make sense of it.

Once you started thinking along those lines, it was easy to convince yourself you were being watched. Amina nodded to herself, feeling an abrupt shiver of excitement. This could be a serious story after all.

The first thing to do was to check his account of the bombing in Tarpan. Even if the *Chronicle* didn't do a piece on it, a report must have come in over the wire. There had to be something about it in the back issues of one of the papers, or even on the web. If she played this right, she might escape the horoscopes page a lot sooner than she'd hoped.

All of a sudden, Ivor McMorris had become a much more interesting character.

The meet was at a bench in front of the war memorial on Swift Square. But Chi Sandwith knew better than to take a direct route there. Getting a bus south from his street, he changed to another one going east and then hurried into an Underground station to take a train back into the centre of town. Once there, he mingled with the crowds, shuffling one way and then another, before catching another bus to Swift Square, all the while keeping an eye out for anything suspicious: maybe a face that appeared in two different places on his trip, somebody pointing a camera in his general direction, or somebody changing direction whenever he did.

The meeting place was a square of urban greenery surrounded by purple-leaved maple trees. Chi had tried to dress so as not to stand out, but he was sufficiently ignorant of modern fashions to prevent him from doing this effectively. His long, frizzy blond hair was tied back in a ponytail and topped with a Metallica baseball cap. At six-foot four inches, he was noticeably tall, and the dark grey trench coat he wore emphasized this, while contrasting with his black combats and Doc Martens. The aviator sunglasses were the final touch in sabotaging his desire for anonymity.

The square was crowded at this time of day, which was important for avoiding curious ears. The war memorial was a marble statue of some heroic mariner wearing a sailor's jacket and tri-cornered hat. Chi passed the bench twice, doing a circuit of the area before sitting down next to the young man who was already there.

'Nexus,' Chi greeted him, without looking directly at him.

'Hi, Chi, how's it hangin'? You got the thing?'

'Sure. You got the goods?'

'Course.'

They both looked warily around the square, and then each of them cast an eye up at the sky as if it might offer more than a few clouds and a jet trail or two.

Nexus was small, pale and skeletally thin, but similarly dressed. His mop of dark hair looked permanently greasy and unkempt. They both tried to move their lips as little as possible when they spoke. The square was surrounded by office buildings, from which any number of people could be watching with long-lens cameras, tracking what they were saying by reading their lips. There was also the chance of being listened to using parabolic microphones that could pick up sounds from a distance of over three hundred metres.

But both young men were too experienced to discuss their business out loud.

'I need to hear it before I make the trade,' Chi said gruffly.

'No problem.'

Nexus had a discreet pair of black earphones in his ears, the cord running into an MP3 player concealed in his hand. He took out one of the earphones and offered it to Chi, who took it and held it at arm's length in disgust. The nub-shaped piece of plastic was covered in earwax.

'Jesus, Nex! Ever heard of cotton buds?'

'What are you, my mother?'

Chi wiped the earphone on the sleeve of Nexus's coat and then stuck it in his ear. Nexus pressed 'play' and Chi listened for a couple of minutes.

'Sounds like the real deal,' he said with a nod.

'That's what I've been tellin' you, my man,' Nexus said in a whisper, covering his mouth as he spoke. 'And there's over an hour of it: names, places, dates. I swiped it straight off Counter Terrorist Command. Their security's a joke. They've an isolated server with the really hot stuff, but their administrative staff are accessing it all friggin' day. I got a program that pools all the references—'

'Yeah, yeah, I hear you,' Chi said sourly.

Nexus was the better hacker and he took every opportunity to rub it in. But Chi had the savvy and the contacts to use the information his friend dug out of all those high-security databases.

He palmed the MP3 player, disconnected the earphone cords and stuck it in his pocket. With an equally furtive movement, he attached an identical player to the earphones and slipped it back into Nexus's hand.

'Here's what you want. Use it wisely.'

'I'm going after the military next,' Nexus muttered. 'I think I've got a lead on a bunch called the Triumvirate. I think they're trying to smuggle a weapon—'

'Enough,' Chi cut him off. 'You're talking too much . . . *again*. You've got to be more careful, man, or you're gonna end up as just one more chump on Suicide Beach. Just get on with it and keep it quiet. Let me know if you get anything I can use.'

'Will do. Watch the skies, man. Catch you later.'

'Stay safe, brother. Watch those skies.'

Chi took another careful look around and then got up and left. A minute later, Nexus walked off in the opposite direction.

Amina sat in front of Goldbloom's desk, waiting for his reaction. She had done what he'd asked: she'd written the story up and handed it in. But she'd also checked out the news reports of the bombing that had injured Ivor McMorris's crew and it had happened just as he described – despite his claims to the contrary. Now she wanted to make more of the story and that meant asking for a new deadline, which would give her time to root through Ivor's past. Goldbloom was sitting staring through the glass wall at the newsroom beyond.

He had asked to listen to the recording and had remained expressionless as it played. Now Amina waited for his decision. Part of her hated this, having to await judgement, but she also knew that office temps didn't normally get this level of attention from the managing editor and she was going to make the most of it.

'He didn't offer any proof for what he thinks might have happened,' Goldbloom said at last.

It wasn't a question.

'I don't think he has any,' Amina replied. 'But it might be worth digging up some facts on this. Even with what I've got, I—'

'I don't think so,' Goldbloom sighed, shaking his head. 'We could get into serious hot water making allegations like this against the military. Believe me, I've been there. So has your mother – ask her to tell you about the Harding story some day. Without concrete proof we'd just be setting ourselves up to be sued for libel. Even if McMorris had offered *something*, some kind of documentary evidence, other witnesses . . . but he's got nothing.

'No, it's got no legs. Leave the text with me – I'll have to cut it down a bit, take out the most contentious bits. It's too long anyway.'

Seeing her disappointment, he gave her an encouraging smile.

'You did a good job, Amina. It's well written and there's no harm in pushing a bit sometimes, but you'll have to let this one go. And don't worry, we'll find you something else to work on. In the meantime, get me a coffee, will you? You know how I take it.'

Amina left the office feeling utterly deflated. Too long? The article was barely two hundred words – there was no room to cut anything out. Making her way over to the newsroom's canteen, she yanked the jug out of the coffee machine reserved for the senior staff. Pouring out the stale brown remains at the bottom, she rinsed it and put it back in the machine. She took a new pack of filters and some freshly ground coffee from a cupboard, slamming the door closed. Then she set about making a fresh brew. Her anger percolated along with the gurgling machine.

'Too bloody long, my *arse!*' she shouted at the top of her voice to the empty canteen. 'If I can't fit the whole goddamned story in, what's the point of writing the bloody thing at all?'

'That's the spirit!' a woman's laughing voice called from somewhere outside. 'We'll make a reporter out of you yet!'

4

She should have left it until later before taking the train home. There were hundreds of thousands more people than usual on the Underground system that Friday afternoon because of the peace marches and she had to jostle for a place on the train when it pulled up to the overcrowded platform. The doors beeped as they slid shut, people pressing up against the windows as if they had been vacuum-packed.

Amina heaved a sigh and opened her book in the cramped space, trying to read it without leaning it against the back of the business-suited man in front of her. Her station was near the end of the line and she'd probably be standing for most of the half-hour journey.

By all accounts, the marches around the country had been uneventful. There had been a few anarchists – she hated the perversion of that term – breaking windows, throwing things and trying their luck with the police, but the crowds had been pretty docile for the most part. The police had blocked off any access to streets with government buildings and channelled the protestors along smaller streets so that they could be dissected into manageable groups.

Some of the people on the train had been on the marches; there were crudely designed placards banging against the ceiling, silly costumes and painted faces. A good-natured chatter filtered down the carriage and at the far end, a few hoarse voices were chanting protest songs with more beat than melody.

The train rocked slightly, vibrating with the movement of the wheels on the rails. There was the occasional screech audible from beneath the floor where the fit of metal against metal wasn't perfect on the turns. The darkness outside in the tunnel meant that the lighted interior was reflected in the windows, showing people how they looked on their way home.

Amina could smell body odour and half a dozen different perfumes and aftershaves. She tried to keep her attention on the page in front of her – a chick-lit paperback, the kind she could read in a day or two and dump in a second-hand bookshop

– but her mind kept coming back to Ivor McMorris. She felt sorry that she couldn't make more of his story. He seemed so desperate to get it out in the open. It wasn't her fault he was going to get such a brief airing, but she felt responsible anyway. She supposed it was like this all the time: striking the balance between how much space a story demanded and how many valuable column inches the editors were willing to give it. Her mother said it was worse in television, where reports were often measured in seconds.

Amina's left shoulder was leaning against one of the poles. The train slowed abruptly, and as it did so, the weight of the passengers shifted, the movement passing through the carriage like a swell through water. Bodies pressed her against the pole, making her wince with discomfort, and then the pressure eased again as everyone righted themselves. She shifted her bag up higher onto her shoulder and patted it to check the clasp was still closed.

The train was still deep in the tunnel. Outside the windows, there was nothing but a grey expanse of concrete wall. They came to a gradual stop, no doubt waiting for another train to clear the station ahead of them. She rolled her eyes, impatient for the journey to be over so she could get out of this stuffy, muggy carriage.

At times like this, Amina's mind sometimes turned morbidly to thoughts of the trains that had taken people to the concentration camps during the Holocaust. She often imagined herself back in dramatic periods of history, daydreaming about what it would have been like to be a reporter covering those stories. She had long been fascinated by reports of war atrocities. And the Nazis were the ultimate bad guys.

They had herded whole families, whole communities, up ramps into stock wagons like cattle. Thousands were transported at a time, packed so close that they could not sit down, often travelling day and night without food or water; there were no toilets, no drains, so the prisoners would have had to make do with a bucket or nothing at all, with only the draughts to feed fresh air into the wagon.

Pressed in as she was among all these bodies, Amina could imagine how it might feel to be trapped like that for hours on end. In summer it would have been unbearably hot, airless and probably stinking to high heaven. In winter, it would have been freezing cold and damp. People died on those journeys, but there was no way of disposing of the corpses – not until the train stopped at its destination and the soldiers unlocked the doors. Amina wondered what it would be like to spend hours, even days, pressed against a dead body. How long did it take before a corpse started to smell? And what if it was your best friend . . . or one of your parents? How did people *deal* with that? Amina had a tough time handling an overcrowded Tube train. She felt guilty sometimes for not having endured some great trauma of her own.

And none of the prisoners would have known where they were being taken, but there would have been rumours. Rumours of vast camps surrounded by fences and armed guards. And yet, somehow, millions of decent, ordinary Germans had remained blissfully ignorant.

Amina stared out of the window at the concrete wall beyond. She was sure she would have stood up, if she'd been alive back then. She wouldn't have fallen for the lies. But there were no Hitlers around any more. The Western world wouldn't tolerate that kind of thing. Politics was a lot more complicated nowadays.

The train still hadn't moved. People were starting to talk about it now. They had all waited in tunnels before, but this was taking too long. The carriage's speakers clicked and the driver asked for their attention:

'Ladies and gentlemen, apologies for this delay,' he said in a halting voice. 'But there's been an incident on the track ahead of us and we've been asked to hold here until further notice. Once again, we're sorry for the delay.'

Amina heard some anxious voices further down the carriage; word about something was being passed along. She heard somebody gasp in alarm. A middle-aged businesswoman close to Amina leaned over to listen to what was being said and then relayed it to those further up.

'Somebody was on the phone to their friend . . . before we went into the tunnel and lost the signal,' the woman said. 'He said there's been a bomb scare, but it wasn't specific. All they know is that it's in one of the stations in the south-west. All the stations ahead of us are being closed and searched. We could be here for hours.'

The tall man in the suit in front of Amina swore under his breath. Others started to talk excitedly.

'Did they say who planted the bomb?'

'How many bombs are there? Does anybody know?'

'Are they just going to leave us down here?'

'What if the bomb's on one of the trains?'

'Don't you remember the bombings a few years ago? Nobody knew anything until it happened. And then when people tried to escape from the trains, the fires spread through the tunnels.

I heard the firemen couldn't even get into some of the tunnels it was so hot.'

'But there's nothing in the tunnels that would burn!'

'There's *us*. *We'd* burn.'

'Oh my God!'

Amina felt her pulse quicken. It was an ideal time to bomb the Underground if you wanted to make headlines – the rush-hour crowds were swollen with peace protestors. If you were aiming for a high body-count, this was the time to do it. It didn't matter that the protestors were demanding some of the things the terrorists wanted. Terrorists were lunatics; they didn't care who died, as long as it made shocking headlines and gruesome tele-vision. Terrorists wanted publicity.

Her piqued imagination was already cramming her mind with morbid thoughts. If a bomb went off on the train, the emergency services could take hours to reach them. Aside from the blast, the biggest killer would be the smoke; more people died from fumes in fires underground than from the flames themselves. Even if a bomb went off in a tunnel nearby, the smoke might be enough to choke them before they could escape to the surface.

Amina tried to make more of a space around her. At five foot five inches tall, she was smaller than most of the people surrounding her and she was beginning to feel penned in. Everyone was restless now; there was a sharp smell of fresh sweat in the air, feet shuffled on the floor. Was it getting warmer in here too? Amina leaned back against the couple behind her to try and get them to shift a bit, but they were against the door and had nowhere to go. There seemed to be less air in the carriage now. She was finding breathing more difficult. That was to be expected; everyone was anxious, so their breathing would be faster.

'Does anybody smell smoke?' the middle-aged woman asked. 'I think I smell smoke.'

'I don't smell anything,' the man in front of Amina replied. 'Let's not get worked up about nothing here.'

'I'm not worked up, I just think I smell smoke.'

'I think I smell something too,' a shabbily dressed teenage boy spoke up.

A debate began about whether there was or was not a smell of smoke in the air. Amina craned her neck to peer over people's shoulders. She just wanted to see everyone's faces as they talked. It was frustrating not being able to see who was speaking. Her hands were pressed against the back of the man in front of her and she pushed a bit too hard. He stumbled forward and looked back at her, a Roman-nosed horse of a face with fair hair and reddening ears.

'Whoa there, young lady! Easy.'

'Can people make room, please!' a concerned voice called from further down the carriage. 'There's a woman who can't breathe, here. I think she's hyperventilating, or got asthma or something.'

'*Where* are we going to make room to, may I ask?' someone else snorted.

'Everybody just calm down!' the horse-faced man cried.

'You calm down!' the middle-aged woman retorted. 'You're the only one shouting!'

Amina squeezed her eyes shut. She could feel her own chest tightening up. A wave of dizziness swept over her. If only they'd all just shut up!

'I think we should get off the train and start walking!' the man declared.

'We can't get off the—'

The speakers clicked again and the driver's voice came through:

'All right now, folks. Apologies again for the delay, but I'm happy to say we've been cleared to go through to the next station. There's been a bomb alert, but there's no need to panic – it's nowhere near us. They're going to be shutting the stations down to be on the safe side, but there will be a bus service laid on to get you to your destinations. We hope this hasn't caused too great an inconvenience and we look forward to having you travel with us again soon.'

It seemed to take for ever to get to the platform, and when it did, the passengers bulged and were spat from the opening doors, hurrying for the escalators in a hustle of movement that fell just short of a panicked sprint. Amina let herself be carried by the mob, over the tiled floor and past the framed advertisements offering holidays, recruitment services and expensive cosmetics. The grooved metal steps of the escalator glided up slowly, but some people pushed past, walking up them with frantic movements. Amina waited for her turn to slide through the ticket barrier and then rushed out onto the street with its foul, exhaust-filled air. She breathed it in like it was the countryside in spring. Around her, police officers armed with sub-machine guns watched with impassive faces as the people flooded out.

Amina took a few more breaths and then looked around for a bus to take her home.

Chi took a circuitous route of train and bus journeys back home, but after getting off the last bus, he made the mistake of walking down the main street, rather than taking the longer way through the park. That was how Gierek spotted him.

'Sandwith, you little rat!' a voice bellowed across the street.

Chi turned in alarm to see a burly skinhead charging through the traffic at him. Horns blared but the man with the army surplus clothes and the muscle-packed body ignored the oncoming cars, so intent was he on trying to get his hands on Chi Sandwith.

His quarry had already taken to his heels. Chi knew he couldn't outrun Gierek for long. The man was a survivalist and a fitness fanatic. He could pound right over Chi in a hundred-metre dash. But Chi was not unprepared.

When you lived life on the edge of society and you came in regular contact with the kind of information the government would kill to protect, you had to have some contingency plans. Chi would normally have anticipated having to escape *from* his house rather than flee *to* it, but it was a straightforward matter of adapting to the circumstances and reversing the route in question.

He was already breathing hard as he turned the corner and made for the park. Dodging around pedestrians who had no idea they were witnesses to a chase that could affect the course of their nation's history, he sprinted through the gate and over the grass towards the trees on the other side. Behind him, Gierek was wasting his breath shouting abuse at him, but it didn't seem to be slowing him down much. His face was flushed red and screwed up in rage. His meaty hands were curled into claws that promised unrestrained violence. Chi could hear the man's army boots beating a relentless rhythm that was steadily gaining on him.

Chi dug into his pocket and pulled out a padlock. He was into the trees now, dead and dried foliage crunching under his running feet as he pushed himself to keep up the pace until he reached the three-metre-high wall on the far side of the park.

Gierek's shouts drew closer, his boots running over the same soft ground now. Chi staggered to a halt at the wall, yanking open the gate in the low doorway he found there. He stepped through, bolting it shut behind him, fumbling with the padlock before finally snapping it closed just as Gierek crashed into it. The enraged man wrenched helplessly at the gate and then tried to reach through, snatching at Chi's clothes.

Chi gave him an apologetic smile and tapped his temple as he struggled to get his breath back.

'Brains over brawn, my friend. They win every time.'

And then, deciding that he was pushing his luck, he started running again.

11

It took Amina over two hours to get home. The bomb scares had thrown the city into chaos as all the people ejected from the Underground emptied onto the streets. It had already occurred to her that the whole thing might be a hoax.

She and her younger brother, Tariq, had gone through a phase of ringing up taxi companies in the evenings and sending cabs to imaginary addresses on their street. It was a laugh, watching the unfortunate cabbies drive up and down the street trying to find a house that didn't exist. After a while, she had started to feel ashamed of what they were doing and stopped it. Tariq and his mates had kept it up for a while longer.

The terrorists could well have done the same thing on a bigger scale to a city easily spurred into fear. With the way things were now, a single phone call warning of a bomb could bring the whole city to a standstill. Just one phone call.

Her father was making dinner when she got in; her mother was upstairs in the study, still working.

'Be ready in five minutes!' her dad called as she hung up her coat. 'You OK, love? You weren't on the trains, were you? Go and prise your mum from the telephone. I'm starting to think it's become welded to the side of her head. And call your brother down too.'

'Mum! Tariq!' Amina yelled up the stairs. 'Dinner!'

'I meant go *up* and tell them,' her dad sighed. 'I can shout just fine myself.'

Martin Mir was a tall man with the upright posture of a career soldier. Despite his trim physique, he had a chubby face that regularly split into an easy smile. It wasn't unusual to see him cooking. His wife couldn't cook if her children's lives depended on it (and some would say that it had once been a close thing) and he took pride in providing them with a good square meal. When Martin wasn't there, the housekeeper would do the cooking or the kids would feed themselves. Helena Jessop – she still worked under her maiden name – had little time for mundane chores such as feeding her family.

Since he had been posted to the Ministry of Defence, Amina's father had been travelling less and had started working civilian hours, so his children got to see a lot more of him. He and his wife were both in their fifties – they had started their family late in their lives – but neither showed any signs of slowing down.

Some families bonded by praying together, others by gathering round the dinner table; the Mir family watched the news. Taking their customary seats around the living room, they sat before the television, eating their dinner of lamb kebabs, falafel and spiced basmati rice off plates resting on their individualized lap-trays. Amina and Tariq shared the couch, leaving the two armchairs free for their parents.

Martin had timed the serving of dinner exactly so that they were sitting and ready as the seven o'clock news started. Helena appeared just as the headlines were being announced, expressing her appreciation of her husband's cooking by giving him one of her impish smiles as he gave her the tray and a napkin.

The coverage of the peace protests was over-shadowed by the bomb scare on the Underground. This was just as well, as Amina was far more interested in the latter.

'Typical,' Martin commented, as he tore some lamb from a skewer with his teeth. 'It's always the bad stuff that makes the headlines. It was probably a false alarm too – to put the wind up all those protesters. Not that it's needed.' The screen showed a marching crowd waving banners. 'Look at them, it's daft! Some of 'em don't even know which direction to march in.'

'I don't see why they bother going on these marches anyway,' Amina snorted. 'It's not like it does anything.'

'No, that's not true,' Helena said, shaking her head. 'A protest march is a bit like swearing.'

Amina and Tariq glanced at each other and then gave their mother their full attention. She could swear better than anybody they knew, even their dad – and he was a career soldier.

'How is it like swearing?' Tariq asked with a straight face.

At fifteen, he thought he knew all he needed to about the art of cursing, but he was willing to take advice from a master.

'It's important to know when to use foul language,' Helena declared. 'Swearing is an excellent way of emphasizing an expression, but if you do it constantly, it loses its effect. It's like shouting all the time – in the end, you'll just irritate people and they'll stop listening to you.'

She put down her knife and fork so she could gesture with her hands, as she did when she was on television.

'Sometimes, it's not enough to use rational debate when you're having an argument. There are times when you need to throw a bit of a tantrum . . . or *swear* to show how angry you're feeling. Because if the object of your anger is failing to listen to what you're saying, then they need to be shocked into realizing that.

'And if you save it up for the appropriate occasion, a swear word can have a great effect. But you have to use it right. And a protest march is like that. It's like the nation throwing a little tantrum. So sometimes, when the government doesn't seem to be listening, and the people are really, *really* pissed off, they have to give up rational argument and get out on the streets. They have to stand out there in their thousands, block the traffic, give their leaders the metaphorical finger and say "FUCK YOU!"'

Having made the accompanying gesture, she picked up her cutlery again, pausing before pointing at the television with her fork.

'But these people have gone about it all wrong, because they don't know what they really want. Half of them haven't a clue what's actually going on in Sinnostan and the ones that do can't agree on what to say about it.' She tucked into her food once more. 'This lamb is lovely, darling. What did you put in the marinade?'

★　★　★

The phone kept ringing. Tariq was awake and as dressed as he was likely to get on a Saturday morning, but he kept on reading his movie mag by the light of his bedside lamp. After waiting long enough to see if anyone else was going to get it, he grunted and emerged from his black-curtained room like a cave dweller, blinking in the light. He didn't know why he was bothering. It was hardly ever for him, and not one of his few friends would be awake this early on a Saturday. It was barely past eleven. In fact, the term 'Saturday morning' was not a term they were at all familiar with any more. The phone was all the way downstairs, in the hall.

'Hello?' he said.

'Hi, can I speak to Amina please?' The voice had the sweetest Edinburgh accent he had ever heard.

'Dani?' he asked, his face brightening up. 'Hi, it's Tariq.'

'How's it goin', Tariq? Is Amina there?'

'She's in the shower . . . hang on . . .'

He held the phone to his chest.

'Amina!' There was no answer. 'AMINA!' he roared again.

The bathroom door at the top of the stairs opened and some steam drifted out.

'What? I'm in the bathroom!'

'It's Dani!'

'Oh. Tell her I'll call her back in a few minutes.' The door closed again.

This presented the kind of opportunity Tariq had been waiting for, but now there was every chance he would lose his nerve. Dani was one of Amina's best friends and he had been eyeing her up for the last year or two. She was more of a character than most of Amina's crowd, more alternative, favouring fashions that suggested she studied as much witchcraft as the social science she was doing at uni. She and Mina had met at school, at an Amnesty International meeting back when Amina was into that whole anti-establishment student thing. But Dani still took her campaigning pretty seriously – Tariq had always found fanatical girls appealing.

The fact that she was drop-dead gorgeous didn't hurt either. Although she was a bit on the cuddly side, her natural sandy-blonde hair, laughing eyes and big, juicy lips gave her an unconventional beauty. He had chatted to her at Amina's last birth-day party and thought he was in with a chance, despite the age gap of three years.

His heart started thumping so loudly he was worried Dani might hear it over the phone. He lifted the receiver from his chest.

'She'll be down in a minute,' he lied. 'So how's life?'

'Life's good,' Dani replied cautiously. 'Y'know . . . full of experiences. Just can't believe I can cram so much excitement into each day. How about you?'

'Great, great,' he said, nodding even though she couldn't see it. 'So . . . eh . . . eh . . . listen, you want to go out for a drink sometime?'

'Mmmm,' she said in that I-had-a-feeling-this-was-coming type of way. 'I'm . . . I'm flattered, Tariq, really. But I have a boyfriend, you know? You met him at the party?'

'Oh . . . I didn't know that was still on,' he said, the lead weight of embarrassment and failure settling in his stomach. Then he added lamely, 'Hey, you could bring him too!'

'Yeah. Thanks anyway,' she said in a voice intended to be kind, which just made him feel worse. 'Ehm . . . is Amina going to be long? I could call back.'

'No, seriously,' he persisted, with a recklessness born of having no more pride to lose. 'He could come along. I'd like to meet him; I don't have enough friends anyway. We might have a lot in common – we both like you; that's a good start. What's he into? Does he play any games?'

'You have things in common all right,' she chuckled – Tariq loved the way she could chuckle with a Scots accent. 'He doesn't take "no" for an answer either. And I am afraid, my dear, that you both love games more than you love me.'

'Really? What's his highest score on Tech-Shot Extreme?'

'He doesn't play it.'

'Dump the swine. Really, dump him. He obviously can't handle a real game and he's just, like, going out with you because your scrumptiousness helps prop up his fragile self-esteem. He'll end up snapping and . . . y'know, finding God or something. You should go out with me instead. I have a much more interesting set of inadequacies.'

'Is that right?' Dani asked, and he could almost hear her arch an eyebrow. 'And in what *fascinating* ways are you inadequate?'

'I live life in a . . . y'know, like, a virtual fantasy world because real life has little attraction for me,' he told her in a serious voice. 'I seek the shelter of darkness, away from prying eyes, so that, like, my sensitive nature won't be bruised by human contact.'

'My, aren't we articulate all of a sudden – now that we've been rejected by the bonny lassie?' Dani retorted, and there was a smile in her voice. He had won a smile, even if it was over the phone. 'And how can I save you from this virtual oblivion then?'

'Your intelligence, your wit and your kindness can be the shining light that will guide me out of the darkness,' he crooned. 'And your breasts will give me something to hold on to.'

Dani burst out laughing, pulling the phone away from her head to try and muffle the sound. Tariq bit his lip, knowing he had scored a point. She came back a moment later, trying to stop laughing.

'They're not *handlebars*, Tariq!'

He was in with a chance after all. Make them laugh and you were halfway there. Clenching his fist in victory, he was framing his next remark when the phone was grabbed from his hand.

'Hey!' he exclaimed.

'I said I'd call her back!' Amina said, prodding him in the arm and giving him her big-sister smile, then enunciating each word with a prod: 'Stop. Trying. To. Chat. Up. My. Friends. It's embarrassing. And you're soiling the phone with your dirty adolescent mind.' Then, into the phone, she added, 'Hi, Dani? Yeah, yeah, I know. I think I just saved you from a fate worse than death. You're in danger of becoming my little brother's next obsession. Yeah? He did, did he?'

She looked at him. He waved his middle finger in her face and folded his arms, waiting to have this out with her when she finished the call.

'Yeah,' she said, returning the gesture. 'He can be pretty funny when he wants. But then, it helps that he's funny-*looking*. Apparently he was born arse-first. And he's been trying to catch up with it ever since. So, were you talking to the girls? Are we going out tonight or what?'

Tariq gave his sister a half-hearted kick in the backside and headed for his room. As he was climbing the stairs he could still hear her talking:

'He said what? God, they're all the same, aren't they? No, I'm in between at the moment. Getting a bit tired of boys, to be honest. They're such kids, y'know?'

Amina pencilled a number into the box and then rubbed it out again, massaging her temples and wishing her post-Saturday-night headache away. The paracetamol did not seem to be having any effect at all. This, combined with her bad mood, was having severely detrimental effects on her powers of sudoku. She and her friends had failed to get into the Lizard Club in Leicester Square again. It was the hottest place in town and they'd tried three times over the last few weeks with no luck. They had decided they were too cool for the place anyway, and had gone somewhere else. The rejection still stung though. How hip and gorgeous did you have to be?

'Journalists can learn a lot from Hitler,' Helena declared.

A few years ago, Amina would have risen to the

bait. It was one of her mother's trademarks to make an outrageous statement in order to get your attention before qualifying it with some well-reasoned justification. Gone were the days when Amina would react in shock at her mother's apparent political incorrectness; now it was consigned to the same area of disdain reserved for any parent's attempts to be controversial, or worse yet . . . cool. This latest declaration had been prompted by an article in the paper in which a prominent neo-Nazi compared the flood of Sinnostani immigrants to the West with the Jewish 'infestation' of Germany before the Second World War. Not long ago, he would have been dismissed as a crackpot. Now he had just been elected a member of parliament in a by-election.

'Really?' Amina asked in response to her mother's declaration. 'Hitler bit of a newshound, was he?'

She winced at the trite remark. She hated being smart with her mother, but something about Helena always brought out the sarcasm in her. Perhaps it was the way Helena substituted lectures for proper mother – daughter chats. And being hungover didn't help.

Now she and her mother were sitting at the kitchen table with their cups of coffee, having divided up the Sunday paper; Amina was doing sudoku while her mother browsed the headlines and worked her way through the crossword. They would read the paper through afterwards, passing pages back and forth. This was one of the few rituals they still shared together, mostly on Sunday afternoons, and even though there might be hardly any conversation at all, they both made an effort to keep it up.

'No,' her mother replied with a patient tone. 'I mean he knew how to use information. He could convince ordinary people to commit acts of extraordinary evil.'

'And that's *exactly* why I want to be a reporter,' Amina said.

'My, aren't we feeling sarky today!'

'Well, I didn't catch it from the water. Can I read that after you?'

Helena slid the folded page over to her. Half the articles in the paper were related to Sinnostan. Amina thought about Ivor and his claims that the army – or somebody connected with it – had brainwashed him. She had dipped into the archives to search for similar claims and had found a few, none of which had offered any more evidence than Ivor could himself. Amina idly wondered if there might be something to Ivor's story, but she was sure the truth would turn out to be something far more mundane. The human mind had limits, and there was no shortage of people who snapped because of the things they'd seen, or done, or had done to them.

Ivor McMorris. She found herself thinking of his sad smile, and those slightly haunted eyes. Haunted eye, she corrected herself. Could a glass eye have an expression? She reminded herself that her interest was in the story, not the man. Although he was in another league compared to all the boys who had been vying for her attention the evening before in the club.

She felt a tingle of excitement as she thought about her article again. She hoped they wouldn't edit it too much. It was still part of the whole journalism thing that grated on her nerves. You could write what you thought was a brilliant piece and then someone came along and told you it was too long, or too subjective or not what the paper was looking for, so they changed it.

Helena Jessop, renowned for her work as a war correspondent and later for her investigative journalism, had famously decided to become a journalist after watching a single documentary about the Holocaust. The turning point in her career had come in Bosnia during the break-up of Yugoslavia. She had made a report on the discovery of a mass grave: twenty-two men, women and children butchered by Serbian soldiers. An elderly imam had led her through Serbian-held territory to show her the site.

Despite the horrors she had seen – and some considered these genocidal maniacs to be the Nazis of the nineties – Helena still considered Serbia's people to be no better or worse than anyone else.

'We make decisions about our lives based not on the world around us, but on our perception of that world,' she said, putting down her pen and cupping her hands around her coffee mug. 'Hitler understood this. Every leader does. Control all the information and you control how people make decisions. If you can control it well enough to convince the majority that a certain action is necessary – even a monstrous one – then you can carry out that action and the people will not only let it happen, they will enthusiastically support you. And all it takes are the right words and maybe some pictures to help them along.

'Hitler and the war he started are perfect examples of the power of words. He was a master of propaganda and he knew the importance of influencing education too. Get 'em young. That was why he started the Hitler Youth. Start persuading them as soon as they're able to understand your words. Empower the kids – make them feel part of the fight.

'Millions of people were executed, not because

he was an evil mastermind or a madman – but because he had the power to *convince*. He could turn a nation's fear into hysteria with his rousing speeches. He made ordinary Germans feel as if they were under attack – not just from enemies in other countries, but also from the Jews he claimed were seizing power from within.

'In fact, by portraying him as an evil monster, we do people like him a favour. We kid ourselves that if another Hitler turned up, we'd spot him long before he could commit the same sort of horrors again. I mean, it'd be obvious he was a monster, right? Which is why this shit keeps happening. It's more likely that the next Hitler will manage to convince us we are under attack from someone else long before we realize what he really is.

'That's why a good journalist can learn a lot from Hitler. He wasn't the devil in human form, he was just a man. But he was a superb manipulator, and that's what journalism is up against. And it's why a country's most important defence is not the armed forces or a nuclear deterrent or even diplomacy; it's a free press – a bunch of bloody-minded journalists who are determined to tell people what's really going on, so we know the real enemies from the false ones. They are the first line of defence against tyranny.'

Helena did not need to point out that she was

one of these and took her position as defender of the nation's freedom extremely seriously. She and Amina had versions of this conversation on a regular basis, with just enough variation to avoid completely repeating themselves. It was a grown-up equivalent of her mother sitting beside her in bed and reading a favourite storybook to her night after night.

'And what about all the *other* journalists?' Amina asked. 'The ones who don't agree with your point of view?'

'They should all be shot,' Helena responded. 'Failing that, well . . . I suppose they have to have their say too. Though frankly, the world would be a better place if only everyone would just listen to me.'

Amina suspected she was only half-joking.

35

Ivor had endured this nightmare many times. He knew there was nothing about it that should have scared him and yet the terror set in again as soon as he recognized the spinning numbers over their alternating red and black backgrounds.

There should have been nothing frightening about a roulette wheel, even if this one was dazzlingly ornate and swung with the gravity of a merry-go-round, the numbered slots flashing past with dizzying speed. There was something about the numbers themselves that filled him with a sense of horror, but he could not say why. He was looking across the top from a low angle, suddenly riding in one of the slots, when the little white ball fell in and started to bounce around the wheel.

The perspective yawned away from him. As the ball bounced into the distance, it retreated in size until it was little bigger than a grain of sand, then expanded to several metres in diameter as it neared him again, crashing down on the wheel at each bounce with the weight of marble. If it landed in his slot he would be crushed. He could not move, no matter how hard he tried. He was strapped into the slot by invisible bonds.

The ball crashed past, its passage blowing back his hair, its tremendous weight sending a jolt along the wheel and up the bones in Ivor's backside. Suddenly he was airborne, looking down on the wheel from above. He had played roulette just once, in a casino in Kurjong. In a normal wheel there were thirty-seven randomly placed numbers, including one slot labelled zero.

He remembered hearing the legend that one of the developers of the game of roulette had sold his soul to the devil to learn its system. This was why, if you added up all the numbers from one to thirty-six, you ended up with 666 – the Number of the Beast.

The wheel in his nightmare had 101 slots. He had no idea what this meant.

He always expected to feel pain from his empty eye socket in these dreams, but instead he still had his right eye. It was his teeth that began to come loose. He wailed, trying to keep his jaws still as his teeth split and crumbled like chalk, shards sliding down his throat and spilling from between his lips.

Even from the relative safety above the wheel, the ricocheting ball held him in a trance and his eyes followed it with a grinding feeling of inevitability. Don't let it fall on number twenty, he prayed. Not number twenty.

The wheel slowed. The ball lost momentum, its bounces getting shorter and lower. It clattered into its final resting place with what sounded like a death rattle and Ivor screamed himself awake.

It always took a minute or two to realize that the dream was over. He slowly became aware that the sheet beneath him was damp and he sniffed it tentatively. It was just sweat. A couple of nights after arriving at the hospital in Kurjong, he had wet the bed. Chronically embarrassed, he had tried to steal away and wash the sheets, but was caught hurrying down the corridor to the bathroom cradling the urine-stained linen. The nurses had been sympathetic; they had seen it all before. Compared to some of the psychologically damaged cases they had on their hands, Ivor was an ideal patient.

He looked at the time: it was after five in the morning. His glass eye felt too big in its scarred socket – he normally left it in when he slept. The socket ached and he tenderly rubbed the skin around it. He wouldn't get back to sleep now. That was fine; he preferred going out first thing in the morning before the rest of the world was up. It made the watchers easier to spot and he had learned to amuse himself by wandering around aimlessly, changing direction at random and seeing them struggle to remain anonymous as they took turns following his antics.

It was Monday morning. Amina had said her article would be printed today. The early editions would be out soon. There was a twenty-four-hour shop down the road, so he could drop in and see if his story had been printed. Would they know already? They had to, if they were as powerful as he thought they were. And if not, they soon would. The online version of the paper would be up for sure; he'd check it out himself, but he needed the excuse for a walk.

Ivor dressed without turning on the light and, grabbing his jacket, he headed for the door. Going outside alone in the early hours of the morning was probably not the wisest thing to do, but after long sleepless nights of uncertainty, he just didn't give a damn about anything any more.

He checked the hallway through the spy-hole and then opened the door, but stopped before step-ping outside. Leaning over to the side table behind the door, he pulled out the drawer, took out his stun-gun and slipped it into his jacket pocket. He already had the metal bar from a dumb-bell in his other pocket.

Just because he was verging on suicidal didn't mean he'd let himself be taken without doing somebody some serious harm.

Amina and Tariq were always up later than their parents and, as a result, had only to compete with each other to get to the bathroom. And compete they did. There was another bathroom downstairs, but it didn't have a power-shower. Tariq got there first this time and Amina had to wait impatiently for her turn.

'I have to go to work, y'know!' she called through the door.

'I have to go to school, y'know!' he sang back.

He was going through a goth phase and spent ages every morning working his black hair into a carefully arranged untidiness. Looking at her watch, Amina was almost ready to give up on the shower when he finally unbolted the door and came out, his gothic look contrasting with his prissy blue-and-grey school uniform. She emerged from her room and stopped dead when she saw him.

'Are you wearing eyeliner?' she asked.

'No,' he replied, bowing his head as he strode past her.

'You are!' she gasped, grabbing him by his jaggedly spiked hair and holding his head up. 'Ha! My little brother – the new Marilyn Manson! It'll be white face-paint next. You could cover up those spots. Or . . . no! Black lipstick!'

He brushed her off with a petulant gesture and hurriedly made for the stairs.

'Hey, wait a minute.' She turned to follow him, her smile disappearing. 'Is that *my* eyeliner? Oi! Do you know how much that stuff costs?'

He was already down the stairs, pulling on his jacket and grabbing his school bag, its grey canvas daubed with the hand-drawn logos of half a dozen death-metal bands.

'Get your own bloody make-up!' she yelled as he slammed the front door after him.

But twenty minutes later, she was still smiling about his new look as she waited for her train. She had gone through her own rake of rebel fashions, but working in an office had put a stop to that. Now she was wearing a smart black trouser-suit over a pin-striped white shirt, eager to be taken seriously by the professionals in the newsroom. Her long dark hair was still a bit damp, so she had left it down to let it dry. She would pin it up before she got to the office.

The first thing she did when she arrived at work was grab a copy of the morning edition.

It was available online of course, but she got a particular thrill from seeing her work in print. It took her a couple of minutes to find her article, tucked into the side of a page halfway into the paper.

On reading it, she wondered if her mother's philosophy regarding swearing at one's leaders applied in this case. The story had been cut to ribbons:

LOTTERY WINNER AFRAID TO SPEND HIS MILLION
by Amina Mir

Jackpot winner Ivor McMorris claims that he has hardly spent a penny of the 2.4 million pounds lottery prize. One of three winners, McMorris is the only one still living a modest lifestyle. Apparently, he is worried about what people might think of him. Speaking yesterday, he said: 'I'm afraid to spend the money. I don't want to make anyone angry.' A veteran of the conflict in Sinnostan, McMorris has since become a recluse and now resents the attention his winnings have brought him.

Amina ground her teeth as she read the article. Ninety-four words; that was all Goldbloom had given her in the end. And half of them weren't even hers. She wouldn't have minded if he had kept the essential elements of the article. The whole reason Ivor had come to them – the reason he was afraid to spend any of his money – was because of his suspicions about the events leading up to his injuries in Sinnostan, and they had been completely removed from the story.

Throwing down the paper, she stormed up to the copy-room. There was photocopying to be done. One of the entertainment correspondents had given her a set of listings to copy and bind, but she was still getting her head around the state-of-the-art, multi-functional copy machines. Any one of these monsters could do two-sided copying, automatic loading, automatic resizing, sorting, stapling and – so she had been told – had a shatter-proof glass top in case you fancied photocopying your backside.

As she jabbed aggressively at the little touch-screen, trying to get it to do a *simple bloody photocopy*, her mind seethed with the unfairness of it all.

Helena had warned her that this kind of thing happened all the time, but this was the first time it had happened to *her*. It wasn't right! Even if Ivor was a bit of a crackpot, she'd promised to do her best and he had trusted her. She would have felt better if Goldbloom had just shelved the story altogether – at least that way he wouldn't have made a liar out of her.

For some reason, the copier seemed determined to print her A4 copies out on A3 paper. She shoved the sabotaged copies into the recycle bin, changed the paper setting back *again* and pressed the green button. The copies came out on A3 for a third time.

Amina was not a complete turnip when it came to technology. She could deal with all manner of problems with her PC at home. She could programme the DVD recorder and use every function on her mobile phone. But this machine seemed determined to disobey her instructions.

'Bugger this!' she growled, resisting the urge to kick it.

Goldbloom should have told her he was going to change the whole context of the piece. It was still her story. Even if she was just starting off, she had the right to know what was going on. As the copier started to spit out copies printed in mirror image, she swore again.

'Problem?' a voice asked behind her.

It was Rob, one of the paper's youngest reporters, a West Indian wide boy with big aspirations.

'Nothing in this bloody building prints the way you want it to!' she told him, folding her arms as if daring him to argue.

'Yeah, it's like a big conspiracy, innit?'

He walked up to her, leaned past, giving her a patronizing smile, and reset the copier. Then he touched the screen twice. The pages started sliding out the right way up, the right way round and on the right paper.

'Yah just gotta know which buttons to press, girlie!' he said in his best Yardie accent.

By the time she had delivered the bound copies to the boardroom, the editors were all getting settled and looking for teas and coffees. Amina dutifully took their orders and hurried off to fill them. She reminded herself that noting down all the various combinations of lattes, cappuccinos, espressos, decafs, half–cafs, sugars, sweeteners, soya milks, along with the confusing arrays of herbal teas, was excellent practice for her shorthand. Her mother said it was vital to have the old skills. Some day she might get caught without a recorder and have to take notes fast.

And if the whole reporting thing didn't work out, at least she could turn to waiting tables.

She was halfway through preparing all the various beverages when Judy on reception buzzed her to tell her there was an Ivor McMorris on the phone for her.

'Bugger,' she said with a resigned expression.

She had barely picked up the phone at a free

desk when Ivor's irate voice blared out at her.

'I'm "afraid to spend the money because I don't want to make anyone angry!"?' he snapped. 'Is this what you call reporting? What the hell happened to everything I told you about my memories? You didn't even mention the bombing! Put Goldbloom on the phone, I want to speak to him. Do you know the risk I took in talking to you? Have you any idea what that meant?'

Amina winced, letting him run out of steam before she replied. She knew some journalists who made it a policy not to speak to the subjects of their stories after the articles were written. Sometimes it just wasn't worth the hassle. But she thought it was a crap thing to do to somebody, even if the mistakes in the article weren't hers.

'I'm really sorry you're not happy with it, Ivor,' she told him. 'But it was felt that we couldn't print the kinds of allegations you were making without some kind of evidence. Maybe if you had some way of proving—'

'Let me talk to Goldbloom!' he cut in.

'Mr Goldbloom's in a meeting, he won't be free for some time. And he'll only tell you what I'm telling you. You can't go accusing the military of brainwashing people without some kind of proof. Just think about what that would *mean*. You were a journalist . . . sort of. You know how this works.'

'I know you printed an inaccurate story about me in a national paper and deliberately misquoted me,' he snarled. 'And I know I'm rich enough to afford some serious lawyers. Tell Goldbloom that and tell him to ring me when he's free.'

The line went dead. Amina sighed and put down the receiver. It was a hollow threat. They hadn't said anything bad enough about him to be sued for libel, but she had to tell Goldbloom anyway. Helena had once said a journalist wasn't doing their job properly if they didn't get sued from time to time, but Amina doubted that this was what she meant.

She was a little hurt by his tone too. She had kind of liked him. Still, you needed a thick skin to work in this business and it didn't develop overnight. Pushing Ivor McMorris out of her mind, she tried to remember what she had been doing before he called.

'Amina! Call for you on line six!' a voice shouted.

'Thanks, I'll take it here!' she replied.

Hopefully it was Ivor calling back to apologize now that he had calmed down a bit. She picked up the phone again and pressed the lighted button.

'Hello?'

'Is this Amina Mir? My name's Chi Sandwith.

I do some work for the *National News*. Maybe you've heard of me?'

Amina rolled her eyes. The *National News* was a rag full of lowbrow sensationalist stories and celebrity gossip. The last issue she'd seen actually had a blurred picture of a UFO on the front page.

'Sorry, no. I don't read the tabloids.'

'Right, well, I believe in reading a bit of everything and I noticed your article in today's paper: "Lottery Winner Afraid to Spend His Millions".'

'Yes, what about it?' she asked guardedly.

'Well, you mentioned that Mr McMorris was a veteran of Sinnostan and I was wondering if maybe he had more to say. It was a very . . . brief article and I just thought he might want to expand on—'

'I'm sorry, but we don't give out contact details,' Amina said in a clipped tone. 'Thank you for calling.'

She put down the phone before he could say any more. Poor old Ivor. He'd probably get hundreds more pest letters over this, from people eager to offer guidance on how to spend his money. Slouching in the chair, she tilted her head back and stared at the ceiling. She couldn't get hung up on this. The story'd had its shot and now it was time for her to move on. There were too many other things to do.

'Oh, bugger! The coffees!'

She took off out of the chair so fast it spun.

Despite his frustrated anger, Ivor was relieved when he read the article. His threat to Amina had been just bluster and he was regretting it already. He winced as he wondered if she'd taken it personally – a part of him still held out hope of seeing her again. What was it she'd said? 'You were a journalist – *sort of*'? Smirking, he shook his head. Cheeky cow!

He knew how the system worked and he should never have expected the story to be printed as he told it. Of course they needed proof. But his hands were shaking as he put down the phone and he couldn't tell if it was due to fear or fury.

Maybe this was for the best. He had tried to tell his tale and failed miserably. Perhaps the watchers would leave him alone now. He had been shown to be impotent in their eyes and they could rest easy knowing he was no threat to their operations . . . whatever they were.

He went to each of his windows and looked out onto the street below, but there didn't seem to be anything out of the ordinary. As ever, he caught fleeting glimpses of people at windows, in doorways and on the street corner, but nothing he could be sure about. Everyone seemed to be just minding their own business.

Letting out a long breath, Ivor went to his fridge and took out some milk. This occasion called for some hot chocolate. He hadn't decided what to do with the rest of his day; do a workout, watch a film or two, surf the web. Maybe he'd pick up one of the books he was halfway through reading.

Then the buzzer on the door's intercom rang.

Ivor glared at it. He wasn't expecting anybody. He continued looking at it until it buzzed again and then he reached out and picked up the handset.

'Yes?'

'Ivor? Hey, partner, it's Ben. Sorry for showin' up out o' the blue like this, but I really needed to talk to you . . . and, uh . . . well, I didn't want to do it over the phone.'

Ivor went to press the button that unlocked the door to the street, but then hesitated.

'You on your own, Ben?'

'Sure, man.'

'Sorry, you know how it is. Come on up.'

Ivor pressed the button and put down the handset. His hands were steady now, but his nerves were even more on edge than before. The timing was just a little too weird. Had Ben seen the article yet? There was a knock on his front door and Ivor checked through the spy-hole before opening it.

Ben was alone, as he'd said. That didn't do much to set Ivor's mind at ease. He opened the door and ushered his old colleague inside.

Ben Considine had been Ivor's cameraman in Tarpan, seconded from the US army. Back then, he had been a real ladies' man, with his sun-bleached blond hair, his tanned, roguish good looks and his macho Texan drawl. He could find the humour in any situation and had been Ivor's guide to the nightlife in Kurjong's backstreets. But that was all before the bombing. He was a different man now.

Ben rarely went out without some kind of hat on to conceal the burn scars up the left side of his neck and head, which had left that side of his scalp bald. After numerous operations on the left side of his face, his flesh looked misshapen and the shape of his stubble was all wrong because the skin-grafts had been taken from his thighs. He had been standing closer to the bomb when it went off, framing Ivor in the shot of the street.

He had always dreamed of being a cameraman in Hollywood and would joke about how he'd make a great movie star himself. Ivor had admired him for the way he could hold his nerve and keep the camera steady in any situation. Now, Ben rarely did any camera work and when he did, it was always in a studio, never out on the street. He couldn't stand the way people stared.

'What's up?' Ivor asked.

'Just needed to talk,' Ben replied, making himself comfortable on the couch. 'Not many people I can talk to about . . . y'know, this stuff. Got any beer?'

Ivor fetched a couple of beers from the fridge. It was early yet, but he wasn't one for obeying conventions. He sat down opposite the couch and handed the bottle over. Neither of them used glasses.

'Been havin' a lot o' problems lately,' Ben told him. 'Hallucinations, paranoia, and some absolutely mindbendin' nightmares.'

Ivor nodded. They'd talked about this before.

'Still no roulette wheels, I'm sorry to say,' Ben added, giving him a distorted version of the ol' charmer's smile. 'A lot o' tiled corridors and faces in surgical masks . . . watchin' the lights whisk by overhead. Kept seeing these coloured flares that made me want to blow chunks. The hallucinations were new, though . . . and they were the freakiest – there's nothin' that screws with your brain like seein' spaced-out crap in broad daylight.'

'Like what?' Ivor asked.

'Well, first I just kept thinkin' people were watchin' me,' Ben said. 'Guys with no faces, y'know? Like you used to talk about? I'd look around and they'd just be disappearin' round a corner, or liftin' a newspaper up in front of 'em. But then I got to seein' worse things too.

'The first dead body I saw lyin' on a path in the park, I thought it was real. It was this pudgy guy in a shirt and trousers lyin' there with no visible wounds. Just dead. Couldn't understand why all these folks kept walkin' past him . . . even steppin' over the dude without reactin' to him at all. I actually went over to check his pulse and that was when I discovered he was a Sinner – one of the corpses we'd filmed in Tarpan. I turned him over and screamed and then I was lookin' down at an empty bit of pavement and people all around me were starin' at me like the nut-job I was.

'After that, I started seein' other corpses that I'd filmed in war zones, walkin' past me in the street – still torn up with their wounds, but walkin' round lively as you please, like they were just wearin' special-effects make-up or something. I learned not to react to them eventually, but you can just imagine how I was feelin'.'

'What about the smudge-faced guys?' Ivor pressed him. 'D'you see them much?'

'Hell, yeah!' Ben guffawed, some of his old spirit showing through his scarred face as he nearly sprayed beer everywhere. 'It got so everybody I looked at had this blurred face that I couldn't see. Like havin' a lump o' Vaseline smeared on your camera lens. Felt like the whole goddamned world was goin' blank on me. Even the pizza delivery guy just had these eyes starin' out of this flesh-coloured smudge – and he's like a buddy, he's round so often!

'Then, last week, I got a call from my pop. I got the webcam and everythin' set up for him, y'know? And there I was lookin' at his face on the monitor and I couldn't recognize a goddamned thing about him. My own *father*. That was when I went back to see Higgins.'

Ben knocked back the last of his beer. Ivor went to get him another without being asked.

'Higgins said I was repressin' a whole load of stuff and I had to work it out o' my system. I swear to Christ, every goddamned shrink you ever talk to tells you that. He put me through some o' that regressive hypnotherapy . . . you know, where they put you in this trance and take you back to the past? Ever done that?'

Ivor nodded.

'Didn't turn up much,' he said quietly. 'It was all pretty confused. And Higgins said it can be as much fantasy as reality. It's useful, but you can't really trust the results.'

'Yeah, well, he said that to me too,' Ben snorted. 'Still *did* it though. Probably charges the army extra for it. Anyway, he puts me under and probably has me talkin' about every time I'd jerked off when I was a kid, or cheated on a girl, and then I come out of it and he's smiling at me.'

'Yeah? How come?' Ivor asked.

'Reckons he's got me figured out. See, the Scalps guys? They're all the people I blame for my injuries. Not that the actual folks I see are to blame . . . it's more like . . . I need a conspiracy to explain why I was hurt. I can't accept that it was just dumb luck I was standing there when the bomb went off; it doesn't satisfy my sense o' outrage. You know, like . . . sometimes this crap just happens to you and that's life. So my mind has kind o' spun together this ring of conspirators who hurt me as part o' their master plan and now they're watchin' me 'cos they're afraid I'm gonna come back at 'em. It helps my subconscious make sense o' my injuries. Sort o' like believin' in God 'cos it gives us comfort, knowin' we're not just arbitrary sparks of momentary existence – if you get my drift.

'But he said the biggest thing I had to work out was the fact that I blamed one person above all the others. He said if I dealt with that, the other stuff would start slidin' into place.'

'So who was the culprit, then?' Ivor chuckled.

'Oh, that was *you*, buddy.' Ben nodded at him.

'But I didn't plant the bomb,' Ivor said, taken aback. 'Why would you blame me?'

'Hell, man! It doesn't have to make sense! It's just my mind lookin' for someone to hold responsible, that's all. You were there and you were callin' the shots, so I blamed you. Don't take it all personal! So I'm just here to say that I know I'm a screwed-up basket case with wild delusions of persecution, but I'm *dealin'* with it. And I needed to tell you that I've spent the last few months blamin' you for all this, even though I know it ain't true.'

'Right. Well . . . thanks for your honesty,' Ivor muttered. 'Ben?'

'Yup?'

'Did . . . did anyone . . . suggest that you come round here and tell me all this?'

'Yeah – Higgins.'

'No. I mean . . . I mean anyone from the top brass.'

'Ivor,' Ben sighed, leaning forward and putting the half-empty beer bottle on the coffee table. 'We both know you're goin' through the same crap. You just haven't been as honest with yourself yet. You've got yourself holed up in this poky little dump, con-vincin' yourself that "they" are out to get ya 'cos . . . 'cos you're on the point of findin' out what they did to you. But there is no "they" – at least, not outside of your *head*. You gotta deal with your demons, partner.'

Ivor gazed out of the window, lost in thought. Ben still hadn't mentioned the article. Maybe it was just coincidence that he'd called by hours after it had hit the streets. But there was no way to be sure. Ivor yearned for a time when he hadn't been so suspicious, so fearful. He knew he was being paranoid.

Yeah, he thought, but am I being paranoid enough?

21

Tariq hated school. Every teenager thinks they hate school, but for the most part this isn't true. They dislike the early mornings, the rigid routine, having to sit still in regimented classrooms, struggling through tough or boring classes, enduring the overbearing discipline and any number of other things. But for most kids it is also a place that gives structure to their lives; while they treat it with open contempt, it is a place where they can meet up, play sports, flaunt the latest street-gear (as far as uniforms allow), pick up new slang, gossip and flirt and check each other out. It is a place where a boy can learn how to fight and eventually how not to fight, and where a girl can begin learning how to wrap boys around her little finger. It is an arena for proving themselves to their peers and it gives them tolerant authorities to rebel against so that they can define their individuality without fear of extended imprisonment or physical injury.

It can also, on occasion, provide some education.

But Tariq *despised* school. As Martin Mir had been moved from one post to another, so his children had moved schools to follow him. It had been OK for Amina; she was pretty, outgoing and vivacious and life was easy for girls like that. Tariq had been moody long before he became a teenager and he was slow to make friends. Apart from English, he spoke German and some Arabic, but he could rarely find anyone he considered worth speaking to. He had a few friends at this school, but mostly they were fellow victims and he didn't actually like them very much. Darren, his best mate, was in the year above him and they only saw each other at break times.

Even though he always left home on time, Tariq tried to get to school as late as he could. The less time Noble and his mates had to hassle him the better. He was just in time to get to Geography, the first class of the day, walking in through the double front doors of the building, past the office and the labs and the canteen and on down the glass-walled corridor towards the classroom in the next block.

Students milled around in the corridor, some

trying to look as if they had somewhere to go, others looking like they didn't care where they went, as long as it wasn't lessons.

The usual sick feeling weighed in the pit of his stomach. His face was tense, his teeth clenched together. Alan Noble and his mates didn't bully Tariq. Bullying was what happened to kids – it was an insufficient word for the torment Tariq suffered on a daily basis. He would never have believed the power of humiliation; he had always been an out-sider in school, but this place seemed to thrive on the misery of anyone who didn't fit in. He under-stood there had to be bullies in every school, but why did everyone else have to laugh?

He reached the classroom just as they were going in.

'Well timed, Tarmac!' Noble called out, much to the amusement of his sidekicks. 'Whass wrong, you forget where Geography was?'

That got another few chortles and one of the others repeated the line as a sign of appreciation. Tariq ignored them and joined the back of the group as they trailed into class. 'Tarmac'. Noble had called him that once because of his spots. When they laughed, he'd warned Tariq that the name would stick. 'Stick – like Tarmac. Geddit?' That had them in stitches . . . And so the nickname *had* stuck. Tariq flinched at the memory; it wasn't like Noble didn't have spots of his own. They hadn't noticed Tariq's eyeliner, but it was only a matter of time. He'd done it deliberately. The more they slagged him off, the more he was determined they could all go to hell.

There was some pushing as they pressed through the door and Noble took the chance to dig his knee into Tariq's thigh. Tariq suppressed a grimace but Noble heard him grunt in pain and that was enough. He looked up towards the board but Ms Maijani, the Geography teacher, had seen nothing.

The students were surprised to see a man standing beside the teacher. He was wearing an olive drab army uniform. Tariq noted that although there were medal ribbons on his chest, the man wore no insignia to show his unit or regiment. He was like a picture from a recruitment poster; his face was lean and tanned, his brown hair was cut tight to his skull and he looked impressively fit.

'Now then, take your seats please,' Ms Maijani said in her heavy South African accent. 'Quietly!'

Once they were all seated, she gestured to the man beside her. There was a reluctance in her manner, as if she was less than pleased to be introducing him, but her voice had that fake enthusiasm that any good teacher could summon at a moment's notice:

'This,' she said brightly, 'is Lieutenant Scott. He will be taking you for Geography today. Our school has been *lucky* enough' – she laced the word with sickly-sweet emphasis – 'to have been chosen to test-run a new project, in conjunction with the Military in Schools Scheme. You will remember it was one of the changes brought in by the Drawbridge Act. I'll leave it to the lieutenant to fill you in.'

She graciously stepped aside and sat down in her swivel chair with a face like frostbite. It was clear she was not happy about surrendering her territory to some jumped-up squaddie.

Scott took the floor with a smile that immediately won him the approval of half the girls in the class. Melissa Denning whispered that he could fill her in any time. Her friends had to cover their mouths to contain their laughter.

'Ladies and gentlemen,' Scott began, clasping his hands. 'As you know the army was originally asked to get involved in schools to help with issues of discipline, but we always felt that we needed a more integrated role in education. After all, I can't just get you all to hit the floor and give me twenty press-ups, can I?'

He beamed at his own joke. Tariq swore under his breath and looked out of the window for something more interesting to catch his attention.

'No, we wanted to get more involved on a developmental level,' Scott went on. 'In fact, we were getting concerned about the poor state of education our new recruits were demonstrating when they joined up. And the program I'm going to tell you about is a result of years spent designing a way to correct this problem.

'We have come up with a computer game that was originally intended to instruct in battlefield strategy, but we have since found to be extremely beneficial in education . . . in fact, in any area of teaching. We call this game program *MindFeed*. We think of it as . . . ammunition for the brain.'

He grinned again. A number of the boys exchanged glances. This was the kind of education they were looking for.

'Over the next few months,' Scott continued, 'you will be given the opportunity to take different classes through the playing of games on *MindFeed*: Maths, History, Science . . . but today we're going to start with Geography.

'The point of all this is to improve your receptiveness to these subjects by making them *fun*. We all learn better when we're enjoying what we are doing, and boys in particular tend to thrive in a competitive environment. *MindFeed* will also improve your hand—eye coordination and will contribute to your computer skills.

'Now, with Ms Maijani's permission, I'd like to take you all down to the computer room, where we'll set each of you up with a player identity.'

Ms Maijani's permission was grudgingly given and there was a rush for the door as the boys raced to get to the computer room to nab the best PCs. Tariq was more interested than he wanted to admit, but as he went to follow the mob out of the room a hand pulled him back.

'Tariq,' his teacher said. 'I'd wipe off that eyeliner before you join the class, if I were you. I don't think they approve of that kind of face paint in the army. What would your dad say?'

'He'd say you're right; the army's got too many poofs already,' Tariq replied. 'But then he is a marine.'

Ms Maijani burst out laughing and he made his escape before she could pull him up for his homophobic language.

Amina was exhausted by the time she got home, so she was in no mood for one of Tariq's explosions of adolescent enthusiasm.

'But you should see it, it's brilliant!' he told her excitedly. 'It's like taking your classes on a PlayStation! We played this Geography game where they picked countries at random from the syllabus, right? And you could choose to bomb places or drop aid parcels. But to make the drops in the right place, you had to learn about the country, so you could recognize the drop-zones. It was cool! I learned more in one class than I normally do in a month!'

'I'm delighted for you,' Amina sighed, as she looked around the living room for the TV remote control.

She noticed the remains of the eyeliner on his lids and made a mental note to keep her make-up under lock and key from now on. She had barely got in the door when Tariq had cornered her and had launched into his spiel. This was what she got for asking about his day. Switching on the TV, she flopped into an armchair, focusing her entire attention on a music programme, hoping her brother would get the hint.

He didn't.

'But they said this game was only one part of it,' Tariq went on. 'There's a driving game for Geography too, and a speedboat one. Tomorrow we're going to be doing Biology using a shoot-'em-up game. You have to name the parts you're hitting on the bad guys – y'know, like all the organs and stuff—'

'That's gross!' Amina protested, turning the volume up.

'That's what some of the other girls said, but

they still want to try it,' he said, nodding. 'Then there's a counter-terrorism . . . er, spy-type game for some of the foreign languages and—'

'OK, I get it, it's the best thing since sliced bread!' Amina snapped. 'Now quieten down or get lost, I'm trying to watch telly!'

He sat on the arm of the couch, visibly pent-up, and tried to watch the dishevelled guitar band wrangle music from their instruments. Music wound out of the entertainment system's waist-high speakers, fading from the indie band as the screen changed image into cello strings stirring as if deep beneath ocean waves. A jagged power chord tore across the melodic sound, shattering the soft intro as the latest hit from Absent Conscience, 'I Love Hurting You With Honesty', grated into the living room. Amina tutted and went to change the channel.

'Oi!' Tariq cried. 'I like this one!'

'It's rubbish!' she retorted.

'How would you know? You don't even listen to their music! You switch off as soon as they come on!'

Amina tossed the remote to him and strode out of the room. Behind her, in their harsh mixture of death metal and hip-hop, the self-proclaimed 'junk poets' snarled their opening lyrics:

'*You've hated me since the day I was born / Tried to*

drown my dreams, tried to send me to war/But you love me now 'cos you need my power/So I tighten my grip with each passing hour . . .'

She grabbed her phone, dialling Dani's number as she headed upstairs to her room. Dani had her phone switched off. Amina scrolled down through her friends' numbers, but then gave up, deciding she didn't want to talk to anyone after all. She put on her stereo and started reading instead.

Amina had grown out of her angry music phase and as the Absent Conscience bass beat pounded through the floor of her bedroom, interfering with her own tunes, she hoped Tariq would soon follow her example. She was surprised at his excitement over the army's 'learning game'. Tariq had rebelled against their father's hopes to raise another marine, expressing a complete lack of interest in all things military – but then, growing up on military bases took much of the idealism out of soldiering. Now her brother seemed determined to seek out every antisocial habit that would annoy his parents at home and make him an outsider in school.

Whatever, she thought. He'll mellow out eventually. We all do.

The news was filled with reports and debates on the War for Freedom. What had begun as a concerted campaign to wipe out Muslim extremists across the world had become a never-ending series of reactions to any revolutionary movement that didn't like Western foreigners meddling in their country's affairs. And those movements were growing steadily in number.

Sinnostan featured regularly on the news reports. A barren, mountainous country, its deeply carved valleys and ridged hillsides were thought to offer hiding places to camps training terrorists, who then swarmed to Western Europe and the United States to do their worst. Its poverty-stricken people – the Sinnostanis, as they were known to the soldiers cursed with patrolling their godforsaken country – barely scratched a living from the unforgiving landscape. They were thought to be ripe for the mixture of religious extremism and fanatical nationalism that made the most dangerous revolutionaries.

Ivor sat in his black-leather lounger and watched the reports. They didn't tell half the story. For a start, you couldn't get into the damn place. Half the roads were only passable by mule or packhorse. Making an assault on any of these camps meant hauling troops hundreds of miles across formidable terrain, which made them vulnerable to ambushes. Flying was a risky business too. Nowadays, every self-respecting mountain fighter carried a surface-to-air missile launcher or two.

The mountains roasted you in summer and froze you in winter. The wind up there had to be experienced to be believed. Ivor still shivered at the memory of it cutting like knives through his parka on the rocky slopes of Myapin. It did have its advantages: apparently the cold could help keep casualties alive – they lost less blood when they were hypothermic.

And there were plenty of casualties, but not so many that the politicians had to call it an all-out 'war'. With the fighting happening in small, savage, isolated clusters, less than a thousand soldiers had been flown home in body bags. Body armour that protected the torso meant there were more amputations than deaths – not that you saw much of that on the news. The government was a bit sensitive about images of men and women with missing limbs and many of the news agencies voluntarily censored their own footage. Ivor's hand went up to his right eye, touching the hard glass beneath his eyelids.

One of the reasons the news organizations were so helpful was that it was almost impossible to get reporters into the areas where the fighting was taking place. They had to have a military escort, because killing reporters – or better yet, taking them hostage, releasing video footage on a website and *then* killing them – was a sure way to get headlines. And terrorists loved headlines. Like everyone said, there was no such thing as bad publicity.

Reporters who tagged along with the troops had to behave themselves. Anyone who filed a story that was too critical of their hosts didn't get to ride in any more helicopters.

It was easier still to let literate soldiers like Ivor do all the 'investigating' and then the real reporters could just sit and wait for the military press briefings. Why risk your life going looking for a story when it could be delivered straight to you? Besides, it was expensive to send someone halfway around the world.

But Ivor knew how accurate his stories had been once the top brass had filtered out all the juicy stuff.

It felt good to despair at the poor quality of the news; it took his mind off his mind. Ben's visit had shaken him up more than he wanted to admit. Ivor had been absolutely sure, he had known with concrete certainty, that somebody had screwed with his head. Now, he was plagued by doubts.

If Ben was right, there was no conspiracy. If there was no conspiracy, then Ivor really was out of his mind. He had turned it over and over in his head, trying to make sense of it. But the more he thought about it, the more confused he became.

Suspicions, questions and paranoia fed on each other, breeding new and more complicated forms of themselves.

Was he really being watched, or was it all in his imagination? What about the things he'd seen: the faceless people, the vehicles following him down the street? He was never able to get close enough to these watchers to talk to them, but was that just his mind making excuses so that it could prolong the delusion? He didn't even know why they were watching him. If somebody had him under surveillance, why did he assume that they meant him harm? Maybe they were just studying him, or even wanted to protect him from . . . well, anything. Protect him from himself, perhaps.

He was sure of what he had seen, and of the sense of menace that sent prickles of tension across his skin. But wasn't that the whole thing with delusions? Your brain interpreted your perceptions, so if something went wrong with it, you might be the last person to know. The human brain was not designed to diagnose its own illness. It was like trying to look down your own throat.

The worst part about this was that there was no way to know for sure if he was mad or not. But if the mental kaleidoscope he was experiencing was sanity, he didn't feel much better about it.

Ivor held his head in his hands, swearing

violently and pulling at his hair. He found himself crying again. He was exhausted from all this. With few friends and no job to keep him busy, he was in danger of losing it completely if he didn't do something.

Lifting his head, his gaze fell on a scrap of notepaper lying on the coffee table. Amina Mir's number was written on it. He had stopped wearing a watch, so he looked at the clock on the wall in the kitchen; it was after midnight.

Tomorrow. He'd call her tomorrow.

He decided to go to bed. He knew that even if he slept, he would have the nightmares again, but he was too tired to worry about it. Let them come; tomorrow, he was going to start asking some serious questions. After all, if he was insane, what harm could it do?

16

Contrary to the belief held among the newsroom staff, Amina did not have a problem with changing the cartridge in the photocopier. Any idiot could change a photocopier cartridge, even if they couldn't read the cartoon symbols printed both on the inside of the copier door and on the cartridge itself. That bit was easy.

She did have a problem with paper jams. For a start, she was amazed that a machine that cost a few thousand quid and weighed almost as much as a small car could be thwarted by a simple sheet of A4. She was also bothered by the fact that she couldn't reach the plug to disconnect it before she stuck her hand into the machine. Most people just left it running, but she was unnerved at the way it sat and hummed at her as she reached her slim hands in between those heavy rollers. So she always turned it off first.

Sometimes, you could wind the paper out by turning the rollers' handles, but other times you had to get your fingers right in and just wrench it out, hoping it didn't tear.

This time it tore, and Amina sighed to herself as she got down on her knees and pulled the pieces out one by one, careful to avoid the heated rollers and shaking her head as she got carbon dust all over her fingers.

When she'd finished wrestling with the copier, she returned to the desk where her next job was waiting: a pile of readers' complaints letters. There was also a message in her inbox telling her to call Ivor McMorris when she got a chance. She took one look at the complaints pile and decided that this seemed like the perfect time.

As it turned out, he was very apologetic about their last conversation and she found herself apologizing in turn.

'I'm really sorry about the article,' she told him in a low voice. 'They edited it to death. I mean, I suppose they had to, but I hated—'

'It's OK, it's OK,' Ivor assured her. 'To be honest, I'm glad in a way. I think . . . I think there might be another angle to the whole thing . . . if you're still interested.'

Amina settled back in her chair as he related the conversation he had had with his friend, Ben

Considine, and how it had caused the doubts he was having now. Ivor wanted to know if there was any way she could use the resources at the paper to see if there were any other Sinnostan veterans suffering the same symptoms as he was. Perhaps there was more to this than just post-traumatic stress? Amina nodded to herself, thinking of the Agent Orange controversy in Vietnam. The health of thousands of US soldiers (and presumably one or two Vietnamese) had been affected by chemicals – particularly one called Agent Orange that had been used to clear the leaves from jungles, which could hide those pesky Vietcong.

There had also been stories about chemicals tested on soldiers in the Gulf War in the 1990s that had caused all kinds of side effects. Amina breathed out softly at the thought that Ivor might have something along the same lines. This could be the making of her . . . if only she could come up with some hard evidence.

'Is there anything you haven't told me?' she asked. 'Maybe something you might have left out before.'

'I don't think so,' he said. There was a pause and then: 'Did I mention my tooth?'

'No – what about it?'

'Somewhere between the bombing and waking up in the hospital, I lost a tooth—'

'Well . . . you were caught in an explosion,' Amina pointed out gently.

'Yes, but I'm sure that the tooth was still solidly in place when I was in the helicopter. Like I said, the memory is absolutely vivid. I tasted blood, but all my teeth were still there.'

'Maybe it was loose, and it came out afterwards?'

'I dunno. I was lying on my back the whole time. If I'd been unconscious, I would have choked on it. And I'm sure if I'd felt it coming out, I'd remember, y'know? I mean, losing an adult tooth is a serious thing.'

'Yes, but you had just lost an eye. I'd say that would be quite a distraction.'

'Even so, I'm sure I'd remember. So that could mean one of two things: either these vividly real memories I have are my mind's way of blocking out some other trauma, or . . .' His voice trailed off.

'Or what?'

'Or if these are . . . are implanted memories – and I'm only saying "if" – then maybe I can't remember losing the tooth because I lost it during the process and they didn't know, so they didn't account for it when they manufactured the memories. They didn't know to add a scene to explain why I was missing a tooth.'

'But who are "they"?'

'Well, obviously I don't know. That's the whole point with conspiracies. No doubt it's army intelligence, some shadowy government department or a cabal of power-hungry fiends from the military-industrial complex – you know the way.'

'Yeah; goes without saying really.' Amina smirked.

He told her about the people he thought were following him, and how he could never get a look at their faces.

'You mean, you can't see them? Like they're wearing masks?' she pressed him.

'No. It's more like . . . it's like I can't focus on their faces,' he said, struggling to describe it. 'In fact, that doesn't even . . .' He paused for a moment. 'It's like their faces are blurred – the same way they do on TV when they're hiding somebody's identity, y'know . . .'

'Yeah, I get it.' She nodded to herself. 'Like when they're keeping a reporter's source anonymous.'

'Yeah, like that,' Ivor said. 'Except I can see their eyes staring out at me. Just their eyes.'

Amina was already writing all this down. He told her about his nightmares then too, but neither of them could understand the significance of the roulette wheel, unless it symbolized the arbitrary nature of death or something like that. Amina said she'd look it up in a book about interpreting dreams, but he said he'd tried that and it got him nowhere. And besides, he thought most of the people writing those books were talking out of their arses.

He'd done a lot of reading up on memory loss as well. Apart from amnesia caused by physical trauma, there was psychogenic amnesia, which came about through psychological factors. Either could apply in his case. He had also learned that your 'episodic' memory could be affected, causing you to forget certain events, or even things like your name, your friends and family, while leaving your 'semantic' memory intact, so you could still remember how to read and write, and that Paris was the capital of France.

With some reluctance, Ivor told Amina that he had also done extensive reading on mind control: everything from the Chinese attempts to brainwash US prisoners of war in North Korea and the CIA's MK-ULTRA programme in the 1950s to modern-day subliminal advertising. But the biggest culprits these days were thought to be religious cults who indoctrinated naïve new converts.

None of what he had read could explain the vivid memories he was so convinced were false. People could be coerced through a variety of ways into saying and doing things that were completely out of character, but it always depended on what they believed. As soon as they started questioning these beliefs themselves, the programming's hold over them began to weaken.

Ivor had been questioning his memory for nearly a year and the events surrounding his injury were still sharp, fresh and exact in his mind.

When Amina finally put down the phone, her head was spinning. For the first time, she thought there might be some truth in what Ivor had said about his memories, and her conversion had nothing to do with all his research or reasoning. It was his tooth that had changed her mind.

Her hand went up to the right side of her mouth, rubbing her bottom lip and the incisor that lay beneath. It was an implant – the original tooth had been knocked out in a hockey game in school. She remembered how she had felt at the time. Ivor was right; it was serious. For the first time in her life she had felt truly vulnerable, aware of how badly she could be hurt. There was something deeply personal about losing an adult tooth. The fact that she had been permanently damaged – if only in this small way – caused her to cry on several occasions afterwards. It just wasn't like losing your baby teeth, those rootless little white nubs you put under your pillow for the tooth fairy; teeth that you knew would be replaced by stronger, adult versions.

Having an adult tooth knocked out left its mark . . . and not just as an empty hollow in your jaw. Ivor was right. You would remember.

The phone rang again, making her jump. She picked it up:

'Hello?'

'Amina? That Chi Sandwith guy is looking for you again.'

'Oh, sorry, Glenda, could you tell him I'm out?'

'I've told him that twice already, dear. He's been very persistent . . . and I'm afraid I only normally field crank calls for anyone of editor level and above.'

Glenda was the suit-clad godmother in charge of reception and Amina had been warned not to get on her bad side.

'Right, sorry.'

'Just this last time, then. I'll tell him you're in an editorial meeting. We can all dream, eh?'

'Great, thanks.'

8

It seemed Chi Sandwith didn't take 'no' for an answer.

Amina came out of the the *Chronicle* offices with a renewed sense of purpose. She had asked Goldbloom if she could follow up Ivor's story from a mental-health perspective and he had agreed, but with reservations. She had to keep up with her grunt work in the office and she had to use some discretion in her enquiries. He didn't want some fumbling temp traipsing around using the name of the paper to open doors. Having agreed that she would hold up her end of the office work and keep her traipsing to a minimum, Amina was given her chance to see how much more she could make of the story.

A tall guy with wiry fair hair, wearing trendy narrow-framed glasses and a dark grey trench coat intercepted her as she exited the front door of the building.

'Hi, Amina Mir?'

'Yes?'

'I'm Chi Sandwith,' he said brightly, extending his hand. 'We spoke briefly on the phone? I've been trying to reach you for the last couple of days.'

'How did you know my name?'

'I did a search for you on the web. Your school team won a national hockey trophy two years ago. The team photo is proudly displayed on the school's website. Congratulations on your victory, by the way.'

She shook his hand, and looked around discreetly for an escape route.

'Twenty seconds,' he said.

'Sorry?'

'You're looking at me like I'm a double-glazing salesman. I'm not. Give me twenty seconds to explain my angle and then if you decide you never want to see or hear from me again, I'll honour your wishes.'

Amina blinked slowly, biting back a smile, and gave him a noncommittal nod.

'OK.' He grinned, nodding back. 'Ivor McMorris. He's a Sinnostan war veteran, right? Let me guess — he's showing symptoms of post-traumatic stress: hallucinations, nightmares, mood swings, paranoid delusions, yeah? Doesn't like going out? Thinks he's being watched?'

'You could just be—' Amina started to say.

'I could be fishing, yeah,' Chi cut her off. 'But I'm not. He was injured, wasn't he? Does he have unnaturally accurate memories of the period of two or three days when he picked up his injuries? Feels like an unchanging film in his mind?' He could see from Amina's face that he had scored a hit. 'He has, hasn't he? Have there been any periods since his discharge from the army when he feels like he's lost a day or more but can't explain why? No? Has he said anything about a group of people called the Scalps? No? Has he ... has he seen any UFOs? No? Definitely not, huh? OK ... these people who're watching him – does he have trouble seeing their faces? And I don't mean they're hidden or masked, I mean he could literally be looking straight at them and still not see any features on their faces ... except maybe their eyes. Does he get that? He does, doesn't he?'

They were staring at each other now.

'He does,' Chi muttered again, almost to himself.

'That was longer than twenty seconds,' Amina said.

Chi didn't answer. He was gazing at her with a strange smile on his face.

'All right.' She lifted her chin. 'What do you know?'

She was a bit wary of letting Chi take her back to his house. He wasn't a very threatening type – slightly nerdy, a couple of years older than her, maybe twenty or so – but he was a big guy and showed definite signs of being a little unstable. They took a taxi, and he made a point of sitting behind the driver so he could look in the rear-view mirror, as well as casting his eyes out of the window on either side. Each of his hands, legs and head took turns jiggling to an imaginary beat, as if he couldn't bear to sit still. He didn't tell her a lot on the way there, preferring to try and tap her for information instead. Amina didn't give him much. She would wait to see what he had to offer first.

The house was impressive. A sprawling asymmetric building of rough stone and floor-to-ceiling windows, it spoke of comfortable, unassuming wealth. The shallowly sloping roofs extended into a veranda on the south side, over-looking a spacious garden.

Inside, it was a contrasting mix of areas; some dressed in trendy ethnic décor from around the world, others filled with a more homely clutter. Chi explained that he lived in the house with his parents, who were separated. They still shared the place, but arranged never to be there at the same time. His father normally lived in Switzerland and his mother in Florida. Both were computer geeks who'd made their money in the dot-com boom of the 1990s. Neither of them left much of a mark on the house and he couldn't fill it all by himself.

'So, Chi Sandwith, huh?' Amina commented as they strolled through the hallway and kitchen and into a wing of the house where the clutter had long dominated. 'You get many cracks about cheese sand—'

'Never. Never heard that one before,' Chi interrupted her. 'What can I say? My folks had more spiritualism than sense. Suppose they thought that calling me "life energy" was pretty cool.'

'OK. Weeeellll . . . let's see what you've got.'

Judging by the shelves of disks, the plans chest and a full wall of filing cabinets, he had a lot – but Amina wasn't sure how much of it was actually going to be relevant . . . or even real. Her heart sank when she saw the poster that hung on one wall. It was a photo of a blurred image of what was presumably a flying saucer against dusky clouds. Why was it that UFOs never showed up when there was a competent photographer around armed with a long-lens and tripod? Across the bottom of the poster were the words: WATCH THE SKIES.

There were no windows in this room. A

powerful PC with a stack of servers, peripheral hardware and three monitors occupied one desk, and another was taken up with tools and half-built electrical devices she couldn't identify. A ginger cat with white belly and paws wandered in after them and jumped up on the computer desk, watching Chi as he moved about the room. He had taken a gadget about the size of a television remote from his pocket and was walking methodically back and forth across the room, waving it around.

'Counter-surveillance,' he muttered. 'Checking for radio signals. Can't be too careful.'

'No. I suppose not.'

Amina continued to look around. The place was dusty and cluttered, but not untidy. It looked like Chi was particular about his organization. Everything was labelled with a series of letters and numbers that suggested a reference system of some kind. One wall was taken up with photographs and newspaper and magazine clippings, as well as print-outs from websites. Most of the pictures were of soldiers in Asia, the Middle East or North Africa. There were also some drawings: figures with smudged or blurred faces.

'OK, we're fine,' Chi declared with a satisfied grunt. 'Let's get down to business.'

They settled down on comfortable leather swivel chairs in front of the computer screens so that Chi could click through various windows while he talked.

'Ivor McMorris is not alone. I have interview material from more than twenty Sinnostan veterans who suffer from similar symptoms. Each of them says they know others like them – the tally could run into the hundreds, maybe even thousands. I got some of this information from the *National News* – I do the odd article for them – but most of this I've picked up myself from interviews, veteran support sites, as well as television reports and articles like yours. These things lie around the edges of the big stories but I've spent the last couple of years distilling them . . . building them into a bigger picture.

'There are some common threads that run through each of these people's stories: the two or three days of memories that seem unreal – or *too* real; the certainty that they are missing some part of that time; hallucinations or nightmares of being wheeled along a corridor while bound onto a hospital trolley, of being paralysed while dark figures operate on them; some are convinced that they're being watched and just a few cases have experienced what your guy McMorris has talked about: seeing people with blurred faces. Blurred faces with eyes. I think those cases may be the ones who really *are* under surveillance.'

As he spoke, he clicked through photos of the people he had spoken to, or the reports he had drawn his information from.

'It's taken me a long time to separate out all of the relevant stuff, I can tell you. War generates all kinds of paranoid conspiracy theories. There are a lot of nuts out there.'

'I can imagine,' Amina said. 'So what's your theory?'

'I'm only getting started,' Chi replied, motioning with his hands to urge patience. 'One guy I spoke to has some of the symptoms, but he wasn't a soldier. His name's Stefan Gierek and he was a truck driver in Sinnostan, a civilian contractor. And he's different from the others. He was with a platoon of Royal Marines just outside Kring-Jintot when it was attacked. Like so many of the other engagements in this little war, it was out in the middle of nowhere. I've read the reports on it; all of the surviving marines tell the story exactly the same way: they were driving in a convoy through a severe storm when they came under fire in a narrow gorge not far from the village. They returned fire and called for air support but couldn't get through on the radios. They eventually got out of the valley and made a fighting withdrawal to the village where they were based.

'But Gierek swears there was no attack. He was

bringing up the rear of the convoy and he was late. He says that when he pulled up, he saw the vehicles stopped in the gorge – the front APC had run off the road. Everyone was slumped in their seats or on the ground around the vehicles. He thought they were all dead until he checked a couple of them and discovered they were asleep. Gierek is a complete survival nut; he had better gear than half the soldiers there. He kept a detailed journal of his experiences in Sinnostan and one of the pieces of kit he carried was a webcam concealed in the rim of his helmet. His memories of the incident are much the same as the soldiers', if a little more conflicted. But this is what his camera saw next.'

Chi clicked on a file and a movie-player window appeared. The camera was looking from Gierek's point of view as he climbed out of the cab of his sand-coloured truck. The picture was low resolution and moved jerkily, the view changing constantly as he looked around him. His movements were confused. There was sound: Gierek swearing to himself, breathing heavily, dust and small stones blowing against the truck and the huffing of a strong wind across the microphone. It was hard to see anything in the low light of the storm, but it was clear that there were bodies lying around the vehicles ahead. One other military-style, four-wheel-drive truck was visible, with its distinct chunky wheels and high chassis, and ahead of it, the more angular shapes of two armoured personnel carriers with roof-mounted heavy machine-guns. The rest of the gorge was hidden in the blustery clouds of dust.

'Look like a raging fire-fight to you?' Chi asked quietly.

Gierek hurried forward, the camera bouncing with his movement. He came upon the body of a soldier in full combat kit, semi-automatic rifle still held in limp hands. Gierek's hand reached down and checked for breathing and pulse. He stood up and ran on, checking others. Two, then three more were found to be unconscious.

Amina was riveted by the film. Had Ivor gone through something like this? It was hard to picture him out there: a recognizable face, a real human in this surreal scene. She was struck by memories of her own, of something she'd seen years ago.

Gierek's movements were becoming erratic, panicky. He suddenly reacted to something, swinging round to look behind him. There was a bright light and then something knocked him to the ground. The light scorched the scene white and then the film ended.

Amina found she was leaning forward towards the screen. She sat back and crossed her arms.

'OK, I'm intrigued,' she admitted. 'So what was going on?'

'I don't really know,' Chi replied. He looked at her warily for a moment, and then shrugged. 'My contacts and I think we're looking at an honest-to-God alien abduction.'

Amina tilted her head, but otherwise her expression remained unchanged.

'You think that's stupid, I can tell,' he said to her.

Yes, she thought to herself. I think you'd really have to be looking for an alien abduction to find one on that film. You'd have to be a full-on UFO conspiracy nut to believe something like that.

Her phone rang, and she took it from her bag, thankful for the interruption. It was Dani.

'Sorry, I just have to get this,' Amina said.

This was a chance to get out of here – to say she had to meet her friend, before the conversation became even more absurd. But still, she couldn't help wondering about that film . . . The phone kept ringing.

She gazed at the screen for a moment and then answered the phone.

'Hiya! Listen, can I call you back? In a meeting. Yeah, OK. Bye!'

Putting the phone back in her bag, she

regarded the screen for a couple of seconds and then looked at Chi.

'OK, look . . . I don't think your theory's stupid,' she said carefully. 'I just think it's a big conclusion to jump to based on this film. I mean . . . there are a lot of other, much more down-to-earth explanations.'

'Like what? Did you see the way an entire platoon of hardcore Royal Marines were lying around like they just collapsed into a deep sleep?'

'Yes,' Amina responded. 'And it's absolutely weird. But isn't it more likely that they were just gassed or something? You know, like the terrorists in the siege of that theatre in Moscow?'

In 2002, a group of forty-two Chechen terrorists had taken eight hundred and fifty people hostage in a theatre in Moscow. Russian special forces had pumped an aerosol anaesthetic into the building to knock out the occupants before launching an assault. Most of the terrorists had realized what was happening and put on respirators, but more than a hundred and twenty hostages had been killed by the 'knockout' gas. Most of them were thought to have choked on their own tongues as they slumped unconscious in the theatre seats. The thought that you could die so easily had terrified Amina for days. She had sat up with her parents, watching the reports of the aftermath of the siege with morbid fascination.

Your body would always correct its own position when you were asleep, but if like these people you were comatose and sitting with your head hanging back, the limp muscle of your tongue could flop back over your windpipe and stop you breathing. Contrary to popular myth, you could not 'swallow' your tongue – it was attached to the bottom of your mouth, after all – but it could still block your breathing and kill you. Amina remembered one Russian doctor saying that most of these people could have been saved if somebody had just tipped their heads forward. It was funny how the little details stuck in your mind.

She imagined herself in the theatre, walking along between the rows of seats, thoughtfully tipping people's heads forward or lying them on their sides in the recovery position, ready for the paramedics.

'The Russian military were really secretive about the gas they used,' she pointed out. 'They wouldn't even tell the doctors treating the hostages.'

'You can't release gas in the middle of a storm,' Chi argued. 'It would all just . . . y'know . . . blow away. And anyway, most were in their vehicles.'

'Maybe the gas was *released* in the vehicles,' Amina suggested. 'That would be a good way to do it, wouldn't it? And . . . and . . .' She threw her hands up in exasperation. 'Look, why would anyone assume this had been done by aliens? What have aliens got to do with anything? Why can't this just have been done by *people*? Why does it have to be mysterious spaceships covered in flashing lights?'

'They're not covered in flashing lights,' he said sulkily. 'Those are always the hoaxes. If someone wanted to observe mankind in secret, do you really think they'd stick great big lights all over their vehicle? No. Think stealth bomber and you're closer to the truth. The lights are some kind of *weapon*.'

Chi was looking severely disgruntled now. Amina pulled herself up; she had to be careful not to get him on the defensive. This could definitely tie in with Ivor's story. Before showing Gierek's film, he had referred to 'the surviving marines'. She wondered what the others had died of.

'I knew this was a mistake,' he muttered. 'There's too much you don't know, and I haven't got time to make a believer out of you just now. This is too enormous to get your head around in one go.'

'Why don't you show me what else you've got?' she pressed him. 'I could bring a fresh perspective to it; you've got some compelling stuff here, I just think you need to take a more grounded view of all this.'

'My view's fine,' Chi retorted. 'It's yours that's

been clouded by the conventions of a blinkered society. There are agencies at work here that never show their faces in the light of day. This whole Sinnostan thing is only part of a bigger picture and you don't get it yet . . .'

His voice drifted off and his shoulders slumped. Amina saw doubt cross his face for the first time.

'I do sound like a crackpot now, don't I?' He chuckled sadly. 'Jesus, when did that happen?'

He raised his head and gave her a rueful grin.

'Why don't I stick the kettle on?'

'That's a brilliant idea,' Amina replied.

33

Ivor's phone rang while he was peering out of the window with his binoculars. It was Ben.

'Howdy there, bud, what's new?'

'Not a lot,' Ivor replied warily. He had not forgotten Ben's last visit. 'How about you?'

'Yeah . . . fine, fine,' Ben responded, forgetting his own question. He was speaking quickly, as if he had something he had to say, but he couldn't seem to get the words out. 'Eh, so listen . . . uh . . . how y'all fixed today? You busy?'

Ivor still had the binoculars pressed against his eyes. There was a window across the street that always had its curtains closed, leaving a gap just wide enough for a camera lens. Or maybe the telescopic sight of a rifle.

'No, I've nothing urgent on,' he said. 'In fact,

I'm definitely starting to think I've too much time on my hands.'

'Great. You wanna meet up? I got somethin' to tell ya and I'd rather not do it over the phone. It's about what I told you the other day. Y'know . . . about the suppressed anger an' all?'

'Yeah?'

'Yeah,' Ben went on, and there was a definite shake in his voice now. 'You know how you asked me if anybody had sent me? Well, truth is, partner . . . somebody did. I'm sorry, man, they really had me over a barrel and now . . . well, I just got some bad news and I don't give a damn about all this other crap any more. I got stuff to tell ya, but I don't want to do it over the phone. Can you meet me at that place we used to go to? You know the one? And . . . and I need some money, man. I wouldn't ask, only . . .'

'No problem,' Ivor said. 'What time and how much?'

The place they used to go to was a little Lebanese café in the East End. The front opened out onto the street. Ivor chose a table out on the pavement, next to the blackboard advertising the specials. He ordered a small cup of the viscous coffee, blowing on the brown frothy top as he killed time waiting for Ben to arrive.

He had played with the idea of asking Amina to join them. If Ben had something important to say about what they both remembered – or didn't remember – it might be worth having someone objective on hand. But it might have put Ben off being completely honest . . . and besides, even in his scarred state, he was still a charmer. Ivor's self-esteem had dropped like a lead balloon after he'd lost his eye, and the thought of having to compete with Ben for her attention made him uncomfortable.

He found himself thinking about her all the time. She had the same straight black hair that he had loved in the women in Asia, the same warm colour to her skin. He wondered if his eye bothered her. It seemed to disturb most women. He reminded himself that she was only interested in his story – there might have only been a few years difference where their ages were concerned, but their lives were oceans apart. There was no point getting his hopes up on that front.

When half an hour had passed and Ivor had reached the muddy sediment at the bottom of the cup, he ordered some mezze, picking without an appetite at the selection of olives and cheeses. He waited another hour and a half, regularly checking his mobile in case he had somehow missed a call. It took a full bottle of mineral water to rinse the taste of a second coffee from his mouth. Still Ben did not show. Ivor's right eye began to ache.

He did not want to leave. There had been a fatalistic note in Ben's voice, one he recognized from other men he had known in the veterans' hospital. It was the tone of voice a man had when he had given up on life. Ivor knew there was no other meeting place Ben could have meant. It was in a busy side street, always bustling with people, and Ivor suspected his friend had picked it because it was safe and anonymous. There was little question why he wouldn't talk on the phone; neither of them trusted phones or email any more. If Ben really needed the ten thousand pounds in cash Ivor had in his bag, something was badly wrong – and it was connected with the conversation they'd had the day before. And what did he mean: 'I just got some bad news and I don't give a damn about all this other crap any more'?

So Ivor rubbed his aching eye and continued to wait for two more hours, becoming increasingly anxious about his friend as the time passed. Five o'clock came and the café was closing. Ivor reluctantly surrendered his seat and stood up to put on his jacket. As he did, he noticed that somebody had written something on the ground behind him, using the yellow chalk from the specials board. He gazed down at the words, a queasy feeling rising in his stomach. They read:

'You still have one eye left.'

10

In an isolated, windowless room in a nondescript government building close to Whitehall, three people sat down at a worn, but solid, mahogany table. The laminated wood-panelled walls around them held modern art prints, with the artists' names emblazoned across the bottom like designer logos. A flip chart stood ignored in one corner and on the wall at the same end, a slightly shabby roll-up screen hung, ready for a projector to light up its life. This was a small conference room on a corridor of small conference rooms and as such attracted no unwelcome attention.

Each person had a laptop, plugged into a hub in the middle of the table. The hub was not connected to the network in the building and the three participants in the meeting deliberately avoided using any kind of wireless technology. They would take their laptops with them when they left. No minutes were kept at their meetings.

The room was neutral territory; none of them worked in the building. After their conference, it would be used by another group for a seminar in the use of some kind of database software. But the coming together of these two men and one woman was quite different in nature. ▮▮▮▮ opened the meeting, reading through the most recent list of names. With his upright bearing, his grey hair trimmed close to his scalp and the way he spoke in confident, clipped tones, the shorter of the two men obviously had a military background – although he was not wearing a uniform today.

The other two listened with disinterest. Hearing the names was a formality they all went through in an effort to 'keep a perspective'. ▮▮▮▮▮▮-▮▮▮▮, the taller man, had the look of a bureaucrat or politician, his stocky body turning slowly to fat, his dark hair parted just so, his hands soft, pale and chubby. Sleepy, heavy-lidded eyes hid a keen intellect and a deep-rooted cynicism. His background was intelligence – both gathering it and countering it.

The woman, ▮▮▮▮▮▮▮▮, used the time to review her sheets of figures. This was unnecessary as she had compiled them herself and had a photographic memory, but the order of the information in its neat columns gave her pleasure. Dressed in a bulky woollen sweater, her mousy brown, curly hair cut short in a practical asexual style, she looked every bit the fuddy–duddy academic. Among her many scientific qualifications she could boast doctorates in medicine – specializing in neurology – and psychology. The programme she designed and supervised formed the core of this particular group's activities.

'That's that,' ■■■■ finished at last. 'Has the room been swept?'

'Of course,' ■■■■■■-■■■■ replied in a bass croak of a voice.

'Who wants to start then? ■■■■■■■■■, you have the status reports?'

'Yes,' the woman replied, her tone slightly tetchy. This was no indication of her mood; it was simply the way she spoke. 'I don't see any need to go over them. Here they are.'

The documents appeared on the men's laptops. They flicked through them quickly, but left the study of the details until later. ■■■■■■■■■'s reports were exhaustive and packed with data. The men would need their own experts to help them make sense of all the information.

'Let's talk about threats then,' ■■■■■■-■■■■ suggested. 'Top of my list is this lottery winner. I'm sure you all saw the article?'

The others nodded.

'Not exactly a revelation,' ■■■■ commented. 'There was nothing in it to excite any interest.'

'It's the principle of the matter,' ■■■■■■–■■■■ replied. 'He's taken a first step towards making waves. And if he's unhappy with the article, as our surveillance suggests, then he could take more drastic measures. He's had contact with the journalist' – he checked his notes – 'Amina Mir, since the article was published – twice that we know of. And then this photo was taken yesterday.'

The others looked at the picture he had sent to their desktops. It was the young journalist, standing on the street talking to a tall youth about her age. They all recognized him.

'Sandwith,' ■■■■ breathed. 'He just keeps popping up, doesn't he?'

'This could work in our favour,' ■■■■■■■■■ spoke up. 'If Sandwith takes up McMorris's story, it will get an airing, but it will fall automatically into the realm of the conspiracy theorists and UFO freaks and, as such, will lose all serious credibility.'

'I don't like it,' ■■■■ said, shaking his head. 'And I especially don't like Sandwith. He's a crackpot, but he's not *enough* of a crackpot. If he keeps making connections, sooner or later he's going to make one that threatens to expose us. I'm sure he's connected to all these hackers who've been probing the military databases recently. They've only been pulling out chaff so far, but . . . I think we should do something about him.'

'There've been too many direct actions lately,' ██████-████ responded. 'We risk creating patterns that people can spot. Sandwith is a useful distraction as he is. If something happened to him, it would focus the attention of all of his cronies on his avenues of investigation – including McMorris's story. Better that we leave them guessing.'

'And McMorris?'

'He's shown himself to be a cautious one, and he's had a warning.' ██████-████ shrugged. 'I say we leave him be, but keep the surveillance on him and the reporter in case one of them does something rash.'

The others nodded their agreement.

'What are you doing about Shang?' █████████ asked. 'He's been missing for nearly a week now. I thought your people were supposed to be efficient.'

'We have several leads,' ██████-████ retorted frostily. 'The man's a former operative and it seems he hasn't forgotten his tradecraft. We'll find him.'

'Before the shipment arrives in Sinnostan?' █████████ persisted. 'We don't know where he is. We don't know if he's going to act against us. We don't know if he's acting alone or with others. Your people haven't found anything useful at all, have they?'

██████-████ bit back an angry reply. He knew she cared nothing for his irritation. For her, emotions were phenomena to be observed and studied and nothing more. He and ████ exchanged looks. They had grown used to her behaviour, but it still galled them at times. There could be nothing more aggravating on this earth than a genius with no empathy and no social skills; someone whose own work was exemplary and who had no compunction in pointing out the flaws in everybody else's. She had no idea – and little inter-est in – how much effort it took to ensure her work remained the stuff of science-fiction mythology.

'We'll find him,' he said again.

'I hope you do,' she told him.

'All right,' ████ cut into the argument with his characteristically brusque manner. 'What's next?'

'I'm unhappy with the level of rejections,' █████████ said. 'The more subjects I have to work with, the more I can narrow down the imperfections in the process.'

'We don't have a limitless supply,' ████ informed her sternly. 'Our sole purpose in all this is to protect the nation – not to provide you with all the human test subjects your heart desires. Besides, as ■■■■■■-■■■■ pointed out, we want to avoid patterns that are too easy to spot – and an escalation in hostilities would be more than the public would stand at the moment. This conflict is becoming unpopular enough as it is. You'll just have to improve your success rate.'

'I thought the purpose of my work was to eliminate hostilities altogether,' the doctor replied tartly.

'They said the same thing about the atomic bomb,' ■■■■■■-■■■■ muttered drily.

27

Tariq normally remembered to knock before walking into his dad's study, but his mind was still buzzing on finishing *Tech-Shot Extreme*. He stopped in his tracks when he found his father on a prayer mat, performing *salat*. Tariq felt awkward for a moment, as if he had walked in to find his dad in his underwear.

Martin lifted his head up from the *sajjada*, his characteristically benign expression somewhat dulled, as if he were waking gently from a sleep.

'What's up?' he asked. 'From the look on your face, you'd think I had two heads or something.'

'No . . . it's just . . . it's nothing,' Tariq stuttered. 'I just didn't know you, eh . . . you still prayed, that's all.'

'Try looking away from the screen from time to time,' Martin replied, then added in a more sheepish tone as he glanced at the Qur'an lying open on his desk: 'Actually, I haven't done much lately – but I should. And it still helps when times are trying.'

Tariq nodded, but didn't say anything. He knew that times tended to be at their most trying when his parents were having one of their bust-ups. Martin expected Helena to stay at home more, now that she was getting older, but she was having none of it. For all his alpha-male tendencies, Martin always gave in to his wife's stubbornness. She had made it clear that she wouldn't convert to Islam when they married and she had been winning most of the arguments ever since. Tariq thought his dad could be a bit of a wuss sometimes.

He wondered sometimes if his father had lost his edge after giving up active service and becoming a 'spokesman'. Tariq suspected that Martin would always be a bit embarrassed about it. The mates he had served with – all of whom ran their own units now – certainly took the piss out of him from time to time. But then, Martin earned more money . . . and he was still married, which was more than could be said for any of them.

Anyway, Tariq hadn't noticed any 'domestic' problems recently. That said, the folks kept their disagreements to themselves for the most part.

There were times when Tariq resorted to

prayer too. Not that he'd ever admit to it, but it was hard to give up the habit.

'Listen, could you give me a lift down to Rent-a-Vision?' he asked. '*Tech-Shot Mutant* is out and I just finished *Extreme*. Darren sent me some short-cuts so I can get straight onto the level with the zombie elephants.'

'Cool!' Martin said, doing his best impression of gawky teenage enthusiasm. When it met with Tariq's effortless look of disdain, he tried another tack: 'I'm off down to the range. Why don't you come along? Do some real shooting for a change.'

Tariq had been going to the practice range for over a year now and though firing his father's automatic still hadn't lost its thrill, paper targets just couldn't compete with cutting-edge graphics. He was already a better shot than Amina, even though she had started even younger than he had, what with being Daddy's little pet. Tariq put that down to his on-screen accuracy.

It made him think of *MindFeed*. With the army in school, he wondered how long it would be before the kids were training with real weapons. The government was always going on about how people had to be ready to defend themselves against the terrorist threat.

'Well?' his dad prompted him. 'How about it?'

'Do they have zombie elephants?' he asked.

'They *swore* to me they were getting them in next week. Big rotting corpses with mad eyes and sticky-outy ribs and ears like . . . like sheets of rancid meat hanging off them. But they can't guarantee they'll be halal.'

'Gross. Maybe next week, then,' Tariq responded. 'So . . . ? Can I get that lift or what?'

His father tried not to look disappointed.

'It's a fifteen-minute walk and it's a lovely evening. You could do with the exercise . . . not to mention a bit of fresh air. When was the last time you went for a run, or even a walk for that matter?'

'Right,' Tariq said, trying hard not to grit his teeth. 'How about you let *me* decide how I'm going to misspend my youth? That way, you can still give me a lift down to the shop where I can rent another violent PlayStation game, *and* have the satisfaction of telling me you told me so ten years from now.'

'How about you do without lifts to Rent-a-Vision for the rest of your misspent youth?'

Tariq went to slam the door, but stopped. He tried to quell the unreasonable anger rising inside him. His lips were pressed tightly together, his hand gripping the door handle like a claw. It was stupid. He and his father did this a lot now, and he was disappointed at how easily they had slipped into the whole teenager-versus-parent thing. He liked his father. In fact, if he were pressed, he would have to admit that he thought his dad was cool. His friends had always thought so. So how did they always ended up sniping at each other like this?

'I'm sorry, Dad.'

'Me too,' Martin said, nodding.

There was a long pause while they each waited for the other to speak next.

'So,' Tariq relented, 'we still on for going to the range?'

His father did not smile, but his expression warmed up.

'Yeah, we can shoot guns and bond like men. Maybe I'll call Geoff and tell him to bring down his L85A1 so we can lay down some heavier fire. Could even go out into the countryside, smoke some cigars and shoot us some dairy cows.'

'Cool.'

Chi followed Amina up the stairs and found Ivor McMorris waiting with his door open. There was a look of resolute bitterness on his face.

Amina made the introductions as they were ushered inside.

'We're sorry about your friend,' she said softly. 'Had he . . . had he been very unhappy?'

Ivor said nothing for a moment, and then

shook his head as if trying to clear the thoughts from his mind.

'It wasn't suicide,' he said firmly.

Ben Considine was dead. His body had been found on Beckford Strand the day before, at the mouth of the River Sliney. There was an old iron footbridge that crossed the river further upstream, at its narrowest point, where the currents were strongest. It was known as Suicide Bridge, and Beckford Strand – where the river's victims often washed up – as Suicide Beach. There were few places in the country more popular with those who had given up hope.

Ben's death had warranted a small article in the *Chronicle*, but only because he had friends in the press. Ivor had asked Amina to come over as soon as he'd seen it; she thought it was as good a time as any for him to meet Chi.

'Ben wasn't ready to kill himself,' Ivor insisted. 'It may have been on his mind – he was dealing with a lot of bad stuff – but I'm sure he had business to see to first.' He took a shuddering breath. 'I heard it in his voice, you know . . . I thought I'd get to talk to him . . .'

His voice cracked and he fell silent, looking faintly embarrassed by this hint of grief. Amina put her hand on his, suppressing the urge to offer words of comfort. Sometimes it was better to just be there, without making your presence felt; to let a person find their own time to talk. Ivor savoured the contact, not wanting to move his hand away from hers. Was there something more than pity there? Again, he reminded himself: she was in it for the story. Don't let yourself think you have a chance here. It's just sympathy, nothing more.

It was still a moment worth holding onto . . . But Chi had too much to say.

'He's not the first,' he blurted out, much to Amina's annoyance. 'Your friend – he's just the latest in a string of suspicious deaths.'

'Maybe we should give it a minute—' Amina started to say, but Ivor interrupted her:

'No, it's OK. Let him talk. I'll just sit here brooding otherwise. I have too much time to think as it is.'

Chi nodded and collected himself a bit, belatedly conscious of the solemn mood.

'I've been tracking down Sinnostan veterans over the last two years,' he told them, opening his laptop case and booting up the computer. 'Particularly ones who've been vocal against the war, or who've been reported to be suffering post-traumatic stress.'

'How would you find that out?' Ivor asked. 'We don't go round wearing labels.'

'Eh . . . actually you do – in a manner of

speaking.' Chi gave a hesitant chuckle. 'It's in your medical records.'

'Jesus, you hack into our medical records?' Ivor exclaimed. 'That's as personal as it gets, man. How the hell do you—'

'No, no.' Chi raised his hands in defence. 'I have *some* principles, you know. But there are friends of mine who don't. *They* hack into medical databases and we . . . well, we trade information. Ever since the government set up the National Database – combining our medical, tax, criminal records and all that – it's a piece of cake. You hack into a local council office and you've got access to information, like, anywhere in the country if you can pinch a few passwords. Plant a program on their system that records keystrokes and feeds them back to you and you're in. And given the monkeys they've got running tech support for these places, it's easy to . . .'

He noticed that they were staring at him.

'Right. Anyway. What I'm getting at is that your whole life is there for anybody who really wants to see it, and that includes your medical records. So I got the names of all the veterans who'd come out bitter, twisted and raising a racket and you know what I found?'

Chi leaned in closer to them, but then stopped, his mouth still hanging open. To think he'd almost forgotten – he had taken no precautions. Standing up, he took his bugfinder from his pocket and started combing the room for signals. He wasn't happy with what he found. Hoping he hadn't already said too much, he motioned to the others and opened the front door, watching the readout on the bugfinder. He ushered them up two flights of stairs to the landing in the floor above and then gathered them close, speaking in a hushed voice:

'Ivor, your place is crawling with surveillance. I counted, like, six devices at least. Chances are I didn't even find them all. You need to take measures, man. I'll come back with some gear tomorrow.'

Amina maintained a sceptical expression, but Ivor looked neither surprised nor frightened.

'Look, get on with it,' Amina urged Chi impatiently. 'Tell him about the soldiers.'

'Yeah, well I started seeing some interesting patterns,' Chi said, still whispering. 'As in, scary-coincidence type stuff. Guys would come home from Sinnostan with PTS symptoms and start mouthing off, demanding investigations into what had happened to them . . . and then they'd stop. Like, really clam up. One minute they're, like, fanatical rebels, the next there's not a peep out of them. Others . . . well, others just plain *died*. Nothing overly suspicious: a house fire here, a road traffic accident there, men having heart attacks despite being in peak physical fitness, a few drug overdoses.

'And at least four of them,' he continued, watching Ivor's face, 'ended up on Suicide Beach.'

He paused for effect, letting this dramatic information sink in.

'OK,' Ivor said cautiously. 'But this could be nothing. This is how conspiracies get started: you pull out random bits of information, dump the ordinary, obvious explanations and start making connections that aren't there. How do you know these weren't all just normal deaths?'

Amina drew a breath to say something but didn't get it out in time.

'UFOs,' Chi replied grimly. 'A large proportion of these men reported seeing a UFO not long before their deaths.'

'Riiiight.' Ivor leaned back, glancing at Amina.

'OK, OK.' Chi held his hands up again. 'Let's overlook my geeky obsession with the paranormal for the moment, all right? You reckon something's been done to you, but you don't know what. I'm telling you there's others out there suffering from the same symptoms. You want to know more, yeah? Well so do I.'

Ivor regarded him for a minute, a guarded expression on his face. Then he relaxed and nodded.

Chi gave them both a brief smile, but he could feel his heart pounding in his chest. Finally, he had some allies who didn't fall into the typical abduction-nut category. He couldn't tell them everything yet – not until he had their trust and he was sure they were committed. His hands were in his pockets. The fingers of his right hand fidgeted, playing with a metal disc about five centimetres across. He itched to show it to them, desperate to test it on Ivor, but it was too soon. There would be time yet.

'I still don't understand what it's all for,' Amina said softly. 'If half of what we're talking about is true, there's a massive cover-up going on. But *what* are they covering up?'

'I have some theories,' Chi said. 'I think these false memories are part of a programming process. Whoever's doing this has to make these soldiers disappear for three or four days. But what's the point of making them disappear? I think it's so they can be programmed as sleeper agents – y'know? Like in *The Manchurian Candidate*?' He looked furtively at Ivor. 'Each one is being given a task and they'll be activated by a phone call or something like that. The false memories account for that missing time.'

'That still sounds far-fetched to me,' Amina said, shaking her head. 'I mean, what are these guys being programmed to do? Are they spies or . . . or assassins or what? And if so, why not just pay professionals to do the job instead of trying to rely on some dodgy mind-control process? How could the brainwashers be sure these pawns of theirs would do what they're supposed to do? And besides, I just can't see the military allowing hundreds of their soldiers to be treated like this. I know you think everyone in the establishment is a cold-hearted manipulator, Chi, but it's just not like that. Most senior officers are decent, honourable men.'

Watching the incredulous expression cross her pretty features, Chi was relieved he had not further expounded his theory on experimentation by alien abductors. Now that he had her respect, he was keen not to lose it. He had already spent too much time in the company of pale-skinned nerds raging about shadowy government agencies responsible for everything from the Martin Luther King assassination to the Bermuda Triangle. But even so, he was concerned that the fact that her father was an officer in the military gave her an unbalanced view of their activities.

'I think it's got to be something more mundane,' she went on. 'Have you noticed how the news reports on the war are always going on about how few innocent civilians are being killed? There are plenty of people who say the figures aren't accurate, but nobody can get in there to do a proper survey, 'cos it's too dangerous.

'Every war has its atrocities, but there hasn't been any really big story about Western troops committing something that could be considered a war crime. There haven't been any photos of torture or . . . or leaked memos on human rights violations or any of that. I think these guys are having their memories erased because they're *witnesses* . . . or even the perpetrators – no offence, Ivor.'

'None taken.'

He was sitting there, gazing at her. She stared back pointedly and he looked away. Did he just blush? With his complexion, it was hard to tell.

'I don't think the military would use their troops like guinea pigs for some kind of dangerous experiment,' she added. 'But I wouldn't put it past them to try and cover up war crimes. They've done it enough times before and they're getting better at it. There are always a few bad seeds that get out of control and do something really shocking. I think this mindwipe thing is just a really sophisticated form of damage control.'

'All right,' Chi said grudgingly, looking over at Ivor. 'So from your point of view, there are two questions we need to be asking: What might you have seen or done to make them mess with your memory? Or: What might you be programmed to do and when are you supposed to do it?'

They both waited for Ivor's opinion. He said nothing, staring down the stairs as if lost in thought.

'I don't know about any of that,' he said at last. 'I can't deal with all this . . . this . . .' He waved his hands around in a frustrated manner. 'All this about war and conspiracies and all that. It's too big, too distant to get my head around. I just want to know *what* they did to me and *why*. And I want to find out who killed Ben. That's it.'

He told them about how he had waited for Ben at the café, and about the threat written in chalk on the pavement behind his chair. Amina went pale, but Chi's breath quickened; he started pacing back and forth.

'This is proof,' he said excitedly, his voice louder but still trying to sound quiet. 'They've slipped up. If they're worried enough to be making threats, you *must* have rattled them. This is great!'

'I'm glad you think so,' Ivor said drily. 'Personally, I want to keep the one eye I have left. I'd like to see how excited you'd be if you found out an assassin was sitting behind you at lunch.'

Chi was loath to admit he found this prospect genuinely thrilling. In his line of work, death threats were considered the highest accolade; an acknowledgement from your enemy that you were too close for their comfort. He knew only two other people first-hand who had received bona fide death threats, and they were at the top of their game. People in this category were proud to wear the label 'Targeted'.

'Still, you've got to admit, it's encouraging,' Chi said, shrugging. 'They wouldn't be threatening you if you were just a delusional lunatic.'

'Unless the writing was a hallucination,' Amina put in.

'Thanks for that vote of confidence,' Ivor sniffed. 'OK, so what do we do next?'

'We concentrate on your story,' Amina told him. 'We dig up as much information as possible and see if there's anything about the bombing that doesn't make sense. So far, all the reports I've found have sounded too alike – almost as if they're all getting their information from the same source.'

'I have a friend who could hack God's data-base,' Chi added. 'I'll see what he can come up with.'

'Oh, good,' Ivor said as they headed back towards the stairs. 'I'm sure God will know what's going on. Hey . . . Chi Sandwith. I suppose you must get a lot of jokes about cheese sandwi—'

'No. Never. You're the first person to ever say that – really.'

19

Amina stared up at the three monkeys sitting on their plastic plinth on the shelf above Goldbloom's desk. The ornament was a cheap tacky souvenir; the type you'd pick up in a tourist area while you were buying your key ring, fridge magnet and novelty T-shirt. If it was British, it would have a Union Jack stuck on it somewhere, but this one was Japanese. She wondered if this piece of kitsch was actually made in Japan – as so many British souvenirs once were. More likely Vietnam or somewhere like that. The monkeys on the plinth had names: Mizaru covered his eyes, Kikazaru covered his ears and Iwazaru covered his mouth. See no evil, hear no evil and speak no evil.

Her mother had a framed picture of the three monkeys on the wall of her study. She said it was a reminder. They were supposed to symbolize the idea that if you refused to acknowledge evil, then you would not commit any. In journalism, her mother said, it kind of worked the other way.

'No, we can't publish details from medical records,' Goldbloom said, waking her from her reverie. 'As well you should know. I don't think any veteran would thank you for making his haemorrhoids, halitosis and STDs public. And people are particularly sensitive about mental-health problems. You know you can be sued for far more money if you sully someone's reputation than if you cut their arm off? Go figure. Anyway, where do you think you're going to get these files from?'

'I know someone who knows someone,' Amina informed him.

He smirked at her.

'Well, well. Aren't we connected? I'd be careful, love. There's no harm in knowing people who are willing to bend the rules on your behalf, but you've got to be careful about where it can land you. If you break any laws, this paper will not back you up, y'understand? Don't go doing anything stupid – and I say that in the full knowledge that youth is all about doing stupid things you'll tell stories about in your old age, but I'm serious. Don't screw around with this.

'If somebody volunteers *their own* medical files, that's fine, but it's illegal to obtain them any other way. If you're going to succeed in making a credible mental-health story out of this, you need interviews from the "victims" and some expert testimony. See if you can get a shrink to give you some quotes on post-traumatic stress – all the better if he's done work for the military.'

'OK, Joel. Thanks.' She turned to leave.

'Amina?'

'Yes?' She turned back.

'This could potentially be a real story,' he said, eyeing her as he tapped the desk with his pen. 'Tread lightly, love, all right? Don't go stepping on any toes and don't do anything to make me regret letting you take this on.'

'I'll be on my best behaviour,' she said, giving him a reassuring smile.

'And don't think you can melt me with any of your mother's smiles; I've seen 'em all and she does 'em better. Now leave me be.'

Amina scooted out of the office in her exaggerated impression of a lowly office temp. She hadn't told Goldbloom anything about Chi, or their theories about mind-control experiments on abducted soldiers. As long as he thought she was only working on a mental-health story, he might leave her to get on with it. If he suspected it was more serious, he would probably pull it off her and give it to an experienced journalist.

She was determined that that would not happen.

It hadn't escaped her notice that he was giving her a lot of attention. The managing editor did not normally waste time dealing with office temps; there were enough junior editors to do that. Amina had heard plenty of stories about him from her mother and suspected that he had been in love with her years ago. It would be understandable if he felt a bit paternal about her daughter. And Amina was happy to accept any help he could give her.

She was passing his secretary's desk when she heard Cathy give a startled gasp. Amina turned back and saw the middle-aged woman staring in shock at an open envelope. Her hands were shaking. It took another moment for Amina to notice the small pile of coarse brown granules sitting on the pine-coloured plastic desktop. Cathy lifted her head, confused fear in her eyes.

'I just opened the letter,' she said.

Amina stared for a second and then pulled Cathy from her chair. The woman wrenched her back and grabbed her handbag. Amina pulled at her again in frustration. They had to get out of there . . . fast.

'Hold your breath!' she cried, and then to the people in the press room, 'Somebody call the police! There's a letter here with brown powder in it! Call the police!'

At first, everybody's reaction was to crowd in and see what all the fuss was about. But then someone said the word 'anthrax' and everything changed. Within seconds, the fire alarm was ringing and people were running for the stairs and elevators. Amina held Cathy's hand as they hurried down the stairs. Cathy was crying, her breaths coming in short gasps.

'I'm sure it's just a scare, Cathy!' Amina said to her as they turned to take the next flight down, both of them stumbling in their high heels. 'It'll be fine. It's just someone looking for headlines.'

Cathy was wheezing badly now. The alarm bells created a sense of barely controlled panic in the scuttling evacuees. Amina and Cathy reached the ground floor and joined the crowd making for the door. Cathy could barely breathe. Amina looked at her in alarm. Could anthrax work that fast? Maybe that weaponized stuff that armies developed in secret fits of madness. Was this for real? Suddenly, Amina wanted to be away from this woman and her tortured breathing. She wanted to be out of this building now. NOW! She felt a tickle in her throat and coughed. For the first time in years, she raised her eyes and uttered an urgent prayer to Allah.

They burst from the building into lashing rain that soaked them in seconds. Amina's thin blue shirt was heavily peppered with dark drops as she looked around for a sheltered place to stand. Cathy was hauling in strained breaths. Amina sat her down on the edge of concrete plant pot in the relative shelter of an abstract rusted iron sculpture in the shape of a ship's bow. Cathy was struggling to open her bag, but then she found the zip, tore it open and dug an inhaler out of one of the pockets. She sucked in a couple of blasts and her breathing started to return to normal.

Amina watched with a mixture of relief and embarrassment. She had been so caught up in her desire to save this woman's life from a would-be terrorist attack, she had almost killed her. All around them, police sirens were howling, cars screeching to a halt. Amina sat down beside Cathy and put her arm around her. Water dripped from the sculpture above them, soaking them still further, but neither felt like moving just yet.

Chi strode down the alleyway that led to Nexus's building. This was a complete breach of protocol. They were supposed to steer clear of each other's bases – better that they work as independent cells with as few connections as possible. But Nexus had been adamant; he had something Chi *had* to see and it had to be done here.

The rain ran down on his shoulders, dripping from his soaked trench coat. His baseball cap offered little protection, but at least it kept the worst of it off his glasses. The galvanized steel door in the grimy brick wall was daubed with graffiti. Chi rapped on it, pulling his collar up to stop the drops running down the back of his neck. He heard two sets of footsteps coming down the stairs inside – sounded like Nex had company – and then the door scraped open.

Nexus was looking as unkempt as usual. Several days of sparse, fluffy brown beard clung to his face and there were bags under his eyes. Chi would have bet that the GREEN DAY T-shirt he was wearing hadn't been changed in a while.

'Man. Hey,' Nexus said dully, his head twitching to one side as he spoke. 'You're early. Eh . . .'

'Can I come in?' Chi asked pointedly, raising his eyes to the sky in a meaningful fashion.

'Sure! Sure!' Nexus opened the door and stood aside, his head still twitching as if he had some kind of nervous condition. Too much time staring at computer screens.

Chi had barely time to register his relief at being out of the rain when a fist slammed into the side of his face. He was thrown against the door-frame and his glasses fell to the floor before another blow to his chest hurled him back out into the rain, landing him hard on his back in the mucky alley-way, knocking the air out of his lungs. He winced, feeling a bolt of pain go through the backs of his ribs. He struggled to get to his feet. The ground was hard, cold and wet beneath him but he was barely able to move. Stefan Gierek's snarling face appeared above him.

'Ah. Gierek,' Chi wheezed. 'Give us a hand up?'

The fist came down like a brick against his face. Chi had never known such stunning pain. Most of what followed was obscured by the headache from hell. In flashes of juddering nerve endings, he felt himself being dragged through the door and up the stairs. His wrists and ankles were bound with duct tape and then he felt a rope go round his ankles too.

'Hey . . .' he mumbled.

The rope went tight and he was hauled feet-first into the air. His headache went from fireworks to high explosives and he wailed like a child.

'My badge,' Gierek said in a grating voice, as Chi's senses began to come back and his eyes opened. 'I want it back, Sandwith, you little pencil-necked fudge-packer. And I'm not going to ask twice.'

'Is there anything else you can tell us, miss?' the detective asked.

Amina sighed and shook her head. She had given her statement about the anthrax letter – the *fake* anthrax letter – three times now. She knew that this was how the police did it, making you repeat yourself to see if your story differed each time. Never trust a single telling of any story. But it didn't make it any less aggravating. The detective, Sykes, who was taking the statement, was one of a team from Counter Terrorism Command. A thin, mousy-haired man with large freckles and a perpetually sardonic expression, he had been questioning her in painstaking detail for over half an hour; more than enough time for her to adequately describe the few seconds she had been standing in front of the opened envelope, before draining the last vestiges of oxygen from Cathy's panicked lungs by rushing her down several flights of stairs.

She wanted to get out of there, to see her friends and talk to them and maybe even have a bit of a cry, and have them hug her and comfort her. She was desperate to get rid of these shuddering remnants of shock and relief that boiled around inside her.

'That's all I know,' she said, in case a shake of her head wouldn't be enough to convince the detective.

His eyes lifted, wrinkling his brow in a way that suggested there was far more she could tell him if she would only try a bit harder, but he pursed his lips and thanked her. All around them, in a room on the ground floor of the *Chronicle* building, people were being interviewed. Cathy was in the seat just over from Amina. She too was being thoroughly grilled.

Sykes stood up, patting down his crumpled grey suit, and shook her hand.

'We're almost done examining the newsroom,' he said to her. 'We'll be taking all of your post away, but you can go back to work in a bit, I'm sorry to tell you. Pity you couldn't have got the whole day off, eh? Nice thing about these emergencies: everybody gets a bit of a holiday. Not us obviously. But normal people like yourself. Thanks again for your time, Miss Mir. We'll be in touch if we need anything more.'

She nodded to him, and was just getting to her feet when he turned back to her.

'Oh! Nearly forgot,' he said, pulling a photograph from his breast pocket. 'Happens sometimes, you know. We're supposed to have these great memories – police officers, I mean – but mine's like a sieve. Expect you've an excellent memory, doing all that journalism training . . .'

Amina regarded him with a quizzical frown, unsure if he was mocking her or not.

'Can you tell me, have you seen this man around at all?' He held up the photo.

It was a picture of a middle-aged man with

oriental features. He was clean-shaven with a small, sharp goatee. Wide, black-framed glasses enlarged inscrutable eyes and his black hair was swept back from a jagged widow's peak.

'I don't think so,' she replied. 'Who is he?'

'Name's Anthony Shang – that's S-H-A-N-G,' Sykes told her, slipping the photo back into his pocket. 'Chinese national. A mercenary scientist with known ties to a number of terrorist organizations. Intelligence sources believe he may have slipped into the country recently. He's a biological weapons expert; this would be just the kind of thing he could pull off.'

'But the letter was a hoax, wasn't it?' Amina pointed out.

'Only one of many,' Sykes replied. 'The *National News* got one too, as well as a number of MPs. It'll all be coming in over the wire as we speak. But we think this may have been a dry run. They want to see how we're going to react.'

'Oh,' Amina said, wondering why he was telling her so much.

Counter Terrorism Command only gave out information when it suited them. If they were talking openly about this Shang character, then he had to be on the terrorist watch list. She made a mental note to check him out. The country was suffering continuous terrorist alerts, seeding a near-constant atmosphere of fear, particularly in the cities. Any threat of attack was always guaranteed to make the headlines but, like most people, she had never made any attempt to put faces to the source of that fear. After today, she would start paying more attention.

First, though, she needed to start going through the paper's archives in search of articles on Sinnostan. She would be meeting Ivor and Chi this evening, and she hadn't yet made any headway on her mental-health enquiries. Amina was desperate to be taken seriously as a journalist and it was vital that the two young men she was working with did not outshine her. She had to show them that she was a force to be reckoned with.

'Amina, can you make me a coffee?' one of the editors asked as he walked past her. 'I'll be in my office. Decaf latte with two sugars, yeah?'

2

Chi felt like his guts were digesting broken glass. Gierek had only hit him three times, but the guy had hands like lump hammers and the blows had a peculiar penetrating quality that Chi was sure had sent shockwaves all the way through to his spine. The rope around his ankles was biting into his flesh and he thought he could feel the joints dislocating under his weight. Ankles were made to be stood on, not hung from. His head throbbed unbearably. His charcoal trench coat hung down over him like the wings of a misshapen bat.

'Ahh . . . ahh,' he gasped. 'I . . . was just coming back to you on that, man . . . Gierek. I didn't even realize I had it until a few days ag—' Another punch to his abdomen stopped him dead. He moaned and coughed painfully.

'You stole my badge. I want it back. NOW, numb-nuts!'

Gierek's mix of Polish and north London accents was strong enough to make him sound like a ham actor playing a Cold War bad guy. He had failed to get into no less than three armies (Polish, US and British) on mental-health grounds, but had nevertheless embraced military living with gusto – right down to his drill-sergeant dialogue.

'Fine,' Chi grunted. 'Happy to oblige. If you could just cut me down—'

'You get down when I say you can, you piss-blooded bottom-feeding crackerjack! WHERE'S MY BADGE?'

Chi would have pointed out that Gierek had originally said he wouldn't ask twice, but it didn't seem like a good idea just then. In Chi's view, the man was overreacting wildly to his theft of the badge in question. Granted, it was the one piece of evidence that Gierek possessed to prove he wasn't going mad, but it wasn't actually any good to him unless he could figure out how it worked. Which was why Chi had taken it – without permission from its owner.

'It's back at my place,' Chi wheezed. 'I'll take you there.'

Gierek cut the rope and Chi dropped to the floor, all his weight coming down on his right shoulder and back. He cried out again but decided against further protest, waiting while the Pole cut the duct tape from his ankles.

Nexus was sitting miserably in a chair nearby. There had been no need for Gierek to tie him up. The maniac had simply threatened to smash Nex's computer gear if he made any funny moves. Nex sat there like a meek kitten, watching his friend get pummelled. Chi glowered at him. There was little that sixty kilos of computer nerd could do against a survival nut twice his size, but he could have made an *effort*.

Nex's place had once been a sweatshop where illegal immigrant workers created fake, gaily coloured designer-label garments. Despite some renovating, it still had a seedy quality to it. Nex had inherited the building when his father was convicted of people trafficking.

He was now intent on healing his karma by helping the needy of the world fight government corruption, particularly in the form of dark, shadowy agencies that operated beyond the law. The concrete walls of the workshop were plastered with papers, photos and cuttings from his various investigations, along with posters of indie bands and a tricked-out synthesizer with an intimidating sound set-up. One corner of the room was filled with a state-of-the-art computer system that made Chi's look like a ZX Spectrum. The rain could be heard rattling on the metal roof above them; the yellowing perspex skylights gave out onto a mottled sky.

'We're goin' to get that badge, you puckered-up lily-livered ass leech,' Gierek barked. 'And if you try anything stupid, I'll hit you so hard your whole family'll die!'

He checked that Chi's hands were still tied firmly behind his back, and then went to open the door at the top of the stairs. Chi saw Nexus lean over and press a button on his keyboard. As Gierek's hand grabbed the door handle, his whole body went rigid and a strangled hissing noise burst from between his gritted teeth. He let go of the handle and collapsed to the floor.

'You electrified the door handle?' Chi asked in amazement. 'How long's it been like that? You never told me!'

'Can't take chances.' Nexus shrugged as he walked over to Gierek's unconscious body and checked for a pulse. 'He'll live. Sorry about that, man. Nutter nailed me as I was coming back in from the shops. Made me call you up and get you over here and then kept a knife jammed against my arsehole when I went to answer the door. I couldn't do anything until his attention was focused on you.'

'Took your time,' Chi muttered miserably. 'You gonna untie me or what?'

'He really did a number on you, didn't he?' Nex said as he sliced the tape off Chi's wrists with a box-cutter. 'Here, help me get him taped up and then we can put him somewhere safe until we figure out what to do with him. That cupboard over there should hold him.'

Once they had the Pole bound up and locked in the metal cabinet, they relaxed. He was starting to wake up and they listened anxiously as powerful blows thudded against the cupboard's aluminium walls. Enraged screams unleashed strings of Polish swear words.

'We can't keep him in there for ever,' Chi commented. 'And now he knows where you live.'

'I'm moving tomorrow,' Nex declared. 'I'll move to bloody Thailand if I have to.'

Chi looked at the cabinet shaking with each blow.

'May not be far enough,' he said.

Ivor found Chi's house without too much trouble, but there was no answer when he rang the front doorbell. The rain had stopped, so he sat down on the polished granite step of the porch to wait. It was a sprawling, high-class residence in a wealthy neighbourhood, but he did not feel safe. He was sure he had been followed; there had been fleeting glimpses of people looking away as he glanced at them, reflected figures in shop windows that changed direction just as he did and, more than anything, the shivery, instinctive sense of being watched. His fingers went up to his glass eye and he remembered the warning left in chalk on the pavement.

Amina showed up not long after and it felt good to have someone there with him. He wondered if she noticed how he stared at her, but then decided she was probably used to it. You couldn't look that good and not be used to turning heads. He had no doubt the watchers would be getting an eyeful too. She was in a black trouser suit with a deep blue shirt and her long black hair hung loose, draped over one shoulder. She smiled at him.

Ivor was abruptly conscious of how he himself was dressed. Back in the day, he had been a sharp dresser, but ever since leaving the army he rarely tried harder than hiking boots, jeans and a T-shirt or baggy sweater. Maybe he should put some more effort in.

'Hi!' she said, and he stood up as she stepped into the porch. 'He not home then?'

'Nope. Not unless he's locked himself in his safe-room or something.'

'Yeah. If I get much more paranoid, I'm going to need one of those myself,' she chuckled.

And just as she said it, a man walked past along

the road. He was dressed in a casual jacket and cords, and as he passed, he glanced once up at the house. Ivor tensed, his hands clenching in fists. Amina saw his reaction and turned to look. The man disappeared behind the willow trees overhanging the garden wall.

'Did you see it?' Ivor muttered through tight jaws. 'Did you see his face?'

'I only just caught his back as he was walking away,' she told him. 'Why? What was wrong?'

'It was one of them,' he hissed. 'His face was gone . . . smudged like . . . like he was a painting and somebody'd rubbed their thumb across his whole face. There was nothing there!'

Amina took off at a run down the driveway, stumbling to a stop at the gate. But the guy was gone. She came back up, a look of concern on her face.

'You think they're watching us?' she asked.

'They're always watching,' he replied.

He noticed she was looking uncomfortable; he couldn't be sure if it was because of the surveillance or the fact that he had apparently seen a man with no face. Chi appeared a few moments later. He was looking decidedly uneasy and was sporting a massive bruise around his left eye.

'Jesus, what happened to you?' Ivor asked.

Chi waved the question away, unlocking the

door, disarming the intruder alarm and ushering them inside. He led them down to his study and quickly scanned the room for surveillance. His cat came in, sitting at the door, licking her crotch and gazing at them occasionally as if daring them to judge her. Chi picked the cat up and put her on his lap, stroking her as if he needed to calm his nerves.

He wouldn't say who had beaten him up, so Amina went ahead and told them about the anthrax scare at the newspaper.

'I saw it on the news,' Ivor told her when she was finished. 'Two newspapers, BBC Television Centre and four MPs. They were all fakes – the letters, I mean, not the MPs – but they had the desired effect. Lots of news coverage. Now everybody in a public position will be thinking twice about opening their post.'

'It scared the hell out of me,' Amina admitted. 'I didn't know how easy it was to catch, but . . .'

'Pretty easy,' Chi mumbled, bringing the news report up on screen on the *Chronicle*'s website. 'I haven't read the reports on this yet, but the letters that were sent in the US after September the eleventh caused five deaths and put seventeen people in hospital. Just a few grains of powder. You have to hand it to those headcases; here's the West coming up with all this sophisticated, multi-million-pound technology for tackling terrorists and they're taking over airliners with box-cutter knives and sending diseases through the post.

'Mark my words: the next real terrorist attack, when it comes, will be something *simple*.'

'You should phone the police and tell them immediately,' Amina urged him. 'It could be the breakthrough they're looking for.'

'Oh, ha ha.'

'Maybe some of the terrorists are aliens,' Ivor mused. 'Maybe they're only using primitive techniques to hide their superior technology until they're ready to unleash it on the world. De-stabilizing the planet before the fleet of mother ships arrive. I bet there's a great big flying saucer lying buried in sand somewhere in the mountains in Sinnostan. Been there for thousands of years, lying dormant, waiting for the signal to awaken an army of clones in cryogenic suspension.'

'And the soldiers who've gone missing have accidentally discovered the ship,' Amina added. 'They have to be captured and reprogrammed so they don't give the game away.'

'Look, you can laugh—' Chi burst out, but Ivor interrupted him.

'And the ship is defended by human agents of the aliens, like desert vampires being protected by human slaves. You know "Osama Bin Laden" is an anagram for "Alien Sand Mob"!'

'Go on then, get it out of your systems,' Chi said, scowling. 'I know you've been dying to have a go. And you're wrong, by the way – your anagram is missing an "A". And for your information, there *have* been sightings of UFOs in Sinnostan, including some by veteran chopper pilots who were reluctant to report them. But more have been sighted over *London* than Sinnostan and you should be asking why. Because that was one of the things your fellow soldiers had in common when they started asking questions, Ivor. Over a quarter of them reported seeing an object in the sky that hovered like a helicopter but had no visible means of propulsion, and when it did move, it did so way too fast to have been a balloon or an airship. So put that in your pipe and smoke it, Cyclops!'

Chi stopped as he realized what he had just said. Ivor stared back at him. The younger man had been incensed, eager to score a hit after being mocked. It didn't mean anything, but Chi had turned bright red.

'God, I'm sorry, man. I—'

'It's OK.'

'I didn't—'

'It's OK, Chi. I'm not sensitive about it, all right? It's cool.'

Ivor saw the expression on Amina's face and knew that she was angry about it – offended on his behalf. And he didn't want that either. He didn't want her to pay any attention to his disfigurement. But how could she not? How could she ignore the fact that this guy in front of her had a glass ball stuck in one of his eye sockets? Now Ivor did feel embarrassed, and the anger that rose because of it reminded him why they were there: to find out who had planted lies in his brain about the day he had lost his eye . . . and why.

That was when his gaze fell on the computer screen and he saw the photo displayed on the news site.

'Who's that?' he asked.

'Some guy named Shang,' Amina told him, eager to change the subject. 'He's wanted in connection with the anthrax scare; supposed to be a biological weapons expert. Funny, though, he's not on any terrorist watch list.'

'I've seen this guy before,' Ivor said, shifting his seat closer. 'I'm sure of it. It was . . . I think it was in the hospital in Sinnostan, before I was flown out. He stuck in my mind because I remember being scared of him, but I couldn't figure out why.'

Chi was frowning. He slid the window of the web browser to another screen and started searching through the folders on his hard drive.

'Shang,' he muttered. 'Doctor Anthony Shang.

I know that name. Where the hell have I heard it before? You think he worked at the hospital in Kurjong? Maybe that's . . .'

His hand worked the mouse quickly, opening one folder after another until he came upon the document he was looking for.

'This is it,' he said at last. 'An article in *Paranormal Monthly*.'

Ivor and Amina avoided looking at each other. *Paranormal Monthly*? Chi went on to give an outline of the article:

'A nurse working for the British army in Kurjong became convinced there was a Chinese Communist plot to place moles in the British armed forces by abducting wounded soldiers and replacing them with perfect doubles. Hope you're paying attention here, Ivor. One surgeon that she considered particularly suspicious was a Chinese guy named Anthony Shang. The army sent her home, citing – you guessed it – post-traumatic stress, but she's popped up a couple of times on conspiracy websites and blogs. Her name is Agatha Domingues, she's a forty-three-year-old Filipino lady and she's now working in London as a psychiatric nurse.'

'You have to love the irony of that,' Amina commented. 'OK, I'll go talk to her, seeing as I'm the least likely to believe her story.'

'I'll come with you, 'cos I think it'll be entertaining at least,' Chi told her.

'I'm going to make some phone calls,' Ivor said. 'I've a friend in the Media Operations Unit in Kurjong who owes me a favour. I'm going to see if anybody there has heard of a surgeon – or a bio-weapons expert – named Shang.'

'Use my phone,' Chi told him. 'It's clean at this end at least, but try and be as vague as possible – you should see the gear they have in Government Communications HQ nowadays. If there were starlings perched on a telephone line in the Outer Hebrides, GCHQ could hear them singing.'

As they got up to leave, Ivor leaned over the desk, picked up a pen and scribbled some words on a scrap of paper. He stood up straight, smiling slightly.

'You were right,' he said to Chi. '"Alien Sand Mob" is missing an "A". "Osama Bin Laden" has three. How did you know?'

'Breaking codes is what I do,' Chi replied with a smug grin. 'Next time, give me something harder.'

34

Gierek was still locked in the cabinet when Chi returned to Nex's place early the following morning. A night of imprisonment had not improved his temper. Chi and Nexus stood gazing at the metal cupboard for some time before gathering the courage to do what needed to be done.

'Gierek?' Chi called out. 'You still with us in there?'

The reply came back in robust fashion.

'I'm gonna chew the meat off your spine like a goddamned kebab, you weasel!'

'OK. Do you want out or not?'

Chi was rewarded by a fuming silence.

'Right. We'll make this as painless for you as possible.'

Gierek must have wondered about that one – until Chi and Nexus pushed the cabinet over onto its side and started to slide it towards the door.

'Hey,' an uncertain voice called out from behind the metal panelling. 'What you doing?'

After much exertion, they made it to the door, jerking the cabinet over the threshold and shoving it to the top of the stairs.

'Hey!' Gierek bellowed.

Chi climbed over the cupboard and hurried downstairs to open the outer door. Then he climbed back up to stand just beneath the front of the cabinet.

'All right, careful now,' he muttered.

He pulled and Nex pushed. The cabinet tipped over and started to slide down the stairs. At first they thought they were in control of the weight, but Nex's fingers slipped and Chi, suddenly faced with being caught underneath the bulky metal box, stepped to the side, still trying to hold it in place. He failed.

The cupboard clattered down the steps, hit the ground at the bottom with a sickening jolt and slammed into the doorjamb. Gierek screamed blue murder. Chi gave Nex a fearful glance and nodded. They crept down – as if they might avoid the Pole's abuse if he couldn't hear them – straightened out the cabinet and shoved it out into the alleyway. Chi put a stainless steel badge and a data disk on the ground beside the cabinet. Putting the key in the cupboard's lock, he turned it and ran for the door. Nex pulled it closed and bolted it.

'You're both dead men!' Gierek yelled as he crawled out of the cramped prison.

'I'm calling the police!' Chi shouted back. 'You can stay till they get here, or get lost now! Remember I've got my face as evidence, you animal! I've left your goddamned badge out there, along with a disk of all the files I've collected while working on your case. We're sorry it's come to this. You left us no choice. The material's all yours, just go away!'

They watched through the small dirty window in the door as Gierek glared balefully in their direction and then picked up the peace offerings. A police siren helpfully sounded in the distance and he looked in the direction of the sound.

'I'll be back!' he called out to them.

As he strode away, Nex let out a huge sigh of relief.

'He will be back, you know.'

'Tell me about it,' Chi said, shuddering. 'I don't even want to think about what he'll do if he ever finds out that badge I gave him is a fake.'

'Dunno, but I'd say that chewing the meat off your spine like a kebab will play some part in the process.'

★ ★ ★

Tariq got into school early. This was a mistake.

The school had once been an award-winning piece of architecture, but like so much cutting-edge design, its time had come and gone and now the bluff concrete slabs, slatted windows and sterile green areas were simply depressing. It was not a place to raise your spirits first thing in the morning. He made his way up to his class's assembly area; he had homework due for English class in the afternoon and he intended to use the next half hour to get it done.

As he walked around the corner into the wide hallway, four boys his age jumped him.

'Hold him! Hold him!' Alan Noble shouted.

Tariq fought like a wounded cat, lashing out at those around him. He caught Jim Harris a wicked punch on the nose and slammed his shin into Winston Garret's balls, but most of his blows glanced off or were smothered as the four boys piled on top of him. They laid in a few thumps for good measure, Harris kneeling hard on his upper arm and making Tariq gasp in pain. Three of them held him there as Noble took out his camera phone and started taking pictures of Tariq's face. Garret held his head by the hair, twisting it this way and that to give Noble the angles he wanted.

'That's it, gorgeous!' Noble sneered. 'Give us a pout there. Show us your profile! Look at the sweep of that neck. And the skin! Like bubble-wrap! Ha ha! You've got skin like bubble-wrap, you spotty muppet!'

The other boys laughed like their lungs would fall out. When Noble was satisfied with his shots, the boys picked themselves up, each throwing in a parting kick for good measure, and then they left Tariq where he lay. He stayed lying there for another few seconds before getting up. He didn't want to know what they were going to do with those pictures. He just didn't want to know. Picking himself up, he found a quiet place to sit against the wall and get his homework done, but it was impossible to keep his mind on it. He would have to finish it at lunchtime.

First class of the day was Maths, and they were doing geometry through a *MindFeed* game in the computer room that had the students aiming artillery using grid references, angles and trajectories. It was demanding, but the graphic depictions of the explosive damage their shelling caused made it all worth it. Sometimes they got to fire rockets, not only at stationary targets, but at vehicles and aircraft too. There was also a version of the game for pacifists: you could pretend to be a dolphin doing a marina stunt course.

There was a tedious test that you had to do at the beginning of each *MindFeed* game: two round-edged squares came up, one that lit up and another that showed different patterns. Every now and then, the second square flashed white at the same time as the first and when it did, you were supposed to tap the left arrow key. Other times, the first square would flash up a pattern that matched the one in the second square. Then you tapped the right arrow key. The squares regularly changed sides. This was supposed to improve hand-to-eye coordination and help customize the game to your individual needs. Tariq just thought it was a waste of time and got through it as quickly as he could, but he found it was getting easier over time.

Lieutenant Scott was still there for most of the classes, supervising, offering help and advice and accosting them with his bland charm. Tariq didn't like the lieutenant. He had grown up around soldiers and, despite his rebellious tendencies, he had a great respect for what they did. He liked the blunt, in-your-face squaddie humour and even the macho codes of honour they always boasted about – though they offended his teenage cynicism in equal measure. There was just something . . . *straightforward* about them. His father had been hopelessly indoctrinated by the marines – he didn't take kindly to jokes about them – but at the same time, he had found a purpose in his life that had chilled him out in a way Tariq envied.

Even though his dad had moved to press office duties years ago, he had still done his time in the field and he had seen action in places like Kuwait, Sierra Leone and Iraq. He loved the marines almost as much as his family, and Tariq could understand why. You knew where you stood with men and women who wanted to go out and do their duty and not let their team-mates down.

But Scott, he was more like an advertising executive, or a PR consultant. That smile of his would have fitted on the face of any politician and his friendliness and back-slapping manner were so fake Tariq couldn't understand why any of his classmates bought it.

Just at that moment, the lieutenant snapped his fingers to get their attention. All the games were put on pause and heads raised above the flat-screen monitors to look at the officer. Tariq ran his hands through his spiked hair, letting his fringe fall over his eyes. He found it hard to keep the contempt off his face.

'Ladies and gentlemen,' Scott began. 'You're all flying through this course, so I thought it might be time to move things up a notch. I have no doubt you'll be *fascinated* to know that aspects of all the *MindFeed* games can be customized.' He stopped to deliver a smile. 'In the game you're playing now, you can change the locations of the artillery battles from desert to open sea to jungle and so on; you can paint words on the sides of your rockets and paste pictures onto the armour of your cannons – give them names and everything. Oh, and those of you playing with dolphins, you can change the colours and patterns on their skins and even customize the walls of the lagoon. All of these settings can be saved for future games, of course. It just gives you a chance to bring some of your own personality into the mix.'

'Cool!' Noble chortled.

'We think so.' Scott grinned back. 'Have a look through the options for the next few minutes, before we get back to the *agonizing* process of learning! After all, learning is as much about building character as soaking up facts, and *MindFeed* is designed accordingly.' He wandered across the room, stopping to look down at Tariq. 'What do you say, son? You look like you're itching to express some individuality. How about it?'

If my dad heard you calling me 'son', Tariq thought, he'd kick your army ass right out of here, you gimp.

'Sure, sounds all right,' he muttered, shrugging.

'That's the spirit!' Scott gave him a playful punch on the shoulder. 'Get on with it, then. OK, everybody, let's see you get creative!'

★ ★ ★

Agatha Domingues lived in Brixton. She was off work that afternoon and eager to talk about her experiences in Sinnostan, so Amina made an appointment to meet her, hooking up with Chi outside the Tube station before walking to the address they had been given. It was a Georgian house that had been broken up into cramped cardboard-walled flats with thin caravan doors and barred windows. Domingues answered the buzzer over the intercom and came out to the door to let them in, putting the chain on the battered, chipped-paint door before opening it. Amina and Chi had to show their identity cards before she would close it enough to take the chain off and Amina began to wonder how many of these suspicious, fearful people there were in the world.

Domingues was a small Filipino woman with a shrewish face and a short nurse's haircut. She moved with a nervous energy that was almost childlike. Her flat was down some narrow stairs in the basement, its single window looking out on a neglected garden. She informed them that she did not have tea or coffee, offering them cocoa instead. Chi took her up on the offer, but Amina settled for tap water.

As the little woman busied herself in the kitchenette, Amina sat down on the couch and laid her recorder on the coffee table. She noticed that

Chi had opened his laptop, which he was using to record too, complete with webcam. She did not know if he was showing off his high-spec equipment or just being thorough, but she definitely wanted to keep her own record of this interview.

'So you want to know about Sinnostan, eh?' Domingues asked, an exaggeratedly canny look on her face as she brought over the drinks on a tray. 'You're not the first, y'know. You saw the article in *Paranormal Monthly*, right? It's been getting a lot of attention.'

I doubt it, Amina thought to herself.

'Yes, we've seen it,' she said. 'It was fascinating. We're particularly interested in one man you mentioned – a Doctor Shang?'

'*Mister* Shang,' Domingues corrected her. 'He was a surgeon, and you call surgeons "Mister", not "Doctor". Yes, Anthony Shang. He was definitely involved.'

'Involved in the . . . the plot?' Amina prompted her. 'You talked about some kind of Communist plot.'

'Oh yes,' Domingues said, nodding. 'I didn't see much of Shang; he didn't work in the main hospital. He was always off somewhere else, but he showed up every now and again to consult on some of the patients, but I never found out where he spent most of his time. I didn't like him from the moment I set eyes on him. Creepy sort . . . and he was Chinese, of course.'

'Not too fond of the Chinese?' Amina asked.

'Don't get me wrong,' Domingues assured her. 'It's not because they're *Chinese* that I don't like 'em. I'm not a racist, y'know! I don't like 'em because they're all *Communists*! People talk like the Communist threat disappeared when the Berlin Wall came down. But they're wrong; it's looming larger than ever on the horizon and it eats its dinner with chopsticks.

'It's on track to be the most powerful country in the world now; over a billion people, all brainwashed into hating the West! That Shang was a typical example. He sometimes worked with the trauma surgeons. Plastic surgery was his thing, y'see? Making awful injuries look normal again. Manipulation of the flesh. *Fooling the eye*. And he was good at it; I could tell by the way the other surgeons treated him. That was what made me suspicious at the start. Anybody needing plastic surgery was sent back to the hospital in Germany. So what was he doing in Sinnostan, eh?'

She leaned forward, sipping her cocoa and tapping the table in front of her.

'The Chinese don't like us being in Sinnostan. It's too close to their border, but they won't go in and clear out those terrorists themselves. Why not?

Because they're allies! And the Russians too! Notice how they're not committing many troops. And it's almost in their back yard too! Communists, the lot of 'em! And don't tell me the Russians stopped being Communists; a leopard can't change its spots. It's in their blood, the red swines!'

The irate woman stopped to take a breath and sip her cocoa.

'So . . . anyway. Shang. Right. There were a lot of wounded being brought in at night by chopper and it was hard to keep track of it all. Then one night, I was out on the roof having a smoke when a chopper landed on the helipad. Shang was on board with a couple of medics and they called me over to help them. Nobody seemed to wonder what a plastic surgeon was doing on a chopper coming from a battle zone. There were six wounded and one had just sprung an arterial bleed in his leg. Blood everywhere, like a garden hose!

'I climbed into the chopper to help with the other wounded while they tended to the bleeder. It was a typical batch; shrapnel injuries mostly. I think a landmine had gone off under an APC or something like that. Ugly business. One soldier's dressing had come loose – on his arm – and I went to change it. That was when I noticed something odd.'

Domingues leaned forward again and spoke in a not-so-quiet whisper.

'The wound was clean. *Perfectly* clean. Ever seen a wound caused by an explosion? I mean up close, fresh after the event?'

Amina and Chi shook their heads.

'They're filthy. They've been caught in a blast, right? Apart from the shrapnel, there's bits of dust and sand and stone chips, sometimes glass or worse. Major risk of infection. You normally have to pick out the big bits with tweezers and then scrub the small stuff out with soap and a stiff brush. Not a job for the squeamish, I can tell you.'

Amina went slightly pale. Chi relished the gritty details of the horror that was war.

'But this guy's wound was lovely and clean. Shang and the others were busy, so I took a peek at some the others' wounds. Same thing. Battle wounds, but *without the dirt*.'

Domingues sat back and folded her arms, raising her eyebrows at them. Amina glanced at Chi and then sat further forward, her eyes opened a little wider to display riveted interest.

'But what does it mean?' she asked.

'Somebody cleaned the wounds before they were put on the chopper,' Chi mused.

'Or . . . *or* the wounds were *grown* there,' Domingues exclaimed with one finger raised.

The two journalists sat and waited for the next line, knowing it was going to be a cracker.

'I think that Shang is creating doppelgängers,' she went on. 'The Chinese have come up with a technology that allows them to change a man's body to exactly match another's. Like a photocopier for humans. They are taking Chinese agents and re-forming their bodies into perfect copies of genuine wounded soldiers.'

Amina exhaled softly. What was it with some people that the simplest answer was never good enough?

'Think about it,' Domingues continued. 'These soldiers are coming in from a supposed war zone with nice hygienically clean wounds. They're confused, they doubt their own memories, they're being supervised not by a trauma surgeon, but by a *plastic* surgeon. After their injuries, many suffer abrupt changes in personality. It all fits, see? The Chinks are sending in sleeper cells – moles who will return to the West and wait for the day they're to be activated.

'You see, I heard him talking about it once. I was coming out of the ladies' room and I saw him coming and hid back behind the door. Shang was with one of the other weirdo doctors who followed him around sometimes; he thought they were alone in the corridor, but I could hear him just fine. He was really hacked off about something and he was saying: "It sometimes takes three *days* to break them down and rebuild them! After that we have a few *hours* to make sure their injuries fit their stories. Does she think I can work miracles? We're not dealing with modelling clay here! If she thinks she can do a better job with her . . . her *zombies*, let her come down here and try!"' Domingues paused for a second. 'And then just as he was walking round the corner, Shang says: "Still, it's nice to know they'll all be taking a little bit of China back home with them, eh? Ha ha!"'

Domingues finished the last dregs of her cocoa, then slumped back, regarding her listeners with a triumphant expression.

25

Amina stood in front of the photocopier, hypnotized by the light sliding from one side to the other under the cover, the soft hasty clacking of the originals being fed in, the whishing, clucking sound of the copies sliding out.

Communists. For decades, they'd been the bad guys. For her grandparents' generation, fear of the Red Menace had clawed its way into the daily lives of everyone. The Reds weren't just behind the Iron Curtain, they were among us. It could be anyone – your friend, your neighbour. They plotted against us. Everyone was afraid of what might happen. Fear of 'The Bomb'. It was hard to get her head round; the idea that the Russians could have attacked the Americans, or the Americans could have attacked the Russians and that would have been it. The end of the world. Nuclear holocaust. She had read a lot about it. It had come closer than most people ever suspected.

And yet it hardly seemed real now. Fear of Communism had spawned thousands of spy thrillers and action films and science fiction stories. But it was difficult to think of the Russians as the bogeymen now. For a start, she knew too many of them on a first name basis.

As she often did, Amina imagined being back in that time, when everyone was so afraid. It had reached a level of hysteria in the United States in the fifties. People would be accused of being Communists and to prove they weren't, they would point their fingers at others. It's not me – it's him. It's her. The accusation was enough to ruin somebody's life. Blacklists were made. Suspicion ruled.

Amina was sure she would never have betrayed others like that. Who knows, back then she might even have been a Communist herself – a socialist revolutionary!

She found herself thinking about Ivor again. It was hard to know whether it was the man or his story she found so intriguing. There was something . . . haunted about him. Even more than the injuries, she thought, it was the sense that he'd been betrayed that troubled him. It had made him older than his years. She would have liked to see him in uniform: younger, arrogant, fearless.

The light from the photocopier swished back and forth, lulling her into a trance. She didn't believe Agatha Domingues' story about Chinese sleepers. The Chinese were not the new Russians, or the new Nazis. They were not the new alien invaders. There were no foreign devils coming over the horizon.

Somebody was lying about this war, and that was a betrayal of the men and women who went to fight in it. The thought outraged her. She was a soldier's daughter – she knew that the safety she enjoyed today had been paid for down the generations with the lives of soldiers.

All they would ask in return was that we remember their sacrifice – and try and stop it from happening again.

Ivor snapped awake with a cry, his limbs twitching as the nightmare faded. The bloody roulette wheel again – he wished he could figure out what it meant. He had fallen asleep on the sofa waiting for his friend in Kurjong to text him. There was a sour taste in his mouth, so he went into the kitchen to get himself a glass of water.

He had got into the habit of taking a nap in the afternoons. When you didn't have to work for a living, it was amazing how easy it could be to fill all that time. Since being discharged and getting his disability benefits, he had been unable to get work and then, when he won the lottery, there was no need. But the boredom had started getting to him and when he began to suspect he was under surveillance, he gradually sank into the scared numbness that had prompted his desire to tell his story to the press. Now he had a new purpose and he was relishing the activity. But he still enjoyed the odd nap.

Amina had called to tell him about the interview with Agatha Domingues. Ivor had assured her that, to the best of his knowledge, he was not a surgically altered Communist spy. But if Shang had carried out some kind of operation on him, it might explain why Ivor had vague, but disturbing memories of the man. The idea that he might be some kind of *Invasion of the Bodysnatchers*-style double made to replace his original self was just a little far-fetched. Just because he had recently discovered he was being watched by shadowy government agents did not mean he was going to buy into every conspiracy theory going. You had to have standards.

He was in the middle of boiling milk for a hot chocolate when a vibration in his pocket alerted him to a text. Opening it, he read that Jenny was ready for his call. He grabbed his jacket and a minute later he was on the street, making for the Tube station.

Chi had gone over his flat and shown him the surveillance devices he found there. It had been a chilling experience. While it was gratifying to discover that he wasn't completely paranoid – they were watching him after all – it was terrifying to know that there really were people out there who might mean him harm, and who had invaded the privacy of his home. He could not help thinking back to all the embarrassing things they might have picked up since he had won the lottery – or even if they had been listening in before that.

Ivor wanted to remove the bugs, but Chi told him there was no point. They would be replaced. On top of that, parabolic microphones, lasers bounced off his windows and other long-range listening devices could all be used and kept out of his reach. It was better to know what was there and watch what he said. Chi said it encouraged good habits anyway. You never did know who could be listening. He said this quietly, under the cover of loud music from the stereo.

So Ivor had phoned Jenny from a cheap calls internet café a few miles from his place, and she had said she'd text him when she found something out. Jenny was an ex-girlfriend; one of those who didn't bear him a grudge. She owed him too.

The British army didn't tolerate bullying, but there were still some young recruits being driven to suicide by constant abuse. The army considered this a military problem and kept the public in the dark about it. Jenny's little brother had been victimized during basic training and was on the edge of despair. Ivor was in the same platoon. He dealt with the problem by picking out the worst offender and gently placing his hand in a bowl of water while he slept one night. The bully woke up in the morning to find he'd wet the bed. Ivor disposed of the bowl of water before it was discovered. Nobody took the bully too seriously after that.

Jenny was a lieutenant in the Signals Corps now, working in the Media Operations Unit, and still had a soft spot for him.

The internet café, imaginatively named Mr Internet, was a dingy place with Silicon Valley aspirations.

Plastic chairs were pulled up in front of old wood-laminate school desks. The computers were old, but in good working order, and each one was slightly different, suggesting that the place had evolved over time from spare parts rather than being built to design. Mr Internet was run by a pair of young Pakistani brothers, who had probably put all these machines together themselves. It was open twenty-four hours a day and there was always at least one of the brothers behind the counter, along with two or three other members of their family.

Ivor sat down in a white, chipboard-walled booth, put on a headset and logged on, punching in Jenny's home number. She picked up on the first ring.

'Hi, babe,' she chirped. 'How's the rain?'

'Cold and wet,' he replied. 'It would make you homesick just to see it. What have you got for me?'

'Yeeeessssss,' she muttered, and from the sounds he could tell she was tucking the phone under the side of her head while she reached for her keyboard. 'Anthony Shang. Couldn't find anything on him in the personnel database – but that's not surprising, if *anything* of what you told me is true. I dug around for anything in the usual channels and got nothing. Then I tried a web search on the inconceivable off-chance that you hadn't. You didn't do a search, did you?'

Ivor frowned.

'No. I figured anything on him would be . . . y'know, secret.'

'Nothing's too secret for the web, babe. I *love* it. I know you didn't do a search because if you did, you'd have found out he has a *book*! *Making Faces: How China's Leading Plastic Surgeon Became a Secret Weapon in the World of Espionage.* I'm sending you the link now.'

Ivor opened his email and clicked on the link. The cover of the book came up, showing Shang –

definitely the same guy – in a white coat, leaning nonchalantly against a blank white wall with his arms folded. He wore a smug grin and an expensive haircut. The blurb for the book read:

Ten years ago, Anthony Shang defected to the West. He brought with him an extraordinary tale of cosmetic surgery, Chinese politics and high-level espionage. As the most celebrated Chinese surgeon of his generation, he led a double life: giving facelifts to top-ranking Communist Party officials while also working for Chinese intelligence, using his unparalleled skills to change the faces and fingerprints of key spies infiltrating Europe and the US.

Judged by British intelligence to be the most valuable defector in decades, Anthony Shang tells his story here for the first time. Welcome to his world.

'Bloody hell,' Ivor exclaimed.
'Yeah,' Jenny chuckled. 'Nothing like keeping a low profile, huh?'

18

In Loving Memory

The meeting place was different, but they were there on the same business. ████████, ████ and ███████-█████ were in a four-star hotel suite, sitting in armchairs around a low table with their laptops on their knees. On the table was a tray of tea and coffee and a large plate of sandwiches cut into neat quarters and served with garnish.

The room itself was neat, clean and impersonal. There were tasteful prints on the off-white walls and an abundance of creatively framed mirrors. Each of the three people had conducted their own checks for surveillance. It was not a good idea to trust anybody in this business.

'So, still no sign of Shang,' ████ was saying. He was in a Royal air force uniform today, despite the fact that he had never served in the air force.

'This is getting to be a real problem.'

'He'll be found,' ███████-█████ sniped back in his bass voice. 'The man's arrogant and he's an attention-seeker. He'll make a mistake somewhere.'

The other two did not look satisfied.

'He'll be found,' he said again, with certainty.

'Do we still go ahead with Operation Renewed Faith?' ████ asked, looking at each of his colleagues in turn.

'Yes,' ██████████ replied.

'Yes,' ███████-█████ agreed, his heavy-lidded eyes opening a little wider. 'It's too important to put on hold just because of an upstart surgeon. He doesn't know enough to compromise the operation, and we can discredit him if he tries to talk afterwards. The package has been shipped?'

'It's on its way,' ████ told them. 'Due in eight days. It's aboard a Dutch-registered freighter with no ties to Britain. There are two minders, but no one in the crew knows what they're carrying.'

'Good,' ███████-█████ muttered. 'I have to admit, I'll be glad when it's secured again. The risk of it being hijacked—'

'—Is well worth it,' ████ assured him. 'The nation is losing faith in the war. If that happens, they'll drop their guard and the British people will become easy targets for any fanatic who wants to try his luck. That can't be allowed to happen.'

██████████ was surprised to see that both men looked anxious. The contradictions of the human mind never failed to fascinate her. These men had planned all this from its inception, and had known the scale of operation they were undertaking. Only now, as it was coming close to realization, did her colleagues seem to consider the risks they were taking. She had only a small, but important, part to play in the delivery of this shipment and had been nervous about it for some time. She was not comfortable working outside of the controlled conditions of her laboratories. These men, on the other hand, should be used to this kind of thing.

'Other business,' ████ said abruptly, as if keen to change the subject. 'You say McMorris has started avoiding your surveillance?'

'Doesn't everybody?' ██████████ murmured, much to ███████-████'s annoyance.

'We think Sandwith made him aware of the devices in his flat, and all three of them are careful about what they say when they're together,' he reported, shifting his large body in the small arm-chair. 'The easiest one to keep track of is Amina Mir. She uses the phones and computers at the newspaper and we've been tapped into them for over a year. She's talkative too.'

'Her mother could be a problem if she gets involved,' ▉▉▉▉ cautioned him.

'She won't. The girl's fiercely independent. She could use her mother's name a lot more than she does, but she's obviously keen to go it alone. The little tart has no idea what she's getting herself into.'

'Then maybe she should be given a hint,' ▉▉▉▉ said quietly. 'Nothing loud enough to get the mother's attention. I won't have this nation's security compromised by another loudmouth reporter.

'And do something about Sandwith too. I don't like the way his friends have been sniffing around the Central Database. God knows what kind of dirt they could be digging out of there. It's time we started to tidy up all these loose ends.'

It was Saturday morning, and Amina was enjoying a well-earned lie-in. She loved her bed. Her purple duvet was piled up around her and a collection of quirkily shaped cushions supplemented her pillows to create a plush boudoir effect, echoed by the terracotta-coloured walls. Despite the cynical attitude she was keen on developing as part of her journalistic persona, she was an avid chick-lit fan and stacks of books on the pitfalls and perils of modern relationships lined her bookshelves, along with books on uncompromising reporters like Edward R. Murrow, Nellie Bly and George Orwell.

Her stereo's timer clicked on at 10.30 a.m., playing her favourite morning radio show, but she stayed under the duvet, resisting the DJ's jovial efforts to kick-start her day. It was only when the staccato lyrics and rumbling bass beat of Absent Conscience started reverberating through the wall from Tariq's room that she finally sat up and faced the day.

'Tariq!' she yelled.

'*They say love is blind, but I see just fine/You're tryin' to sell me a world when it's already mine/You are my first love but not the last you see/I love hurting you with honesty . . .*'

'TARIQ! TURN. IT. DOWN!'

The volume dropped until it was merely a muffled annoyance and Amina flopped back into her pillows. That was it; she was awake now. The lovely fluffy fog of half-asleepness was lost. She wondered if she could persuade her dad to bring her breakfast in bed. He did sometimes, when he was in a mood for spoiling her.

But one look at her PC was enough to motivate her into getting up and putting on her snug mauve dressing gown over her peach silk pyjamas. She had promised herself she would spend some of the day writing up her notes and putting together the beginnings of an article on what they'd found so far. But not before she'd treated herself to a nice breakfast and an hour or two of lounging on the sofa with a good book.

She didn't spot the envelope until she was opening the bedroom door.

It was a plain white square, leaning against the base of the lamp on her bedside table. Her parents were usually up before her, but they left any post for her on the kitchen counter. One of them must have left it in here while she was asleep. She wasn't mad about the idea that her parents were still sneaking into her room; apart from the fact that she was old enough to demand her privacy, she had been bringing boyfriends home for some time now. Having her latest romantic endeavour interrupted by one of her parents – particularly her overprotective dad – was a scene she could really do without.

For a moment, Ivor flickered into her thoughts. She could only imagine what her dad would make of him. He was only a few years older than her, but a far cry from the jack-the-lads who'd had the misfortune of running into Martin Mir. And her dad had never been keen on her dating soldiers – even ex-soldiers. 'They're dogs,' he would say simply. When asked what that made him, his reply was always the same: 'An *old* dog.'

Picking up the envelope, she noticed that although it had her name and address written on it, it didn't have a stamp or postmark. It must have been hand-delivered. She slit it open with a nail file and pulled out the card within. It was a funeral card. Frowning, she opened it. There was no inscription inside, just a couple of lines printed in fake handwriting:

> *Sending you our deepest condolences on the loss of your mother. Our thoughts are with you and your family at this difficult time.*

With a start, Amina dropped the card on the bed and stepped away from it, her hand covering her mouth. It was a threat. Somebody was threatening her mother. No – they were threatening *her* with the death of her mother. But it couldn't be. Surely it was a mistake or . . . or maybe a joke . . .

It wasn't a mistake and it wasn't any joke. With trembling hands, Amina picked up the card and slid it back into the envelope, holding it by the edges in case it might have the perpetrator's fingerprints on it. What was the name of that detective from CTC? Sykes, that was it. She would take it to him and explain about the story she was working on . . .

No, she wouldn't. Feeling suddenly cold, she sat down on the edge of the bed. For the first time, she realized what this story they were working on could actually mean. If they really were scratching the surface of a criminal conspiracy, they were interfering with some very serious people. People who would do serious harm to anyone who got in their way. People who might have powerful influence in the police force, or the courts, or the intelligence services. The fact that Sinnostan was thousands of miles away had made all of this something of a fantasy. She had never considered that she might not be safe here, in nice, civilized London.

This was why Ivor was scared and Chi was paranoid, but she had completely failed to appreciate the risks they were taking. It had all seemed like an adventure. She felt suddenly sick. Had somebody come into their house – into her *room* – to deliver it? Somebody who stood over her while she lay there in a deep sleep? Maybe they had even prowled through the house unseen in the night, peering into the bedrooms of her parents and her brother; noting where they slept. The house had an alarm, but that wouldn't matter to people like this, would it?

Amina looked around her room to see if anything had been disturbed, but it all seemed the same. What about bugs? Was she under surveillance now? She cursed her own stupidity. *Of course* she was being watched. Chi had shown her the bugs in Ivor's flat. She remembered being excited by the whole thing – like a bloody idiot. She was only ever careful of what she said around Ivor and Chi because *they* were careful. When she was alone, she brushed off their suspicious tendencies and acted like she didn't have a care in the world. She'd never taken any of it that seriously. Were the watchers tapping the phones here? What about the phones and emails at the newspaper? Mobiles were easy to listen in to – she had to assume anything she'd said on hers had been picked up.

Just as the thought crossed her mind, her phone rang, making her jump. God, this was it. This was where some deep, garbled voice on the phone told her to stop asking questions if she knew what was good for her.

But it was Dani. Amina answered, relief flooding through her.

'Hi . . . hiya. What? Sorry, no . . . no . . . I forgot we were going out tonight. Listen, I don't think I'll be able to make it. No. I . . . I just can't at the moment. Look, I'll call you back, OK?'

Dani had hardly replied before Amina rang off. The more she thought about the funeral card, the more anxious she became that she might already have dug herself too deep a hole. She needed to talk to Ivor and Chi – show them the card and see what they thought.

First, though, she needed to see her family and find out if any of them had left the card in her room. If not, her whole life had just changed.

26

Chi woke to the sound of the doorbell ringing. It rang again impatiently as he slowly registered that he had fallen asleep at his desk again. Lifting his head from his folded arms, his elbow nudged the mouse on the pad beside him and the PC woke up with him – but considerably faster. He reflected that it was time he got himself a new girlfriend; he didn't want to end up as one of those guys who only had a relationship with their computer.

The doorbell rang again. It sounded louder this time, even though he knew it couldn't be. His clothes had that constricting, crumpled feel to them from having been slept in. Standing up stiffly, he stretched and started for the door.

'OK! OK, I'm coming!'

Most people gave up after the first four or

five rings; these guys must be pretty sure he was here . . .

That made him stop for a moment, but he shook his head and hurried out to the hall and down to the front door. He wasn't so uptight yet that he was afraid to answer the door. Not yet. He was in his bare feet, and for some irrational reason he wished he'd put on his boots. There was something about being barefoot that made you feel vulnerable.

He opened the door to find a man and a woman standing there. He could tell immediately that they were old bill. The man was thin and freckly with pale brown hair and a slightly superior, but absent-minded air about him. The woman had 'career' written all over her. She was black, with her dark hair cut short, her navy blue suit and pin-stripe shirt carefully pressed – unlike her partner's – and a look on her face that said 'Go ahead . . . make my day'.

'Come on in,' Chi said, before they had even raised their IDs. 'Coffee?'

The man's name was Detective Sergeant Sykes, the woman's was Detective Superintendent Atkinson, and they were from Counter Terrorism Command. They were here to investigate a tip-off that Chi had been involved in the recent anthrax scare at the *Chronicle* building. He had been spotted on CCTV footage recorded a few days before the incident and had made scathing references to the paper's political ties in his weblog, *EyesWideSideways*.

'And where did this tip-off come from, exactly?' Chi asked as he gestured at them to sit down at the kitchen table and waited for the kettle to boil.

'We're not at liberty to say at the moment, sir,' Atkinson replied.

'Anonymous, huh? Or intelligence sources maybe? Come on, give me a clue.'

'We'd appreciate it if you would just answer our questions, sir,' Sykes told him. 'It's just a formality, you understand. We have to follow up every lead, even if it's to eliminate you from our enquiries.'

'Of course.' Chi filled three mugs with coffee and set out sugar and milk.

The mundane act of making the drinks gave him time to think and helped hide his nervousness. Somebody had decided to turn up the heat on him, and heat didn't come any more serious than the CTC.

If they decided they had enough evidence to arrest him, they could hold him for weeks without charging him. Even if they didn't have enough evidence to charge him, they might still be able to get a restraining order and put him under indefinite house arrest. They could hold him like that for years, or put an electronic tag on him, take his computer gear, his files, all without a trial. The only question was, what had they been fed to bring them to his door?

All the phone calls he made to Nexus and his other mates were encrypted. He was very careful about what he said on any other calls and he hardly ever used his mobile. But then there were all the sites he'd visited on the web. They could be traced. The police and intelligence services were permitted remote access to any server or database in the country. The new Drawbridge Act gave them power to do all of these things and much more.

Even so, the police had to play by the rules. One of the advantages of having wealthy parents was that he had lawyers ready and waiting to defend him against any trumped-up charges that came his way. But if the intelligence services were involved, then the gloves came off. They could feed the police information that Chi and his lawyers would never be allowed see. After all, if you had a spy in a terrorist organization, you could hardly go around telling everyone who they were. He could be put under house arrest without ever knowing what they had on him.

Sitting down at the table, facing the two detectives, he readied himself for what was to come. But all the while, he was itching to get back to his PC, contact his network and have them start stretching out their feelers. He needed to know what was coming.

The detectives' questions were direct and to the point, and he answered them without expression. No, he had nothing to do with the anthrax scare at the *Chronicle* or anywhere else. No, he did not have any medical or laboratory training. No, he did not have a grudge of any kind against the newspaper or any of the other targets of the anthrax scare. As he was questioned, Chi's mind raced. He knew that if they got a warrant to search his house they would find all his files. With all the information he had gathered over the years, they were bound to dig up something to make them suspicious. One wrong connection and he was stuffed. And his files were full of all kinds of connections to suspicious activity. That was the whole point.

No, he did not support, nor have any affiliation with, any of the groups on the terrorist watch list. No, he had never received any training in weapons or explosives. No, he had never searched for information on these subjects on the web (which wasn't exactly true – he had just never been stupid enough to do so from his own computer. He couldn't help being curious). No, he had never subscribed to any of the publications on the list Atkinson showed him. No . . . no . . . no . . .

'Do you know this man?' Atkinson held up a photo.

'He's been on the telly,' Chi replied. 'Chinese guy. They say he's into biological weapons or something. Don't know him personally, no.'

This was all fishing. They didn't expect him to admit to any of these things, they just wanted to provoke a reaction, to size him up. He clasped his hands around the coffee mug to stop them trembling. Tension tightened around his shoulders and neck. His jaw clenched and unclenched and he tried to relax, conscious that they would be reading all of this.

'What were you doing at the *Chronicle* building?' Atkinson asked then.

Chi hesitated. If he had been caught on CCTV, they probably knew he had met Amina. It didn't make sense to lie about it anyway.

'I'm working on a story with one of the junior reporters there; a girl named Amina Mir.'

The two detectives exchanged looks but didn't make any comment. Chi knew she had been questioned after the anthrax scare; they probably remembered her.

'What's the story?' Sykes enquired.

Chi's first instinct was to give the line that he and Amina had agreed on: that they were investigating a pattern of mental-health problems in Sinnostan veterans. But then he realized that he had a chance here to divert the detectives' suspicion from him. Better to be a harmless nut than a subversive terrorist suspect.

'Actually, it's part of an ongoing investigation I'm carrying out,' he said with fake enthusiasm. 'I've been following up reports of mysterious abductions in battle zones in Sinnostan and places like that – and the subsequent stories of mind-control experiments related by the abducted soldiers after they return. It's all in conjunction with the increasing reports of UFOs over the UK and the US, as well as over Sinnostan itself. I'm playing with a theory that the soldiers are being abducted, experimented on and maybe even replaced with alien doppelgängers in preparation for the seeding of an alien population on Earth. I can see you're sceptical, but the evidence is extremely compelling. Would you like to have a look at some of it?'

This time the detectives were less subtle in their exchange. Chi knew that look too well. The sidelong glance, the raised eyebrows, the carefully suppressed smile.

'Sure,' Atkinson said. 'Let's have a look.'

They wanted any chance to see his place without having to get a search warrant. That was to be expected. He took them down to his study, glad of the big WATCH THE SKIES poster on the wall. He sat down at his PC and clicked on a blank folder. This was his 'Completely Bonkers' file. He kept it for laughs, but now he could pretend it formed the backbone of his work. A few more clicks and a range of articles filled the screens.

'These kinds of abductions and experimentation have been going on since Roswell in 'forty-seven,' he explained, flicking at speed through the outlandish collection of documents. 'You think our governments are running things? Think again. There's a network of dark agencies working in a global conspiracy to undermine the human race and create ties with an alien race that's desperate to colonize our planet. These men see the future and they know it's not human. And they want to be part of the ruling class, rather than be consigned to slavery like the rest of us.'

Chi had to be careful here. He had to come across as crazy, but not *unbelievably* crazy.

'Look at all the key figures of the second half of the last century – the icons who could have really unified the world with their ideas. John F.

Kennedy: assassinated. Martin Luther King: assassinated. John Lennon: assassinated. Mikhail Gorbachev: overthrown. Bob Geldof: accused of selling out. And do you really think the South African government would ever have let the *real* Nelson Mandela out of prison? Like hell! They were all working for a unified Earth and were therefore a threat to the aliens' plans. The invaders needed us to be divided and weak so they could take over our governments one at a time. You know they have weapons that can duplicate the effects of natural disasters? A few signals to a satellite and they can create earthquakes, tidal waves, forest fires, avalanches, volcanoes . . . OK, maybe not volcanoes . . .

'Then there's the documentary proof that George W. Bush never actually existed, that he was in fact an animatronic puppet—'

'We get the idea,' Atkinson interrupted from behind him. 'I think we've seen everything we need to, don't you, Sykes?'

'I think Mr Sandwith has important work to get back to,' Sykes replied. 'Thanks for your time, sir. And good luck with your story.'

Chi nodded and walked them out to the door. When he closed it after them, he pressed his ear against it and heard their chuckles on the other side. He turned and leaned back against the wood, heaving a sigh of relief. They were gone, for now, but he was sure that those who had sent the police had more moves to make. And unlike the two detectives, they couldn't be fooled into thinking he was harmless.

30

Nobody in the house had left the envelope in Amina's room. Each of them assumed one of the others had dropped it in and she let them go on thinking that. She resisted the urge to tell her parents her suspicions; like all of the leads she had gathered with Chi and Ivor for their story, there was no solid evidence to prove that somebody had come into the house during the night. They would say she was imagining things, or that she must have picked up the envelope inside the door and carried it up with the rest of her post. Or something like that.

It was hard to know which was scarier: the thought that an intruder had come into her room while she slept, or the fact that after all the time she had spent working on this story, there was still not a scrap of proof to show that anything was actually happening. It was as if the more she tried to get a grasp on what was going on, the more it slipped through her fingers. When she turned it all around in her head, she wasn't even sure what the story *was*. Ivor had his implanted memories and his night-mares and the disturbing Scalps people who were watching his every move. Chi had been investi-gating for a couple of years and had plenty of . . . material, but no sense of the true nature of the con-spiracy – if that's what it even was. When she really thought about it, they had nothing tangible. Maybe they never would. Maybe there was no great conspiracy, just a bunch of mentally disturbed war veterans and the theories of some over-imaginative conspiracy nuts.

But then there was the card that had been left on her bedside table. Sitting down on her bed, she looked at it again.

Sending you our deepest condolences on the loss of your mother. Our thoughts are with you and your family at this difficult time.

A shiver ran through her and she crumpled up the funeral card, tossing it into her wastepaper basket. She needed to talk. Her first thought was to call Dani or one of the other girls; but it would be too hard to explain, to make them take it seriously. Then she considered Ivor, who would understand what was going through her mind at least, but . . . no. It would be a bit weird. And she was in danger of crying and she didn't want to seem weak to him; she didn't want to lose his respect. For a moment, she thought about calling Chi – and rejected that idea immediately.

Deciding she didn't want to be on her own, she went next door to Tariq's room.

The nihilistic phase he was currently exploring had taken its toll on his decor. The walls were painted a dark red, almost black, and were marked with scrawled graffiti in marker, chalk and even some scratched into the plaster with the point of a compass.

LIFE IS DEFINED BY DEATH.

GOD IS A CREATION OF MAN TO EXPLAIN HIMSELF.
DON'T READ THIS!

WE HAVE CEASED TO EVOLVE. NOW OUR WORLD ADAPTS TO SURVIVE US.

And there were plenty more, all equally morose and reflecting her brother's prematurely world-weary personality. She dearly hoped he would cheer the hell up soon. This was worse than those six months when he'd decided to start taking Islam more seriously and berated the rest of the family for failing to show the proper respect to Allah. He was always going around, squawking '*La ilaha illallah!*' (There is no God but Allah!) in his adolescent about-to-break voice, and kept waking her in the middle of the night to pray. He only stopped when she threw a fit and threatened to hit him with her hockey stick. A few months before that, he'd complained about not being Christian like all of his friends on the base where they'd been living. And before that, he'd been expelled from two different schools for getting into fights. He had a savage temper.

Even so, there was something comforting, something lovely and *normal*, about Tariq's teenage angst. Absent Conscience was still playing on his stereo when she walked in. He was dressed in his black gothic best, lying on his bed and reading Sun Tzu's *The Art of War*, probably just so he'd be able to impress people by quoting from it. Amina was sure he would already have underlined some of the best bits.

'Hey,' she said.

'Hey.'

'What's up?'

'Not much. What's up yourself?'

'Nothing. Stuff,' she said, shrugging. 'Y'know.'

Tariq noticed how she was standing, leaning against the wall with her shoulders hunched. She wasn't dressed yet and it was almost lunchtime.

She looked pale too. He sat up, put the book down and crossed his arms.

'OK, I'll bite. What's wrong?'

'Nothing,' she assured him.

And then she started talking.

She told her brother about Ivor and Chi, and about the story they were all working on. It all just came out of her, even though she hadn't meant it to. She knew she was being indiscreet. The Scalps could be listening to every word she said, but they had just shown her they were one step ahead no matter what she did. Maybe they would leave her alone when they heard how frightened she was.

She told him about the Sinnostan vets with fake memories and hallucinations, the three-day disappearances in the war zones, the film of the unconscious soldiers from Gierek's helmet camera, about Ben Considine's apparent suicide, about the plastic surgeon named Anthony Shang and the unrealistic wounds that Agatha Domingues had found on the soldiers. Amina described the surveillance they were all under, telling her brother about the devices in Ivor's flat and the watchers with no faces and the message left on the ground in chalk at the café. And then she told him about the card. By this time she was crying.

She went back into her room and took the card out of the bin, bringing it in to show Tariq. He had an incredulous look on his face, but it was obvious that she was genuinely upset. Taking the crumpled card, he flattened it out on his desk and looked at it and then back at her.

'Wow,' he said softly.

Amina just nodded, wiping the tears from her face. She felt better, having got it all out of her system, but now she'd got Tariq involved.

'I'm in over my head,' she said to him. 'We all are. None of us have any idea who these people are. Even if we did, we don't have any evidence – any *believable* evidence – that something is going on. We don't even know *what's* going on.

'I feel like I've been acting out some bloody *Famous Five* adventure and now I've just discovered these are real villains – the kind who don't care that you're just a kid; who'll . . . who'll . . . wrench out your teeth and smash . . . your . . . your kneecaps and dump your cut-up body in a canal. You know: the type nobody ever reports to the police because they know where your family lives and you're terrified they'll . . . they'll . . .'

She stopped, feeling suddenly drained. Tariq exhaled softly.

'You need to tell Mum and Dad about all this,' he said. 'If half of this is true, you're in deep shit here, Mina.'

'I'll talk to Ivor and Chi first,' she replied

hoarsely. 'And maybe Goldbloom too, although I hate to think what he'll make of all this. You know, Mum was threatened on a bunch of occasions 'cos of the stories she was working on, but I never really thought about what that meant. There were a couple of times when Dad actually asked her to drop a story. She never did.'

'Yeah,' Tariq muttered. 'But we've never had anyone break into our house to deliver a funeral card before. That's really freaky when you think about it. No broken windows or locks, no alarm . . . they just came in and left without a trace.' A look of realization came over him. 'Bloody hell, Mina! What if this wasn't the first time!'

'Don't, Tariq,' she moaned, holding her hands up. 'I may never sleep again as it is.'

The trip to Chi's house on the Underground seemed to take for ever. Amina tried to ignore the feeling that someone's eyes were crawling all over her. The train was about half full and whenever she looked up, there always seemed to be somebody just turning to look the other way. She was an attractive girl; she was used to being looked at. But this was different. Now all of the men who eyed her up no longer wore expressions of excited interest or concealed lust; they all appeared more intent in their observation. The women — and she knew it was always the women who stared more — were no longer measuring her up as a rival; they were assessing her as a target.

There was no way to be sure about any of this. It could just have been her imagination, her newfound paranoia reading into things. They couldn't *all* be watching her. Most of these people — if not all of them — were just going somewhere; taking the Tube with no thought of tangled conspiracy plots. But now Amina was looking at the world through new eyes and was suspicious of everything she saw.

The gaunt-faced man in the suit sitting across from her, with the briefcase lying on the seat beside him. Could there be a weapon in that case? She had caught him looking at her a couple of times already. Or the young woman with the hair-wraps and the backpack standing near the door, holding onto the rail, her body swaying with the motion of the train. Amina could see her face clearly in the reflection on the window, which meant that she could see Amina's. Or the stocky man with the beard further down on the other side, tapping on the screen of his PDA with its little plastic stylus. There were a few occasions when he lifted it high enough to get a picture of her with its camera.

Allah help me, she thought. I've caught Chi's disease.

Chi was not surprised. She babbled out her fears as soon as he opened the door, showing him the funeral card. He in turn told her about the visit from the CTC officers. Amina suggested they take what they had to Goldbloom and see what he made of it. They needed help with this.

'No,' Chi said, shaking his head. 'This is our story; if we get mainstream people involved, the corporate interests will come into play. They won't do anything if they think they'll be taken to court, you know – or lose their precious advertisers. And half the time they just take the government's word for everything anyway. But we're wild cards! Unpredictable! The fact that somebody's worried enough to threaten us means we've got them rattled now.'

'We've got *who* rattled?' Amina threw her hands up in exasperation. 'Rattled about *what*? We're snatching at shadows here—'

The doorbell rang. It was Ivor, and he was grinning. Chi followed him back into the study and watched in bemusement with Amina as Ivor whipped three copies of a paperback out of his bag and held one up.

'He wrote a bloody *book*!' he exclaimed. 'Anthony Shang wrote a bloody bestseller! So much for being top secret!'

He looked at their faces.

'What's wrong now?' he asked.

★ ★ ★

After the three of them had talked it out, they still could not come to any consensus about what to do. Chi was keen to chase up on the leads they had without any outside involvement; Amina wanted to get help from Goldbloom and the *Chronicle*; Ivor was worried for his two younger friends and asked them to give up on the story before something more serious happened. He felt he had nothing to lose, but he didn't want to put them in any danger.

In the end, the three of them decided to hold off making any decisions until after they had all read Shang's book. Amina still had plenty of articles to search through from the newspaper's archives and Chi wanted to get back to his contacts to see if they had any news. Ivor had already tried to get in touch with some of the other veterans he'd known in Sinnostan, but none of them would admit to suffering the same symptoms. He said he'd try again, and this time he was going to offer rewards for any solid leads. It was time to start spending some of his money.

'This is what I've been afraid of doing all along,' he told them. 'It's why I'm being watched – because rich people can cause more problems than poor ones. But you two need to look like you're backing out. I'm going to get all the wrong kind of attention for this and there's no point you taking any more risks – at least' – he raised his hand against their protests – 'until it's absolutely necessary. So don't call me, don't email me, don't come near me until I tell you it's OK, right?'

The other two reluctantly agreed.

Ivor and Amina took the Tube back into town. He sensed that she was uneasy and noticed how she kept looking around her. Overcome with a sense of sympathy for her, he chatted with her about normal, everyday things. She was just a kid with big ambitions, much as he'd been a few years ago. But she'd been living in a sheltered world and now it had been tainted by the pervasive fear he had endured ever since he'd returned from Sinnostan. It was deeply unnerving to know that something was wrong with the world around you, but you didn't know what.

'So it must be handy, having a famous correspondent for a mother,' he said, when she mentioned her mother was working on a story about arms companies working in Sinnostan.

'I could make more of it, I suppose,' she admitted. 'But I want to do this on my own, not because I'm her daughter. Still, they definitely cut me more slack at the paper because of who she is, and I'm not above using that. She's always saying I should do whatever it takes. There's pressure though, too. It means I've a lot to live up to.'

'What about your dad? He's in the media too, right?'

'He's a marine. Well . . . technically. Nowadays he does more press releases than assault courses. That's how they met; they were both working in Iraq and he chatted her up after a press conference. Mum jokes about their marriage being a conflict of interest. Only sometimes she's not joking.'

'And you haven't talked to them about any of this yet?' Ivor asked. 'They might be able to help.'

He didn't point out that Amina should have told them as soon as she thought there was any risk involved in working on this story. It would have done no good – he was much the same at her age; he had figured the less his parents knew about his activities the better.

'They'd want me to stop, they'd say it was too dangerous,' Amina sniffed. 'But that's the whole point, isn't it? The ones who break the big stories, they don't stop for anything. When I think about what some reporters have had to go through: death threats, beatings, imprisonment, torture . . . just for trying to tell the truth, I always wonder what I'd do in their place, you know? I'd like to think I'd be brave enough to do the same.

'It should be easier for us, shouldn't it? We have democracy and a free press and all that. But now I don't know. You look back through history and so much of what went on seemed black and white. Now it's complicated – it's all about versions of the truth. We don't have any dictators or secret police or . . . or censors telling us what is and isn't true. Do we? So why do I have this growing feeling like . . . like . . .'

'Like everyone's treating you like a mushroom?' Ivor grinned.

'What?'

'You know – keeping you in the dark and feeding you loads of bullshit.'

'Oh, right.' She smiled back at him. 'Yeah, like that.'

Ivor looked out of the window as the train slid squealing into a station and the doors clunked open.

'I don't think it was ever simple,' he mused. 'Hindsight's a wonderful thing. We have the luxury of looking back at history and thinking we'd do it better. But there's as many different versions of each story as there are people to tell 'em and we normally only get to hear from the ones who were left in charge after the smoke settled. History as told by the losing side is a real eye-opener.

'As for being brave, I think it's a rare event when you can make that great, courageous gesture that gets you noticed. Most of the time it's just about plugging away and making all those tricky little decisions that come at you every day. That's how it was when I was in the army.

'And I'd be lying if I said I hated giving boring stories a dramatic touch, or simplifying the background information so it could be given in catchy sound-bites. I figured this was reporting for the MTV generation and I was good at it. News these days has to be less like a documentary and more like a movie or a video game. It's got to look good and still fit between the ads!'

His eyes were on the dark walls of the tunnel as they swept by.

'And war is the most entertaining news of all. It's the best story. Human drama, action, explosions, cool machines, medical emergencies, heroes and villains, dramatic locations and constantly changing situations . . . tragedy and triumph. It triggers the most extreme emotions. Everybody wants to report on a war.'

'If everybody wants to report on it,' Amina asked quietly, 'why can't we find out what's really happening over there?'

'War is loud,' Ivor replied. 'If you want to distract people's attention from something, there's nothing better than a bit of death and glory. Isn't this your stop?'

They had agreed to say goodbye publicly, to make it look like they might not be seeing each other again. He stood up to see her off and gave her a hug.

'Maybe I'll see you again sometime,' he said.

'Yeah, let's keep in touch,' she replied.

On impulse, she kissed him on the lips. Ivor was so taken aback, he almost forgot to wave as she got off. She turned to watch him through the window as the train pulled away.

There was a man standing behind her wearing a leather biker jacket and jeans. His face was a blurred smudge. The train moved away into the tunnel before Ivor could do anything to warn her.

9

Ivor tried to reach Amina on his mobile as soon as he came out of the station, but he couldn't get through. She was probably on the connecting train home. Deciding a text or message on her voicemail would do more harm than good he hung up, swearing under his breath.

Frustration, fear and rage whirled through him in a confused mass. He wasn't thinking this through. They knew they were being followed. They had said the safest thing to do was to avoid contact for a while. The man he had seen behind Amina probably wasn't there to harm her, but even the slightest chance that he might be was enough to terrify Ivor. What should he do? Try and reach her at home? He knew where she lived. He had the solid steel bar from his dumb-bell and his stun-gun in his pockets in case of trouble. But maybe this was a test. The man on the platform might have known the effect he would have – he could have been attempting to get a reaction out of Ivor, to see what he would do. If Ivor sought Amina out, he could be endangering them both. Perhaps he shouldn't react at all.

But the thought that she might be in danger ate into him, making his skin tighten, searing him like acid. It was all he could do not to seek out a taxi and drive straight to her house.

It was starting to get dark. Ivor jammed his hands in his jacket pockets and walked quickly with his head down, trying to get his thoughts into some kind of order. He became aware of somebody walking behind him. Out of habit, he checked the darkened reflection in the window of a designer clothing shop as he passed. It was a short, stout man wearing a woollen cap and a bomber jacket. There was nobody else on the street. Ivor stopped suddenly, pulling his hands free and patting his pockets as if searching for something. He glanced at his watch and then looked back the way he had come, giving the impression that he was thinking of going back for whatever he had forgotten.

The man behind him had no face. Ivor was careful not to react. Instead, he made a disgusted expression and started back along the path. As they passed each other, Ivor turned, pulled his stun-gun from his pocket and fired it into the man's back.

The two darts pierced the man's jacket, embedding themselves in his skin, trailing two wires from the gun. Two hundred volts shot through his body, jolting him rigid. He collapsed to the ground with a gasp. Ivor gave him an extra shock for good measure and then grabbed the man by his collar and pulled him into an alley around the side of the shop.

It took a little over a minute for the man to come round. He was obviously in good shape. Ivor could not see his face, no matter how hard he looked. Just the eyes were visible, blinking slowly. It had a sickening effect on him. What the hell had they done to him?

'Who are you?' Ivor hissed at him, brandishing the stun-gun, which was still wired to the man's body. 'Who are you working for?'

There was no way of telling what expression the man was wearing, but his voice said it all.

'I don't know what you're talking about,' he grunted, his eyes staring up at Ivor. 'You just attacked me for no reason. I have no idea who you are.'

The words were clear enough, but it was how he said them that rattled Ivor. He was far too calm. It was as if he was lying without any attempt to make it convincing. There was no fear or confusion or outrage in his voice, as there should have been if he were telling the truth. But there was an edge to it; one that implied that he was in control of this situation, and not Ivor. To persuade him otherwise, Ivor punched him where his nose should have been. He felt a satisfying crack.

'I'm going to ask you one more time,' he snarled. 'Then I'm going to keep triggering this thing until the battery runs out, you get me? Who are you? Who are you working for?'

'This is all in your head,' the man told him. 'You're having a nightmare you can't wake up from because you *are* awake. You need help, Ivor. And we can give you that help.'

Something big and heavy piled into Ivor from behind, knocking the wind from him as he slammed into the damp, uneven ground. His face scraped across gravel. His right arm was pinned behind his back and the stun-gun was wrenched from his grip. He kicked out, catching somebody's shin and knocking them off-balance enough to weaken their hold on his right arm so he could twist his left hand into his pocket and seize the steel bar hidden there.

Two hard blows hit him on the side of the head. A memory exploded in his mind: a white tiled wall and floor. A few drops of blood close to his face. There was shouting, the smell of rubber, vomit as well as antiseptic, bleach and other chemicals. The door – he had to make it to the door.

Then he was back in the alley again. He swung the steel bar behind him with all his might and connected with something that felt like an elbow. There was a cry of pain and he kicked and lashed with all four limbs until he was able to struggle onto his feet. There were two of them – the one he'd caught and another taller, leaner one with darker skin. He could not see their faces. In the dim light of the alley, he took in as much as he could: their size, their colour, their hair, their clothes. It was vital he remembered every detail of this encounter. This was his enemy. As his hand gripped the bar, feeling the reassuring solidity of its weight, Ivor was struck with an overwhelming need to hang on to at least one of them. He would kill one if he had to. Anything to hold on to them – to prove they were real.

They were only a few paces away. The taller one reached into his jacket and Ivor screamed, charging towards him. He saw the gun with its silencer in the instant before he brought the bar down on the man's outstretched arm. The man let out a squeal as his forearm broke, but Ivor hit him again, knocking aside the other arm as it came up to fend him off. The third and fourth blows hit the man on his shoulder and head. He fell back heavily, hitting the ground with a meaty thud. He didn't move again. Ivor was tripping over him in his haste to reach the other one. This one already had his gun out. He looked in pain, but he was still lifting the weapon to aim.

The first hurried shot went wide, the crack of the bullet off the wall behind Ivor louder than the shot itself. The second shot took him in the side, but by then he was within reach, swinging the dumb-bell bar over the man's arm and into the side of his face. He shrieked in triumph as he watched the man fall, everything in slow motion, slowing . . . slowing . . . slowing . . .

He woke up to the sound of sirens. There was movement around him, under him, through him. His eyes opened, looking up at the roof of a small room. No. A van, or bus. No. An ambulance. Of course – the sirens. A face blocked out some of the harsh light as it leaned over him. The expression gave him some comfort, the professional concern of a paramedic. The man's hand gripped his.

'Yuh gowna be awight, mate,' the man said. 'Stay still, yeah? Yuh got a wound in yo' side. What was it mate? Gunshot, was it?'

'The other two,' Ivor gasped. 'Where are they? The other two who were there.'

'It was just you, mate,' the paramedic said. 'Was someone wiv you? Two of 'em yuh say? We'll have the bill check the area. You was alone when we found yaw.'

Ivor's head sank back and he closed his eyes. He could feel a wobble in his teeth where his ceramic implant had been knocked loose. The tooth he had lost in Sinnostan. His tongue prodded at it. Shouldn't really do that, he thought, I'll have to get that fixed. He pushed at it again – he couldn't help himself. The man was asking him questions. Did he have any medical condition? Could he squeeze his hand? Could he feel that? Could he . . .

It was a relief give in to the nothingness.

Chi switched on the twenty-four-hour news channel in a window on his desktop, in time to see a clip of Nexus being led out of the door of his warehouse by two uniformed police, and into the back of a waiting police car. One of the officers put his hand protectively over Nex's head as he got into the car. Chi snorted miserably; they had to be sure he didn't pick up any bruises on the way to the station. In the band along the bottom of the screen, other headlines scrolled across, telling of more bombings in Sinnostan. The female newsreader was already narrating the story of Nex's arrest:

'. . . David Fogarty, who calls himself "Nexus", is thought to have stolen hundreds of thousands of pounds, possibly millions, from several high-street banks over the past four years. Detectives are still piecing together the full extent of his activities. Using a program that removed only a few pounds from each of hundreds of accounts each week, Fogarty quietly gathered a small fortune that police say was intended to fund terrorist operations. Fogarty was an active member of Live Action, the banned animal rights group . . .'

Chi shook his head in amazement. Nexus had been to a few animal rights protests at a guinea pig farm, but he'd never done anything more than shake a banner and shout slogans. And as for robbing banks, he held himself above such materialistic hacks. Nexus was a truth-hound; he got his thrills from cracking secrets, not bank accounts. And banks did not publicize the fact that they'd been hacked into – it happened all the time, after all – they'd lose too many customers. Who'd want to keep their money in a place where it could be stolen over the phone lines?

For a moment, he wondered if Gierek had informed on him, but it was unlikely. The Pole had nothing but contempt for law enforcers; they were corrupt beneficiaries of the tax he refused to pay. No, Nexus had been brought down by someone on high. The last project he'd been working on had something to do with a bunch he called the Triumvirate – three mysterious figures he suspected of smuggling weapons into Sinnostan. Chi wondered if they were the ones who had set him up. Not that it really mattered now.

'Jesus, prison. The poor sod.'

Nexus would not be able to cope with prison. A small weed like him with no hard friends would be a plaything for the kind of predators that ruled behind bars. Nex had been bullied at school; he said it had been like living in hell. That would be nothing compared to the treatment he could look forward to inside. And, of course, he wouldn't be allowed within a mile of any computers. Chi wondered how long he would last and shuddered at the thought. He'd need money. The network would see that he had enough cash to get by.

And they would work to clear his name; for it could have been any one of them getting the knock at the door.

Chi checked his emails. There was one from Nexus. Like all their communications, it was encrypted with a key that only he and Nex shared. Chi hesitated for a moment, then opened it up and read it:

'Chi. They've rumbled me . . . Haven't time to get out. Watch the skies, my friend.

Nexus.'

Chi studied the line of text. It had seven full stops, one comma, two apostrophes and the letter 'n' appeared twice in lower case. 7 – 1– 2 – 2. Both he and Nex kept back-ups of certain files in safety deposit boxes. They each had a key to the other's box, but only part of the number needed to access them. They had arranged this simple code as a means of sending the missing numbers in case something happened to either one of them. It was vital that their work be carried on after their . . . retirement.

Undoing the screws holding on the round, hollow steel drawer handle, he pulled it off the front of the drawer and tipped a key out into his hand.

Chi sat back in his chair, running his hands through his hair. Roswell, his cat, jumped up into his lap and he stroked her back absent-mindedly.

'Hey, Ros.'

Nexus would get years for this. God help him, they'd make mincemeat of him in there.

'Stay safe, brother,' he said softly, gazing down at the key in his hand. 'We'll be thinking of you.'

O

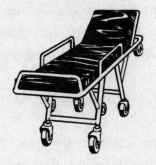

Amina meant to talk to her parents as soon as she got home, but she was intercepted by Tariq when she walked in the door. He had been thinking over her mind-control conspiracy and had come up with a theory of his own.

'School!' he exclaimed. 'They're trying to brainwash us at school!'

Amina arched her eyebrow at him, focusing the full glare of her intolerant-big-sister expression at him. But its effects on her little brother had been waning for some time. Tariq glared right back at her.

'No, I'm serious,' he insisted. 'You know the *MindFeed* software they've got us using? I'm sure there's ... y'know, like, subliminal stuff in there that's soaking into our brains. I'm telling you, they're up to something.'

Sweeping past him, she walked into the kitchen, where their father was cleaning his stripped-down automatic pistol. This Browning Hi-Power 9mm was his own weapon – press officers did not need to be issued with side arms, but Martin Mir believed in keeping his skills honed.

'Hi, Dad. Tariq thinks they're brainwashing him at school.'

'That's what school is for, love.'

When he had finished cleaning out the barrel with the long thin brush, he laid the components out on the cloth, pressed a button on his stopwatch and began assembling the weapon with practised ease. Slapping the thirteen-round magazine into place to finish the drill, he put the gun down and checked his time. He looked mildly pleased. He stripped it down to its parts and started again.

Tariq came into the kitchen looking sullen. His eyes were on his father, watching as the gun clicked together.

'Are you going to tell him, or not?' he asked Amina in a petulant tone.

She scowled at him. She'd prefer to do it in her own time, but maybe it was better to just get it all out in the open now. Martin put down the weapon and looked up from the table.

'Tell me what?'

'I need to talk to you and Mum,' Amina said reluctantly. 'It's about what I've been working on. I think I'm in over my head.'

Helena was called down and they all sat down in the living room. Amina got off to a faltering start, glancing constantly at her mother as she explained about meeting Ivor for the first time and how she had got more involved in the story from there. By the time she reached the point where she was describing the warning Ivor had found written on the ground, Martin had his head in his hands and Helena was staring at her far too intently for her liking.

Then she told them about the funeral card. When she took it out of her bag, Martin drew in a sharp breath. Helena did not say anything, she just took the card by its edge, so as not to smudge any fingerprints, and examined it closely.

'What in God's name were you thinking?' Martin asked, exasperated.

He always said 'God' – hardly ever 'Allah'. He had entered the military when it wasn't a good time to be a Muslim.

'I was doing my job!' Amina retorted. 'What would you expect me to do?'

'You're an office temp on a summer job!' her father barked at her. 'You're supposed to be making coffee and learning how to write! Who the hell are these people who've got you involved in this? I want to meet them . . . By God, I'll . . . I'll skin them alive! And what about your bosses at the paper? How much do they know about this? Do they know you've been threatened?'

'Well, that's the end of it,' Helena told her. 'You're not up to this, Amina – at least, not yet. You're too young, too inexperienced and you should have known better than to get mixed up with a bunch of cranks. Do you realize how you sound? You've let yourself be drawn into the delusions of some mentally disturbed veteran—'

'There not delusions and . . . and he's not disturbed!' Amina protested. 'I mean, he's a decent guy and if he is . . . if he's mixed up about anything it's because of what bloody Sinnostan has done to him!'

'You've taken these *delusions*,' her mother continued, 'and tangled all that up with some fruitcake's wild conspiracy theory for good measure. You need to step back and start seeing things clearly.

'If this threat is real – which I seriously doubt – you should have told us immediately. But I can't honestly believe somebody came into our house last night to leave a funeral card by your bed, honey. I just can't. The more time you spend with these kinds of schizos – and believe you me, I know their type well enough – the more you get infected with their mentality.'

She stood up.

'You should have filled Goldbloom in on this "investigation" before it went this far. I'm going to call him now, to ask him how he's let my daughter get duped like this while she's supposed to be in his care—'

'I'm not in anybody's bloody *care*!' Amina shouted back at her, lunging to her feet. 'And this is not a delusion! Goldbloom gave up his right to take over this story when he cut my article to shreds. But at least he still trusts my judgement enough to let me keep digging. This stuff is real, and I don't know where it's taking me, but I'm not going to let *you* get in the way, you domineering cow!'

'Amina!' Martin shouted. 'Amina, don't you dare speak to your mother that way!'

But she was already gone, storming from the room before she said something she'd really regret. Because at that moment, she felt nothing but burning hatred for her mother. The woman had put her career before her marriage and children all their lives; always travelling, missing birthdays and proud moments, staying too long in her study in the evenings and never remembering the names of their friends. She had been Amina's idol, but so rarely her mum. And now, when Amina had started to show the same qualities she admired in her mother, Helena had recoiled at her own reflection.

Now that she was in danger of having this story taken off her, Amina realized she couldn't bear to give it up. She had to see it through to the end . . . whatever that end might be.

Ivor couldn't tell if it was a real tooth or a ceramic implant. It depended on when this was happening. It shifted in the left side of his mouth whenever his tongue brushed against it. Once he had become aware of it, it was impossible not to probe at it, wiggle it. It was a real tooth, he decided. He wouldn't have the implant until later, when he was back in London. And it was clear he was still in Sinnostan.

He could see flashes of the future. In that future, he was lying in a hospital bed with a drip in his arm. He was dimly aware of a slight lump on his side, which he knew was the dressing covering the gunshot wound. That had been one of the Scalps men, before Ivor had hit the gunman with the bar from his dumb-bell. The ambulance had brought him here – he remembered part of that. But all of that was in the future; it would not happen for some time.

His tongue wiggled the tooth. The gum around it was sore, with a sharp pain sometimes when the pointed prong of the root brushed against a nerve in its socket. This was in a different hospital now. He couldn't remember how he had been brought here. In this hospital, he could not feel anything. Not his fingers or toes, nor anywhere on his limbs. There was no sensation of any kind throughout his body. Nor could he see or hear anything. That was worrying him. Despite all this, he knew he was in a hospital.

The order of things was mixed up in his head, confusing him. One thing he was sure of was the impact that had loosened his tooth – his real tooth, in the here and now, not the implant the watchers would knock loose in the future – so he went back to that moment. His real tooth had been loosened when his face hit a tiled floor. His arms were held behind his back so he couldn't catch himself as he fell; he couldn't protect his face. There was a soldier pinning his arms. The soldier's weight fell with him, on him, making the impact against the cold hard floor even worse. His ribs hurt and the breath was forced from his lungs.

The soldier was holding him down because he was out of his bed. Ivor had waited with his eyes closed until they came to undo the straps that held him. It was coming back to him now, but the order of things was mixed up. He saw the roulette wheel . . . No. That didn't happen yet, he told himself. He was confused. He had to remember things in the right order.

Go back to the start, before his tooth was knocked loose – in the first hospital. In Sinnostan.

He woke up in a bed in a room with seven other beds in it. There was a drip in his arm and a sensor on his forefinger. His arms and legs were bound, attached by straps to the bars on the side of the bed. Why had he been restrained? His thoughts were fuzzy, unclear even though he was waking up, and he recognized the feeling. Some kind of sedative – he had been drugged. The room had concrete walls painted hospital green. There were no windows. Each bed had a full intensive care set-up: a trolley with machines monitoring life-signs, oxygen tanks and masks, those vacuum tubes for sucking vomit out of the airway . . .

All the beds were occupied, but the men in them were unconscious – or at least they appeared to be. Ivor's head slowly cleared. Moving very slowly, he looked to one side and then the other. To his right was a door. It was closed. What was he doing here? Had he been hurt? His last memory was of that little village . . . Tarpan; a depressing little patch of life in the arsehole of nowhere. They'd gone there to report on a unit of para-troopers who were helping the locals rebuild an orphanage. He and Ben had gone out to find the orphanage, driven by a local guide. On the way, they had been stopped at an army checkpoint. Ivor had pulled out their identification and their orders . . . That was the last thing he remembered.

He didn't feel any pain, lying there in the hospital bed. Flexing his fingers and toes, he tensed and shifted his torso slightly from side to side. If he had been hurt, he couldn't detect it now. His breath quickened. Something was wrong here. Why had he been restrained? He raised his eyes to the ceiling. Big square air-conditioning vents breathed over the inert patients. The door opened suddenly and he closed his eyes, feigning unconsciousness. Whoever it was strode over to the bed opposite his. Two sets of footsteps.

'What's happening to this one?' a man's voice asked.

'Burns to the neck and torso,' another man replied. 'Supposed to look like an IED, I suppose.'

'Another messy one,' the first voice said wearily. 'All right, get him into the blast room. Have the OR ready. I'll do the touching up after lunch. And check the dosages on the others, I don't want any more wakers. Half these goddamned grunts are so pumped up on steroids or some other fix they're damn near impossible to keep under.'

'Yes, sir.'

Ivor listened to them, trying to make sense of

what he was hearing. It was almost as if the man they were talking about wasn't wounded yet, but was *about to be*. What was going on? They said it was supposed to look like an IED – an improvised explosive device, the insurgents' favourite weapon. It was what caused most of the injuries to Western troops in Sinnostan. His heart thudded against his ribs. He understood one thing: he wasn't supposed to be conscious. That wasn't a huge surprise; he'd been hooked on sleeping pills for a few months now – he'd knock back six or seven a night, sometimes more. Anything to sleep. His nerves had been on edge ever since he'd arrived in this goddamned country. The more pills he took, the higher his tolerance, and with a higher tolerance, a normal dose of sedative wouldn't keep him under. The pills were black market, of course, so they wouldn't know about his resistance to the sedative without tests.

More men came in, along with the squeaking wheels of a trolley; he heard the sounds of them removing the man from his bed – 'one, two, three and *up*' – the limp body flopping onto the trolley, its metal frame creaking slightly. He waited for them to leave and then pulled at his restraints. They didn't budge. He lay still and waited again, trying to suppress the waves of fear surging through him. This wasn't right. If he'd been wounded, he'd know about it by now. His head was clearer. There was no numbness in his body now; he had no sense that he had been given painkillers.

If he wasn't supposed to be awake, he would pretend to be unconscious. Until he knew what was happening, he needed to play every advantage he had. Ivor didn't know why they had been talking about that man's wounds in the future tense, but he wasn't going to wait here and find out. The door opened. He shut his eyes and lay still. Footsteps approached, stopping by his bed.

'What's this one down for?' a voice asked.

'Number twenty,' another answered. 'The right one, with minor shrapnel scarring.'

'Poor sod. Well, at least he's just losing the one. Right, let's get him in there.'

Hands started to undo the straps. Ivor remained limp. He had no idea how fast he'd be able to move after lying here for all this time, but he was going to get out of this bloody room if it killed him. The restraints were taken off. He hoped they would not look at the monitors, notice how fast his heart was going . . . The sensor was slipped off his finger and hands took him by the shoulders, hips and shins. There were at least three men . . .

'One, two, three – *up*!' one of them barked.

He was hoisted over onto the harder, flatter mattress of a trolley. A faint gasp escaped from his lips as he flopped down and he thought he'd given himself away, but they paid no attention. Unconscious bodies did that too, sometimes.

Someone leaned over him: he could sense the shadow on his closed eyelids and their breath on his face.

He heard the snap of the trolley's straps being unwound. Ivor opened his eyes and snatched at the head above him, seizing it by the hair with both hands. With all his might, he butted the man in the face. The drip tore from Ivor's arm, the wound spitting blood.

There was a second man by his feet and Ivor kicked him in the chest. With a strength born of terror, he sent the man sprawling across the floor. Ivor rolled off the side of the trolley, away from the third man, who grabbed him by the flimsy hospital tunic he was wearing. Ivor swung his elbow back into the man's teeth and tore himself free. The door. He had to make it to the door. His legs wobbled under him at first, but sheer desperation got him to the doorway. The men, who were dressed in order-lies' scrubs, were already coming after him. He slammed the door after him, nearly running into another trolley outside. Pulling it over, he kicked it back into the path of the orderly nearest him, knocking the man off his feet.

Ivor ran, his bare feet slapping over the

linoleum, his ripped tunic hanging open at the back. Whimpers slipped from his throat as he sprinted for a set of double doors ahead of him. A man in a soldier's uniform came through just as Ivor reached them and Ivor hit him with the flats of his hands, hurling the soldier back through the doors. Ivor brought his knees down hard on the man's chest, grabbed his head and banged it on the floor. The uniform had no insignia. Who was he with? A private security contractor? Special Forces? The soldier was wearing a side arm and Ivor yanked it from its holster, flicked off the safety, turned and aimed it straight at the chest of the man behind him. The orderly skidded to a halt, his two colleagues nearly running into him as he did so.

'Back off!' Ivor shrieked at them, his voice high and frantic. 'Lie down! Down on the floor!'

The men did as they were told; their faces were masks of restrained frustration. The soldier was on security detail; Ivor found one set of handcuffs on his belt and some plasticuffs in a pouch. He quickly bound the wrists of all four men, interlocking their arms so they were tangled together. Then he started running again. Behind him, the men were already shouting for help.

Reaching a crossroads in the corridor, he stopped, heaving in breaths. Which way? Jesus, which way? How did he get out of here? A normal hospital had signs in the corridors and hallways, labels on the doors. There was nothing here to tell him which way to go. To his right, a door opened at the end of that hallway. Ivor ran towards it as a man came out. Ivor lifted the gun, putting his fingers to his lips, demanding silence as the man's shock registered on his face. The man was dressed in pale blue surgeon's scrubs; he raised his hands in reflex when he saw the gun. Ivor seized him by the shoulder and spun him round, his arm around the surgeon's neck, pushing him back through the door, holding the gun to his temple.

There were two other men in the room and one woman, all dressed in scrubs. They stood up as Ivor barged in with his hostage. He looked around in bewilderment, not understanding what he saw.

It was a bizarre mix of a military strategic planning room and a doctor's consulting room. On two walls were physical and political maps of the various trouble spots in Sinnostan, as well as a table with a plasma display currently showing the region around Tarpan. There were a number of computer terminals and two free-standing transparent displays down the middle of the room. The tables were littered with reference books of different types. On the other side of the room were a number of easy chairs and couches, along with anatomy charts, pharmaceutical charts, a white board, wall-mounted light-boxes displaying X-rays as well as what looked like diagrams of different kinds of armaments: rifle and handgun ammunition, grenades, artillery shells, rockets, all accompanied by photos of the kinds of wounds they caused. Three cups of coffee stood incongruously on a low table between the couches.

'What the hell's going on?' Ivor wheezed. 'Who are you people?'

That was when he noticed the roulette wheel. Set into a dark wooden counter in the very centre of the room, it was so out of place he didn't realize what it was for a moment. But there was no mistaking it now that he stared at it. It was big; there were at least a hundred slots . . . no, he could see the number 101 from where he was standing. What was a roulette wheel doing in a hospital? Was this even a hospital at all?

Nobody had answered his question. There was an oriental man with slicked back hair and a goatee in front of him. The others were looking at him. He was probably in charge. Ivor pointed the gun at him.

'Who are you?' he demanded.

'I'm just a doctor,' the man replied calmly, his accent a mix of Chinese and American. 'I can see you're confused. That's just the medication – it's making you a bit addled, that's all. Why don't you put down the gun? You're scaring everybody. Nobody here is going to hurt you. You've been brought here for treatment. You're disoriented and you need to calm down. Please, put down the gun.'

'Treatment for what?' Ivor hissed at him, his tight grip on his hostage's neck causing the man to choke.

'Post-traumatic stress,' the doctor said in a gentle voice. 'Please put down the gun.'

'*Bullshit!*' Ivor snapped.

He caught the doctor's gaze flick over to the wall to his left and Ivor glanced round to see what he was looking at. There, on the wall, was another chart. It listed different types of injuries, each one assigned a number. The last number was 101. Ivor frowned, frantic thoughts racing through his mind. His eyes opened wide as realization came over him. Ivor got a glimpse of number twenty before he caught the doctor looking past him and spun round in time to fire a shot through the opening door behind him. A woman collapsed in the doorway, a flower of blood blooming through the shoulder of her pale blue tunic. The shot echoed down the corridor.

'How do I get out of here?' he snarled at his hostage, pressing the hot barrel of the gun against the man's temple.

'Agh! Out and to the right, but—'

Ivor shoved his hostage at the Chinese doctor and pulled the door open, jumping over the injured woman. He heard the clatter of running feet. An alarm sounded. Turning right at the junction, he sprinted for the double doors at the end. I just shot someone, he thought. What the hell is going on? Why did I just shoot that woman?

There was no time to wonder if what he'd done was right. He had seen number twenty. He knew what they were going to do to him, even if he didn't know why. What had the orderly said as they picked him up? 'At least he's just losing the one.' Ivor ran like he had never run before.

Slamming through the swing doors at the end of the corridor, he reached a T-junction. Finally, an exit sign to his left. The sound of hurrying footsteps behind him. He turned and put two shots through the door to slow them down. This weapon had eleven shots. He had eight left.

He reached the next door in seconds, pushing through it to a large, high-ceilinged vehicle bay beyond. Two military-style trucks and three APCs were parked there, but they were not army or marine vehicles. Who were these people? He could hear the thumping roar of a powerful helicopter outside the big steel shutter doors barring the exit to his right. No way out in that direction – besides, he couldn't afford to get caught in the open.

He heard shouting behind him. Another door led down a different corridor, one that looked like it might skirt the building, maybe to a quieter exit. Following it for fifty metres, he came to a steel service entrance. It was locked. The only other door led back into the building complex. Ivor panted for breath. Three men in security uniforms appeared at the bottom of the corridor. They moved like professionals. They were all carrying semi-automatic weapons.

Ivor shoved through the interior door and started running again. The corridor was cold and sterile, its walls and floors lined with white tiles that felt slippery under his feet. He didn't see the alcove to his left until it was too late. A heavy body hit him, driving him against the opposite wall as his right arm was skilfully twisted into a lock, pinning the gun against the wall. As he tried to resist, the man grabbed his other arm and the gun went off, shattering tiles and causing his attacker to flinch aside. They both fell forward, the soldier's weight on Ivor's. Ivor hit the ground with his arms locked behind him. His face struck the tiles, blasting a burst of pain across the left side of his head.

That was when his tooth came loose.

24

Then he was on a trolley, restraints on his wrists and ankles. They had given him a drug of some kind but he wasn't unconscious, just dulled. Number twenty, he thought. Jesus, aren't they even going to knock me out first? The lights of the corridor whirled by overhead, the glow seeming to drag from one fluorescent bulb to the next as if following him. He screamed. They paid no attention. He shrieked and kicked and thrashed around on the trolley, but it made no difference. His movements were weakened by the drug, his screams little more than whimpers. Nobody was paying attention to him, even if they did hear.

They had taken away his voice.

The sedative they had given him was too weak again, they were saying. They gave him another shot. Closing his eyes, he waited for unconsciousness.

It did not come. Were they going to operate on him like this? One of them noticed that Ivor's eyes were still opening from time to time. Someone else said it was nothing to worry about.

He was taken into a room lined with eight metal tanks. A breathing mask was fitted over his face, and clips attached to his twitching eyelids to keep them open. The clips dripped saline solution into his eyes – presumably to stop them drying out and obstructing his vision. There was something they wanted him to see. The mask was strapped on and he suffered a terrible feeling of claustrophobia. The sides of the mask covered his ears completely, blocking off his hearing. His senses were numbed, but he felt his restraints being removed and then he was lifted off the trolley and lowered face first into the tank. His wrists and ankles were slipped into sleeves of rubber, bound from four points each with what felt like soft bungee cords. Their grip was yielding but firm. He could move, but not enough to touch the walls of the tank, or even his own sides. His body was so numb he was barely aware of his own limbs.

He could hear his breath inside his head and smell the rubber edges of the mask, the faint scent of old sweat and some other, chemical odour. The rubber sleeves and a girdle around his waist supported him as the hands let go and water started to fill the tank. He wanted to scream again, but he was too weak. As the water covered his mask and he knew he was going to be able to breathe, he relaxed slightly. Then they covered the top of the tank and everything went black.

The sedative was wearing off. He could tell because he was able to count up to one hundred without losing track. His limbs still felt numb. There was no sensation but the sound of his breathing, the smells in the mask and the growing pain in his jaw. He knew why they had hung him face down; it was to stop his tongue slumping over his throat and suffocating him if he fell unconscious. The thought frightened him more than anything that had happened so far.

What were they doing to him?

He prodded at his loose tooth with his tongue and felt a dart of pain go through his jaw. Despite the discomfort, the feeling gave him relief. It was real, part of him. Something they hadn't taken away. As fear closed over him, he clung to the sound of his panicked breathing, the fading smells inside the mask and the pain in his gum caused by the roots of his tooth. He wiggled at it again – his friend, the pain.

Ivor screamed until his throat was raw. The noise did not stop. It seemed to go on for ever.

Sometimes the lights flashed into his eyes at the same time, sometimes the white noise deafened him so much he couldn't tell if the lights were strobing across his eyes or not. It was so loud he couldn't understand why his eardrums hadn't burst. With no sense of touch or smell or taste, his mind clutched at any sensation. Whenever the noise disappeared, he relished the silence. But not for long. Soon his ears ached for some kind of sound, anything to pull him out of the deaf, blind and empty void that his senses had become. Anything to tell him he was still alive.

The lights burned their way into his brain, making him feel sick with their pulsing. He retched, but there was nothing to throw up. But when they were gone, the glow scorched into his retina assured him that whatever else, he was not blind. Soon that would fade and he would strain his eyes for anything, anything to focus his mind on. He had heard of this kind of thing: torture that didn't leave a mark. It was mental conditioning, sensory deprivation, normally used for interrogations. But nobody was asking him any questions. Left alone, he had no idea how long he had been there, or whether he was going to be left there. Was anybody coming back for him? Were they going to leave him here to die? How much time had passed? It felt like weeks, but he would surely have died of thirst by then.

He screamed again, just to hear something. His throat was dry and painfully ragged, as if he'd been swallowing sand. He prodded his loose tooth with his tongue again. It was almost out, just hanging by a thread of flesh. There was a certain satisfaction in feeling it dangle on that strand of skin.

A film started playing on the glass of his mask. Some kind of heads-up display. It was a scene in Tarpan, what looked like a market.

'Ivor McMorris.' A man's calm voice spoke into his ears. Ivor was absurdly happy to hear another human being. 'You have been hurt. This is what happened to you. Listen carefully. This is what happened to you. You were filming in Tarpan when a bomb went off, injuring you and your colleague, Ben Considine.'

'No,' Ivor croaked. 'I don't know . . . I don't know what you're doing, but I know I wasn't hurt. You're lying and I'm not falling for it. Tell me what's . . . what's really going on here.'

The display disappeared. The white noise cut through him, roaring until his ears seemed like they would implode. He screeched until his voice gave out. Then there was complete silence. He waited: blind and deaf and senseless. His tongue pushed at his tooth. It almost came out and he pushed it back in again. Biting down, he felt the roots stab into the bottom of the socket. The strand of gum was so thin now, easy to break, but he just wiggled the tooth back and forth instead, saving the sensation for as long as possible.

The waiting seemed to go on for ever.

'Say something!' he rasped. 'What . . . What are you trying to do to me? I don't . . . I don't . . . I don't understand what's happening. What do you want?'

'I want to tell you what happened,' the man said gently. 'Listen carefully.'

The market scene in Tarpan reappeared. It was inter-cut with scenes of a bombing, but Ivor could tell that these shots were from a different place. As the pictures flicked back and forth, lights pulsed behind them and he started to find it hard to keep his thoughts coherent. The voice was gentle, soothing, almost hypnotic as it spoke to him. He stopped wiggling his tooth and listened more carefully. He started to recite the words as he was told.

'We were sent to the scene of a car bomb in a marketplace in the middle of the village. It was gruesome; the injured had already been rushed to hospital, but there were still a few charred corpses in the burnt-out cars around the site of the explosion. Men with hoses were washing the blood off the road and into the drains. We started filming, even though we knew the insurgents – or the resistance, whatever you want to call the bastards – had a nasty habit of launching follow-up attacks on the people and the soldiers who gathered around these bombsites . . .'

And the more Ivor heard of the story, the more it made sense. Of course this was what had happened. He couldn't believe he'd forgotten. Why had he been denying it? He should have trusted the voice sooner. Every now and then, he bit down too hard and the roots of his loose tooth dug into his gum, making him wince. When that happened, he had moments of doubt about what was happening – but they were just moments. He was comfortable here, listening to this man's voice telling him what was what.

The voice told him they were going to take him out of the tank. It told him he would not remember any of this. It continued talking to him as the top of the tank lifted off and light turned the water around him into white fire. He was lifted from the tank, the rigging taken off him, his eyelids sticky against his eyes after being held in place for so long. Clenching his eyes shut against the light, he was already forgetting what it had been like in there.

'He really hung in there,' someone said. 'That one took nearly six hours.'

'Well, he's done now,' another one replied, as

they started to ease him onto a trolley. 'Let's get him into the OR. Shang's going to throw a hissy fit if he misses dinner.'

Ivor retched, leaning over the tank, but nothing came out. The water was starting to drain away. He spat into it, and felt his tooth fall from his mouth. Watching it sink to the bottom of the tank, he wondered how it had come out. A minute later, as he was led out of the room, he had forgotten about the tooth. A few minutes after that, he had forgotten about the room.

17

Chi spent the Sunday morning online, catching up with his posse and trading information. He couldn't go and check Nexus's safety deposit box until the following morning, so he could only guess at what Nex had done to get himself nobbled. Although knowing Nexus, that could have been anything.

Chi finished up his online liaisons and then picked up Shang's book. Ros appeared and jumped onto his lap, curling up in the warmth as he read. Shang had led an extraordinary life, if you were to believe everything he wrote. This was difficult because he wrote with such opinionated smugness that you didn't *want* to believe anything he said.

His career in intelligence had begun while he was studying medicine in Boston, where he had been tasked with gathering information on bioengineering research at the world famous Massachusetts Institute of Technology. From there, he went on to study at Queen's University in Belfast, learning under some of the most experienced plastic surgeons in the world, who had honed their skills during nearly thirty years of the 'Troubles'. His Chinese masters had little interest in Northern Ireland, however, and once he qualified as a surgeon, he was persuaded to take a post in London, where he continued getting involved in research programmes and feeding the information back to his government.

Most of the beginning of the book, *Making Faces: How China's Leading Plastic Surgeon Became a Secret Weapon in the World of Espionage*, consisted of one boasted achievement after another. Shang's career went from strength to strength until the day he tried to carry out the world's first face transplant on a burns victim and it went horribly wrong. He was sued by the unfortunate patient, hounded by the media and ostracized by the medical establishment, accused of suffering from 'God Syndrome'. In the book, he described all this with suitable outrage and not a hint of remorse, pointing out that if he had succeeded he would have been hailed as a hero. He returned to China and built up a successful practice making the country's new generation of millionaires beautiful. Soon, he began working on key government figures too.

By late afternoon Chi was suffering from ego overload and in need of some food. His cooking skills did not extend much beyond putting a plastic container in the microwave or sticking a bread-crumbed something under the grill, and he felt like he should get some proper nutrition, so he decided to go out for dinner.

There were only a few places where Chi felt it was safe to eat. It would be all too easy for some-one to slip him some kind of drug in his food – a move that could lead to all sorts of compromising situations. One of these places was Kato's, a Japanese sashimi restaurant where you could choose dishes from a conveyor that glided around the oval-shaped counter. Chi made a point of picking dishes at random, just to be on the safe side.

Chi sat alone at one end of the counter, as he usually did, watching the other punters watch the chefs. There were a lot of couples, and he felt pangs of loneliness as he observed the little affectionate touches they shared, the way some pairs looked comfortable together, talking casually, while others were obviously new to each other, self-conscious and attentive. They all looked so blissfully unaware of the kind of world they were really living in.

Chi was not a typical conspiracy nerd. A

mixture of wealthy upbringing and cosmopolitan parents had given him the kind of social confidence sadly lacking in many of his comrades, and his journalism work meant he got enough chances to meet people. He had broken up with his last girlfriend a few months ago, for the usual reason: his obsession was too much for her. She told him he needed to get a life.

His thoughts turned to Amina. There was a girl who shared his obsessive nature, but he'd seen the way she had been looking at Ivor lately. It didn't really surprise him; Ivor had the appeal of being a more . . . *experienced* man, as well as having that sadness, that haunted quality that girls seemed to swoon over. It didn't hurt that he was loaded too, of course. None of this stopped Chi from daydreaming about her; a selfish part of him assured him that her attraction for Ivor would end the first time she saw him without his glass eye. The fact that she was a social girl and was probably surrounded by admirers did little to subdue Chi's fantasies.

By the time he left the restaurant, it was after eight and an overcast sky meant it was already quite dark. As he walked home, his eyes moved ceaselessly, ever watchful for anything suspicious. Once again, he felt lonely. He was tired of all this. There were times he wished he was unaware of all the games that were being played beyond the public eye. He could be living a much more peaceful life if only he'd grown up a little less suspicious.

It was his father's fault. Back when Chi was only ten and his parents were still together, his father – then only a talented programmer yet to make his fortune – had told him about a database he was debugging for the Royal Air Force. The information stored on it included UFO reports by air force pilots. There were hundreds of them. Chi's father, in direct violation of his contract and the Official Secrets Act, had brought a few of these reports home to show his son. After one night of reading, Chi was hooked. Four years later, he was able to hack into the systems at RAF Headquarters in High Wycombe and have a look around for himself.

Trudging along the road towards his house, Chi thought about those first reports he read, years ago. He could explain a lot of them now, having become something of an expert on the subject. Most UFOs were cases of mistaken identity, misinterpretation, hallucinations or drugs. But there were a few – a fraction of a percentage – that defied explanation no matter what way you looked at them. The RAF pilots' reports still impressed him the most. These were men and women who had to keep cool heads while flying at high speeds with jet engines roaring behind them. They were trained to observe and report accurately. They could identify the shapes of other aircraft, judge their speed and bearing, track them on radar – if possible – and even chase after them if they chose to. They were not given to making sensationalist claims. Most did not want to be associated with UFO sightings and were reluctant to call them in. Those were the reports that had changed Chi's life.

A movement near the roof of a house caught his eye and he looked up ... just in time to see something flicker out of sight behind the roof's gable. The sky was a gunmetal grey, mottled with black, and Chi stared for a minute or two, searching for the source of the movement. There was a line of trees silhouetted against the house lights from the next street and he was just about to turn away when he spotted something gliding along just beyond and below the tops of the trees. Then, in a sudden spiralling motion, it rose straight up into the sky and disappeared.

Chi stood motionless for some time, willing the thing to come back. Strangely, he felt inclined not to believe what he had just seen. He tried to rationalize it, to work out what ordinary, everyday sight he could have misinterpreted. After all, hadn't he just been thinking of UFOs? Was there some part of him that wanted to see one so badly it would twist his own perceptions to fool him? Had he been chasing shadows for so long he was actually starting to see them?

In a state of disappointed confusion, he made his way home.

It took some time to convince Ivor, once the sedative wore off, that he was in a normal, over-crowded, understaffed NHS accident and emergency ward and not some secret military installation. And even then, he insisted on hobbling outside to take a look around and satisfy himself that the doctors and nurses were telling the truth.

They were equally bemused by the fact that he was more concerned about the loss of a ceramic tooth implant than the danger that his glass eye might have been damaged, or indeed, the bullet wound in his side. There were two police officers waiting to take his statement – bullet wounds had to be reported – but they were forced to humour him first by escorting him to the exit while he carried out his confirmation of the staff's claims about their so-called hospital.

When he gave his statement, he kept it vague, being careful not to mention the fact that he had started the fight, or that the assailants' faces were invisible, saying instead that they had been wearing tights on their heads. The constables did not seem satisfied, but they took his details and said they'd be in touch if they had any more questions.

His wound had been dressed; the grazes down his face where it had hit the ground were too minor to need bandaging. One of the junior doctors – a round-faced Indian woman with a cute, gurgling voice – sat him down and asked to take a look at his glass eye and the eye socket, to ensure that the impact had not caused any damage. Ivor took the eye out, examined it carefully and declared that it was fine. With everything that was going on in his mind, the mash of images, memories and sensations, he found it hard to concentrate on what the woman was saying:

'Sorry, what?'

'Can you hold back the lids for me, so I can have a look inside?'

'Oh, right.'

Ivor obliged, pulling the lids open so the doctor could point the light of her examination lens into the socket. She rotated the light from one side to the other, tilting it to examine the roof and floor of the empty hollow in Ivor's head. She frowned and leaned in closer.

'There doesn't seem to be any recent damage,' she told him. 'And there's no sign of infection. But there's a mark here that looks a bit odd to me. It could just be part of the original scarring, but . . .'

Grabbing a piece of paper and a pen, she drew

something on it. Then she stared at her own drawing for a minute.

'It looks almost like . . . Hang on a second.' She called over to another doctor on the far side of the room, an oriental man who looked about fifteen and had a haircut that would have looked more appropriate on a skateboarder. 'Joe? Can you have a look at this for me?'

'Anything for you, Immy,' he replied with mock gusto as he came over. 'What's up?'

'Does this look like a Chinese character to you?'

He studied the drawing for a moment.

'Could be. Could be,' he mused. 'It's hard to tell – your penmanship sucks, baby. Where'd you get it?'

'It's in here,' Ivor told him, pointing towards his empty socket.

Joe picked up the examination lens and peered into the socket.

'Yeah,' he chuckled. 'That's the weirdest thing. Like seeing Christ's face on a mossy wall, huh? It's a word all right. Could mean a few things, but . . .'

'Does it say "Shang"?' Ivor asked.

Joe leaned back, lowering the lens.

'Yeah. That's what it could be. How did you know?'

Ivor thought about what the Filipino nurse had heard Shang saying once, some time ago: 'It's nice to know they'll all be taking a little bit of China back home with them.' Ivor shook his head at the arrogance of the man.

'The bastard signs his work,' he said.

31

'It was Monday morning, and Amina sat in abject misery while Goldbloom listened to all of her recordings and read her notes. His face was impassive, but she knew her mother had been on to him and Amina doubted it had been a pleasant phone call.

'This was supposed to be a mental health piece,' he said at last.

'I followed it where it led,' she replied.

'Following doesn't mean going around with your eyes closed,' he snapped. 'You've got nothing here except conjecture and wild leaps of imagination. You can't print anything without some kind of evidence and—'

'That's why I didn't want to show it to you!' Amina retorted. 'I *know* it's not ready.'

'I rang some of my contacts in the Ministry of

Defence this morning,' Goldbloom told her. 'I asked them if the army or the intelligence services had ever carried out mind control experiments and they *laughed*. They laughed! You see, it's not that nobody's tried it – hell, everybody's tried it in one form or other – it's just that it never works. It's the stuff of movies and spy novels and conspiracy theories.'

This was becoming a sensitive subject for Amina. She was starting to worry that even if she did find some evidence to back up Ivor's suspicions, nobody would believe it because of Chi's fanatical conspiracy network. If their story got lumped together with the likes of Area 51 or the Princess Diana 'assassination', it would never make it to print. She'd have to talk to Chi and Ivor about that.

'So you asked them and they said "no" and you're leaving it at that, are you?' Amina snorted. 'Whatever happened to investigating a story?'

'Don't take that tone with me, girl. You're on thin ice as it is.'

'Did Mum tell you about the funeral card?'

'Yes, and she doesn't believe for a second that it's for real. We've run into the likes of Chi Sandwith before. They have a tendency to get a bit caught up in their own stories.'

'It was left in my room while I *slept*,' Amina said through gritted teeth.

'And you couldn't have picked it up somewhere by mistake and dropped it there somehow? Somebody couldn't have slipped it into your bag, or into your pocket, without you seeing? You need to keep your wits about you in this game, Amina. There's a lot of sharks out there looking to pull a fast one on an inexperienced young girl.'

Amina bridled at his tone. Could he have been any more patronizing?

'I'm handing this story on to Rob. He'll follow up your leads and see where they take him, but I promise you this is all going to turn out to be the ravings of a few would-be mental patients. I'll make sure he keeps you informed — you've put a lot of work into this and you'll get a byline if it ever goes to print.'

Amina scowled. Rob wasn't much older than her, and he'd be too precious with his new brief to let her get involved. Now, on top of the humiliation of having an investigation taken off her, she'd have to put up with him lording it over her in his wideboy way.

This wasn't the end of it. She would call Ivor this afternoon. There was no way she was going to be left out of this now.

'And don't think you're going to go it alone,' Goldbloom said, reading her thoughts. 'You're back on office duty full-time. If I catch you posing as a

Chronicle reporter to anyone, you're out of a job, d'you understand me?'

She glared at the floor, grinding her teeth.

'Yes,' she said. 'I understand.'

Despite Goldbloom's insistence that she return to her role of office temp, Amina discovered there was a lull in the need for coffee, photocopies or typing, so she was left to her own devices. She used the time to go back over the archives on the server, searching for stories on Sinnostan or any mention of Anthony Shang. There was a review of his book in a back-issue of the *Sunday Literary Supplement*: 'A self-satisfied, conceited and barely believable trip through the memoirs of one of this century's leading surgeons. Compulsive but cringe-inducing reading.'

There was also an article on his 'defection' to Britain, eleven years before. He had flown to London for a conference and then refused to go back. He claimed that the Chinese had tried to have him assassinated on a number of occasions, because of the sensitive information he had gained through his contacts with his nation's leaders. Apparently, he had only escaped these murderous attempts through sheer cunning. The Chinese had claimed he was a fantasist and naturally dismissed his claims as hogwash. Shang had gone into hiding and it was rumoured that he was now working with British intelligence.

British intelligence? She sat back, staring at the screen. Amina remembered how the police had handed round Shang's name and photo to all the reporters in the paper, claiming he was a terrorist – some kind of bio-weapons expert. She wondered why nobody had recalled this article. Had they just forgotten, or were they inclined to believe the police over their own sources? If Shang had been working for British intelligence, could they be involved in whatever was going on in Sinnostan? Maybe some secretive little branch with their own agenda? Then, if the police were looking for Shang because the intelligence services were saying he was a terrorist . . . Amina tilted her head up and gazed up at the ceiling. Had Shang done a runner? Maybe he had and they were afraid he'd talk. He could be thinking about writing another book.

But what she couldn't understand was why nobody else had picked up on this gap between his old story and the police's new one. Anybody could find out what she'd just discovered. Of course, they'd have to be looking—

A two-inch-thick document slammed down on the desk, making her jump. Marie, one of the crime correspondents, was standing over her. She was a curiously asexual woman, with a short practical haircut, no make-up and a rumpled blue suit that hid her shape. Like many reporters, she always looked like she needed more sleep.

'Sorry, did I wake you?' she said, smiling. 'Copy that for me, Amina? Drop two copies in to editorial and one into legal?'

Amina got a lot of that. A command with a question mark tagged on the end to be polite. She nodded and picked up the document.

'Quick as you can, thanks!' Marie grinned again as she walked away.

Ten minutes later, Amina was wrestling with the photocopier again. A page had got lost inside the machine. It seemed to have completely disappeared. The symbol on the little screen told her there was a paper jam, but it refused to tell her where. After a careful look inside the machine, she tried to switch it off and switch it back on again. The copier politely reminded her about the paper jam, reiterating its point that it could not work until its insides were sorted out.

Sitting on the floor, she braced her feet against the wall and heaved the machine out far enough to allow her to reach behind it and pull out the plug. Then, after waiting a few seconds to ensure that the last dregs of electricity had drained from the machine, she opened the copier and began feeling around between the heavy, finger-mashing rollers.

Amina was so absorbed in what she was doing

that it took her a minute or two to notice what was going on in the newsroom outside. The place was erupting into activity. She leaned out of the door and looked around. Everyone was on their feet, grabbing jackets, notebooks, recorders and cameras and making for the doors. Goldbloom and a couple of the other editors were shouting orders.

'Amina, I have to go to Heathrow,' Marie called to her, stuffing a bottle of water into her bag. 'Can you do something for me?'

'Eh, sure. What's going on?'

'Terrorist alert. There's been some kind of threat reported against the airports. The army's surrounding them all – big bloody tanks and armoured cars and everything. Goldbloom wants everyone to drop what they're doing and get out and see what's going on, but I promised this old woman I'd see her today. It's just a small story, but she's a sweet old bird and I've cancelled on her twice already. Here are the details.' She handed Amina a piece of paper. 'Apologize for me, yeah? I'll give you a byline, OK? See ya!'

And with that, she was gone. Amina looked down at the sheet of paper. Goldbloom had made it clear she wasn't to do any reporting, but this hardly counted. It wasn't to do with her own story and anyway, she was covering for Marie at her request. It would be a shame to let the old lady down.

Amina turned her back on the photocopy room, put on her jacket and picked up her bag. She scribbled a note explaining where she had gone and left it on the desk she'd been working at. It would be a good idea to check with Goldbloom, but he might say no, and anyway, the woman didn't live too far away. The newsroom was almost completely empty. Amina should be back before anybody noticed she was missing. She hurried out, biting back a smile.

After Chi and the clerk used their dual keys to open the safety deposit box, the clerk pulled out the drawer, leaving the lid closed. She took Chi into a small room and left him alone to open the drawer, which was about the size of a box of A3 photocopy paper. He watched her close the door before lifting the lid.

As he expected, the box was full of disks. Nexus's back-ups. Here was what he called 'the Essentials Collection' – all of the most important, most sensitive information he had gathered, along with the theories he was putting together on the various plots he was intent on cracking. To Chi's surprise, there was also a Ready-to-Go mobile phone and a disguise kit filled with wigs, different kinds of facial hair, make-up and even contact lenses for changing eye colour. Tucked into a pocket in this kit were a couple of false passports with credit cards in the same names, some cash in pounds, euros and dollars and a small can of Mace pepper spray. Chi would have expected to find a gun among all this fugitive paraphernalia, but that wasn't Nex's style. Deep down, he was a gentle soul.

Chi put everything into his backpack, slipping the Mace into his pocket, and was about to close the lid when he paused. There was a certain finality in the act, as if by committing it, he was taking over Nex's life. He grimaced and clicked the lid shut.

His mobile rang as he left the bank and he lifted it to his ear.

'Hi, it's Ivor. We need to meet up.'

'Fine. My place in an hour.'

'See you then.'

'Bye.'

Chi hung up. It was best to keep phone calls short and mobile calls even shorter. So much for keeping their distance. Chi wondered what had prompted Ivor to break their short-lived silence.

3

Mrs Hilary Atkinson seemed to suffer from abysmally bad luck, as Amina was soon to discover. And being mugged wasn't the half of it. When she answered the door of her maisonette – a well-tended little seventies affair with window boxes on the ledges and hanging plants on either side of the door – she was squinting out through a black eye that wouldn't have looked out of place after a heavyweight title fight. The black was fading into a purple, its stain of yellow spreading well beyond the main lump. Amina almost winced when she saw it.

'The swellin's gone down a bi' now,' Mrs Atkinson said, spotting Amina's reaction. 'Me 'ead woz the size of a wa'ermelon las' week. I woz chewin' parace'amol like they was Smar'ies. If my son ever gets 'is 'ands on the little snots who done this, they'll wish they was never born, I tell yah. You Marie then?'

'My name's Amina, Amina Mir. I'm afraid Marie couldn't make it because of the alerts at the airport, but she asked me to come in her place. I'd very much like to hear your story, Mrs Atkinson.'

'Right then. Come on in. Kettle's on.'

The house was comfortable in a worn, old-fashioned way that would have reminded half the adults in the country of their mother's place. Bad watercolours of birds hung in the hall; in the sitting room were pictures of children or grandchildren, and over the fireplace, a picture in a laminated frame of two cockerels woven out of some kind of fabric. The furniture was old but well cared for, and the ornately patterned carpets and wallpaper could not have been bought in this country in the last twenty years.

'The muggin' was just the icin' on the cake, really,' Mrs Atkinson began as soon as they sat down to a tray of tea and biscuits and a mineral water for Amina. 'Those kids've bin actin' up for the last couple o' years. Most of it was just mischief to start wiv; smashin' windahs or lettin' air out of people's tyres an' all 'at. Y'know, just playin' up. But lately it's bin gettin' worse. I woz onto the bill abou' 'em, but they're just too busy wha' wiv all the drug dealers and people smugglers an' the terrorists an 'at. My sister's eldest, Jimmy – lovely boy – is a copper, an' he spends all 'is time fillin' out bleedin' forms. I ask yah, is 'at wha' it's all abou'?'

Amina shook her head. She should have asked Mrs Atkinson questions to keep her focused, but found she was enjoying the old woman's banter.

'So I was walkin' along the alley, and I sees these two li'l snots comin' towards me. An' I knows I'm in trouble, 'cos they're the same two who smashed all me garden gnomes last year and Mary-across-the-road says they're bad seeds and they're sproutin' into right li'l villains and them not even sixteen. They did 'er gnomes an' all, an' I'm sure they was the ones who set fire to me shed in the winter just gone. Li'l snots! Mind you, it was the warmest I got that winter, what with the pittance they giv yah for fuel allowance these days. My next-door neighbour froze to death a year ago! Can you believe 'at? *Hypothermia* they call it, but it's a fancy word for *freezin'* to death if y'ask me. Who'd a thought it in this day and age? Sometimes I shiver so much me dentures sound like a pair of wood-peckers goin' at it!'

Amina resisted the urge to look at her watch. She took a sip of water and continued to listen, letting the old dear get to the point in her own good time.

'Mind you, the 'eat can be as bad! Y'know how many people died in the 'eatwave last year? Nearly three thousand! Know how many were killed by terrorists? None. But you didn't see the army out surroundin' old people's 'ouses and fannin' 'em to keep 'em cool, did yah? Hear all the politicians on the radio talkin' about keepin' us safe? Y'know what would keep me safe? *Air conditionin'*!'

She stopped long enough to take a sip of her tea. Amina knew there would be very few people in the world who would be allowed to make Mrs Atkinson tea using that teapot. It would have to be done just so.

'So I'm in the alley and I can see the two li'l snots comin' towards me. And it's only about seven in the evenin' but it's already dark under the trees and the council's been promisin' to put lights on 'at path ever since my *brother* was mugged there two years previous, but of course they 'aven't. So then . . . sure you won't 'ave some tea, love?'

'No, thanks,' Amina replied with a polite smile.

'Suit yourself. Never saw the appeal in drinkin' plain wa'er meself. So then, these two boys come up – 'oods up, you know the way – and they ask me if I 'ave any fags and I tell 'em I don't. I gave 'em up after I caught pneumonia a few years ago.

'So then they laugh and ask me for me 'andbag. And I tell 'em they're not 'avin' it.'

Mrs Atkinson took a sip of her tea, her hand shaking only slightly.

'And . . and then they started 'ittin' me. Really 'ard, like, and I'm on the ground in no time and they're *kickin'* me. Then one o' the li'l snots stops and takes out 'is phone – y'know the ones with the cameras?'

Amina nodded, swallowing as she felt her throat tighten.

'An' 'e *films* it!' Mrs Atkinson's voice shook. 'It was the last thing I saw – 'im lookin' at me on the . . . the . . . the li'l screen on 'is phone an' gigglin' away to 'isself.'

She didn't cry, but Amina could see the effort it was taking to hold it in.

'And they were arrested?' she prompted gently. 'You told Marie that the police picked the two boys up the following day?'

'Course they did,' the old lady quavered. 'Kids 'adn't a brain between 'em. Tried to use me pension book, didn't they? Said they were collectin' it for their granny. Idiots. As if that pension's worth a damn anyway, since the fund collapsed. Know what the li'l snots said when they were nicked?'

She sniffed and then started laughing –

high-pitched, almost hysterical laughter, and Amina didn't know whether to smile or not.

'You know wha' . . . ha-ha-ha . . . wha' they said? They . . ha-ha . . . they said, "Wasn't our fault! We're just products of the system. We never 'ad a chance!"'

Her laughter stopped abruptly, and an expression of what could have been pity settled on her features.

'Still, it could be worse, I suppose. Not every-one's 'ad my good fortune. You seen those ol' dears livin' in their bombed-out ruins in Sinnostan? Gawd love 'em. Some people have the worst luck.'

Biology was taught on *MindFeed* using a shoot-'em-up game. You had to name the parts of the body as you blasted them. There was an alternative that taught the science using first aid instead, if you weren't of the trigger-happy mentality. Tariq went straight for the guns.

The enemy soldiers came thick and fast and the crosshairs could pick out chinks in their body armour, but you had to choose the name of the body part from a drop-down list. Tariq was among the best in the class at this and he was revelling in his new-found expertise. His hands danced nimbly across the keyboard, blasting one target after another. He wished he had a proper cordless controller handset like he had at home, but the school's computers weren't set up for games . . . yet. If there was one thing he knew about the military, it was that they knew how to spend money on hardware.

His hair was long enough, with his shirt collar turned up, to hide his earphones. As he gunned his way through the virtual city street, Absent Conscience thudded in his ears.

'*You said I was your guiding star/But I'll be daylight to your vampire's heart/Say you love me while you suck me dry/So I'll burn your soul and your poisoned lies . . .*'

Tariq finished his game and got ready to start a new one. First he had to do the hand-to-eye co-ordination test, tapping the arrow buttons as the two squares on the screen flashed up alternate lights and patterns. He turned off the music because he couldn't concentrate enough with it on. There was a sound element to the test now too; a beep you had to react to whenever you heard it.

He had just completed the test when he heard cackling from a group of the guys at the other end of the room. There were thirty terminals in four rows, but some of the others were empty as Noble and his mates had gathered around a single screen. Lieutenant Scott was not in today. Mr Quinn, the

Biology teacher, was sitting at a desk by the door, engrossed in a science magazine. Unlike some of the other teachers, he did not resent the intrusion of this military project into the school curriculum. As far as he was concerned, the less time he had to spend trying to drum facts into the heads of obtuse students the better.

There was more cackling, and Tariq caught a few sidelong glances his way. It was smarter just to ignore them, but he put his game on pause and stood up.

'Can I go to the toilet, sir?' he asked the teacher.

'Mm-hmm,' Quinn replied without looking up.

Tariq walked towards the door, passing the gang of four boys crowding round Noble's terminal as he did. He stopped when he saw what was on the screen.

Now he knew why they had held him down a few days ago and taken his picture with their phones. The enemy soldiers charging towards them on the screen all wore Tariq's face. They even had a grimacing one for when the shots struck. Noble was proving to be an apt student of Biology, blasting away one Tariq after another. The boys gave an extra cheer when any of the charging figures were hit in the face.

Tariq watched from behind them, completely unnoticed. Suddenly, he really did need to go to the toilet. Suddenly, he needed to be on his own. His breath rasped through gritted teeth as he walked down the corridor.

23

Chi got home not long before Ivor was due. He went through his normal routine of sweeping the place for bugs, then laid out a bowl of food for Roswell, whistling to her to come in from the garden. She sauntered through the cat-flap and brushed back and forth between his legs, indicating that she would eat when she was good and ready. He loved her contemptuous manner.

The terror alert at the London airports was all over the news. The rumour was that the authorities had picked up email traffic about a possible attack on planes landing or taking off around the city. A simple surface-to-air missile fired from the shoulder could bring down any commercial airliner. The airports had been surrounded by troops, tanks and armoured cars. Helicopter gunships swooped overhead. Nobody was quite sure what all this heavy armour was supposed to achieve, but it was an intimidating sight.

Chi watched the reports on his PC as he waited for Ivor. A correspondent was describing the frustration of the people trapped in the airports until their planes could be given clearance to take off, when the doorbell rang. Chi kept one ear on the television as he went out into the hall, punched a code into the alarm and opened the door to let Ivor in. But one look at his guest's face made him forget the news broadcast.

'I need you to turn that off,' Ivor told him, as they walked into the study. 'There's something you're going to want to hear.'

And then Ivor began to relate the flashback he had experienced in the hospital. Chi listened in rapt fascination as the story unwound – about Ivor waking up in the military hospital, escaping from the orderlies and finding himself in the medical/strategy room, surrounded by surgical staff. As Ivor told of his recapture and the patchy memories he had of the hours of conditioning in the isolation tank, Chi could not hide the smile that crept across his face.

'And all because you lost a tooth they didn't know about,' he chuckled. 'Bloody hell, Ivor. This blows this thing wide open! And you're sure you saw Shang?'

'It's hard to be certain.' Ivor shrugged. 'Maybe my mind was just putting his face there, 'cos it fitted . . . I don't know. But I'm pretty sure all of this is what got buried under the false memories. It's all still a bit woolly. I don't know what I was doing there, or what the story was with the roulette wheel.'

'Shang's a roulette fiend – he spends a fortune on it,' Chi replied. 'It's in his book.'

'OK, but what . . .' Ivor's fingers went unconsciously to his right eye. 'What's it all for? Jesus, you don't think I was a stake in some kind of twisted casino gig, do you? That's all I need: I lose my eye 'cos some rich old fart was using me as a gambling chip.'

'I don't know,' Chi said, lost in thought. 'It's hard to be sure, but like I said before, it's one of two things. Either they're brainwashing you to make you *forget* something, or to make you *do* something. I'm still trying to figure out the UFO angle in all of this—'

'Oh, for God's sake, Chi!' Ivor snapped, suddenly losing his patience. 'When are you ever going to give up on that crap? Get serious, will you! We're not living in the bloody *X-Files* here.'

Chi glared back at him for a moment, saying nothing. If Ivor wanted to see 'serious', then maybe it was time to show him. Chi hadn't trusted anybody but Nexus with knowledge of his prize possession, but this was as good a time as any to test it on Ivor.

'Stay here,' Chi said. 'I'll be back in a minute.'

Striding out into the kitchen, he knelt down and opened the pots cupboard. Taped into the lid of an old coffee percolator was Gierek's badge. The real one. The badge Chi had given him had been a copy. It wasn't difficult: the badge was simply a blank chrome-plated disc about five centimetres in diameter with a safety pin set into the back. Chi pinned it onto the right breast of his black MEGADETH T-shirt and walked back into the study.

Ivor was watching the news on the computer screen and did not look up immediately. When he did, his first response was one of utter shock. His second reaction was a wild punch that caught Chi on the cheek and knocked him back against the doorframe. Ivor hit him again, nearly dislocating his jaw. Two more blows landed before Chi could pull the badge off his T-shirt and hold up his hands.

'Stop! Agh! Stop! It's just me! Let me explain!'

Ivor grabbed him by his hair and dragged him across to the desk. There was a letter opener in a cup with some pens and Ivor seized it and pressed the point against Chi's throat.

'It better be a *good* explanation. If you're one of them . . .'

He didn't finish the threat. He didn't have to.

'I'm not, all right?' Chi protested, holding up the metal disc. 'It's the badge. Gierek caught one of his watchers once and pulled this off his jacket. This is what's making you see . . . what you're seeing.'

Ivor looked at the chrome badge as if he'd only just noticed it. He took it off Chi and held it up to the light. He was wincing and pressing his hand against his side as if he was in pain, but he didn't say anything about it. Looking back at Chi's face, he frowned in thought.

'What did you see?' Chi asked, with a hungry expression.

'Your face . . . it was blank. I could only see your eyes. It was like you were one of the Scalps.'

'It's the badge,' Chi said breathlessly. 'I think it may be alien technology. It looks innocent enough – there's no visible circuitry, or . . . or transmitter – even under a microscope – but it's definitely sending out some kind of signal. I think anybody who's been through the same process as you can pick up that signal – maybe they've put an implant in your brain that can read it – and it makes you unable to see the face of someone wearing this badge. It's like it gives you a blind spot. To anybody else, it just looks like a blank chrome disc.'

Ivor was still staring at the object with a mixture of amazement and confusion.

'What if it's much simpler than that?' he said softly. 'I couldn't see the badge when you were wearing it. What if I've just been programmed with some kind of post-hypnotic suggestion? When I see the badge, I'm supposed to block out the person's face and the badge itself.'

Chi opened and closed his mouth like a gold-fish for a moment, his heart sinking.

'I never thought of that,' he admitted. 'Damn. Damn, I thought I finally had some proof that there was something out there.'

'You have,' Ivor replied, pinning the badge back on Chi's chest and regarding him with an unsettled expression. 'You've proof that somebody out there's been messing with my head. I . . . I can't see your face, man. This is scaring the shit out of me. But why would anybody do this? I mean, I can't tell who you are, but I can see you've got no face! It's not exactly subtle.'

'Maybe that's part of the plan,' Chi sniffed. 'Creating a myth. Can I take this off now? You're looking at me funny.'

'Huh! Look who's talkin'.'

Amina's mind was whirling when she returned to the newsroom. The place was quiet; only a few people were at their desks. Everybody was still out covering the alert at the airports. She wondered how many other stories like Mrs Atkinson's weren't getting written today because of the terrorist alerts. Then she wondered how often this happened. She remembered what Ivor had said: 'War is loud. If you want to distract people's attention from something, there's nothing better than a bit of death and glory.'

She wished she could call him up – just chat to him. There was so much to talk about and her friends would never understand. They wouldn't even believe half of it. It was a lonely feeling.

The War for Liberty made the news in some form every day. It was big, scary and affected everyone. Their very way of life was under threat, or so they were always being told. The terrorists were out to get the people of Britain simply because they were trying to impose peace on some of the most troubled regions in the world. The more she thought about it, the more it seemed like the plot of some Hollywood action thriller – evil villains with paper-thin motives of world domination threatening the peace-loving democracy. She thought about Mrs Atkinson again and how her story had been eclipsed by a bolder life-and-death drama and asked herself what other stories were being blotted out.

Chi had said Ivor's brainwashing had to have one of two purposes: to cover up something that he had seen or done, or to programme him to carry out some task at some point in the future. But what if he was only partly right? What if the cover-up was still going on? Maybe the whole war was a diversion to hide something that was going on in Sinnostan?

Once again, Amina was struck by how little she knew about the country. It was constantly in the news, but she didn't know anyone except Ivor who had been there – or at least had been outside the safe areas – since the war had started. Any reporters who didn't travel with the military had to get their news from local Sinnostani reporters who risked their lives going into the isolated mountain regions where the insurgents operated. That was another thing: the insurgents were supposed to be trying to overthrow the government, but all the action seemed to be happening in areas of the mountains where hardly anybody lived. What was that all about?

Everything about this war seemed to be held at arm's length. It was so far away and yet it dominated the news like some kind of gruesome soap opera. And then every now and again, a terrorist group would commit some atrocity in Britain or Europe or the States and rattle on about the West's crimes in the East, just in case the news coverage of such a distant, alien place was beginning to lose its flavour.

Amina decided she needed to know more

about the place itself, from someone who knew it well. The memory of the funeral card was never far from her mind and she knew Goldbloom would not take kindly to her persistence, but she had to know what was really going on over there.

Charlie Stokes, one of the paper's longest-serving reporters, was sitting at his desk, typing away. He was a painfully thin chain-smoker who had to take regular fag breaks out on the roof to get him through the day, and would drag any in-experienced temp up with him to chat while he did. Like most addicts, he needed company. Amina wandered over to him, trying to look casual.

'Hi, Charlie, whatcha workin' on?'

'All right, Amina? Just putting the finishing touches to this piece – looking back on how the war started. Asking about all that nerve gas the terrorists were supposed to have.'

'Oh, right.' She couldn't come up with a less direct way of asking, so she just came out with it. 'You've worked on a lot of the Sinnostan stories, haven't you?'

He turned to look at her.

'Yeeesss. Why?'

'Who do we have over there – I mean, who has the paper got over there, who really knows what's happening?'

'Tryin' to figure it all out, huh?' He chuckled,

pulling a piece of paper from a drawer and writing a name and number on it. 'Good luck. One of our best guys is actually in London at the moment. His name's John Donghu. His blog is one of the most reliable coming out of that pit and he's a sound bloke when it comes to translating irate natives. Want to meet him?'

'Do you think he'd want to meet me?'

'As far as Sinnostan is concerned, he'll talk to anybody who'll listen. Wouldn't hurt that you're cute either. Buy him lunch and you won't be able to shut him up. Fancy comin' up to the roof for a smoke?'

'I still don't smoke, Charlie.'

'All right, all right. Fancy comin' up to the roof while I smoke then? You can drink some bloody mineral water or something.'

Amina knew it paid to get the old salts on your side. Charlie got his choice of the big stories and he might one day ask for her help on one. Futures were made in the little conversations over coffee or a cigarette. And if Goldbloom found out she was still digging into Sinnostan, she'd need all the future she could get.

'Sure,' she said. 'I could use some fresh air.'

29

████████-█████ was convinced that they had scared off the girl, but ████ and ██████████ were not so sure. It was becoming clear that Sandwith and McMorris were still probing around, however, and something was going to have to be done. Sandwith would be given one more chance. They all doubted that he'd take it. McMorris had been spreading the word around the veterans that he would pay for any reliable information on the events in Sinnostan that had cost him his eye.

'Plus he assaulted two of my men,' ███████-█████ growled. 'He didn't get anything out of them, but it will have given him reason to push harder now. It was something solid to grab onto. The bugger's not questioning himself as much as he was; he's looking outwards instead. He's become too dangerous. I think the conditioning may be cracking.'

'Highly unlikely,' ███████████ snorted. 'The programming was intensive. He tested low on the suggestive scale, but his response scores were excellent. McMorris was needy; he was addicted to sedatives – which Shang missed, of course. Our errant war correspondent's personality had big, gaping holes of need. He didn't *want* to resist the process once it started. You can't go wrong with that kind of foothold.'

'Well, you did,' ███████-█████ retorted. 'Because now he's asking all the wrong questions . . . and he can pay good money for the answers. Who knows what worms will come out of the woodwork when they hear that kind of cash is on offer? Somebody somewhere will talk.'

'So remove him,' she said firmly. 'He's becoming connected to too many other strands. Soon it will be overly complicated to take any direct action against him. Best to do it now while he's still an outsider.'

'He'll be seen to,' ████ assured her. 'We're getting sidetracked here. We still have a week to bring all the pieces together for Operation Renewed Faith. The shipment will be late getting to Sinnostan. The freighter was waylaid at Rotterdam. Customs were doing spot searches, but they didn't find the package. Even if they did, they wouldn't know what it was without testing it.'

'And God knows how many would die if someone uncorked that particular genie,' ██████-████ snorted.

'You're sure nobody at MI5 has a hint of this?' █████████ asked. 'And you said MI6 had some of your people under surveillance in Sinnostan—'

'The deal was done in the utmost secrecy. My people are the best,' ██████-████ told her, glaring at her with his arrogant, sleepy-looking eyes. 'There are a few in each agency who know because they have to, but they also know that what we are doing is in the nation's interest. Nobody will interfere.'

'And we won't be hung out to dry if it goes wrong?' █████████ pressed him.

'It has gone too far for that, my dear,' ████ told her. 'The stakes are too high. If this operation goes wrong, we'll all be found dead in our beds.'

13

John Donghu didn't want to be taken to lunch. He wanted four orders of sandwiches and he wanted them delivered. Amina was happy to oblige and after taking his order over the phone, she had the sandwiches made up at a local deli and put them on the *Chronicle's* account. Donghu gave her an address, which she found with difficulty. It was a garage in a lane behind a row of houses in Chadwell Heath. The rhythmic sounds of machinery carried from inside. When she knocked on the peeling navy paint of the wooden door, she was greeted with a yell over the noise. Pushing open the door, she stepped inside.

The place was warm and heavy with the scent of lithograph printing: oil-based ink, thinners, cut paper and the hot, greased joints of the printing press. It was similar to the atmosphere Amina had grown to love after her visits to the *Chronicle's* printing floor. Seeing the giant web presses in action gave her a sublime thrill. The printing press here was a fraction of the size, but still took up nearly half the space in the small garage, along with a guillotine in one corner, a light desk with its long daylight bulb suspended inside a metal hood and several workbenches and sinks lining the walls. Every horizontal surface was covered in some form of paper or film or discarded metal printing plates. Stacks of printed material, some wrapped in plastic, others simply bound with twine, sat under the worktables.

There were four men. Three of them were white, with two in their fifties and another in his twenties. They were all dressed in old clothes and aprons. The fourth man was small, barely over five feet tall, and had the oriental eyes and broad flat face of a Sinnostani. His skin was weathered a ruddy brown and he smiled with teeth the colour of beeswax. Amina's first thought was that he looked like a stereotypical Eastern bloc Communist, dressed in shapeless slacks, a heavy grey woollen jumper, cheap shoes and a large flat cap. There was something about his face that was immediately likeable and he strode straight over to her to shake her hand with his right one and take the bag of sandwiches with his left.

'You're a star,' he said to her over the whirring, stamping press. 'Lunch is up, lads!'

The men didn't stop working to eat their food, merely grabbing their sandwiches, nodding their thanks to Amina and going back to whatever they were doing. Amina sat up on a stool and tucked into her cheese salad wrap as she watched the oldest man using the guillotine to trim the latest stack of leaflets to come out of the machine. She looked at what was printed on them.

YOUR TAX MONEY
IS THEIR BLOOD MONEY

Below, it listed the arms dealers who were making huge profits from the war in Sinnostan. Amina was not impressed. She knew that these leaflets would be handed out at protests or pasted onto lamp-posts and walls, but most would be thrown away or simply become litter. They did no good and just showed these operations up for what they were: amateurish, badly funded and small-time. Her mother had no time for them and Amina was inclined to agree.

'So you want to know about Sinnostan?' Donghu asked over the sound of the machinery.

'Yes, please. Is there any chance we could go somewhere quieter?'

'I like the noise,' he replied. 'Quiet makes me nervous. Too many years hiding from the secret police in the old Sinnostan, see? Lots of ears around back then. Getting like that here now.'

'I don't think we're that bad yet,' Amina chided him with a coy smile. 'We're a long way from having the Gestapo knocking on the front door in the middle of the night.'

But she was already thinking of the Scalps. Had they followed her here? Were they listening? And even if they were, what harm could she do talking to a man who published all his thoughts on a weblog anyway?

'Used to be that way in Sinnostan,' Donghu told her. 'Now it's different. Now you get a knock on the door in the middle of the night and you don't know *who* it could be. Could be soldiers looking for insurgents, or insurgents looking for "traitors", or kidnappers just looking for someone to ransom. Or it could be some old dear tryin' to find her son who's been out on the town all night. The old women scare me most. Some of 'em have tongues that could cut you in half.'

Amina had already decided to tell Donghu about parts of her investigation. There seemed to be no way around it; he would want to know why she was so curious. She explained that she was working on a story about the mental health of British soldiers coming back from the war.

'This war, is it drivin' people mad? Good question!' Donghu said with a humourless grin. 'Most wars are insane, but this one is making less sense than any of 'em.'

'What do you mean?'

Donghu took a big bite out of his roast beef sandwich and kept talking.

'Gah! It's like a war from some goddamned kid's comic book: good-guy soldiers and bad-guy terrorists. All these heroic-soldier stories and hardly any innocent bystanders with bits blown off them. Up until lately, hardly any civilians killed – only soldiers and "terrorists"! What kind of a war is that? Even Sinnostani reporters say the whole thing is short on dead bodies – and they're really *looking*! We want to show what your news doesn't – which is plenty. It's too weird. War is a nasty, complicated thing. But we watch it on your news and it's like a Hollywood production – all neat and tidy and exciting.'

'But the aerial bombing and the smart missiles are supposed to be really accurate,' Amina put in. 'They go on about it all the time. That's why there've been so few civilians killed.'

'Gah! How do you avoid killing wrong people when you blow up whole *towns*! No, it's weird.

'And very goddamned hard to *find* sometimes

too. It's like they're trying to *hide* the real war. I been out looking for it and it's always somewhere else. I seen fire-fights and stuff, but not much, you know? There been times that I been out there asking the locals about some battle that's supposed to have happened and people just shrug and shake their heads. They haven't seen nothing. But it's on film . . . on the news. I watch reports on Western news about fighting in places I never heard of. And I know my country. There been reports of terrorist attacks in villages I can't even find on a map.

'Like I said, it's a comic-book war. I'm still waiting for them to bring out a range of toys.'

Amina nodded. After reading so much about it, she'd been wondering about all these little, out-of-the-way locations.

'It's a big place though, isn't it?' she said. 'And everyone says it's hard to get into those mountains.'

'Gah! There are people living in those mountains!' Donghu waved his hand dismissively. 'Getting pushed about by soldiers who are leading the reporters around. These soldiers, they're controlling everything the reporters see. Don't want bad press. But even the locals not seeing much terrorists. At least not until lately. Now we got all these foreigners coming in to fight the soldiers for us. Not like we *asked* them, mind you. They just showed up and joined in. Ha! Between them and your soldiers, we got a war of the immigrants! And now it's starting to creep into the towns. Now it's starting to worry us. We goin' to be one of those countries where the big boys come from outside and use our land as a battleground.

'But this happens all the time, I just don't understand why Sinnostan. We got nothing the heavyweights are interested in. Just big mountains and thin soil and people tough enough to live off them. We got a little natural gas, no oil, no minerals worth mining. There's no diamonds or gold in our hills, no tantalum or—'

'You've got terrorists,' Amina pointed out.

'Gah!' Donghu shrugged. 'Like I said, they're not a natural resource – they had to be imported. A lot of those guys don't even speak the language. Even heard rumours that they got something else going on up there – something no one's talking about. Mind you, we know there are Special Forces units working out there – SAS and the like – hunting for the insurgents. But that doesn't explain some of the stories.'

'What stories?'

'Stories about lights in the night sky,' he said, looking at her. 'I mentioned it in my blog a few times, but it hardly gets noticed. You're out in the hills and suddenly you see these lights and a few hours later, you wake up lying on the ground. And some of the people who tell these stories swear that they've been searched, or they've lost time, or even been moved to a different location. A few even claim they been the subjects of some kind of experiment. Weird, huh?'

His eyes were on her, watching for her response. Amina remembered the piece of film taken by the camera in Stefan Gierek's helmet; the flashing light just before he blacked out.

'Not as weird as you'd think,' she replied, as she decided to tell Donghu what she and the others had discovered so far.

The alert at the airport resulted in increased traffic on the Underground. It was starting to look like another false alarm, but that was little comfort to the people whose flights had been cancelled and were forced to make their way home again as rush hour began. A number of bodies had brushed against Ivor's as he travelled home and in his distracted state, he had taken little notice. So it was impossible to tell who had slipped the note into his jacket pocket.

He discovered it as he tucked his hands into his pockets on exiting the station, walking down the road towards his flat. Pulling out the folded piece of paper, he read the words written in a looping, perfectionist handwriting:

I hear you are willing to pay for information on your injury. I can supply a full explanation, with documentary proof and the names of the people responsible. This will cost you £1 million. If you are willing to pay this amount, contact me at the number below at 9 p.m. tonight. Call from a phone box you have never used before. If you say a word to anybody else, or if I think you are going to cheat me out of my money, you will never hear from me again.

Ivor read the number, his heart thudding against his ribs. Was it a trick? Were they playing with him? Were they setting him up? He felt overcome with a sickening fear. It couldn't be this easy. The price meant nothing to him if it could provide him with the answers he was after. He already knew he was going to make the call. But if this person wanted payment, there would be some kind of trade involved and that could mean exposing himself.

Wasn't he already exposing himself? Just returning home after he had been attacked was a risk in itself. He should be avoiding his flat, staying where there were crowds . . .

He shook his head. Whatever this was, he would go along with it. It was too good a chance to turn down. He would worry about the risks when they came up. In the meantime, he had a phone call to make.

Chi had already started rooting through Nexus's back-ups, but had not come up with anything really new. He emailed the others in the network to see if there was any news on Nexus. Then he continued his trawl through the back-ups. One disk was labelled 'The Triumvirate' and was full of surveillance photos. They were badly composed enough to have been taken by Nexus himself. Nex was not a great one for fieldwork. He could disassemble a digital camera and put it back together with his eyes closed, but even with them open, he still couldn't take a decent picture.

Chi checked the dates on the files. The most recent ones were of a nondescript office building on what looked like a London street. He clicked them to enlarge each one in turn. There were a number of people on the street, but the photos were centred on three figures leaving the building, one after the other. There was a lean, sallow-faced man with a grey military-style haircut, dressed in a khaki trench coat. The second figure was a short-haired woman dressed in a brown woollen sweater and slacks who resembled a university lecturer. The third person was a tall, stocky man with the appearance of a politician but the eyes of a wary animal.

The three subjects had left the building separately, but the way Nexus had photographed them linked them together. He had definitely been interested in these people. Flicking back to the woman, Chi thought he recognized her, but he couldn't remember where he had seen her before. 'The Triumvirate'. Nex had mentioned that term a few times; supposedly it was a group of three conspirators who were running some operation he was interested in. Something to do with smuggling weapons. Was this them?

Not that it mattered. He closed the files and ejected the disk. Chi didn't have time to take on any more projects. Ivor's revelations had given him a definite direction and unless Nex had information that was relevant to this investigation, he'd have to wait his turn.

Ivor had told Chi to keep Amina out of the loop for now. They were both uneasy about involving her any further, even though she had already done a lot of the legwork. The fight with the Scalps men had shaken Ivor and convinced him that any threat was to be taken seriously. Chi still felt an urge to call her and tell her what was going on. They couldn't keep her out of it for ever, so how could they protect her? And even if they could, he knew she'd be outraged at the idea. The very thought of it made him smile.

He checked his emails, half hoping that she'd got in touch, but there was nothing from her. In fact, hardly anybody in the network had responded to his emails either. They were normally more prompt than that. Chi wondered if there was a reason for their silence.

It was getting late and he was growing hungry. Putting the PC to sleep, he wandered into the kitchen to find a little present from Roswell lying in the middle of the floor. A dead mouse.

'Ah, Jesus, Ros! How many times do I have to tell you . . .'

Picking it up by the tail, he was about to drop it into the bin when he spotted something sticking out of its mouth. With his fingernails, he pulled the tiny roll of paper out of the limp creature's throat as if drawing a joke from some macabre Christmas cracker. Unrolling it, he read the words that were written upon it:

Knock knock!
Who's there?
Ike.
Ike who?
I could have killed your cat, but I thought it might be a bit predictable.

Despite his trembling hands and chattering teeth, a grin spread across Chi's face. He had made it! He had been Targeted! Holding the dead mouse up like a trophy in one hand and the note in the other, he raised his face to the ceiling and let out a roar:

'Yes! Yes-yes-yes-yes-yes-yes!'

Then, realizing it was unlikely that it had in fact been Roswell who'd left the mouse in the middle of his kitchen, Chi ran back into his study and woke up his PC. From here he could monitor the status of his intruder alarm. It was still active. He opened up the software that controlled the cameras he had installed throughout the house and checked the one in the kitchen. He ran it backwards until he spotted the man opening the back door and calmly walking into the kitchen, holding the dead mouse by its tail. The man was wearing a tracksuit and a baseball cap that hid his face from the camera. Chi watched as the guy put the mouse on the floor and left again.

That had been forty-five minutes ago, while Chi was sitting at his desk. He checked the alarm status again. It was working fine.

'Jesus, they're good,' he said softly, suppressing the urge to be sick.

His breath was coming in stops and starts. He felt dizzy and thrilled and terrified all at the same time. This was it – he was on the edge now. His thoughts went to Nexus and to other martyrs to the cause; all those who'd died in car accidents, or house fires or unlikely suicides – his particular favourite was the guy who'd shot himself in the back of the head . . . twice.

Chi gazed at the man on the screen and his whole body went cold. His home had been broken into while he was right here in his study. He should have called the police, but he thought it might be a bit predictable.

22

Ivor finally found a phone box that was working. He thought he'd lost whoever was following, but he couldn't be sure. He would watch the street on either side of him so that he could at least check they weren't listening. Chi had warned him that he could be tracked by satellite surveillance, so he'd taken a route under as many trees and subways as possible. Holding the digital recorder to the earpiece, he checked it was on. He dialled the number on the piece of paper. The phone rang once.

'Ivor McMorris?'

'Yes. Who is this?'

'That's none of your concern.' The voice was nasal, precise and had a slight American twang to it. 'All *you* need to know is how much I know. All *I* need to know is that you are willing to pay my price. Are you?'

'Yes.'

There was a pause and Ivor sensed the definite air of relief in the other man. Whoever this was, he had his own problems. Ivor might be able to use that.

'I need proof you can do what you say,' he said, his chest tight with pent-up breath. 'If you want this money, you're going to have to be pretty convincing. Tell me what's going on.'

'I'll tell you what's going on,' the voice replied. 'But you're not going to believe some of it. You lost your eye in a bombing, but for a long time you've had the feeling that the memories of the event were too exact – too perfect, yes? That's because – as you've probably worked out – those memories are false. They were implanted by a process of conditioning known as strobe interruption.

'Strobe interruption uses flashing lights to disrupt the brain's neural activity, causing you to black out. It can also be used to disorientate you, confuse you and ultimately leave you extremely vulnerable to hypnotic suggestion.'

'I've heard about something like this,' Ivor said, almost to himself. 'The stories of epileptics having their fits set off by flashing lights.'

'Yes,' the man said, sounding mildly irritated at being stopped in mid-flow. 'The US military learned a lot from helicopter crashes in Vietnam.

The rotors spinning against the sun created strobing effects that caused pilots to black out. Strobe interruption has taken this to its most refined form. Used skilfully, pulsing light at the right frequencies can be used to flick switches in your brain for a variety of effects. Now it has been combined with sensory deprivation. They cut you off from the outside world, assault your senses with abrupt changes between silence and deafening noise, project manipulated imagery into your face and start telling you what they want you to think. It is devastatingly effective in reprogramming the human mind.'

'I know,' Ivor muttered. 'But what's it all for? Why did they do it to me?'

'You are only one of many, Mr McMorris. You are but the smallest pixel in a much bigger picture. It started off with one man. This man had to be convinced that he had seen something he had not.

'Members of the government wanted to pass a law. They were after more power, more control. They wanted to introduce the Drawbridge Act. You know it?'

'Of course,' Ivor said. 'All the . . . the anti-terrorist powers. Searching without a warrant, holding somebody without trial . . . arresting someone for not having their ID card . . . all that stuff. It got passed.'

'Yes. Lots of new powers. It got passed because

of what one man saw. He was a reporter with an international reputation for honesty and objectivity, who was taken to interview a terrorist leader hiding out somewhere in Sinnostan. He was shown an arsenal of chemical weapons intended for Britain. But there was no interview and there were no chemical weapons. A few well-placed intelligence agents set the whole thing up; a group of "black ops" people you veterans have taken to calling the Scalps. That reporter was the first "civilian" victim of strobe interruption. Because of his report, nobody objected to a law aimed at fighting terrorism. They were protecting the country. The Drawbridge Act was passed. The government got more power over its people. Simple!'

Ivor detected a tone of the lecturer in the man's voice. This guy was only getting into his stride. He was *enjoying* talking about this.

'But the plan backfired. All of a sudden, people were asking why nothing was being done about these terrorists hiding in Sinnostan. They demanded action. These maniacs had to be stopped before they came to Britain! But nobody in the government wanted a war – everybody remembered what happened in Iraq. What a mess that was! Years of civil war, hundreds of thousands of innocent civilians dead – all to stop weapons of mass destruction that didn't exist. They couldn't afford to make that kind of mistake again. Sinnostan kept protesting that there were no terrorists, but who could trust them? Their leader was a tyrant and probably a sympathizer!

'Most of the government did not know that the chemical weapons threat was fake, but a few more were told. They were all still convinced they were protecting their country. They concocted a plan to create another illusion to cancel out the first one: they would pretend to have the chemical weapons destroyed and the terrorists all killed by a team of SAS. Simple!

'The politicians didn't ask how it would be done. They didn't want to know. An SAS unit boarded a plane. During the flight, the soldiers were gassed and then brainwashed into thinking they had carried out their raid. Two were even wounded to make it all the more realistic. The destruction of the 'chemical weapons' was filmed and released to the media. Simple!

'But then people began asking how we could be sure that all the chemical weapons had been destroyed? It wasn't long before the conspiring politicians found themselves in an impossible position. They would have to send an invasion force into Sinnostan.'

Listening to this absurd story, Ivor felt a sick sensation building in his stomach. He knew where this was leading; he just couldn't believe it.

'So a force was assembled. The Sinnostanis protested some more. But they were a poor country with only a small army. They were ignored. Britain was backed up by America, Russia and China. In they went. Just a few thousand; enough to make a convincing show of searching the mountains, not enough to actually achieve anything. They had to find some terrorists − otherwise they'd look like fools and warmongers. The Scalps arranged for the occasional patrol to 'make contact with the enemy'. The soldiers came back raving about the terrorists they had seen. Sinnostan protested most vigorously.

'The military felt overstretched in this big, mountainous region. They demanded more troops. The public demanded that all the terrorists be hunted down. While all this was going on overseas, the politicians discovered they could do pretty much *whatever they wanted* at home as long as it looked like they were protecting the country. Anybody who disagreed with them was branded unpatriotic, or even a traitor.

'But to maintain the illusion of a war, there had to be casualties. The Scalps were tasked with keeping up the pretence, but the politicians didn't want to know how. Most of them managed to convince themselves that there really was a war going on out there. The strobe interruption process went into overdrive, with its own base in Sinnostan. A surgical team was brought in to mimic wounds to fake the effects of battle.'

Ivor's stomach gave a heave. His right eye was starting to ache. He swallowed, taking a deep breath. There was no war. There was no war. It was too much for him to grasp.

'But . . . but how could the soldiers just disappear for days?'

'Most didn't, officially. The patrols would be in-country for at least that amount of time. The Scalps called their reports in over the radio whenever it was required.'

'The roulette wheel,' Ivor rasped. 'That was for—'

'A bit of vanity, really. It was imperative that we keep the choice of wounds random, so we used the roulette wheel. A spin of the wheel decided who got what. Each wound had a number – sometimes more than one. Increased odds were given to the most common injuries, some you see in battle more than others. Number thirteen was a head wound, fifty was abdominal. Each casualty got three spins of the wheel. The mind-control process took the spins into account too. Numbers eight or twenty-two were extreme post-traumatic stress, for instance. And twenty . . . well, twenty was the loss of an eye.'

Pain lanced through Ivor's scarred eye socket.

His dead eye felt alive; it pulsed with an agonizing heat, but it felt alive. Ghost pain, the torment of a missing body part. It started to spread through the right side of his head.

'You said "we",' he wheezed.

'What?' the man replied uneasily.

'You said "*we* used the roulette wheel". You're Shang, aren't you?'

There was silence on the other end of the line. Ivor gritted his teeth, trying to suppress the overwhelming rage he felt towards this man.

'You took my eye. For . . . for what? For a fucking *PR stunt*. How many soldiers have you operated on in this "war". How many have you killed?'

'I didn't kill anyone,' Shang retorted. 'That wasn't my job.'

'You bastard! YOU UNBELIEVABLE SADISTIC BASTARD!' Ivor screamed down the phone. 'You took out my *eye*, you fucking monster! You—'

'I was just following orders,' Shang told him calmly. 'You can shriek all you want, I don't care. Frankly, you're the least of my problems. By talking to you, I'm signing my own death warrant. If you want the people responsible for this, I can give them to you. But it's going to cost you one million pounds . . . in cash, of course.'

Ivor slumped against the inside of the booth, exhaustion overwhelming him.

'How could they do it?' he said in a voice that was barely more than a whisper. 'Were they out of their minds? Were they completely bloody mad?'

'Grow up,' Shang snapped at him. 'The politicians got an enemy that keeps the public scared and obedient. That gives them power. And they achieved this by having a war where there are few soldiers killed and almost no civilians . . . Or at least that's what they had – it's started heating up a bit over there. That's why I quit. The military is hunting a threat they believe to be real . . . or rather, they can't admit they're hunting a threat that isn't real. And the Scalps? They're doing what they do best – screwing with people's minds. And they're loving it – they're getting to test all kinds of new toys out there. And all concerned firmly believe they're doing their best to protect their nation.

'But it's all a mess now. It's completely out of control, and the Sinnostanis? We invaded their *country*. It was only a matter of time before the terrorists we claimed were there would turn up for real. There was no war, but there's one there *now*.

'Anyway, we're getting off the point,' he said abruptly. 'Let's talk money.'

Chi sat listening to the recording of Shang's confession with a rapt expression. When it was finished, he played it again. Ivor sat waiting for his reaction. He had informed the bank he'd be withdrawing the money before he'd even made the call to Shang the previous evening, but he still had to wait for that much cash to be prepared. In the meantime, he had come back to Chi to keep him in the loop. After listening to the recording for a third time, Chi pursed his lips and hissed for his cat, who wandered into the study and jumped up into his lap.

'Smoke and mirrors,' he said, almost to himself, as he stroked Roswell's ginger fur. 'There is no war. Jesus, this is bigger than Kennedy, bigger than September the eleventh . . . this is bigger than anything. We've gotta be careful here. Wow . . . Wow! This testimony is going to blow things wide open. We have to assume that they're already out to nail Shang before he talks, and the same goes for us if they find out we've heard this. You're meeting him the day after tomorrow?'

'Nine a.m. in Liverpool Street station,' Ivor told him.

'Smart,' Chi said, nodding. 'Crowds and lots of escape routes. Still, you know that's where it could all go wrong, don't you?'

Ivor shrugged.

'What else can I do? I have to know.'

'Tell me about it,' Chi chuckled. 'We all have to know. There is no war. Jesus – how did I not see this one coming? And this stuff he talked about . . . strobe interruption. That's—'

His face went blank for a moment. His fingers drummed against the edge of the desk and his lips moved but no words came out.

'Aawwgh!' he yelled suddenly, making Ivor jump. Roswell bounded out of her master's lap and turned to give him a hostile glare. 'That's where I've heard of it before! The bloody woman . . .' He stood up and strode over to a shelf full of disks. Pulling several out, he examined the indexes, before choosing one and taking it from its case. Slotting it into a disk drive, he closed the drawer and brought some folders up on-screen. Ivor wheeled his chair in behind him to get a closer look. Chi had opened up a series of scans of magazine articles. Most of them were about experimental technology: things like unmanned reconnaissance planes, microwave weapons, remote-control machine-gun posts and lots on state-of-the-art surveillance devices.

'This is the problem with looking for conspiracies,' Chi said as he searched. 'You gather so much information that you can eventually find links from anything to anything. It's tough to keep any kind of perspective.'

He sifted through all of this until he found the article he was looking for:

'There was an American woman named . . let's see . . . yeah, Ellen Rosenstock, who pioneered this technique called strobe interruption, but she wanted to use it in schools. Claimed you could effectively implant facts into somebody's memory. She has incredible memory powers herself – some say she's borderline autistic – but she's very, very clever. Has almost perfect recall; can tell you what the weather was like on the twelfth of April ten years ago, or memorize a whole phone book. Rosenstock's devoted her life to studying how her own brain works and she claimed she could use this strobe interruption in the form of light pulses to bypass the conscious mind and write memories into the human brain the same way you can record stuff on a computer's hard drive. She designed a computer program to put it into practice and started using it on some of her university students but the tests went wrong. Two of the kids had epileptic fits and one suffered retinal burns . . .'

There was a photo of the woman with the article. Chi opened up the picture he had taken off Nexus's back-up disks, the one with the two men and one woman leaving the office building. The people Nexus called the Triumvirate. It was the same woman in both pictures.

'OK, so that's her,' Chi breathed. 'So who are these two guys? The brainwashing process connects her to the fake war, and she's involved with them somehow. But Nexus didn't know about the war thing — at least as far as I know — so why was he so interested in them? What were they up to?'

'One mystery at a time, man,' Ivor told him. 'First let's milk Shang for all he's worth. We can worry about these guys some other time.'

'These,' Chi muttered, pointing at the screen, 'these are the kinds of characters I worry about *all* the time.'

6

Amina spent the next couple of days after talking to Donghu finding out as much as she could about UFO sightings. She needed to talk to Ivor. It was easy to tell herself that it was so she could tell him about Donghu, but really she just needed to see him to . . . to see him. And besides, they had a lot to discuss.

She still did not buy Chi's alien abduction theory, but it wasn't unthinkable that the military were testing some new kind of weapon out in those isolated mountains. Something that could knock you out from a distance without leaving a mark.

Deciding to be late into work that morning, she took the train to Ivor's instead. The Underground station was busy when she disembarked from the train, and she pushed her way through the sleepy herd that shuffled around her to board the carriage. There were still enough people on the platform to prevent Ivor from spotting her as he got on at the next door up. Amina waved and called out to him but he didn't hear. He was carrying two small suitcases and with a jolt in her heart, she wondered where he was going. Was he leaving? Two cases meant he would be gone for some time.

She slipped back on board the train just as the tinny siren announced the doors were closing. Resisting the urge to make her way up to him, she decided instead to observe the people around him and see if she could spot anyone watching him. Maybe it was easier to catch the watchers out when their attention wasn't directed towards you.

Even at this time of the morning, the carriage was hot, stuffy and smelled of drowsy commuters. It was difficult to move without brushing up against somebody, but at least the full carriage meant that she could stay out of Ivor's line of sight. It was strange, following somebody without their knowing. Amina felt closer to him and, at the same time, slightly predatory. It struck her that even here, in this crowded train, she was invading his privacy somehow by watching him like this. Despite the fact that she meant him no harm – quite the opposite – she doubted that he'd be happy when he found out. She was stalking him like a crazed fan, studying his face, his clothes, his fidgeting hands, having feelings about him while he sat unawares only a few metres away. She wondered if those who carried out surveillance for a living formed a kind of relationship with their subjects. It must be hard not to – a one-sided relationship where the watcher enjoyed a detached kind of power. The subject's life gave you purpose; you could know everything about them while they knew nothing about you. You were untouchable. Their problems were not yours unless you chose to make them yours.

Her phone rang. It was one of her friends. She let it ring out. She'd been doing that a lot lately. Amina gazed at Ivor's scarred face, framed by his untidy brown hair. He needed a haircut and he hadn't shaved. The pressing of his hand against his side told her that he was in pain from something. She loved his sad expression and even with his face set in that mask people wear on the train, she could see that calm resolve in his eyes. He was a man who would see things through.

The urge to touch him came over her – to get closer and reach out and brush her fingers across his back or his arm without him knowing. This must be how stalkers felt, she supposed. To be close enough to share someone's life, but never taking the risk of getting intimate, of being rejected. Amina could see the attraction in it.

In a way, this was what journalism was like: to

watch with detachment – to be a witness and never get involved. There was something creepy about it, when she thought about it like that.

She could make nothing of the people sitting or standing around Ivor. If anyone was observing him, she couldn't spot them. But then, they were professionals after all.

Ivor got off at Liverpool Street and she followed at a safe distance. It was hard to keep track of him in the throng of commuters, some hurrying to make connections as they all squeezed onto the escalators, a few pushing past on the left side in polite haste. Ivor struggled with his suitcases. They were heavy and bulky and his fellow travellers were intolerant of luggage at this time of the morning when they had jobs to get to.

The Scalps were here somewhere, she was sure of it. They could be beside her, behind her. They could be anywhere. Something was going on here and they would be assessing it, judging the threat. If Ivor was acting in any way to compromise them . . .

That's it, she thought. He's making a break for it because he's got something on them he can use. Wouldn't he have told me? No, he wanted me safe. He wanted me out of it. If he's leaving now he's scared. Suddenly everyone she looked at seemed to be looking at Ivor. She became convinced he was surrounded by hostile eyes. They reached the main concourse, swiping their cards through the ticket barriers and emerging into the open space dominated by the information board hanging from the centre of the ceiling. On the right were the lines of platforms for the mainline trains, on the left, in front and behind, the ticket offices, shops, cafés and ways out. Ivor looked around, but Amina stepped behind a pillar in time to stay out of sight. Then he made his way over to the line of boards in front of the ticket offices, the ones holding the timetables. There was a bench next to them. Sitting on the seat with his chin on his chest was a man wearing a bulky Barbour jacket over an expensive, but rumpled, suit. There was a bottle of whiskey tucked into the crook of his arm. The bottle was half empty.

Ivor sat down on the bench facing the other way, sliding the two suitcases in under the seat between them. Gaping at this move, she had to suppress a smile. Ivor was having a clandestine rendezvous, complete with secret trade-off! She wondered what business he could be conducting with a drunk first thing in the morning. Or maybe the other guy's alcoholism was part of the theatre. If that was the case, the whole thing was priceless. Amina was moving in for a closer look when her arm was grabbed and she was dragged back behind the pillar.

Torn between outrage and fear, she spun to face a tall young man with dark dreadlocks and a beard, wearing a multi-coloured woollen hat.

'What are you doing here?' he demanded in a hushed voice.

'Who the hell are . . . ?' Her voice trailed off as she looked closer. 'Chi? Is that you?' She almost laughed at the absurd picture before her. 'Are you in disguise?'

'I'm not supposed to be here,' Chi muttered, looking a little disgruntled that she'd seen through his façade so easily. 'And neither are you. That's Shang over there. Ivor's about to get all our questions answered. Damn it! You're not supposed to be involved in this any more!'

'Blow it out your ass!' she snapped at him, loud enough to make people look round. 'I'm in this thing as much as you are. Have you two been going behind my back? Where do you get off—'

Chi cut her off by putting a finger to his lips while his other hand went to his ear. He was obviously listening to something. She turned to look over at the two figures on the bench as the colour drained from his face.

'Oh Christ,' he whispered.

Ivor thought Shang was just pretending to ignore him when he sat down. There was no mistaking the surgeon's face even with his head hanging down like that.

'I've got your money,' he said, not looking at the other man, but speaking in a normal tone to be heard over the noise in the station. 'Do we need to go somewhere so you can check it?'

There was no response. Ivor knew Chi would be listening on the mic he had secreted under Ivor's collar. A tiny flesh-coloured earpiece hidden in Ivor's left ear would let Chi talk to him if he spotted anything suspicious.

'Don't mess me about,' Ivor hissed at the surgeon. 'Are you drunk? Are you listening to me—'

He turned to glare at the other man, but from this angle he saw just the back and side of Shang's head. The collar of the jacket was up, but it was still possible to see the thin red line of fresh blood leading up the back of his neck to the small hole just inside the hairline. Ivor felt suddenly numb, the skin tightening on the back of his own neck as he stared at the surgeon. The hole was too small to be a bullet-wound – more likely a stiletto, or one of those ice picks you saw in the US. The ghost of Ivor's missing eye began to ache.

He checked Shang's neck for a pulse, knowing he wouldn't find one. He suspected there would be no alcohol in the surgeon's blood either. The whiskey bottle was just to keep people away from the corpse until Ivor got here. He was trembling now, though he would have sworn he was still devoid of emotion. His missing eye burned in its socket. They had killed Shang in a crowded train station – stabbed him where the spine met the skull, tucked a bottle under his arm and left him slumped on this bench as if he'd simply fallen asleep. How did they do that? How could nobody have seen it happen? It didn't matter. What mattered was why. They were sending a message. Crowds didn't make any difference. Public places didn't make any difference. The Scalps could get to you anywhere.

'No, no, no. No, no, no!' a voice sobbed in despair. It was his voice. 'Not now. No! You're not going to do this to me now!'

Ivor jammed his hands into Shang's pockets, frantically searching for the proof the surgeon had claimed to be carrying. There was nothing in the jacket pockets. He pulled open the buttons and began rifling through the man's suit. People passed, glancing down at him in disgust. But they did not stop. They should have tried to stop him, or at least *said* something to him. But they just kept walking. Others paused long enough to look around and see if anyone else was going to take action, before continuing on their way, eyes carefully averted as if Ivor was some homeless guy begging for change . . . or a nutter who might be carrying a machete or worse. For once he was grateful for all these obtuse, blinkered people living in their own detached little worlds.

'Shang's dead,' he told Chi. 'Everything's gone pear-shaped. Get out of here!'

His searching became more panicked. There was nothing in Shang's trouser pockets. Where else could it be? Nothing else mattered now, only the truth – the proof. Ivor snarled in frustration, barking out a string of curses, sounding even more like a madman.

'Goddamn it! Goddamn it, it's got to be here!'

But they wouldn't have left proof sitting in Liverpool Street station for everyone to find. They didn't leave proof anywhere. Ivor was going through the suit jacket again when police officers in body armour, armed with sub-machine guns, came running from all directions. He didn't hear the consternation as travel-doped commuters suddenly found themselves in the middle of a potential fire-fight. He barely heard the voices as they shouted 'Police!' calling for people to get down, to be calm. When they were roaring at him to lie down on the ground and put his hands behind his head, he continued to search. Nothing else mattered now.

'Ivor!' Chi's voice burst into his ear. 'They're going to bloody shoot you! Get on the ground, man!'

Ivor finally woke up to what was going on around him. There were over a dozen weapons pointed in his direction. He sank off the bench onto his knees, raising his hands as he did so. As soon as he was on the floor, four officers pinned him down roughly as his hands were cuffed behind him. A spear-thrust of agony punched through his side from the bullet wound and he cried out in pain. He had to be careful about that. A bullet wound would take some explaining if they discovered it. A man identified himself as Detective Sergeant Sykes and cautioned Ivor:

'I must inform you that you do not have to say anything, but it may harm your defence if you do not mention, when questioned, something which you later rely on in court. Anything you do say may be given in evidence.'

His tone implied that he expected Ivor to do plenty of talking over the next while. Ivor ground his teeth together, clenching his eyes shut. They were going to do him for Shang's murder. Sykes – the name was familiar. He was the one who had questioned Amina and Chi after the anthrax scare at the *Chronicle*. The one from Counter Terrorism Command. The only way he could be here now was if he'd been tipped off. Ivor was being set up.

'For Christ's sake!' he bellowed, tears of frustration streaming down his face. 'This is such a fucking cliché!'

The police cordon was tightening on the main thoroughfare, but it would take several minutes for them to close down all the exits and keep the thousands of potential witnesses contained. Chi and Amina slipped onto the escalators to the Underground station, trying to look as if they weren't fleeing the scene of a murder.

'We can't leave him!' Amina was saying under her breath.

'We can't help him!' Chi retorted. 'What use are we to him if we get arrested too? We're accomplices now and as soon as they find the mic and earpiece he was wearing, they'll be looking for whoever was at the other end of the line.'

He was still listening to Ivor's microphone, but there wasn't much being said now. The crime scene was being secured. London's transport system had slow reflexes; Amina didn't know if the Transport Police would stop the trains leaving the station or not, but what was important was that she and Chi got lost in the crowd. Chi told her it was Sykes who had arrested Ivor and if he spotted the two of them as well, he couldn't help but be suspicious. They reached a Central Line platform just as a train was about to leave. Jumping on board, they waited for what seemed like an age until the doors closed and the train started moving.

'You need to get to work,' Chi whispered to her. 'Turn this back into a normal day.'

She nodded, irritated at having him tell her what to do. She knew what to do. But she couldn't help thinking of Ivor and how they were deserting him. Chi was right, there was no way they could help – at least not yet. Their best hope was making this story as public as possible and quickly. She had to convince Goldbloom to take this on . . . and if he wouldn't, then she'd find someone who would.

'Listen,' Chi said softly as the train rolled into Bank station. 'Come over to my place tonight. Shang spilled the beans over the phone. We've no evidence, but we've got what are almost his dying words. We need to sort out what we're going to do with them. Don't do anything until then, OK? And stay safe, Amina. We're all marked now. They could come for us anytime.'

The doors opened and he slipped onto the platform without looking back. In seconds he was out of sight along the tiled corridor leading to the surface. Amina decided to get off at the next station. She needed to get above ground again, to breathe the open air, no matter how grimy or polluted. Her nerves were on edge, she flinched when anyone brushed against her. Her hands clasped and unclasped and her jaw was tight and tense. Her pulse thudded in her ears. She couldn't go on this way. If she ever hoped to survive this, she was going to need some protection.

And she knew just where to get it.

32

Tariq knew he was becoming a disappointment to his father. Unlike his father, he had no military ambitions. The prospect of a career in the Royal Marines held no attraction for him whatsoever. Who'd want to spend their life getting ordered around and having a loudmouth sergeant bellowing at them for not folding their clothes right, or for failing to do enough press-ups? What kind of a life was that?

Martin Mir was not an unreasonable man. He would have been happy to see Tariq show any kind of ambition at all. But Tariq was not in an ambition frame of mind and he saw no reason why he should be planning how to spend the rest of his life at the tender age of fifteen.

It was hard enough trying to survive school. Amina's mix of looks, brains and popularity made her path through the world of education appear effortless. Tariq, on the other hand, seemed to stumble from one mismatched class to the next, suffering his education much as one would the pulling of a succession of bad teeth.

Now he was going to have to ask to move school again. He couldn't take the torture any longer and he was afraid of what he was going to do. He didn't want to be expelled again. His parents wouldn't stand for it. His father would send him straight to press-up school if that happened.

Tariq knew they wouldn't understand, no matter how he tried to explain. He was in hell. His head buzzed with angry, conflicting thoughts. It was almost impossible to sleep. Most nights, he lay there, drifting between a restless doze and frustrating wakefulness. The coming of every morning meant facing his torment, tired, depressed – already beaten. Something had to give. He had to get out of that school.

To his surprise, Amina was home when he got in. She was coming down the stairs carrying her handbag, looking pale and distracted.

'Hey,' she said.

'Hey,' he replied. 'What's up? Thought you'd be at work.'

'Had to take a half day to do some stuff,' she told him, tucking her bag behind her as if he might grab it from her. 'How was school?'

'Gimme a break!' he snorted.

'I was just asking.' Her tone was distant, as if her mind was miles away. She reached the bottom of the stairs and stopped him before he closed the front door. 'I'm off. See you later, yeah?'

'Sure.' He threw his bag into its place under the stairs. A thought occurred to him. 'Hey! Did you find out any more about that mind-control thing you were working on? It's just that this game they've got us playing in school is—'

'Look, Tariq,' she sighed, putting her hand to her face in an exasperated gesture that reminded him of their mother. 'Nobody's brainwashing you with a computer game, all right? Computer games don't rot your brain. You're a teenager. You'll be screwed up for a few more years and then things'll work themselves out, yeah? Everybody thinks that school is messing with their minds. Look at all those kids who go shooting up their classes with a semi-automatic because they can't cope. They think the world's out to get them. But you know what? It isn't. And believe me, I know the difference.'

Tariq stared at her with a quizzical expression.

'Bloody hell, I can't decide who's more patronizing: you or the army guy in class. At least he's getting paid to talk crap. Why don't you go stuff yourself, you snotty cow?'

Amina went to say something, but held back, turning and walking out the door instead. The door slammed shut and Tariq glared at it for a moment, his face twisted into a sneer. Who the hell did she think she was? A few years older than him and she was acting like one his teachers. Sometimes he felt like just . . . As he stood there, fuming at her words, he was struck with an idea. 'Look at all those kids who go shooting up their classes with a semi-automatic because they can't cope.' Yeah. The schools were terrified of that kind of thing. Everybody was. Everyone was waiting for the next kid to snap and commit another massacre.

Tariq pounded up the stairs to his parents' room, opened the wardrobe and reached up for the lockbox that sat on the shelf above the hangers. He would never hurt anybody – he wasn't crazy – but a good scare would knock some sense into Alan Noble and his mates.

Sitting down on his parents' bed, he ran his hands over the ribbed surface of the graphite-coloured lockbox. It was about half the size of a briefcase and made of hardened steel. This was the box where their father kept his Browning Hi-Power 9mm automatic. Tariq tapped in the combination on the keypad. He had worked out the combination number years ago; it was 1664: the date that the Duke of York and Albany's Maritime

Regiment of Foot was established. The fighting force that would become known as the Royal Marines.

He would just scare the assholes – he wouldn't take the safety catch off. He wouldn't even put any rounds in the clip. It would be a simple matter of catching them somewhere quiet. Point the weapon at them and pull back the hammer for that loud click. For just a few seconds, he'd be that lunatic that every school dreaded. He smiled in grim anticipation. They'd absolutely piss themselves.

The automatic would be back in its box before his father even knew it was gone. Chances were, Noble and the others wouldn't tell a soul about what had happened. The more he thought about it, the more sure he was about doing this. He was a desperate man. Drawing in a shaky breath, he opened the case. Tariq stared for most of a minute before releasing the breath in a gasp.

The gun was gone.

When Amina reached Chi's house, the feeling of being watched was palpable. It was almost as if the Scalps had withheld their presence from her before, but now they were allowing her senses to pick them up on some subliminal level. Her skin was crawling around her neck and shoulders as she rang the doorbell.

Chi let her in without a word and immediately returned to his study, where he began walking back and forth, running his hands through his hair. Amina had the definite impression that he had been doing this for some time. The place was in a state of chaos; she would have suspected it had been ransacked except for the way the untidy piles appeared to have been categorized. He pointed at the PC and she sat down, pressing 'Play' on the media player window that dominated the screen. Shang's hollow, phone-distorted voice told its story. Amina listened, a weight growing in the pit of her stomach. She played it again when it was finished. She had expected to feel relief at finally discovering the reason for everything they had experienced – instead, she felt only a horrible empty fear.

'That's it?' she said quietly. 'There's no war? How . . . how can that be? How is that possible? How can you fake a whole war? God, all those soldiers killed . . . maimed. That's insane.'

Chi nodded. He kept pacing, his lower lip red from where he had been chewing it.

'It wasn't real, but it's real now,' he said hoarsely, as if he had been shouting all afternoon. 'There are terrorists there, there's real fighting. We can't prove there's no war because they've created one out of nothing. The illusion's been replaced by the real thing. We're screwed. All day, I've been trying to work out what we can do, but I can't think of anything. Without proof from somebody on the inside, we are absolutely screwed.'

'But we have this!' Amina pointed at the screen. 'People will have to listen to us if we show them this.'

'They've already done a job on him though, haven't they?' he replied. 'Even if we could prove it really was him speaking, he's been discredited. They've already changed the world's perception of him. He's a terrorist now – nobody can believe a word he says and he's not alive to back it up.'

'It would still stir things up,' Amina insisted.

'Sure, enough to get us killed, maybe,' Chi retorted. 'But enough to bring the whole thing down? I don't think so. I've seen attempts like that before – and for things far less important than this. This lie is so big, nobody will believe it's possible unless they're forced to.'

He stopped pacing and gazed at her with a helpless expression.

'You know what else is getting me? Shang was dead before we got there. We knew he must be desperate to risk exposing himself like that. He really had to have that money. He was so dangerous they would have nabbed him as soon as they found him, but they only got to him when he reached the meeting point. Somehow, they found out about the meeting.

'We can guess they weren't tracking *him*, because they'd never have let us get that close. Ivor called him from an anonymous callbox . . . They could have listened in if they got the number in time, but . . . I don't know. The only other time Ivor would have mentioned the meeting is here, in this house. In *my* house.'

Amina could see that this had disturbed Chi more than he was willing to admit. She supposed that after all his precautions, he had considered his home safe from prying eyes and ears.

'I've scanned the house a dozen times,' he said softly. 'I've turned the place inside out. I can't figure out how they did it.'

Amina felt a deep sympathy for him, seeing his defences collapsing like this. She had learned enough about this business by now to know that they were amateurs playing a professional's game and they had survived this far by sheer luck as much as anything else. Despite his greater awareness of their adversary, Chi seemed to have lived in a bubble of delusion as far as his security was concerned.

'Maybe they've got some kind of transmitter you can't pick up?' she offered helpfully, prompting a dismissive sniff from the disgruntled electronics expert. 'Well, why not? Or maybe it's something they switch on after you've done your scanning? They might know your routine. You know, they could just wait until you're off-guard.'

'It's possible.' He shrugged. 'But the room's insulated against thermal imaging, I've got a copper mesh in the walls and doors that act like a Faraday cage to prevent radio signals passing through, and there are no windows from which to pick up sound vibrations passing through the glass. Even then, I monitor for all forms of transmission and I routinely search the place for recording devices – anything that's new or out of place, any trace of unexplained metal or electrical activity or . . . or . . . anything. If you can think of something I can't, please enlighten me.' He paused for a second. 'That said, I know they can get in without setting off the alarm, so maybe I'm not as smart as I think I am.'

He told her about the man who had left the message in his kitchen.

'A dead mouse?' she exclaimed, shuddering. 'They're pretty twisted, aren't they? Whatever happened to just saying "Shut up or you're dead" or something like that?'

'Suppose it's scarier to be weird.'

'Still, at least your curiosity didn't kill your cat, huh?'

'Ha ha.'

Amina's eyes fell on Roswell, who was curled up asleep in a pile of papers in one corner.

'Hey, maybe Ros is on their payroll,' she said in another lame attempt at a joke. 'She's selling you out for tuna.'

'Oh, you're on form today—' he sneered, but then stopped.

Walking over to where his cat was dozing, he picked her up, ignoring her sleepy, irritated protests. Sitting down at his worktable, he looked her over. She glared balefully back at him, but the hold he had on the back of her neck kept her still. Chi unbuckled her collar and held it up to the light. As soon as he released his grip on the cat, she bounded away to the other side of the room. Squinting at the collar, Chi tilted the buckle one way and then the other.

'Damn,' he said. 'This has been fiddled with.'

The leather of the strap folded round one side of the buckle and was held in place by a stud. He took out a penknife and prised the stud out, but instead of coming out in one piece, the top popped off, revealing a tiny hollow inside.

'Bastards,' he grunted. 'Bastards bugged my cat.'

He picked up a needle and jammed it into the device, disconnecting it. Switching on a magnifying lamp that sat on the table, he peered through the lens at the hollow stud.

'Best work I've ever seen,' he muttered in reluctant admiration, as Amina peered over his shoulder. 'The chip is half the size of anything I could get my hands on . . . the mic is tucked inside the fold of the leather, but it must still pick up sound. I'd love to know how they managed that. Hell, the thing doesn't even need batteries! See these contacts on the underside? It runs on the electricity in Roswell's body. They just wait for her to come outside, attract her over with . . . I don't know, a bit of tuna, and just download the new material. Clever, clever, clever. Damn, they're good.'

He looked up at Amina, fear written on his face.

'I have no idea how long this has been here. I haven't taken her collar off in ages. We have to assume they've been able to hear every word we've said from the start.'

Amina was abruptly conscious of how vulnerable they were here, the two of them alone in this big house.

'Let's get out of here,' she urged him. 'I need some air.'

'Sure, just let me get something upstairs.'

Chi understood Amina's need for people and light and noise, but the complete failure of his counter-surveillance had shattered his confidence. He didn't want to leave the house. He wanted to talk to his mates online, or surf through his files or the web looking for new leads, new connections. What he didn't want was to think about what this all meant.

He had hidden Nexus's stuff in a concealed compartment in the base of his bedroom wardrobe. Pulling out the backpack, he opened it up and checked through it. It would be easy enough to get the fake IDs changed so that he could use them himself. The credit cards were next to useless without the pin numbers, but Chi had enough cash put by in readiness for a time like this. The disguise kit might come in useful, and he was certainly going to keep the can of Mace handy.

He wasn't sure if he wanted to run just yet – maybe they had let him find out just how impotent he was so they wouldn't have to bother killing him. Presumably it was less risky to simply neutralize the threat somebody posed rather than bumping them off altogether. These thoughts flared through his mind, throwing themselves against the wave of fear that loomed on the point of overwhelming him. Maybe they were sitting in a van or rented room somewhere, laughing at him and his pathetic little quest. Maybe he'd never been in any danger at all.

Even so, he wanted to be ready. He and the others in his network always talked about the possibility of having to 'disappear' before somebody did it for them, and he had made half-hearted plans to do just that. But he never really believed it would be necessary. He believed it now.

There was a small gap in the curtains that covered the floor-to-ceiling window. He went over to them, opening them wide to gaze out at the night sky. It was hard to see any stars over the city lights. Chi yearned for the days when he had just been chasing UFOs and aliens. The dark side of human nature was so much more terrifying than extra-terrestrial bogeymen. He felt like he'd been kidding himself this whole time. Why watch horror films when you could read a history book or just turn on the news and see it for real? Because horror films gave you a way out. They told you it wasn't real. Chi chuckled to himself, shaking his head.

He was neck-deep in reality now . . . and all because of an illusion of war.

The sight of a dark grey disc, almost invisible against the evening gloom, made him start. It dropped down out of nowhere to be framed by the window and he stared at it in disbelief. A beam of pulsing light flashed in his face and he blinked, but was unable to take his eyes off the unidentified flying object. It was only as he started to faint that he remembered the significance of the strobing lights. As he collapsed to the floor, Chi could have sworn he heard gunshots and the sound of smashing glass.

Amina. He knew they'd come for him eventually, but Amina was here too. She didn't deserve what they'd do to her. This was his last thought before he blacked out.

28

Chi woke to find Amina kneeling next to him, gently slapping his face. There was the smell of smoke in the air. The smell came from the muzzle of the gun she held in her hand.

'What the hell happened?' he asked, sitting up.

'You've got a UFO out in your front garden,' she told him. 'We better get out there. Your neighbours are getting curious.'

Amina talked as they hurried down the stairs. She had come up to check on him. She probably didn't like being alone in the house and he couldn't blame her. The lights had just started flashing in his face as she walked in and on impulse, she had drawn her father's automatic from her bag and started shooting. Evidently she was a good shot; she had hit whatever the thing was despite standing in a lighted room, shooting through glass at a target hovering in darkness outside.

'Like you said,' she sniffed as she opened the front door. 'If you want to keep a secret, don't stick flashing lights all over it.'

The thing lay on the grass, where the Furmans, Chi's next-door neighbours, were already inspecting it from the far side of their wall. Front doors were opening up and down the street. The gunshots were attracting a lot of attention and Chi was grateful for every bit of it. The more witnesses, the less likely he and Amina were to be dragged into an unmarked van and driven away.

'What's going on, Chi?' Gary Furman asked. 'Bit late in the night for loud experiments, isn't it? You haven't been messing with explosives again, have you?'

'Nothing to worry about, Gary,' Chi reassured him as he stared down at the object, which was about a metre wide. 'It's just a prototype surveillance drone a black ops group have been using to keep tabs on me. It was trying to disable me with strobe lights but Amina here shot it down. I don't think it'll be giving us any more trouble.'

Furman smirked and shook his head, exchanging a look with his wife. They knew enough about Chi's bizarre interests to know when to take him seriously. This wasn't one of those times. Some of the other neighbours looked at each other with the same expression. Chi glanced around and grinned at Amina.

'Sometimes the truth is too much explanation for people,' he giggled softly.

The drone was a cloudy grey disc a little over a metre in diameter. It had four turbofans that could move independently and a series of lenses around its edge that looked like they might be cameras of different kinds. There were three bullet holes in its top edge. Chi lifted it up to look underneath. It weighed little more than a large model airplane. A tube set into the underside looked as if it could project the focused light that had knocked him out only minutes before. The whole thing appeared to be seriously state-of-the-art. He could only guess at what kind of technology lay under its skin. He was going to have fun finding out.

Someone must have called the police. There were sirens wailing in the distance. They would arrive in a matter of minutes.

'What are we going to do now?' Amina asked.

She had a small camera out and was taking shots of the drone.

'We need to get out of here,' he replied. 'We've struck bloody gold. If this isn't hard evidence, I don't know what is. I need you to go home and get those pictures uploaded on the web somewhere, and soon. Distribute them. Make it so they can't be gathered up and destroyed. And then find somewhere safe to lie low for a while. We got lucky this time – they tried to take us on the sly and you caught them by surprise. But these sods won't give up that easy, especially now we've got them by the short and curlies!'

Chi was elated. He'd finally found his flying saucer and he was going to make sure the whole world knew about it – but not until he'd examined every inch of it to find out who'd made the thing. There was a huge, stupid grin pasted on his face and he didn't care.

'What are you going to do?' Amina asked him.

'I'm going to take this to the only man I can trust to protect me,' Chi told her. 'And I think I've got enough to buy my way in.'

■■■■■■-■■■■ stared at the phone in his desk drawer, wondering why it was ringing. That phone was a dedicated line. It wasn't supposed to ring unless something was going badly wrong. It was late in the night, when normal people were at home in bed or out enjoying themselves. ■■■■■■-■■■■ rarely indulged in either activity. The problem was, he had just been about to pick that phone up to deliver some bad news of his own. Now he was about to receive some instead.

With some sense of trepidation, he reached into the open drawer and picked up the handset.

'Yes?'

'The package has gone missing,' ████'s voice informed him.

'What?' he barked, glancing up at the door of his office, to ensure it was closed. Then, in a quieter voice, he hissed: 'What do you mean, "missing"?'

'I mean exactly that. The container that arrived in Sinnostan was full of water. Plain old bloody water. The nerve agent has disappeared and we have no idea at what stage in the shipment. The route was so complicated it could be anywhere. Our people are rounding up all the couriers, but it'll take time to find out who diverted it and where. There's a possibility it never even got put on the ship. I think Cantang double-crossed us.'

'Cantang? Jesus,' ███████-████ exclaimed. 'Hang on . . . you mean he could still have it *here*? But if that's so—'

'There could only be one reason why he'd do it,' ████ said calmly. 'He's going to screw us over – the only question is how badly. We have to shut down everything, cut our losses and get out.'

'That won't be so simple,' ███████-████ replied. 'Amina Mir and Chi Sandwith just got their hands on one of our drones.'

There was a frosty silence on the other end of the phone.

'How the hell did that happen?'

'*She shot the bloody thing down.* Don't ask me how! The point is, we can't shut up shop until we've got the thing back or destroyed it. I presume there's nothing on it that can lead back to your company?'

'No, not directly. But . . . No, no, there isn't.'

He didn't sound sure enough for ██████-████'s taste. There was another long pause on the line.

'Look, we don't have any options on this,' ████ said at last. 'I want scorched earth. Leave nothing behind that can implicate us. In two weeks, I want all of this to be a memory.'

'Easier said than done. We don't want them to be able to follow a long line of dead people back to our door. What about ██████████? She won't be happy about shutting down her precious programme.'

'██████████? I think she's outlived her usefulness and I don't trust her motives. If there's any doubt about her, get rid of her too.'

██████-████ sniffed, allowing himself a bleak smile.

'That one will be a pleasure.'

Amina had come home after Tariq had gone to bed

and she was awake and out before he got up. He
didn't know why she had taken the gun, but
it didn't take a rocket scientist to work it out. She
had taken that funeral card threat seriously. Tariq
was worried about her. Whatever she was mixed up
in, she was way out of her depth. He wished their
parents had taken her more seriously – just as he
wished they'd listened when he tried to tell them
about the *MindFeed* program in school. He was still
taking part, but he was feeling increasingly nervous
about it.

They were doing Physics using a beat-'em-up
game today. Speed, acceleration, momentum, mass,
gravity, energy, they all had a bearing on how you
tackled your opponent. You picked your fights
according to how well your specs compared with
your opponent's and played your strengths against
their weaknesses. As the students lined up for roll
call, Tariq held his phone up, pretending to turn it
off, and used the camera to snap some pictures of
Noble.

Once on the computer, he downloaded the
images. The customizing feature of this game, like
the shoot-'em-up, allowed you to paste a new face
onto your opponent's head. Noble's fit perfectly.
Tariq proceeded to thrash the bugger's image with
well-placed blows.

The class passed quickly and it left him in a

good mood. Destroying your tormentor over and over again was quite therapeutic. For most of the rest of the day, Tariq felt better about school. The other lads ignored him at lunchtime, preferring to spend their break smoking out the back and flirting with the 'bad girls'. It made him think of Dani again and how he could make her laugh, but that seemed to be as close as he'd ever get.

Tariq had always been of the opinion that bully victims – and he hated using that term to describe himself, it was so pathetic – brought a lot of trouble on themselves. He probably shouldn't take himself so seriously; he should relax, laugh a bit more at their jibes and even crack a few jokes at his own expense. This whole thing of relishing being the outsider had backfired on him. Being different was all very well, but he seemed to have gone too far. He hadn't been out with a girl in over a *year*.

As he walked out of his last class of the day, he was already considering a change in hairstyle. He could join a couple of the school clubs too – it would be nice to play some tennis again, maybe even take up a martial art. His father was always on at him to channel his aggression into something useful.

Tariq noticed the smell in the corridor as he went to leave his heavier books in his locker before going home. Other kids were looking around too, sniffing the air with puzzled expressions. Wrinkling his nose, he walked along the bank of grey metal doors until he reached his; marked like his school bag with the names of death-metal bands. The odour was stronger here – crawling up his nostrils in feathery wisps of irritation. His eyes were fixed on the three slits perforating the top half of the door. With his keys out, he hesitated before opening it. He already knew what he was going to find.

With jerky movements, he jammed the key in the lock and turned it, yanking the door open. Inside, spread out on his jacket as if dropped from a height, was bagel-sized curl of dog shit. Some of it had been smeared up the walls of the locker and over his books and the stack of software disks. He gently closed the locker, walking away from it until a wave of dizziness came over him. Feeling nauseous, he knelt down and pressed his brow against the cool metal of a locker door. Rage grew like a ball of needles in his mind, his breath coming in short gasps through his teeth. They were never going to leave him alone.

They were never going to leave him alone.

His nails dragged down the drab, painted metal.

They were never going to leave him alone.

His head leaned so hard against it, he could feel the door buckle slightly.

They were never going to leave him alone.

A gurgling growl uttered from his throat, like the sound of some trapped, despairing animal.

There were no clear thoughts in his head as he strode through the corridors and out of the school. The car park was too small and was always full at the end of the day with parents on the school run. Some parents didn't bother pulling in because they were likely to get stuck behind somebody else who was waiting, stopping instead at the kerb of the dual carriageway that ran past the car park. Kids hung around on the path alongside the main road, watching out for their ride home and horsing around while they waited.

Alan Noble and his mates were just outside the gate. There was a three-metre fence around the entire school grounds, but the railings on the side of the road in front of the gate were suitable for sitting on and Noble's crew often claimed them as their own so that they could sit and look out over the high roofs of the SUVs pulling up to the kerb.

Perched on the top bar of the railing, Noble turned in time to see Tariq coming through the gate.

'Whoa!' he said, laughing. 'Look at the face on hi—'

Tariq's first blow broke Noble's nose. Blood sprayed from his nostrils. The frenzy of punches that followed shocked everyone standing nearby. Noble's friends stood frozen for several seconds. The mother behind the wheel of the car nearest the railings saw the violence break out and immediately pulled out of the space and into the road. Tariq kept hitting Noble around the head, grabbing the bully's tie so that he could wrench him back each time his punches knocked the other boy away. Somebody tried to get their arm around Tariq's neck but he bit as hard as he could into their arm until he heard a scream and the arm pulled away. His left hand kept a tight hold on Noble's tie. The skin of his right fist split around the knuckles, cut by the impacts and by Noble's teeth.

More hands grabbed him and this time someone seized his hair, pulling his head back. His grip on Noble's tie was broken and he was dragged back. A man in a silver, low-slung Mazda, unable to see over the Range Rover in front of the fight, spotted the vacant parking space by the railings, gunned his engine and swung into it just as Noble toppled backwards off the railing. His head hit the tarmac of the road, his neck folding under the weight of his body just as the car skidded over him. His shriek grated across the surface of the road before being crushed against the high kerb.

Nobody who heard the sound would ever forget it.

The hands holding Tariq loosened, almost letting him fall. Their grip released and he stood, suddenly conscious of the empty space that had developed around him. The others were distancing themselves from him, and his vision completed the illusion of suddenly floating in space, tunnelling his focus onto the body beneath the front wheel of the car. Somebody behind him started screaming and then another started and another. The harsh sound was a wall pushing him forwards, pressing him against the railing, forcing him to look down on what had once been Alan Noble. Tariq was overcome with the certainty that he had not done this thing. This wasn't happening to him, but to someone outside of him.

'It wasn't me,' he whispered.

As hands seized him again, pulling him back, forcing him to the ground, he shouted it over and over again.

'I didn't do this! I didn't do this! It wasn't me!'

Amina got out of work when the crowds were heaviest, seeking safety and anonymity in the mass of bodies making for the trains. Despite Shang's very public murder, she was convinced that nobody would come for her as long as she had people around her . . . and if they did, she would scream blue murder.

She had spent the previous night lying awake, holding her father's gun beneath the duvet, trying to work out how she could convince her dad of the danger she was in. Maybe if he could get her onto one of the marine bases, they would keep her safe. But for how long? Was she going to have to live in fear for the rest of her life?

The last few nights had taken their toll on her. In the reflection of the train window, her face looked pale and drawn; there were dark bags under her eyes. She fantasized about being able to lie down and close her eyes without fearing for her life, as she had been able to do only a few weeks ago.

The Underground station wasn't far from her house, but this was where she felt the deepest unease, on the walk home. Every car or van that passed near her set her on edge; she flinched at any loud noise. She had the keys for the front door in her hand while she was still a hundred metres from her house.

Amina was unprepared for the scene that awaited her outside her home.

Over a dozen reporters were hanging outside the garden gate with microphones, recorders, cameras and TV cameras. They turned as one when they saw her coming, spreading out to encircle her like a pack of dogs. The questions came in a barrage of insistent voices.

'What made your brother do it? – Has he had any previous history of violence? – Has he ever suffered any other mental health problems? – Tell us about the mind control experiments! – Have any of his friends suffered the same problems? – Does he have any friends? – What about this mind control? – What have the flying saucers got to do with this? – Who is involved in this conspiracy? – Was your father one of the brainwashed soldiers? – What exactly—'

'Stop!' Amina shouted. 'What do you want? What's going on?'

Some of them shared knowing looks. She hadn't heard.

'Amina Mir.' A woman spoke up, brandishing a microphone bearing the news logo of a radio station. 'Your brother, Tariq, has just murdered a fellow student on the road outside their school. He struck him several times in the face and then pushed him under the wheels of an oncoming car.'

Amina's throat tightened, her stomach becoming a hard knot of wood in her abdomen.

'What? What . . . what did you say?'

'Tariq claims that he was being brainwashed by a computer program that the army introduced into the school. He said that he knows this because of a story that you have been working on for the *Chronicle* – a story about soldiers being abducted and put through mental reconditioning by a secret black-operations unit. He said that they are using the same process in his school and that you have received death threats because of your investigations. Is your mother involved in this investigation, Amina? What about your father? What have his connections in the military and the Department of Defence got to say about all this? Have you any comment, Amina?'

The rush of questions began again, buffeting her with their insinuations. She pushed through the pack, hurrying up the driveway, her keys in her hand. The moment she was inside the house, she snatched her mobile from her bag and dialled her mother's number.

'Hi, Mum?'

'Amina? Oh God, love. Are you all right?'

'Is it true, Mum?'

'Tariq killed a boy at his school, honey. There . . . there were a lot of witnesses. He's already . . . he's already confessed. It sounds like a fight that got out of hand. I'm sure the part where . . . where the other boy – Alan Noble – was pushed under the car . . . I'm sure that was an accident. Hang on—' Her mother turned away from the phone to say something to somebody else for a moment and then directed her attention back to Amina. 'Are you all right? The press are at the house, aren't they? Don't say a bloody word to them, OK? Your dad will be home soon and he'll deal with them. Stay inside until your dad gets home. Don't say anything to the press, do you understand?'

Amina hung up. She sat down on the stairs and gazed out through the patterned glass at the distorted figures hovering outside the gate. It occurred to her that she had better put her father's gun back. But even if she cleaned it he would know it had been fired – and anyway, she had no way of replacing the four missing bullets and he always knew exactly how much ammunition he had in the house.

If the press found out who had fired the shots at Chi's house, her family's reputation for insanity would be confirmed.

Staring out at the reporters, the irony of the situation did not escape her. She had wanted proper publicity for her story and now she'd got it. She had craved the safety of the public eye and now she had it in spades. It was hard to see how things could get any worse.

14

Things got steadily worse. Over the next week, Tariq's assault on Alan Noble continued to be held up by the press as the latest evidence that young people today were violent screw-ups. Helena Jessop and Martin Mir put their media savvy to good use, releasing a carefully measured statement to the press and downplaying talk of Amina's 'investigation' and Tariq's claims about being brainwashed.

But the dogs had their teeth into this now. If Tariq had not mentioned the army's computer program, the story might have faded after a few days – another tragic episode of school violence. Instead, the sniff of a conspiracy added far more meat to this story. But the idea wasn't taken seriously; it was used instead to establish how disturbed Tariq was and how his older sister's outlandish theories had sent him over the edge. The boy remanded to the detention centre in Feltham – bore so little resemblance to her brother, caught in snatched shots by the press's cameras outside the police station that Amina had to look twice at him before she recognized him. Pictures on television of his new face, with its hollowed cheeks and sunken eyes, made him look like a haunted schizophrenic.

The *Chronicle* distanced themselves from Amina, saying that she had been working outside her brief, that she wasn't even a real reporter, just a university student on work experience.

All of a sudden, the rest of the press seemed to know a great deal about Amina and her connections with Chi and Ivor. Too much, too fast. She was told not to come into work for a week and she spent most of the time watching the news and reading the papers online, and she was astounded at how much they knew, how detailed their background information was.

Tariq's poor record in a series of schools, his behavioural problems and the fights he'd got into were all made public. Even his brief foray into Islamic fundamentalism was dragged out. They made a big issue of the music he listened to, especially the 'nihilistic' work of Absent Conscience, whose songs were also being blamed for a school shooting in the States.

Amina's youth and lack of experience in

journalism were highlighted, excusing her for her gullibility in being taken in by more cynical types. But in some reports, she was portrayed as ruthlessly ambitious, willing to weave any kind of fantastic tale in her desperation to make headlines. Girls she'd hardly known in school were interviewed, claiming she had always cared more for her career than for friends or family, airing old grudges against her that she'd never even been aware of. In their opinion, she was not above playing to Ivor McMorris's insecurities in order to use him for his story . . . and his lottery millions.

Even Dani showed up on television, labelled 'Amina Mir's Best Friend' on the banner, describing how Amina had changed in the last couple of weeks, how she had stopped answering her friends' calls, and had become distant, antisocial, a loner.

Chi Sandwith was shown to be a stereotypical conspiracy freak. Much was made of his articles on abduction, on his more bizarre theories and his paranoid lifestyle. His neighbours, none of whom spoke with any ill-will, confided that he was considered something of a harmless nut who was tolerated in his eccentricities as long as he kept his weird electronics experiments under control. His parents' broken marriage was mentioned, as well as his younger brother, who had died in a car accident as a young child.

Ivor was portrayed as an even more pathetic character. Allegedly addicted to sleeping tablets while in Sinnostan, he had been caught in a terrorist bombing that had cost him an eye and some facial scarring that had seen him released from service. It had resulted in him becoming a recluse – a condition compounded by post-traumatic stress disorder, a diagnosis that included hallucinations, delusions and, of course, paranoia. His recent win of over two million pounds on the National Lottery was reported to have made him even more insecure, and now the conspiracy he had been concocting in his mind was being given flesh by all the lunatics his money was attracting. The suicide of his friend, Ben Considine, had apparently cut the last few fragile threads of his sanity.

This kind of character assassination took up most of the space in the reports. The trio's investigation into Sinnostan and the brainwashing process – Amina was really beginning to hate that term – was mentioned just often enough to dismiss it as fantasy. The military ridiculed the idea of soldiers being 'abducted' and experimented upon, consigning the idea to the same realms as UFOs and the Loch Ness Monster. The press had even got hold of Amina's pictures of Chi holding the surveillance drone – she had sent them to a number of servers, including her own email address at the *Chronicle* –

suggesting that Sandwith, an electronics expert, had built the device himself in an effort to persuade the world of the truth of his theories. Naturally, the contraption did not actually *work*.

The army withdrew *MindFeed* from schools, but vigorously defended it, denying that it caused aggression in any way and pointing out that if you wanted to find the source of behavioural problems in any individual, the first place you should look was the parents.

Helena Jessop and Martin Mir observed this onslaught with growing outrage. They were only beginning to come to terms with the fact that their son had killed someone and this made it so much worse. They knew a smear campaign when they saw it and could not believe it was being aimed at their children. Amina was afraid that they would hold her partly responsible for Tariq's moment of madness, but in the beginning they were too concerned for their son and his victim to worry about blaming their daughter. As the attacks in the media continued, they recognized an agenda at work and set about trying to find out who was feeding all of this information to the reporters.

But then came the day when Martin, in a moment of severe stress, settled down to the calming routine of stripping down and cleaning his gun at the kitchen table.

Amina had been meaning to tell him that she had taken it — she really had. She'd just never built up the nerve. He realized the weapon had been fired moments after taking it out of the lockbox and when he discovered that four bullets were missing, he summoned Amina to him with a voice so level and reasoned that it terrified them.

Confessing to her father that she had fired his Browning automatic at a UFO was the scariest thing Amina had ever done. She broke down crying before she finished, but he just stared at her with a stone-cold expression on his face.

'What did we do wrong?' he asked quietly, once she had calmed down. 'Your mother and I . . . we can't understand where all this has come from. You have both . . .' His voice cracked, but he regained his composure before continuing. 'You both seem to have completely lost your minds. But all this madness is going to stop now. Tariq is going to stand trial for manslaughter . . . if we're *lucky*, it'll be manslaughter. The best we can hope for is a plea of temporary insanity, but frankly, your mother has covered enough murder cases and she doesn't hold out much hope. It's very possible that Tariq will be spending the next few years of his life in juvenile detention.

'Amina, tomorrow you are going to take me to where you fired this weapon and you're going to show me this thing you claim to have shot down. And so help me God, if I'm not satisfied with what I see, you'll think Tariq got off easy. Do you understand me?'

That night Amina took the home phone to her bedroom. She knew someone would be listening in on the call, but they weren't going to hear anything they didn't already know. She tried to ring Chi on his mobile four times, but could not get through. On the off-chance that he might have returned home, she called the house too, but only the answering machine picked up. Without much hope, she decided to try Ivor and was surprised when he picked up his phone on the third ring.

'You're home?' she gasped. 'They let you out on bail?'

'The million quid I was going to give to Shang is being held as evidence,' Ivor told her. 'The judge at the hearing thought that was more than enough leverage to keep me around until the end of the trial. Listen, I heard about your brother.'

'Hard not to,' she snorted. 'The news can't seem to shut up about it.'

'I'm really sorry, Amina. How's he holding up?'

'Better than the other guy.' She winced. 'Sorry, that sounds awful . . . Mum and Dad met Alan's parents the other day. It was pretty traumatic. I've never seen Mum cry as hard as she did when she got home.'

'There's something else I need to tell you,' Ivor said. 'I went round to see Chi, but the police are all over his house. There were bullet holes in one of the windows.'

'Yeah. That was . . . that was me,' Amina replied.

She glanced towards her bedroom door; she lowered her voice and told Ivor what had happened, explaining that Chi had taken the surveillance drone and gone into hiding. Ivor whistled in wonder. She didn't tell him where Chi had gone. Not over the phone.

'C'm'ere,' he said. 'Can I pick you up? I've hired a car. There's something I need to tell you. And I'm going somewhere tonight: you might want to tag along.'

Amina could guess what her parents might have to say about that, but at this point she was past caring. Tariq was being done for manslaughter, she was a public disgrace and her story had been ridiculed. Her mother and father held her in thinly disguised contempt. It felt like she had nothing to lose any more.

'Sure,' she chirped. 'Beep your horn when you're outside.'

★ ★ ★

Ivor got there in less than half an hour, drawing up

in a bland, blue Toyota saloon. Thankfully, the reporters who had spent most of the week hanging around the outside of the house were nowhere to be seen. It was cold outside. Amina walked outto the car, turning to look back through the darkness at her parents, who were watching her, silhouetted in the light of the living-room window. Getting into the passenger seat, she hugged Ivor and gave him a kiss on the cheek, and he replied with a squeeze of her hand and an uncertain smile.

'I'm glad you called,' she said, surprised at the shyness in her own voice. 'Not just because of this, I mean . . . I . . . it's just good to see you.'

'You too . . . that's . . . it's good to see you too,' he stammered. He was about to take the handbrake off when he hesitated, turning to look at her. 'Listen, Amina. I know how I feel about you and I think you kind o' like me too, but . . . I have to ask: Is it me you're interested in, or . . . or is it my story?'

She looked away, thinking for a moment. Then she met his gaze again.

'I don't know. Is there a difference?'

He smiled, then an uncertain expression crossed his features and he smiled once more.

'Honestly? I'm not sure. I never thought of it like that before.'

Ivor let it go at that, figuring that she hadn't given him a perfect answer, but it wasn't a half bad one either. Better than he'd hoped. Pulling back out into the road, he started talking quickly.

'The last time I saw Chi, he told me about a woman named Ellen Rosenstock. She came up with a process known as strobe interruption that could be used to—'

'I know, I heard the recording you made of Shang,' she told him. 'So she invented the process they used on you?'

'Yeah, right. Well, she started off using it on university students. Listening to what the news had to say about Tariq's freak-out, I wondered if she might have anything to do with the program the army was using in the school. If that's the case, then maybe he's not so responsible for his actions after all, yeah?'

Amina nodded. She'd already considered the possibility that Tariq had been programmed into doing what he did. Anything was easier than believing he was a killer. That said, if he had been brainwashed, then it might well have been because of the questions she had been asking. That gave her no comfort at all.

It also made her ponder the army's motives for using *MindFeed* in schools. Were they up to something more sinister than education? Perhaps they too were being manipulated by someone else.

'So where do we start looking for her?' Amina asked.

'You're not going to believe this, but she's in the phone book,' he said, chuckling. 'I decided not to call her, in case . . . you know.'

Amina nodded. She knew.

'Instead, I figured we'd just drop in on her and ask her a few questions. She has an address in Fulham.'

'Cool.'

He looked over at Amina and gave her that grin she was growing to love. It was nice to be sitting here beside him, as if they were just out for a drive, or going on a date somewhere. Doing something normal. But there was nothing normal about what they were doing. If Rosenstock was so deeply involved in this mess, she was bound to be well protected. They were taking a big risk in going to see her. Amina could see from the look on Ivor's face that he was feeling as reckless as she was. They had been through so much that they were done caring about consequences. If anything, they were feeling an insane giddiness. All that mattered to them now was getting to the truth and finding the proof to back it up. And if Amina could help Tariq, any risk would be worth it.

As they drove, each filled the other in on what they'd missed. When Amina heard that Ivor had been shot, she insisted on looking at the wound. He was touched by the hurt in her voice, the pain in her eyes. She told him about Donghu. The Sinnostani's view of the war came as little surprise to Ivor now. She asked him about the charges against him.

'They caught me at the scene, but their evidence is thin,' Ivor said, shrugging, his eyes on the road. 'My lawyer says they don't have much of a case so far. The murder weapon was found on the ground a few metres away, but there are no prints on it and I wasn't wearing gloves. They don't have a clear motive and Shang's been vilified as a terrorist so there'll be little sympathy for him. Can't say I've any for him myself.'

His hand went up to his right eye, his fingers brushing against the eyelid.

'Even so, you don't know what they're going to turn up on me if somebody decides to cook up some evidence. I wouldn't put it past them.'

Amina put her hand on his, wishing she could do more than offer this scant comfort.

When they reached the address in Fulham, a large Victorian house on a street of tree-lined, upper middle-class residences, they found a police car and an ambulance sitting outside. Their roof-lights flashed ominously in the gloom, their blue light giving the pleasant street an air of sinister drama. Ivor pulled up twenty metres back on the other side of the road.

'That's the house,' he muttered.

Amina couldn't even muster any shock or surprise at what she was witnessing. A stretcher was being carried down the steps from the front door. There was a body lying still on the stretcher. The head had been covered up.

'Do you think they knew we were coming?' she asked quietly.

'Probably,' he replied. 'But they've been one step ahead of us the whole time. Maybe she was becoming a liability anyway. Either way, it doesn't matter. Everything we try and do, they cut the legs out from under us.'

He fell silent, gazing out at the ambulance as it drove off without haste and without its sirens. A police officer spoke to two people standing on the path for a few minutes and then he left too. There was no attempt to cordon off the scene. There was no suspicion that a crime had happened here.

'What now?' Amina looked at Ivor.

His shoulders were slumped in defeat, his morose expression spoke of a complete loss of hope and it hurt her heart to see it. He didn't answer her. Taking a notepad from her bag, she scribbled some words on it and showed it to him. With a sigh, he read the words: *Let's go see Chi.*

'Where is he?' he mouthed the word to her.

She put pen to paper again, and wrote out Stefan Gierek's address.

'First, though, I want to talk to someone else,' she said.

1

Stefan Gierek maintained a 'city base' with four other survivalist fanatics in an industrial estate in Cricklewood. All five had been casualties of the Sinnostan war and had devoted their lives to resenting the British government because of it. Chi's discovery of the surveillance drone had helped mollify Gierek and bought him sanctuary in the Pole's homemade fortress.

Ivor, Amina and their guest parked the car in a city-centre car park and took a tortuous route through the Underground and by bus and taxi to the address, in an attempt to throw off any followers. There were few people on the streets and train platforms. Stopping at a payphone halfway through their journey, Amina made a phone call to alert Chi and his host that they were coming. A light rain drifted from the sky, dampening everything around them and giving the city a greasy, sleazy feel. The three travellers looked over their shoulders regularly, their eyes constantly scanning for any sign of a threat. Amina wondered again if she would ever be able to walk alone in dark streets without that near-constant edge of fear.

It was almost midnight by the time they arrived at the decommissioned factory that served as home for Gierek and his trucking company. It was easy to see why he'd picked it.

The walls, built to support the weight of some kind of machinery inside, were steel-reinforced concrete. The garage entrance and the few windows on the ground floor were covered with heavy steel shutters. The windows on the first floor were secured with horizontal steel bars, as were the sky-lights in the roof. There were no buildings adjoining the factory and the upper-floor windows had a view of the wide yard on every side. Gierek's four trucks were kept safely in the garage. CCTV cameras and motion sensors surveyed every inch of the floodlit exterior and the compound was surrounded by a high fence topped with razorwire.

A few weeks ago, Amina would have con-sidered this level of security for a trucking company a little absurd. Now, she found it comforting. Gierek came out to greet them, nodding at Amina and Ivor through the bars of the gate. The floodlights created a halo-like reflection around his broad, shaved head. He glared suspiciously at John Donghu, whose little figure stood hunched against the rain in a worn leather bomber jacket.

'Who is that?' the Pole snarled.

'A friend,' Amina told him. 'I told Chi about him on the phone. We can trust him.'

With a grunt that could have meant anything, Gierek pressed a remote and the gate slid open far enough to let them slip through before closing again immediately.

The interior of the building was as severely practical as the exterior. Half of the space was divided into two floors, with offices downstairs and living space upstairs. The rest was for the lorries: two DAF container trucks and two Mercedes tractors with sleeper cabs. They were in immaculate condition. A Land Rover was parked in front of them. There was enough equipment in the garage to carry out all but the most serious maintenance, including a heavy-duty winch hanging from a girder in the roof. A first-floor balcony encircled the garage space to allow access to the windows on all sides.

Amina and Ivor studied the place for a moment and then looked at each other. It gave them a gratifying feeling of safety.

Part of the living space on the first floor was

given over to a gym and the new arrivals followed Gierek upstairs to find Chi working out on a bench press, wearing a vest and tracksuit bottoms. Judging by the pale flab hanging from his chest and arms, this kind of exercise was a new experience for him.

'Hi!' he exclaimed, growling against the strain of the weights. 'They've got me working on my cuts and going for the burn!'

The others waited patiently for him to finish. There was a formidably fit-looking man spotting him, dressed in camouflage T-shirt and combats and sporting a high-and-tight haircut. Another three, equally butch, survivalists sat around the area. One kept his eyes on a bank of screens that showed the views of the surveillance cameras outside. Another was examining Chi's captive UFO, carefully peering through a magnifying lens at some of the electronics. The third one just stood leaning against a doorway, staring at the newcomers from behind mirrored sunglasses.

'I heard about your brother, Amina,' Chi panted, as his training partner nodded to him and he finally finished his reps. 'I'm really sorry. If it's any comfort, I think he may have been set up.'

'No, it's not much comfort and yes, I've already considered that he might have been set up,' she replied. 'Ivor and I went to talk to Ellen Rosenstock this evening. The others got there first. We've hit another dead end.'

Chi's face fell, and he digested this news with a pensive expression, chewing his lip. Then he nodded to himself.

'They're mopping up. But it's not over,' he said at last. 'I think we've really got them cornered now. I bet they thought they were really smart, showing the pictures of this surveillance drone – making it look like I'd built it myself so I'd appear a fool if I tried to go public with it. There are no markings on it – *anywhere* – so they probably thought it couldn't be traced back to them. They were wrong.

'There are five different parts of this machine that have been patented. Why go to all the bother of designing a whole bunch of new bits when you can use existing ones, right? One company holds all the patents; a group called VioMaze. I bought a few shares in the company and—'

'And they sent you a brochure,' Amina murmured.

'Right.' Chi grinned. 'They make military gear – you name it, they can supply it. Even really unusual stuff like, oh . . . I don't know . . . unmanned surveillance aircraft, maybe? They've got knockout gas and other "non-lethal" weapons – plenty of *lethal* stuff too, of course. They can set up mobile operating theatres and build prisons. They can even supply "private security operatives" – that's "mercenaries" to you and me . . . serious ones too – ex-Special Forces. Oh, and you know what else they make? *MindFeed*, the program the army's using in schools. VioMaze is the one-stop shop for everything you need to fake a war.'

'That's great, but that's still not enough of a link to put anybody in prison,' Ivor pointed out. 'Or in Tariq's case, keep them out. What use is it?'

Chi sat back, disappointed with the lack of gushing praise.

'It's a good start,' he retorted. 'We can follow the leads—'

'We've been following the leads since this whole thing started!' Ivor snapped. 'All it's got us is public ridicule, a few dead bodies and our days spent waiting to be dragged into the back of a van and carted off to a disappearance somewhere. I've had enough. I got you two into this and I've been regretting it ever since. It's time to stop before it gets any worse. We don't have enough evidence to finish it and every time we get close, somebody dies, or goes to prison or . . . or . . . I've just had enough.'

It was clear from his posture that he meant it.

'I'm not finished,' Chi insisted. 'The head of this company is a retired navy admiral by the name of Robert Cole. Remember the photo I showed you of Rosenstock and two others? He's one of the guys in the picture. I went through Nexus's disks. Nex found out the Triumvirate were trying to smuggle nerve gas into Sinnostan. Why? Maybe because it'll prove to everyone that we were right to go to war. Who makes the nerve gas? VioMaze. Not in Europe, obviously, 'cos it's illegal. If we can find proof that—'

'But we never find proof,' Ivor interrupted. 'They're ahead of us at every turn. And sooner or later, we'll run out of luck.'

'I love it, the word "war",' John Donghu said abruptly. The others turned to look at him, as if noticing him for the first time. 'This word, it changes everything. After you use it, you can do almost anything and people will understand – they will forgive. You can hurt another human being – call them "enemy" and then murder them. You can commit the worst of crimes and your government will pin a medal on your chest. You can bomb cities.' He made an explosive gesture with his hands. 'Reason is turned on its head at the mention of the magic word: "war".'

Donghu settled into a chair, looking round at his audience.

'Nobody cares enough about this war to stop it, now that it has started,' he rasped. 'It's too far away for them to care. Bad things happen in war, that's just the way it is. Even you don't care enough about this.' He held up his hands to silence them. 'It's not a criticism. You care first about your safety and about your story and that is understandable. I am always the same. But I tell you this . . .' He leaned forward. 'You should be angry because *they* have made you *afraid*. Not just you – all of your people. They gave you an enemy in Sinnostan and wailed about bombings and aeroplanes and nerve gas and you cowered as if you had seen a ghost.

'Me, I am much more scared of car crashes than ghosts. Your trains worry me too, but mostly cars. They are deadly things. It is the same in my country. Many more people are killed by pick-up trucks than bombs. They crash into each other, they run off the road, they roll over. People fall out of the back. Nobody wears seatbelts. But it's very hard to make people afraid of their cars. You cannot declare war on pick-up trucks.

'The powerful ones make you afraid of the bogeyman so that you will be good children and go to bed when you're told. And though there are real bogeymen – real terrorists – they are less dangerous than car crashes or bad electrical wiring or heart attacks. Now that you have started questioning the bogeyman legend, it is the powerful ones who are afraid. But any animal that is afraid will lash out and that's what they're doing now. And they *can* hurt you while there are just a few of you.

'I know this animal and I have fought it before and I can tell you that it *cannot be killed*. Defeat it once, and it will rise again in another shape.'

Donghu rubbed his hands together, his eyes seeing something else in another place – another time. His hands clasped into fists, nails digging into his palms.

'But you can make it afraid of you and that is enough. It is a creature of the night; drag it into the light and you can beat it. You must drag it out where others can see it and they will help you. They will not believe in it unless they see it for themselves.'

There was silence for some time after he finished. Then Amina spoke:

'The press have made us out to be paranoid cranks who believe in flying saucers and make up our stories as we go along. We don't have enough proof to take to a court or a newspaper or television channel – not now that we've been discredited. But we have enough to make people question what's going on and I think we should put that inform-ation where everyone can find it.'

'How?' Ivor asked. 'We could email it to every reporter in the country, but the story's already been rubbished in the media; reporters will avoid it like the plague – particularly if it's coming from any of us. We could email it to everybody we know and ask them to send it on, but it's become a conspiracy theory now. You know how many of those are circulating the web? How many do you pay attention to, when they come into your inbox? Sure they're good for a laugh, but nobody takes them seriously.

'Chi's run a well-informed blog for years,' he went on. 'So has John here. Nobody goes to them unless they're looking for them. We could put all our information on a website, but how will people find it? No reputable paper or magazine will let us advertise this – they won't take the chance of being sued. And anyway, websites and blogs can be attacked with viruses and shut down. You'd have to put it on a dozen websites . . . a hundred. How do we get ordinary people to go looking for them?'

'We create a virus all our own,' Amina told him. 'An information virus. One that will make the news. Let's drag this animal out into the light. We'll need a printing press, some websites . . . and a large sum of money.' She looked coyly at Ivor. 'Money talks. Oh . . . and it would help if it's a slow news day.'

Then she told them what she had in mind.

There were mixed feelings about it. Ivor was willing to fork out the cash, but he wasn't the only one to wonder if this was the best way to use it. Chi wanted to wait until they had more conclusive proof. Gierek and his mates liked the brazen nature of the plan, but were a little too keen on using explosives.

After the details had been worked out, Donghu went home, but Amina and Ivor stayed the night there. Gierek gave up his bed for Amina, and Ivor settled on the floor beside her in a sleeping bag.

'You know,' he whispered to her in the darkness, 'if we do go through with this, we'll be breaking the law. We could be arrested.'

'Then we'll get even more publicity,' she said. As she said it, she realized arrest was a more serious problem for a man already out on bail. Feeling a little ashamed, she added: 'Let's hope we cause enough fuss to justify the crime. We should make the headlines unless something really bad happens.'

'Well then,' he chuckled, 'let's hope the world stays safe for the next few days.'

They drifted off after that. And both of them slept better than they had in weeks.

5

Amina was back at work two days later. She was treated with an uncomfortable combination of sympathy and avoidance by the rest of the staff. Nobody gave her any work that involved writing, editing or emailing. She wasn't allowed to photo-copy sensitive documents. They wouldn't let her anywhere near a computer. So she fetched drinks and breakfast bagels and tried to make herself as useful as possible. There were few advantages to making the coffee, but one of them was the chance to overhear snippets of editorial meetings.

This was how she came to be among the first to hear about the deaths at the Lizard Club.

Goldbloom had called a meeting of all the lead journalists as soon as word reached him. Coffee, tea and mineral water were ordered and Amina duly delivered. Her curiosity was piqued by the subdued mood that pervaded the newsroom. She had never seen this before – it took something horrific to bring the frenetic activity of this hive to a halt. After putting the tray of drinks on the table in the conference room, Amina hung by the door to try and listen in. To her surprise, nobody even noticed her.

Charlie Stokes – visibly restless without a cigarette in his hand – was in the middle of relating what had happened at the nightclub. The rest of the people in the room listened in sombre, respectful silence.

'. . . The medics said it could have been much worse. If the nerve agent had worked slower, more people would have been affected. They were all teenagers out on the town after their graduation ball. Beautiful young kids, all dressed up to the nines in tuxes and ball gowns. You should have seen it – they were still dealing with the casualties when I got there. There were far more girls affected; more of them were drinking shorts and alco-pops. At first everyone thought the ones who were throwing up had just had too much to drink. But others started collapsing soon after and when a few started having convulsions and haemorrhaging around the eyes, then the panic started.

'There was a stampede for the doors because somebody thought it was being caused by gas. More people were hurt in the crush. When they first got there, the medics thought the water might have been poisoned. But the club doesn't serve tap water and, of course, all the individual bottles are sealed until they're served.

'Then they figured out that it was the ice. Somebody had fed some highly potent nerve agent into the ice machine. All of the ones who fell ill had ice in their drinks. Thankfully, the kids stopped drinking when the first few collapsed. That's the mercy of it. If the first ones hadn't died in the club, hundreds more could have drunk from contaminated glasses.'

Charlie looked down at his notes, his calm reserve cracking for just a moment before he collected himself and continued:

'Nobody knows what the toxin is yet, but it's definitely not a chemistry-set job. It may even be a weaponized nerve gas in its liquid form. The amount needed for a fatal dose is tiny – a drop the size of a pinhead. The latest count stands at fifteen dead, sixty-two in critical condition. Doctors don't know how many of those will make it, but there's a strong possibility that even if they do, they will have suffered permanent brain damage. The doctors have no idea how to counter this stuff without knowing what it is.'

He pressed a button on the DVD player beneath the television on the wall and stood back.

'We received this disk this morning.'

The screen came on to show a man wearing a T-shirt emblazoned with a Sinnostan flag. A black balaclava covered his face. His hands were clasped in a relaxed fashion on the table in front of him.

'People of Britain, today you wake to a different dawn. Today you wake to the emptiness left by your dead children. The nerve agent we used on the unfortunates in the Lizard Club was designed and manufactured by your people. You sent it to Sinnostan as part of your war and we have sent it back to you. This operation is only the beginning. There is plenty more poison where that came from. Your arms dealers supplied it in industrial quantities.

'I want you to know fear: in your Underground; in your train stations and airports; in your schools. We can and will strike wherever we choose. We make no demands of you – those will come later. First we want you to be terrified of us . . . because you should be.

'I have no religion. I am not a fanatical nationalist. I am a father, a son, a brother. I have no intention of dying for my cause. That is *your* purpose. You will be hearing from us again.'

The screen went blank. Charlie switched off the television.

'We don't know who they are,' he informed the

group before him. 'They didn't identify themselves – not even a group name. We can assume they're Sinnostani, but that's about it.'

'All right.' Goldbloom stood up heavily, letting out a long breath. 'Most of the photos from the scene were taken on camera phones, but they'll do. Let's put a face on this disaster. They were celebrating their graduation, so see if you can get their grad photos. Pick the prettiest girl on the critical list – I want the front page with a before and after: grad photo and her on the life support machine. "Horror of Young Lives Cut Short" kind of thing. That's it. Get on with it.'

Amina hurried out of the conference room and grabbed her phone from her bag. Dialling Chi's number, she waited impatiently for him to answer.

'Amina?'

'Have you seen the news about the Lizard Club?'

'Of course. There's only been sketchy reports so far, but—'

'They used a nerve toxin. Listen, did Nex have any information on that stuff they were trying to smuggle into Sinnostan?'

There was a pause on the line: she could hear Chi clicking his tongue.

'Could we not do this on your mobile?' he asked. 'Call me back from somewhere more secure and we can talk about it. And we need to keep it short, OK?'

Amina hung up and swore under her breath.

It took her ten minutes to get out and find a working payphone, two streets from the *Chronicle* building. She didn't know why she was bothering – it was barely safer than using her own phone – but she decided it was best to humour Chi. He was much more experienced at being paranoid than she was.

Closing the door of the phone box, she kept looking around her as she picked up the receiver and started to dial. Her head began to swim. Leaning back against the perspex wall of the booth, she put her hand up to her face as her vision blurred. She had time to look out at the street in front of her and see two men coming towards her wearing paramedics' uniforms, striding unhurriedly up to the phone box. No, she thought. Not like this. Amina was barely aware of her surroundings now, but she seemed to be sitting down in the cramped booth. How did that happen? Her thoughts were becoming increasingly confused. The door opened and she blinked, pushing herself back against the inside wall, waving her arms feebly in front of her. She made a pathetic attempt to fight the men who leaned in towards her. Strong hands gently pulled her out and lifted her onto a stretcher.

No, she tried to say. No. Her words came out as a slurred mumbling. She knew what they'd done. They'd booby-trapped the phone somehow – wiped the mouthpiece with anaesthetic or maybe even rigged it to release a gas when she picked it up. Very James Bond.

People on the street watched as the men wheeled the stretcher towards a waiting ambulance. They probably mistook her weak sobs for some semi-conscious, delirious pain. The Scalps were taking her out here, with all these people around. Amina was able to stay awake long enough to see the curious onlookers peering through the rear doors of the ambulance as she was lifted inside. Then the doors were swung closed and she was alone and trapped and terrified. She looked up at the men's faces, crying, begging them incoherently to leave her alone. A mask was pressed over her nose and mouth and it all went away.

Amina's breath panted weakly, hollowly in a mask. Things came and went woozily. Lights trailed by overhead. She was floating down a corridor. No. She was on a trolley. It was all confusing. Where was she? What was going on? Her eyes closed. They opened again. The ceiling had changed. A different corridor. This was wrong. She must try and stay awake. It was hard to remember why it was wrong.

Then it came to her. The Scalps had her. Amina started to panic. She tried to sit up. Her wrists and ankles were strapped to the rails on the sides of the trolley. Another restraint crossed her chest, holding her down. She tried to scream, but it came out like a whimper. Whatever they'd given her had left her partially paralysed.

'She's coming round,' a voice said.

'Put her under again,' another replied.

Ivor had described this to her. This had happened to him before they brainwashed him. Before they operated on him and took out his eye. Amina wailed into the plastic mask, her breath fogging it. She tried to shake it off, but it was held firmly on her face by its straps. The men were not hiding their faces. That wasn't good. Either she wouldn't be able to describe them when all this was over . . . or she wouldn't live to. Her sobbing grew harder. Some of her strength was coming back. She pulled at the straps on her wrists again.

'I said put her under,' the second voice said again. 'I want her out by the time we get started on her.'

Get started on her? Amina's imagination began torturing her. She didn't think of the soldiers who had died in Sinnostan; she thought about the ones who had made it back despite horrible injuries. Men and women like Ivor who had lost eyes, or arms or legs or who'd been burned or had shrapnel embedded in their bodies.

She wondered if she was going to get a turn on the roulette wheel. What were they going to do to her? Whatever they wanted. No matter how hard she thrashed, she was helpless. Another scream rose from deep inside her. The men who were pushing her along on this trolley did not care. She was just another job to be done.

'Don't worry, love,' the first man said, leaning over her. His hand reached down under the mattress and he turned something and she heard a hissing sound. 'No matter how bad it gets, you won't remember a thing.'

Amina started to lose consciousness again.

I will, she swore to herself. You won't make me forget. I will remember. If Ivor could do it, so can I.

But Ivor had a loose tooth that helped him remember. She did not. As her senses began to fail her, Amina bit down hard on the side of her tongue. Wincing, she crushed the flesh between her teeth again, tasting blood.

I *will* remember.

12

Chi waited an hour for Amina to call. After that, he knew she wasn't going to. The Scalps were mopping up. He sat at Gierek's computer desk, his head in his hands, wondering what he was going to do. Despite having five well-armed, hardcore survival enthusiasts at his disposal, he was utterly helpless. He didn't even know where to start looking for her. He could report her missing, but what good would that do? Amina was gone.

She had wanted to try and help the kids who were dying from the nerve agent used at the Lizard Club. The least Chi could do was give the police everything he had on VioMaze. Maybe the company had an antidote. They might even be embarrassed into handing it over – if it could be proved it was their stuff the terrorists had used.

Which, of course, it couldn't.

Even so, he had to try. There was a police station only ten minutes walk away. Chi saved his files onto his MP3 player and, checking his pepper spray was in his pocket, he made for the door.

'Where d'you think you're going, pecker-wood?' Gierek called after him, from beneath the chassis of one of the trucks.

'Out. Don't suppose any of you want to come along?'

'Busy,' Gierek grunted back. 'Don't be long. Your turn to cook dinner.'

Chi nodded and walked out. He had to stand and wait for Gierek to buzz the gate open long enough for him to slip through and then he started along the road out of the industrial estate. He hated Cricklewood. He found the place depressing and even in daylight, he was nervous walking around here. This part of it consisted of half-dead green areas and wide roads, forbidding blocks of flats and high walls encircling factories and goods yards. Razorwire said a lot about a neighbourhood. In the evening, many of the streetlights in the area were out.

His eyes followed any car or van that came too close to him along the road. He had his earphones in, but kept the sound off. It was never a good idea to block out your own hearing. A helicopter passed by overhead and he watched it anxiously. But it was probably just some rich slob avoiding the traffic.

The dog came at him out of nowhere. A Rottweiler, a mound of black and brown snarling muscle with jaws dripping drool, charged up behind him. Chi turned round to face it in alarm and immediately knew it was a mistake. This dog wasn't playing. And it wasn't stopping. Chi put his hand in his pocket to reach for his pepper spray. It would probably stop the animal . . . or it might just make it mad. He bolted for the nearest cover.

Turning down an alleyway between two factory walls, he looked round desperately for something to climb up on. But everything around here was built to be youth-proof. The dog came into the alley after him, dashing towards him with unnerving speed. He had seconds before it was on him. A steel door started to open in the wall to his right. Chi rammed through it and slammed it shut behind him. There was a thud and the scrape of claws on metal as the dog hit the other side. An enraged barking erupted outside.

'Down, Butch,' a man's voice shouted.

The dog fell quiet. The hair on the back of Chi's neck stood on end as he realized that the voice had come from behind him . . . on his side of the door. He turned to find himself in a small utility room with bare concrete walls lined with fuse boxes and pipes. It was dark; there were no windows, just a bare fluorescent bulb that flickered dimly. Another door in the opposite wall was closed, hiding whatever lay beyond. There were four men in here with him, all wearing gas masks. So much for his pepper spray.

None of them looked surprised to see him.

'Chi Sandwith,' one of them said in a muffled, rubbery voice. 'That was your life.'

Chi fought them. There was no hope, but he wanted there to be evidence of a struggle on his body. Anything that could be found in an autopsy: skin under his fingernails, bruising on his body, defence wounds . . . anything that could tell the world he wasn't just another sympathy case who'd done himself in because he couldn't handle living.

But these men were too good. When they finally jammed the cloth over his nose and mouth, his limbs were restrained firmly but gently, in ways unlikely to leave any marks at all. The concrete floor was cold and gritty as it pressed against his skin. The cloth was damp and the fumes from it quickly made him dizzy. Sobbing, he tried to hold his breath, but it was useless. He was grateful when the end finally came.

★   ★   ★

Much to his dismay, Chi woke up. It seemed his ordeal wasn't over yet. He was lying on the floor in the back of a van, with a man sitting on the bench over the wheel-arch beside him. The man was stocky, with a tight haircut, the skin of his scalp and face stained with the dark tinge of one who simply cannot shave enough. Chi's eyes were drawn to the large brown mole on his jawline. It had been cut recently, presumably while shaving. If there was any expression at all in the man's eyes, it was one of amusement.

'He's awake!' he said, over the noise of the engine.

'So what?' someone called from the front.

Chi was lying on his front. As he rolled over onto his back to look around, he felt something hard and square dig into his side, but he couldn't tell what it was. The interior of the van was unremark-able — white, with racks of some sort lining the walls. Two more of the Scalps sat up front. It was dark out. Chi worked out that he must have been unconscious for at least eight hours. His arms and legs were tightly pinned and he gazed down at what was holding them. It appeared to be some kind of shrink-wrap, wound around his entire body from his feet, all the way up to his mouth, which was effectively gagged. Only his nostrils were left free so that he could breathe.

'It's clever stuff,' the guy with the mole told him. 'Dissolves in water. Not too fast, mind you – after a couple of hours or so. Won't leave a trace. As far as anybody will be able to tell, you'll have gone into the river of your own free will.'

'Why do you always have to talk to them?' the driver shouted back. 'He's a muppet – and a dead one at that.'

The stocky one ignored his colleague, continuing to stare down at Chi with a disturbing intensity.

'I put a couple of bricks in your pockets, so you'll sink fast,' Mole said. 'It'll be over quicker if you don't hold your breath. Just open your mouth and suck that water into your lungs. You won't, of course, but I thought I'd say it.'

So that was it. They were taking him to Suicide Bridge or somewhere like it. Chi tried to hide his fear, but it was pointless. He was trembling like a child, his skin was coated in a cold sweat and his bladder was threatening to release its contents into the shrink-wrap. The van slowed down and the driver let out a curse.

'There's people on the bridge.'

Mole stood up and walked forward to look out of the windscreen.

'What the hell are they doing there?'

'Look at the placards.'

'Ha! OK, let's do it further downstream.'

Mole came back and sat down on the bench again.

'Seems like you get a few more minutes. There's some folks on the bridge standing watch. Bleeding-heart parents concerned about all the suicides, by the looks of things. We'll have to take you downriver a bit and drop you in there. Won't be long.'

The van turned onto a rougher road, jolting the floor under Chi's back and causing him to roll from side to side. He could only bend his knees to keep himself still, and even that movement was restricted. Mole stuck his foot out, pressing his heel against Chi's stomach to hold him down. The van drove for what seemed like an age and then stopped. The abrupt silence left after the engine was turned off sent a chill down Chi's spine.

He thrashed about as they opened the doors, but he was too tightly bound to offer any resistance. The three men pulled him out of the van and carried him through a gloomy area of woodland, picking their way carefully, moving without haste. They did not use torches, confident enough to find their route by the faint light of the moon. Soon, he heard the sound of the river. His nose was getting blocked up now and he was finding it hard to breathe. Snot bubbled and burst from his nostrils. As his breathing became strained, he began to hope that he would pass out before they threw him into the water, but it wasn't to be.

They reached the edge of the river. Chi could only see the slight glimmer of the water in the darkness. There was no sense of ceremony, no pause to contemplate the murder they were about to commit. Mole used the point of knife to cut a small hole in the plastic around Chi's mouth. It was important that water got into the lungs, he explained. Then he nodded to the others:

'Right, on three. One . . . Two . . . Three!'

Chi felt their hands release him on the third swing. There was the briefest, frightening moment of weightlessness and then the river hit him, engulfing him. The chill water paralysed his chest, making him gasp. Panic seized him, making him squirm frantically around, his mouth firmly closed against the water. It was all around him, trying to get into him. The shocking coldness made him curl up . . . and it was then that he discovered he could get his head above the surface of the water.

Just barely. He was lying in mud at the edge of the river and here the water seemed to be only a couple of feet deep. By staying still, he was able to lift his head up high enough to get his nose and mouth into the air. He dragged in life-giving gulps of it.

Rolling his eyes back, he stared up at the bank. The three men were gone. Or were they? Was this part of their game? He didn't think so. He should have been thrown from the bridge, but they had taken him to a part of the River Sliney they didn't know instead. They thought it was all as deep as the section under the bridge. Their mistake. Now he had a chance – however small a chance that might be. The cold seeped through his flesh, his muscles, his bones, his marrow.

Doing his best to keep himself on his back, using his pinned arms to brace himself, he bent his knees, dug his heels in and pushed himself up towards the bank. He managed to move about twenty centimetres. The plastic was slippery on the mud of the riverbed, making it hard to stay in position. Every movement risked dipping his head under the water.

He jammed his heels in and pushed again. His feet just slipped in the mud and ducked his head under the surface. He panicked for a moment but then regained the air. Blowing water from his nostrils, he took a few more panting breaths and tried again. Another twenty centimetres or so. The water was a little lower around his head. Its edge encircled his face, reaching just over his plastic-wrapped chin and around to his cheekbones.

After a few more pushes, he hit something

metallic. The water was just shallow enough for him to look round. His head was resting against a large cylindrical shape angled down into the mud. A rusty barrel. Beyond it was the riverbank. One look at the mud bank told him he hadn't a hope of going any further. As he peered through the gloom on either side, it looked as steep in both directions. Resting his head against the crumbling rust of the barrel's side, he felt his heart sink. The Sliney was a tidal river. Judging by the height of the waterline on the bank, the river was due to get a lot deeper. But even that didn't matter, because Chi could barely feel his hands or feet. Hypothermia was setting in. He was shivering violently now and he knew that when he stopped shivering – when his body no longer had the strength to generate warmth – then he would pass out and drown.

How long did the plastic take to disintegrate? Two hours? Too long. It certainly didn't feel any weaker yet.

Chi roared through the hole in front of his mouth, the plastic making a flapping sound. The Scalps must be gone by now. Maybe the people on the bridge would hear him. He let out another cry and then started coughing as water got into his throat. After another few yells, his voice started failing. In frustration, he banged his head against the metal barrel. It emitted a dull boom.

To hell with it, he thought, gritting his teeth against the icy wave of nausea that was climbing over him, I've got nothing else left.

It was the only Morse Code he knew. Three dots, three dashes, three dots. Like they used on the *Titanic*. With his forehead, Chi began to bang out 'SOS' on the corroded barrel's side. He was starting to slip back into the water and he no longer had the muscle control to stop himself. Soon, he was struggling to keep his mouth above the surface. He kept head-butting the barrel. Three quick knocks, three slow ones, three quick ones. Grainy-wet crumbs of rust coated his forehead. Now it was hard to keep his nostrils clear of the water. He had to keep his mouth closed. As he turned his head to the side, his breath sprayed across the surface. He could barely feel the rest of his body; his entire focus was on his head and neck, which were starting to ache unbearably from the tension of holding them in this raised position.

Three quick knocks, three slow ones, three quick ones. Three quick knocks, three slow ones, three . . . three quick ones. Three quick . . . knocks . . . three . . . slow ones, three quick ones . . .

The water climbed up his nostrils. His first attempt to clear them failed. He breathed in water, coughing it out and almost sucking more back in through his mouth. His second breath barely got him enough air to stop his lungs from spasming. Could he hear voices? It sounded like somebody calling out. Three quick knocks ... The water covered his nose and mouth again ...

7

The doctor told Amina that she had been found lying unconscious in some bushes in the park not far from her home. She had a bad cut on her head from where she had probably been hit with some blunt object. Her tongue had needed a couple of stitches too, from where she'd bitten it, presumably when she fell. It was swollen, and she was lucky not to have choked on it. It was assumed that she had been mugged.

She confirmed this; the memory was hard and sharp in her mind, two black home-boys, wearing hoodies and packing knives with knuckle-duster handles. The doctor, a young man with a shy manner and a sexy Eastern European accent, checked her out and declared her to be recovering well, despite being unconscious for what must have been a full day and night. They hadn't found any ID on her – her bag was gone – so the first thing he did after he'd taken her name and details, was to call her parents. Amina spoke to them briefly on the phone and assured them that she was OK. Their concern gushed through the receiver, spilling over her and upsetting her. It was a relief to hang up the phone.

As she waited in the six-bed ward for them to arrive, Amina reflected on this latest bit of misfortune in a whole series of tragic embarrassments that she had been forced to suffer. Being taken in by Sandwith and McMorris and the whole conspiracy posse was bad enough – if she never saw either of them again it would be too soon – but to have her gullibility broadcast across the national media was almost more than she could stand. It would take a miracle to get her career back on track after this. She'd be a target of ridicule when she went back to university – a delusional patsy with a convict for a brother.

Her tongue throbbed and she worked it around her mouth, but sucking on an ice cube was the only thing that helped. Wallowing in her misery, she stayed wrapped in her bedclothes with the curtains drawn around the bed, moping quietly until her parents arrived.

'Oh, honey!' her mother exclaimed, pulling the curtains aside. 'God, we were so scared!'

Her father said nothing, simply enveloping his little girl in his arms so that she had to hug him back and then the tears started. Helena joined in the embrace, driving even more sobs from Amina, despite her best efforts to put on a brave face.

'We're so sorry,' Martin rasped, his throat tight with emotion. 'We turned our backs on you when you needed us most. We didn't believe you. It'll never happen again, sweetheart.'

They stayed like that for another minute or two, before unwrapping themselves, warm and red-faced and feeling like a proper family again.

'I feel like an idiot,' Amina said to them at last, speaking awkwardly around her swollen tongue. 'They fooled me from the start with their talk of mind control and UFOs and . . . and . . . and bloody secret agents. I fell for it hook, line and sinker. I won't be able to show my face at the paper again! I should have stuck to making photocopies.'

Helena and Martin exchanged uneasy glances. None of them had ever heard Amina indulge in self-pity before. Her plaintive tone almost made them cringe. Helena found herself unable to meet her daughter's eyes. Her mothering instincts had never been very strong – her career had always come first. But Helena Jessop knew her little girl and she could always tell when something wasn't right. Looking down with concern at her daughter, Helena resolved to find out what.

There was nervousness in the air of Liverpool Street station as the early morning commuters hurriedly made their way out of the Underground and onto the main concourse. Everyone had seen the broadcast now, the one sent after the poisonings at the Lizard Club. Everyone knew how vulnerable the Underground system was to a nerve-gas attack.

Amina stepped off the rising escalator, allowing those in a rush to brush past her. It was good to be getting back to work again. Her family had been getting on her nerves for the past few days. They had been treating her as if she was on the verge of some mental breakdown. As if she was some kind of new Amina they did not fully recognize. Often she would walk into a room and find them pausing in the midst of a conversation she knew was about her. She was getting sick and tired of it all.

Watchful eyes followed Amina as she came through the ticket barriers onto the concourse. An echoey voice announced a late arrival on platform six. This was the busiest time of the day, when the greatest numbers of travellers passed through the station. People queued up at the counters for fast-food breakfasts of bagels, baguettes, croissants and coffee and smoothies. Faces looked up at the boards, waiting for word from on high. Amina was in the thick of the crowd, making for the stairs that led out of the side entrance of the station.

She caught a side-on glimpse of a man's face as he wheeled a tall, black, heavy case past her. A black plastic hood covered the top half of the case. There was something about him she thought she recognized, but you got that a lot in crowds – your mind sought out the familiar. He looked like a hard-case: a muscular skinhead with Slavic cheekbones – maybe a soldier she had met on one of the bases her family had lived on. She wasn't in the mood for chatting with near-strangers today.

As she turned away, he reached up and pulled the cover off the case, revealing a wide metal tube like a gun barrel protruding from the top of a squat box. There was a hopper mounted on the side of the box, and on the back of the case were two silver gas cylinders. Gas cylinders.

The man looked straight at her and smiled. Her heart gave a mighty thump. His hand slapped a button on the top of the weapon. There was a loud bang. A stream of something erupted out of the barrel. Screams burst from the crowd as the air filled with . . . the air filled with *money*. The machine was a confetti blaster – powered by carbon dioxide. And it was shooting money.

The screams hesitantly turned to laughter and whoops of joy. The people reached up, snatching the ten-, twenty- and fifty-pound notes out of the air. The money swirled around, floating lazily down towards thousands of giddy commuters. Amina joined in, grabbing a fifty-pound note as it spiralled down towards her. She looked at the paper and then over at the man who had fired the cannon. He was laughing. She stared back at the paper again. There were words printed on it in translucent blue ink:

'Web search: There Is No War'.

'Do you remember?' a voice beside her asked softly.

Amina turned to face the man who stood there. It was Ivor McMorris. The man she'd inter-viewed not long ago, who had dragged her into a mess of delusions, lies and paranoia. She should have felt disgust at the sight of him, but instead . . . she felt a need to see him smile.

'Do you remember?' he asked again, his face hopeful.

She rolled her tongue around her mouth, feel-ing the healing scar where she had bitten it. Looking around her, Amina could see that other people were reading the words printed on the money. They appeared puzzled – curious. Many were taking pictures of the scene with the cameras on their phones.

'I . . . I remember . . . that . . .' She struggled to make sense of a memory that didn't fit. 'I think this was my idea. Money talks.'

'Yes,' Ivor said, smiling in that slightly sad way she knew she loved. 'Money talks. This is happening right now in three other railway stations. Thousands of people will pull this money from the air. And it was all your idea.'

It would spread like a virus. Unlike the leaflets she'd seen John Donghu's boys printing, these would never become litter. They would be carried by these travellers to every corner of the city, and to the country beyond. They would never be thrown away, but would instead be spent – passed on to others. Some could circulate for years.

People would begin to search – some with real curiosity, others just for a laugh. The phrase 'There Is No War' would become famous. And even if the information they found was scoffed at, maybe a few – just a few troublemakers – would demand to know the truth. And a few troublemakers was a good start.

'I remember . . . things . . . things about you,' she mused aloud. 'But they don't seem real.'

'Because somebody made you forget,' Ivor said. 'But we'll help you remember.'

Amina did not want to remember. It was uncomfortable to even try. She did not want to fight her own mind.

'Let's start now,' she said, holding up the fifty-pound note. 'Come on. I'll buy you breakfast.'

They walked away through the crowd, watching those around them stooping to scrape up the cash that was littering the floor. And so it was that the word was spread.

████ was packing his bags. He had a private jet scheduled to leave the country from a small airfield in an hour's time. He slapped a clip into his automatic pistol and threw it on top of his jacket, which lay beside the open suitcase. It was an empty gesture. If it ever came time to use the weapon, it would already be too late.

Striding across his severely, but expensively decorated bedroom, he opened another drawer and started pulling out some socks. His mobile rang – the no-nonsense electronic ring-tone making him start. Walking back over to his jacket, ████ drew the phone out and looked at the screen. The number wasn't displayed. People in his business withheld their numbers as a matter of routine. Biting his lip, he took the call.

'Yes?'

'Is this Admiral Robert Cole?' a woman asked.

'Who is this?'

'Admiral Cole, this is Helena Jessop. I was wondering if I could ask you some questions about

VioMaze and the experimental mind–control programme it's running for the military?'

Cole stared at the phone, wondering how the bloody woman had got his number. For a moment he was tempted to go on record. Maybe even go to the police, ask for protection. Get it all out in the open.

But the moment of madness passed. He hung up on her, throwing the phone beside the gun.

'You did the right thing,' someone said from behind him.

Cole's shoulders slumped and he felt a sudden itch in the centre of his back. Turning slowly, he locked eyes with the man in the black tracksuit standing in the doorway. The man held a pistol capped with a stubby silencer. He wore latex gloves and plastic covers over his trainers.

'You don't have to do this,' Cole protested, raising his hands in a pleading gesture. 'You have nothing to fear from me.'

But those were his final words.

ACKNOWLEDGEMENTS

You can't create a story from the outside. So when you've finished it, you need someone to take a look at it and tell you whether the tale you've woven in your head is the same as the one you're weaving in the heads of others. Before any editors get involved, my family are my first critics and I'd like to thank all of them, particularly my wife Maedhbh, for their sound advice, passion and their (mostly!) constructive criticism. They keep my feet on the ground.

My brother, Marek, does much of the work on my website (www.oisinmcgann.com) and keeps me up-to-date with any online developments, gossip and scandal. I tap his brain on regular occasions and basically treat him like a free technical support centre for a range of issues.

Thanks also to my agent, Sophie Hicks, who, with the help of Edina Imrik and everyone at Ed Victor Ltd, guides me through the minefield of contract negotiations. Such straight-talking and diplomacy so rarely go hand in hand.

I've had conversations with many people about the subjects dealt with in this book – too many to name here – but they have all helped to hone and focus my ideas. The worst conspiracies are the ordinary, down-to-earth ones whose results we see around us every day. And there is more than enough truth being told about them if we know where to look. Thanks to all the writers, journalists and film-makers who've asked the awkward questions on behalf of ordinary people, and all those who've made me question my own perceptions of the world.

As ever, the staff at Random House made great contributions during the production of this book and the promotion of the last one. I'm grateful to Nina Douglas and Lauren Bennett for all their help with the publicity for *Ancient Appetites*, and for their patience, efficiency and pleasant demeanours over long, long days of travelling and talks, even when they know they'll be doing it all again next week. James Fraser continues to accept my design input with remarkably good grace and always knows how to do it better.

Clare Argar took over from Shannon Park as editor on this book at relatively short notice, and did so without missing a beat. Changing editor is an unsettling experience for any writer and I'm happy to say that Clare made it an absolute pleasure.

SMALL-MINDED GIANTS

Oisín McGann

Beyond the huge domed roof of Ash Harbour, deadly storms and Arctic temperatures have stripped the Earth bare. Sixteen-year-old boxing enthusiast Solomon Wheat is thrust into a dangerous underworld when his father – a daylighter who clears ice from the dome – goes missing and is accused of murder.

As Sol uncovers the mystery surrounding his father's disappearance, he gradually exposes more sinister secrets when it becomes clear that the Machine which keeps the city alive is running out of power. Strange messages start appearing from the rebellious Dark-Day Fatalists, warning inhabitants of their inevitable fate, while the elusive and dangerous Clockworkers seem intent on protecting the ailing Machine at any cost.

Sol's search leads him into the bowels of Ash Harbour, where street-fights and black-market deals rule its skeletal maze, and the giants of industry who run the city bury their dirty secrets. Along with rebellious classmate Cleo, and Maslow, an unlikely accomplice, Sol faces the match of his life to uncover the truth. The fight is on . . .

978 0 552 55473 2

ANCIENT APPETITES

Oisín McGann

Nate Wildenstern's brother has been killed,
and the finger is pointed at him . . .

After nearly two years, eighteen-year-old Nate returns home to
the family empire ruled by his father – the ruthless Wildenstern
Patriarch. But Nate's life is soon shattered by his brother's
death, and the Rules of Ascension, allowing the assassination
of one male family member by another, means he's being
blamed. He knows that he is not the murderer, but who is?

With the aid of his troublesome sister-in-law, Daisy, and his
cousin Gerald, he means to find out. But when the victims of
the family's tyrannical regime choose the funeral to seek their
revenge, they accidently uncover the bodies of some ancient
Wildenstern ancestors, one of whom bears a Patriarch's ring.
The lives of Nate and his family are about to take a
strange and horrifying turn . . .

SHORTLISTED FOR THE 2007
WATERSTONE'S BOOK PRIZE

978 0 552 55499 2